Seeds of Malice

WILTED KINGDOM DUET
BOOK 1

MAGGIE COLE

Pulse Press Inc.

IMPORTANT NOTE FROM MAGGIE

Dear Reader,

This duet is a dark romance, which may be unsettling for some readers. My characters Dax Carrington and Ivy Ford both evolve through this duet; however, this is not for the faint of heart.

Book one begins when they are in college. This first part of the duet is a college bully, dark billionaire romance. Book two takes place ten years later and continues as a dark billionaire, second-chance romance where Ivy is determined to get revenge for all Dax did to her.

Please note I said dark.

Expect substance abuse, addiction, sexual manipulation, graphic and taboo sexual scenes including multiple partners, dub con, humiliation, bullying, revenge, and heart-wrenching chapters.

If you don't like dark romance, or any of these elements, then I advise you not to read. I have faith you know your triggers.

I promise you that if you decide to read, Dax and Ivy will have their happily ever after. And both of them will redeem themselves in the end.

Thank you for reading (or not if it's not your thing).

XOXO

Maggie Cole

Contents

Contents

Contents

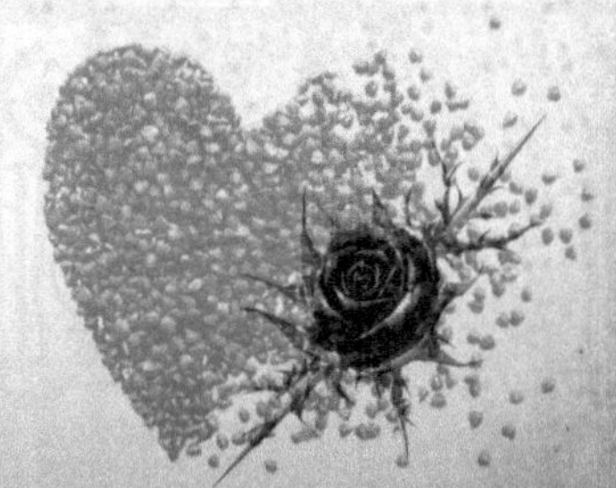

I'm a pawn in a twisted game I never agreed to partake in.

Dax
TIME TO PLAY
Prologue

Dax Carrington

A thick haze of smoke hangs in the air. Red embers burn brighter at the end of the joint as Bobby inhales. He holds the smoke deep in his lungs, then releases it, moaning, "I'm not ready to go back."

"Stop whining," I mutter as I grab the joint, then take a hit of my own.

"Since when do you love school?" He smirks.

I point out, "This is our last year, and we're fucking done. We can join the real world then."

He grunts. "I don't know why you're in such a rush to graduate. We have the rest of our lives to fucking work."

He has a point. Taking over the family floral business isn't exactly my dream life. But I'll be damned if I let my little brother take over. He'll do what he always does, which is put in little to no effort and come up smelling like roses. My mother will gush for the rest of my life about how talented he is while giving me a knowing look of disapproval. So I just agree with Bobby. "School sucks. Shut up so we can enjoy the last few weeks."

"Still don't know why you won't take a year abroad with me," he adds.

I ignore him and glance out the window of the cottage. I claimed it several years back so I wouldn't have to live in the main house any longer.

Fully bloomed flowers in every color dance across the lush lawn. Greenhouses etch the premises full of more foliage. Several workers focus on different areas of the estate.

A loud knock tears me out of my trance.

Bobby arches his eyebrows. "You expecting somebody?"

Am I?

I rack my brain. There are always people stopping over. I don't remember inviting anyone, but that doesn't mean much.

Bobby rises and flings the door open.

Cindy stumbles inside with Marcey in tow.

Not now.

It's the same as always. Both girls have eyes wild with booze, drugs, and the longing expression to get naughty. Their matching bleached designer hairstyles and expensive outfits suddenly look ridiculous.

Same shit, different day.

The summer's haze of partying hasn't changed one bit from the weeknights and weekends of the last three years. The girls' trashed demeanors used to excite me. It meant anything goes and they were all too willing to do whatever Bobby and I wanted. Now, the novelty has worn off. It's boring the fuck out of me.

Bobby grabs Marcey by the back of the neck and pushes her against the wall. She shrieks as he holds her cheek firmly to the crimson wallpaper. He asks, "Looking for some fun?"

Her lips twitch, and her gaze locks on his, begging him to do what I've seen too many times before.

"So predictable," I mutter.

Cindy saunters over to me in a drunken wobble. "Dax, where have you been hiding?"

I stay quiet.

She bends over, takes her finger, and touches my nose. "There you are."

I jerk my head back. "What do you want, Cindy?"

She giggles and drops to her knees in front of my armchair. She slides her hand up my thigh, past the cuff of my shorts, and teases my balls with her perfectly manicured nails.

It used to get me going, but like I said, I'm bored. She's making it too easy. There's nothing exciting about her anymore.

I need a new plaything.

"Dax," she slurs, batting her eyes.

I take another hit and then hold the joint to her lips.

She inhales, then coughs, her eyes watering until her mascara smears black under her lids.

I study her, wishing I could feel what I once did when I looked at her, but I can't. She's washed up and overused, just like my toys when I was five.

She cups my cock and smirks. "Time to play, Dax."

My flaccid dick doesn't respond.

She squeezes it, and her grin widens. "Dax..."

It doesn't take much for me to lose my interest, and if I'm being honest, she went off my radar months ago. I question why I even let her step foot on my property.

"Baaaaby," she slurs.

I grab her hand and pull it out of my shorts. I move it away from my body, claiming, "Not interested."

She purrs, "Oh, sure you are." She slides my shorts to the floor.

"I'm not," I insist.

She bats her eyes, moves her hand back to my cock, and puts her hot pink lips closer while holding my stare and pouting. "I was going to do that thing you love."

"Don't be a fool, Dax. Let her give it to you," Bobby calls out, then drops Marcey's skirt, revealing her yellow thong and boney ass cheek.

I reach over and turn the music up. I'm tired of hearing Bobby fuck Marcey against my wall. The girl shrieks. I don't know how he can fuck her with that loud sound. It's the most annoying noise I've ever heard.

Cindy's wet tongue slides against my cock. I turn my attention back to her. She takes several licks and then coos, "What's wrong, baby? Something going on you want to talk about?"

As if I want to talk to her about anything. She's got a brain the size of an ant.

"We can talk," she offers.

Annoyed and wanting her to stop talking, I palm her head, push it to my cock, and demand, "Do your job and shut up."

She giggles, then sputters as I force my entire cock into her mouth. It's still not hard, but I'm big either way.

"Take it like I taught you," I seethe, pissed off she's here and that I'm not even able to get it up when her wet mouth's where it should be.

She chokes again, then recovers, working my cock like a pro, but I can't seem to get erect.

Several moments pass. More anger replaces my boredom. My cock's barely hard. I miss my days of a raging hard-on, and wonder if I'm aging faster than my twenty-one years. It's not right that a woman sucks on a man and it's not hard as shit, no matter who it is.

Fuck, I've got to get out of my head.

I'm bored and fucked-up.

Is that what this is?

Maybe I do have a problem.

Should I steal the old man's pills again?

I shouldn't need that shit. I'm twenty-one, for crying out loud.

This isn't helping.

Cindy tries to stop, but I hold her down, repeating, "Do your fucking job."

She grips my thighs with her fake nails, and the pain is somehow welcoming.

I glance across the room. Bobby's going full at it with Marcey, pounding her against the wall but holding his palm over her mouth to muffle her shrieks.

At least he remembered my warning about keeping her quiet in my place.

I turn the radio up higher and glance out the window.

Who the fuck is that?

My heart pounds faster. A young woman with dark hair and stunning blue eyes stands beside an older man. She's younger than me, maybe just a year or so, but Jesus, she looks innocent.

My erection wakes up.

Cindy purrs, "There you go, baby."

I grip her head tighter, imagining it's the new girl sucking my cock.

Our head groundskeeper, Benny, motions at her and the man I assume is her father, to go into a greenhouse.

I can barely make out her silhouette, covered in her cut-off jean shorts, tight tank top, and tits that are there but nothing like the girls I'm used to messing around with.

There's nothing fake on this girl. No, hers are real. Maybe a C cup.

When's the last time I fucked somebody with a C cup?

Never. I don't think I've ever fucked anyone with tits that small.

D, double D, that's what the girls around me usually have. I only fuck rich girls who started getting plastic surgery by the time they turned fourteen.

"Yeah, I've definitely never fucked anyone with C cups," I mutter, for some reason, growing harder at the thought.

"What?" Cindy asks.

I barely hear her and push her back down.

The girl steps outside the greenhouse by herself and looks around. She crosses her arms, and a worried expression appears on her face. She purses her lips.

Blood rushes to my dick, making it even harder. I move Cindy's head faster over me.

The mystery girl's old man steps outside, and they exchange words with Benny, then stroll toward my place.

I can't take my gaze off her. She's beautiful but doesn't look like the girls I normally associate with.

She's real.

Suddenly, my cock's harder than it's ever been. I'm no longer bored.

A wave of heat fills me to the point I'm about to break out in a sweat, and I violently come in Cindy's mouth. I ignore her gags, making her swallow everything that doesn't seep out of her mouth. When I finish, I push her off my cock.

She falls to the ground, coughing and protesting. "Dax! What the fuck!"

I rise and go to the window.

I don't know who this girl is or why she's here, but it has something to do with my family's estate. My guess is this won't be the last time I see her.

Benny leads her and her father toward the golf cart, and she disappears.

My life suddenly seems full of hope. I'm going to make it my mission to run into this girl.

My boredom's over.

I have a new project.

Her.

Ivy 1

WHAT'LL IT BE?

Ivy Ford

"So this is Greenwich, Connecticut," I mutter.

I stare around the cottage again and then glance out the window at the huge estate.

This is the first time I've seen so much acreage belonging to one family. Sure, West Virginia has lots of land, but more than one family owns it.

I spot my father near a greenhouse several hundred yards away. His smile's back on his face. I haven't seen it in a while; not since before my mom disappeared. She wanted a better life than my father could give us in West Virginia. So it's ironic that now we're in Greenwich, an uppity place full of money and power.

At least that's what my father says about the town. He claimed my mother would've loved it here, but in my mind, I doubt she'd be happy. It still wouldn't have been good enough for her.

Since she left, we've yet to hear from her. It's been over four years. I try not to think about it, but seeing the glow in his expression for the first time in a long time makes me happy.

He's always loved flowers and gardening. He's a botanist and specializes in making different hybrids of flowers. So when the Carrington family was looking for someone to replace their old botanist, my father jumped at the chance.

When he told me he got hired, I didn't want to move. Unlike my mother, I was happy in our West Virginia town. A few months ago, I graduated high school. I had a job lined up and had enrolled for the fall semester at the community college to follow in my father's footsteps. It would take me longer since I couldn't afford to attend school full-time, but I was okay with it.

Last week, my father told me about his new job, including an all-expenses-paid spot for me at Clifton University. It's like miracles were happening all around us, so I wasn't going to complain about moving out of state.

Now, we're here. But I'm not free of worry. The size of the property makes me think my father will work too hard. He has a heart condition, and they shocked him back to life last year. He seems to be doing okay, and the doctor said his heart's like new, but he's all I've got. So I'll always worry about him.

I tear my eyes off the lawn and focus on the inside of our new home. I have two weeks until school begins, and while I'd love to take a dip in one of the several pools that dot the estate, or explore the dozens of gardens, there's too much to do. And there's no way I'll let my father have more work to do with unpacking.

I open another box, and a song I know comes on the radio. I start to sing when I'm suddenly startled.

A male voice shouts, "Anyone here?"

I spin, and my heart beats so fast I think it might pound through my chest.

A beautiful man stands in front of me. His dark hair has a few expertly positioned blond highlights in it. His cheekbones are perfectly sculpted. Dimples dent both sides of his rough lips, and his light eyes have a hint of blue, but they're almost see-through. He's mesmerizing. His manicured goatee and boyish grin frame his gleaming white teeth. And his arms are built but not overdone.

I squeeze my legs together and question, "Sorry, who are you?"

His grin widens. "I'm Dax."

"Dax?" I question, my face burning.

He's gorgeous.

He saunters toward me, and my pulse beats in my neck. He holds out his hand. "Yeah. I'm Dax, the oldest of the Carrington children."

"Oh, hi. I'm sorry. I didn't mean to be rude." I wipe my sweaty palm on my shorts and take his hand.

He wraps his large fingers around mine and holds longer than normal; at least, I think it's longer than normal.

He sizes me up in a semi-lewd way, which should turn me off, but it doesn't. He asks, "And what's your name?"

"Oh, I'm sorry. I'm Ivy. My dad's—"

"I know who your dad is."

"You do?"

Amusement fills his expression. "Yeah. He's the most talented botanist we could find."

I can't help but swell full of pride. My father is talented. I admit, "Yeah, that's him."

"And why are you staying inside on this nice day?" Dax

questions, crossing his arms so his biceps bulge, straining against his white T-shirt sleeves.

I glance around the messy house at the chaos. "These boxes aren't going to unpack themselves."

"Surely you can have some fun?" Dax asks.

"Nope! I've got to get this done."

"You should come swimming. It's hot after all, and the weather won't hold up forever," Dax points out.

I glance out the window into the sunshine. It would be nice to swim, but I shake my head. "I'm sorry. I can't. I have to unpack. I don't want to leave this for my father. He's got enough to do."

"Are we overworking him already?"

"Oh, no. I'm sorry. I didn't mean it like that. I just meant—"

He holds up his hand and chuckles. "It's okay. We have a huge estate here. I understand if he's overwhelmed."

"He's not. My father wouldn't get overwhelmed. He's a professional," I insist.

Dax looks even more amused. "I'm sure he is."

"He is," I boldly declare.

Dax steps even closer, and the scent of his cologne fills the air. I swallow hard. My mouth turns dry and then waters. I lick my lips, and Dax's clear gaze darts down to study my tongue. The heat burns my cheeks hotter. I ask, "Is there something else I can help you with?"

He tilts his head. "How old are you, Ivy?"

"Eighteen."

"Senior in high school?"

I shake my head. "No, I graduated. I'm going to college this year."

Dax chuckles again. "Yeah, I know."

"You know?"

"Of course I know. This is my estate. I know everything that goes on here." His gaze drifts down my body and then rises to lock on mine.

I stay quiet. I've never had anyone look at me like that. I'm curious if he's interested in me, but the idea is absurd. Men like Dax Carrington don't give girls like me a second thought. He's sophisticated, wealthy, and a tad arrogant.

I'm boring compared to him.

He declares, "I believe we're going to the same school."

"We are?" I ask in surprise. I figured he was at least twenty-five.

He nods. "Yes, I'm a senior at Clifton University. You're a freshman, correct?"

I tilt my head. "Why are you asking me these questions if you already know the answers?"

He shrugs. "Not sure. So what are you going to study?"

"Botany."

He arches his eyebrows. "Apple doesn't fall far from the tree, does it?"

My lips twitch. "No. My father got me obsessed with flowers when I was little. We had a huge garden in West Virginia."

"West Virginia. Bet that was fun," Dax says, but I'm unsure how he means it.

I stare at him.

"Well, was West Virginia fun?" he questions.

I nod. "Yeah, it was a nice place to live."

"So you weren't looking forward to coming to Connecticut?"

"I didn't say that."

"No?" He arches his eyebrow, as if he knows me better than I do.

"I'm very grateful that we're here. Please don't think

anything different," I answer, not wanting to give him the wrong impression and do anything to harm my father's position or my free ride to college.

He studies me for a moment until I'm so uncomfortable I have to shift on my feet. Then he claims, "Ivy, I'm not a prick. You don't have to worry about what you say around me."

I release a breath. "I don't?"

"No. Let me guess. You think because I'm rich that I'm a spoiled brat, and we can't be friends."

I scrunch my eyebrows together. I did think that, but I'm not admitting it out loud. "No, I didn't say that."

"Good, so you're excited to be friends?" he asks, smiling bigger.

"You want to be friends with me?" I question like a moron, confused by this entire conversation.

He reaches toward me, and I freeze. He slides his finger over my forehead, down my cheek, and pushes a lock of my hair behind my ear. Tingles explode under his touch. He murmurs, "Yeah. Are friends bad?"

"No," I barely get out, wondering why a man who looks like him would be interested in being friends with me. I'm just a girl from West Virginia. Surely, he's got women all over him. I may be naive, but I'm not that ignorant. He's gorgeous. He's rich and has power. I bet he's beating women off him with a stick.

"Ivy, you need to take a break. It's summer and hot. There are several pools. And, yes, I need to show you all of them."

I nervously laugh. "Is that so?"

"Yes."

I glance around the house one more time. I'm tempted to give in, but I can't do that to my father. "Sorry, these boxes aren't going to empty themselves. Maybe a different day?"

Dax stares at me for a few moments.

"You're not used to being told no, are you?"

He shrugs again. "Nope, but that's fine. I'll help you unpack. We can hit up one of the pools before the sun goes down."

"You're going to help me unpack?" I ask, confused once more. Why would a man of his stature want to help me with manual labor?

He nods. "Sure. Like you said, the boxes aren't going to unpack themselves, are they?"

"No, but you don't have to do that. I'm sure you have a lot of things to do."

He rolls his eyes. "Oh, I've got tons of things to do. Starting with this box." He grabs one off the floor and sets it on the table. He yanks it open and pulls one of my bras out. "Like this. This looks pretty important for me to unpack."

Horror fills me. I put my hands over my face and groan. "Can you not unpack that box?"

He chuckles. "Why? Do you think it's my first time seeing a bra?"

I move my hands off my face and stare at him. My heart, once again, beats hard.

He chuckles. "Don't answer that. Here, I'll put this in your room."

He picks up the box and saunters past me. I stare at his firm ass and flexed shoulder blades as he disappears down the hall.

Then I come to my senses and follow him, calling, "I haven't told you which room is mine."

He turns his head. "There are only two. I think I can figure it out."

"Oh, duh."

I'm a moron, I reprimand myself.

He picks the right room, sets the box down, then comes back out. He suggests, "Maybe we should work on the kitchen stuff so you're not embarrassed."

"I'm not embarrassed," I claim.

More amusement fills his expression. He gives me a knowing look. "Sure you're not."

I put my hand on my hip. "Are you trying to be nice or make fun of me right now?"

He grins again. "Maybe both."

I don't say anything. He gives me another stare down, then picks up another box labeled "Kitchen." He puts it on top of the table and pulls it open. We quietly work together, taking out pots and pans. I put them into the cabinet.

We get to the next box, and he says, "So, what did you do for fun in West Virginia?"

I shrug. "I like to be outside. Probably the same things you do."

"Yeah? What do you think I like to do?"

I blurt, "Okay. I don't know what you like to do. That was silly of me to insinuate that. I was on the track team."

"Track team? So you're going to run away from me quickly?"

I laugh and shake my head. "Are you always like this?"

"Like what?"

"A comedian."

"Glad you think I'm funny."

"Are you sure you have nothing better to do? I find it odd that you want to unpack my house."

He grunts. "This is the most fun I've had all summer."

"I don't believe that."

"Believe it. It's pretty boring around here," he declares.

I glance out the window again at the beautiful estate. Sparkling lake water peeks through the trees, adding to the brilliance. Part of a sail from one of the boats grabs my attention. I ask, "How could you possibly be bored here? This place is beautiful. You have a lake, boats, and pools."

He adds a set of plates inside the cupboard and turns back to me. He crosses his arms and leans against the counter. "Yeah, I have all that and a bunch of boring people who are overrated and only know how to do the same thing."

"What's that?"

"They know how to be boring," he claims.

"You can't tell me all your friends are boring," I insist.

"Well, Bobby's mostly interesting, although he's getting boring too. But everyone else, yeah, they're boring. But you... Now, you seem pretty interesting," he says with more enthusiasm.

I bite my lip. How am I in any way interesting to him? I'm just a girl from West Virginia.

"Why do you look like you don't believe me?" he questions.

"I just find it hard to believe your life is boring."

His lips curve. "Well, you're going to have to hang out with me and then you can judge my life. But again, I said the people around me are boring. I'm pretty sure it won't be boring if you and I hang out. Like right now, I'm not bored."

I shake my head, pointing at all the boxes. "You can't tell me this interests you...unpacking my stuff."

"Oh, but it does," he claims, breaking down a box. He studies the room, adding, "We'll have the whole kitchen done in no time and then it'll be time for a break."

I reply, "I still have the bedrooms to do."

"The bedrooms will wait. You can't be all work and no play. That's not good for you," he says with mischief in his eyes.

Something about it makes me nervous. I question, "And what is it that you want to do?"

"I told you we can go to the pool. Or if you want, we can go on the boat."

"The boat?"

"Yeah. We can pick one of the boats."

I laugh. "*One* of the boats?"

He shrugs again. "Sure, you can pick. Don't tell me no. I'm helping you so we can go hang out."

Does this guy really want to hang out with me that badly? Surely, his life is not that boring.

He challenges, "Come on, Ivy. What's it going to be? Boat or pool?"

I take a deep breath. "Let's start with the pool. I don't think we have time to go boating when I have to do the rest of the house."

"I'll help you."

"No, I'll do my bedroom and my dad's bedroom myself," I say, for some reason thinking we need a little bit of privacy.

"Okay, suit yourself. Let's finish this kitchen, but we're going on the boat on a different day," he insists.

I try to stop my smile. "Okay, that's a deal." I wonder if my life is really getting this amazing. It's only been a day, and I've already made a new friend. And he's super hot. But I'm not worrying about that because there's no way he can seriously be interested in me. Not with all the girls I'm sure he's around. But it'll be nice to hang out by the pool, and boating does sound like fun. I've never boated except for the few times I went in a row boat one of the kids in my class had.

"You can swim, right, Ivy?" he questions.

"Yeah, I can swim. I used to go in the lakes up in the mountains."

"Ah, all right, good. I don't have to worry about you drowning, then."

"Do you always worry about people dying on your watch?" I tease.

That mischievous grin fills his face again. It makes me uncomfortable but excited in a way I can't explain.

"Yeah, I was worried about that. I thought I would have to lift you up on my shoulders the entire time."

"Ha ha, funny," I say.

He tears open another box and takes out several coffee mugs. One is of me as a little girl smelling a dandelion. He coos, "Aw, isn't this cute?"

I snatch it from him. "Don't make fun of it. It's my dad's favorite."

"I can see why." He smirks.

I smack the back of his shoulder.

"Ouch. Don't hurt the help," he teases.

I ignore him and put the coffee mug away. We continue to work for the next hour until the kitchen and the family room are unpacked. The only thing left are the boxes for the bedrooms.

He picks one up and starts walking down the hall.

I question, "Where are you going?"

"I'm just going to set it inside your room. Chill out," he says, then returns.

We take the rest of the boxes and divide them up between my room and Dad's. When we're done, Dax slides his arm around me and pulls me into him.

My knees wobble.

He looks down at me, and his hot breath hits mine. I do everything I can to stay standing.

Why is he so gorgeous?

Why does he look like he wants to kiss me?

He doesn't.

He does.

He can't.

He gives me his lewd expression again, and a warmth flows through my body. He leans closer, staring at my lips. In a low murmur, he teases, "All right, Ivy, are you going naked? Or are you putting on a bikini?"

Dax 2

EARN HER TRUST

Dax

In the last twenty-four hours, I've learned everything I could about Ivy Ford and her father, John. Ivy's mother isn't in the picture. I've not found any information on her, but it's clear it's just Ivy and her dad. And the fact she's from West Virginia couldn't be more perfect.

She's lived a sheltered life, raised in a small mountain town. As bored as I am, I'm sure it was ten times worse where Ivy comes from.

And I didn't need her to tell me she was studying botany. Her old man won't stop gushing to anyone who will listen about her following his career path.

Luckily for Ivy, when my father hired John, he agreed to pay for her college. Her father doesn't have two dimes to rub together. He lost his shit for a while after her mom disappeared. He even let it affect his corporate job. He's had a hard time finding a decent replacement since. So that meant Ivy's only option was some podunk West Virginian community college.

For some reason, my father decided to give him a chance. My old man claims John's beyond talented with seed selection and hybrid creations, which our family business specializes in.

I couldn't give a rat's ass about John's skills. Except for Ivy, it's just as boring as everything else on this estate.

She's way more innocent and beautiful than I anticipated. Her porcelain skin reminds me of one of my sister's old dolls. I can't decide if I want to bruise it with my lips to claim it as mine or let it stay in perfect condition.

I stare out the window, tapping the sill, feeling borderline giddy. I can't wait to use Ivy in all sorts of ways. I'm going to make her do things she never knew she wanted to do and then take it all away once she becomes obsessed with it.

The "it," being mainly me.

But before I can get to the good stuff, I have to earn her trust and remind myself to focus on my task at hand.

I call out, "Ivy, I'm about to fall asleep out here. Are you blow-drying your hair or putting on that bikini we discussed?"

She steps through the doorway. "Hold your horses. I haven't been gone that long."

My heart almost stops. Her flat stomach, full thighs, and those damn C cups only make her more enticing. Her modest pink bikini covers more than any girl wears around Greenwich, which continues to make Ivy the most entertaining thing I've laid eyes on in a long time.

I whistle.

Her face turns red, something that happens easily. I note how much I'm going to enjoy the others at school using her downfall for my gain.

Once they see how easily she gets embarrassed, it'll be a

challenge between them to see how quickly they can humiliate her. And while there are lots of things I'll do to break her, I'll have their help without even asking. And she'll constantly be running into my arms.

"Is this not okay?" she questions, second-guessing her outfit and tugging a matching wrap around her waist.

"It's perfect," I claim.

"Then why are you staring at me like that?"

I attempt to pull my gaze away from her breasts, but it's hard. All I've been dreaming of since I saw her on the lawn is fitting those boobs into my mouth. I bet her nipples are pink. I can't wait to suck on them till they turn red and get so sore that every time they rub against her bra, all she can do is think of me and squeeze her pussy.

Fuck, I bet that's pink too.

"You're still staring," she murmurs.

I snap out of it and hold her gaze, answering, "Is it wrong that I like what I see?"

The red deepens on her cheeks. I don't think I'm ever going to get used to it.

Jesus, she's adorable.

Too bad I'm going to have to give her lessons in life 101, 102, then move on to the 200s.

"Dax?" She fidgets with her fingers and shifts on her feet.

"What's wrong? Haven't you had lots of men drool all over you?"

She swallows hard.

"Well," I push.

She shakes her head and quietly answers, "No."

"I don't buy that," I declare.

She doesn't say anything.

I chuckle and slide my hand around her waist. "Come on.

The day isn't getting any younger." I lead her out of the cottage and over to my golf cart.

"Ivy, where are you going?" a man calls out.

She freezes, then spins. "Dad, you're home."

"Ivy?" he questions, his eyes turning to slits as he looks me over.

I put on my most charming grin and step in front of him. I hold out my hand. "Mr. Ford, I'm Dax. Everett and Gwendolyn's oldest child. It's nice to meet you. I've heard such amazing things about you and your work."

Her father hesitates a moment and keeps his suspicious expression in place. He finally takes my hand. "It's nice to meet you too. I've heard the same about you."

I bet you have.

Ivy clears her throat. "Dad, Dax was nice enough to come to the house and introduce himself. He even helped me unpack the kitchen."

Her father gives me another look of distrust. "Oh?"

I nod. "Yes, sir. I wanted to show Ivy the grounds and take her to the pool. I thought it'd be nice to introduce her to some people before school starts."

Her father shifts on his feet, reminding me of when Ivy just did it.

"Dad, it's okay, right?" Ivy questions, which I find intriguing. She's eighteen. Does she ask her dad's permission before she does things? I haven't asked my parents' permission since I was twelve.

Her father finally caves and nods. "Yeah, it is. What time are you going to be home?"

"We're just going to be over at that pool." I point to the farthest one on the estate, adding, "I'll take good care of her, I promise."

Her father meets my eyes again. He doesn't like me. He has

no reason not to, but the man is smart. I have to give him credit. He knows that I'm up to no good. How could I be when his daughter's a ripe peach ready for me to bite into? Still, I play the role that I've mastered. It fools most parents, and I decide that I'm going to make it my mission to get him on my good side as well. I vow, "I promise I'll take good care of her and ensure she gets safely back to your place."

"Dad, I'm not leaving the estate. Everything is fine. Don't look so nervous." Ivy reaches up and hugs him.

He wraps his arms around her and finally retreats, stating, "Enjoy yourself."

I slide my arm around her waist and lead her back to the golf cart, feeling his eyes on me.

It takes everything I have not to chuckle from euphoric celebration. This is going to be even better. I love it when parents don't trust me. Fathers especially. It rarely happens. I have most of the town fooled. But every now and then, I have an extra challenge on my hands, and I'm more than up for it.

I wait until Ivy gets into the cart, then turn around and wave. "See you later, Mr. Ford." I go around the golf cart and get in. I slide my arm around Ivy and drive away from him.

We're halfway across the estate when Ivy says, "I didn't know your friends were coming. Are they nice?"

I could tell her the truth, that they're all a bunch of vindictive, mean, very conniving brats, and that they're going to eat her alive, but I'll let her experience it. I lie, "Yeah, they're nice. They're going to love you too."

"Really?" she asks, as if she doesn't believe me.

"Yeah. What's not to love about you?"

She bites on her lip.

"Are you always this nervous to meet people?" I ask.

She shrugs. "I don't know."

"Well, why are you nervous now?"

She shakes her head. "I'm not sure. Probably just jitters of being in a new place."

I take my arm from around her shoulder and put my hand between her thighs.

She freezes and holds her breath.

It's just the reaction I'm looking for. I lean closer. "Well, you know me. I'll protect you against anyone."

She stares at me. Her breath moves in and out in shallow pants.

I chuckle again and rub my thumb on her thigh. "Don't worry, gorgeous. Everything's going to be fine. We'll have a blast today. I hope you like burgers."

"Who doesn't like burgers?"

"You'd be surprised. But we're going to grill burgers with real buns. Tell me you eat bread, please."

She wrinkles her forehead. "Of course I eat bread. Why wouldn't I?"

I squeeze her thigh. "That's my girl."

"I'm confused. Why are you asking me if I eat bread?" she questions.

"Because none of the girls around here do. They're all worried about their carbohydrate intake."

She softly laughs. "Oh. I've not had to worry about that yet."

I move my hand higher, and she shifts. Her thighs are thicker than most of the anorexic bitches around here. It's another thing they'll make sure she feels horrible about, but I'm tired of not having anything to hold on to but bones while fucking. So I'm going to enjoy it until Ivy starts to starve herself to become like them, which she undoubtedly will eventually do. So I honestly agree, "No, you definitely don't. Promise me you'll keep these thighs just like they are." I squeeze them again.

She glances at my hand, and her lips twitch.

I steer the golf cart around the bend, then go through a small, wooded trail. When we come out, the pool's only a few yards away.

Bobby's there, along with my sister Avery and little brother Cooper. Avery's nineteen. Cooper's seventeen.

Ivy asks, "Are those your friends?"

"Just Bobby. The other two I'm related to, unfortunately," I mutter.

"Sibling love. Noted," she says in an amused tone.

I pull the golf cart over, and Avery shrieks, "Don't you dare, Bobby!"

He waves my sister's bikini top higher in the air.

She holds her arms over her breasts.

He taunts, "You shouldn't leave this lying around."

She reaches for it, and he holds it out higher. She demands, "Give it to me, Bobby."

He dangles it, but it's still out of her reach. He wiggles his eyebrows. "What do you want to give me for it?"

"Give her her top," I order.

One thing about Bobby, he's known my sister and brother forever—as long as he's known me. But it annoys the fuck out of me when he flirts with my sister. They have a love-hate relationship going on, and while he swears he's never screwed her, I don't fully believe him. It's one of those things I've not pushed to know. The thought makes me want to hurl.

Avery glances at us, then narrows her eyes. She gives Ivy a once-over, then slowly puts her hands on her hips, showcasing her fake tits.

"Put your top on, Avery," I order.

She shoots a glare in my direction. "Order someone else around, Dax." She refocuses on Ivy. "And who do we have here?"

"Bobby, give her the top!" I exclaim.

He glances over at me.

"Now," I demand.

He tosses it at Avery and turns his grin on Ivy, chirping, "Well, well, well. It's so nice to see some fresh blood around here."

I get out of the golf cart, as does Ivy. I lead her toward them, announcing, "This is Ivy."

Avery gives Ivy another stare down, then asks, "And where did you find her?"

Ivy shifts uncomfortably and tries to avoid looking at Avery's tits.

I put my arm around Ivy's waist and tug her close. "Her father is the new head botanist on the estate. She just moved into one of the cottages. She's going to attend Clifton. Put your top on, Avery."

Avery moves her sunglasses down her nose and peers closer at Ivy.

"Don't be such a snob," I scold.

She innocently proclaims, "What? I'm not being a snob."

"Yeah, you are. And put your top on."

"No, I'm not." She licks her lips and holds her hand out. "How are you doing?"

Ivy clears her throat, keeping her eyes pinned on Avery's. She replies, "Good. How are you?" She takes her hand.

Avery daintily shakes it. My mother taught her that shake, and it drives me nuts.

My brother rises and holds his hand out. "I'm Cooper, their better third."

I groan. "Sure, bro. Keep telling yourself that."

Ivy shakes his hand. "It's nice to meet you too."

I tug Ivy closer. "Cooper's a senior in high school. Avery is a sophomore at Clifton. She's my sister, unfortunately."

"Shut up, Dax," she reprimands.

Bobby steps between us and leans forward. He kisses Ivy on the cheek. "I'm Bobby. Dax's best friend."

I move Ivy out of the way so he's several arm lengths away. The last thing I need is Bobby all over her. I give him a look that she's mine and question, "Did you start the grill? I'm hungry."

Avery rolls her eyes. "Don't we have people for that?"

I point out, "And you claim you aren't a snob."

She huffs. "What? We have enough people working on this estate. There are plenty of peons on our payroll who can do that for us. Why are you insisting Bobby do it?"

"You are such a snob," I repeat. Then, I lead Ivy past her and over to the grill.

"I can do it," Ivy quietly volunteers, a new flush of pink crawling through her cheeks.

I grunt. "No, you're not going to do it. Bobby and I will do it. Just grab a chair." I turn on the grill.

Ivy doesn't move.

"Something wrong?" I ask.

"You sure you don't want me to help?"

"No. But maybe you should get wet!" I pick her up.

She shrieks, grabbing me around the neck. "Dax, what are you doing?"

"Food can wait." I take three steps toward the pool and jump in the deep end with Ivy still clinging to me. We go under the water and pop back up.

She laughs. "Are you crazy?"

"I thought it was time you got in the pool," I say, then dive under the water. I kiss her belly and slide my hands around to her ass. She struggles to get away. But I hold her tight and come up right in front of her lips.

Her breathing increases.

"Oh, Dax has fresh meat," Avery calls out. "Save some for the rest of us."

I ignore her, but I don't miss Ivy's expression. I'll have to convince my sister to shut her mouth around Ivy. I don't need rumors going around about me and other women, even if they are true. And I definitely don't need Avery trying to seduce Ivy. She claims she's bi-sexual, but the only time I ever see her go for women is when she's trying to get something from them. So I'm unsure what her true sexuality is, but I'm not letting her dig her claws into Ivy.

"Hot dogs or hamburgers?" Bobby calls out.

"Hot dog. No, hamburger. No, both," Cooper picks.

"Burger on lettuce, no cheese, only mustard," Avery adds.

I dramatically roll my eyes, and Ivy starts laughing. Like every other girl in this town, my sister is skin and bones. I don't remember the last time she ate a carbohydrate.

I yell out, "Ivy and I will have cheeseburgers with buns. Isn't that right?"

She nods and giggles.

I add, "See? Isn't this better than unpacking?"

She smiles. "Yeah. It's a nice day."

"Sorry about my sister. She's annoying," I mutter.

Ivy glances at Avery, declaring, "She seems okay."

I grunt. "I can assure you she's not."

"Thanks for bringing me with you."

I claim, "No problem. Tomorrow, I'll take you somewhere away from this place."

Her eyebrows arch. "Where?"

"I'm not telling you."

"You're not telling me?"

"No. Don't you know what a surprise is?" I tease.

She bites on her lip again.

God, I want to sink my teeth into it until it bleeds and suck on it until it's swollen. Then all she'll have to do is walk around, and everyone will know it's from me.

She tilts her head. "You're really not going to tell me where you want to take me?"

"Nope."

She raises her eyebrows.

I add, "Don't tell me you're scared of surprises."

She shakes her head and laughs, but the thing is, she should be scared of any position I put her in. Very, very scared.

Ivy 3

VERY LICKABLE

Dax's phone rings. He glances at it and hits the screen. It rings again right away, and he groans.

Bobby and he exchange a glance.

Dax sends the call to voicemail, but it rings again.

"You can get that," I tell him.

"Of course he can. He's not that big of a moron," Avery snarks.

"Shut up," Dax warns.

"Get it so she stops calling," Avery instructs.

My heart drops.

She?

Of course he has a girl calling.

It's probably his girlfriend.

Why is he touching me if he has a girlfriend?

Maybe I'm misinterpreting things.

Dax seethes, "Shut up, Avery!" He turns to me. "Let me take care of this." He walks past me and answers, snapping, "Take a hint, Cindy."

Cindy?

My gut churns.

Avery steps next to me and slides her hand around my waist. Her thumb caresses the curve of my hip, and she murmurs, "Don't be so sad. There are people right in front of you who are way more interesting than Dax."

"I'm not sad," I blurt out, but it's a lie, and Avery sees it.

Instead of calling me out, she purses her lips and leans closer. "You have really nice skin. Very lickable." She drags her fingertips down the front of my stomach.

I jump back and stare at her.

She laughs and steps in front of me. She puts her hand on my cheek. Hurt fills her expression. She softly asks, "Did I upset you?"

My stomach somersaults, and I swallow hard. I'm not interested in women, but I also don't want to offend her. I open my mouth, but nothing comes out.

She drags her finger over my jaw. "You're lucky. You have very sharp features."

I step back to escape her grasp but fall into Bobby's hard frame. "Oh! Sorry!" I squeak.

He positions his arms around me and then Avery, palming her ass and tugging her against me.

"Oh. You want to play with us too, Bobby?" she coos, batting her eyes at me and pursing her lips.

"What?" I exclaim.

Bobby's hot breath hits my neck. He reaches for my chin and tugs my face upward. His gaze drills into my mouth and his brown eyes light with lusty flames. He murmurs, "I'm always up for a good game. You know that, Avery."

Before I can stop it, she squeezes her hands on my hips and claims, "Been a long time since we had anyone with meat on their bones, huh?"

Bobby keeps my chin positioned so I can't avoid him. I'm sandwiched between them, and they caught me by surprise.

But what does she mean by meat?

I'm not fat.

Avery is skin and bones, and I don't think I could ever get that skinny.

"Fatty Patty was the last one. Remember her," Bobby says, leaning into my neck and inhaling deeply.

It gives me the creeps, making my skin crawl.

Avery adds, "She wasn't nearly as pretty as Ivy."

My insides quiver. I try to push against Avery, but Bobby has his hold firm around us.

Cooper's voice interjects. He orders, "Get off her, you two."

Bobby turns his head, keeping my chin pinned. "Mind your own business."

"You heard me. Let her go," Cooper states.

Avery scoffs. "And what are you going to do if we don't, Coop?"

"I mean it—"

"What the fuck, Bobby!" Dax bellows.

Bobby's lips twist. He redirects his gaze to Dax, and in a nonchalant voice, replies, "Don't get your panties in a twist. We're just showing Ivy how much we adore her. Aren't we, Avery?"

"Yes. Total adoration for your new friend. In fact, I was just admiring her body," Avery replies.

Dax's hands move to both sides of me, and he violently thrusts them against Bobby's and Avery's chests. "That's enough!"

"Aww. You're such a party pooper," Avery whines.

"Chill out. It's all in good fun," Bobby declares.

"My ass," Dax growls, tugging me into him. He glances down at me. "You okay?"

I recover and smile, deciding I don't need to make enemies on the first day. But I note that I need to be more alert around Bobby and Avery when I'm alone with them. "I'm fine. They were joking."

"Yeah. We were just joking, Dax," Avery interjects.

"Sure you were." Dax scowls.

Tension builds between the two as neither of them flinch. Dax stands solid, holding me tight against him. Avery keeps her smirk on her face, as strong-willed as Dax.

"Let's not cry over milk that hasn't even spilled," Bobby suggests.

Dax redirects his glare on him.

Bobby laughs and shakes his head. "Let's let Ivy be the judge of this."

Dax stays quiet.

Bobby asks, "Ivy, are you pissed at us for joking around with you?"

I debate about being honest but decide it's best to let it go. I shake my head. "Nope. We're good."

He grins. "See? Ivy's fine. If she's fine, then you should be too."

Dax keeps his disapproving expression aimed at Bobby and Avery.

A different ringtone fills the air, and Bobby pulls his phone out of his pocket. He glances at the screen and groans. "You're fucking up my mojo, Dax." He hits the screen and turns, walking away, answering, "Marcey. You miss me already, babe?"

Avery opens the fridge and pulls out a bottle of hard seltzer. She opens it and takes a sip. Then she grabs another one, removes the cap, and holds it toward me. "Have a drink, Ivy."

"No, thanks," I reply.

She adds, "It doesn't have any carbs."

I refrain from rolling my eyes. All this talk about carbohydrates is annoying me. She's thin as a rail. Why is she worrying about her weight? Instead, I say, "Thanks, but I'm good."

Her eyes narrow. "Don't tell me you don't drink."

I take a deep breath. It's not the first time someone's tried to get me to drink. Something tells me she's going to hold it over my head. Still, I shake my head and answer, "No, I don't."

Amusement fills her expression. She holds it out closer to me. "Then welcome to the Carrington Estate. Time you grew up. Here, start with this."

Dax scolds, "Shut up, Avery. If she doesn't drink, then she doesn't drink."

She snaps her head toward him. "Stop acting like her savior, Dax. You can only keep up your saint-like attitude so long before she discovers the real you. Might as well show her who Dax Carrington is right now."

Her comment pisses me off. Dax has been nothing but nice to me. I step toward her and politely—and forcefully enough to get my point across—say, "I don't drink, Avery. Thanks, but you don't have to offer me any ever again." I turn toward Dax and smile. "You ready to make those burgers?"

He tosses another nasty look at his sister and then smiles at me. He nods, answering, "Sounds good. Why don't you help me after all?"

"Would love to."

He leads me to the grill and mutters, "I'm sorry about them. Don't hold them against me."

My insides warm once more. I can't ignore how much I like Dax.

He has a girlfriend, I remind myself.

"What's wrong?" he asks.

It's better to have him as a friend than not at all.

I smile again. "Nothing."

He spins the knob on the grill. The flames burst under the metal grate. He lowers his voice and says, "Your frown tells me something is bothering you. Is it what they just did?" His eyes darken.

"No."

"Then what is it?"

"Nothing. I'm fine."

He looks at me like he doesn't believe me.

I blurt out, "How was your phone call with your girlfriend?"

"Cindy?"

"Yeah."

"She's not my girlfriend," he claims, then clenches his jaw.

Relief fills me. Still, I question, "No?"

He shakes his head. "No. Sure, we had a thing once, but that's been over a long time."

"Oh."

His lips twitch. He studies me.

The butterflies in my stomach take off. I ask, "Why do you look amused?"

His lips curve into a bigger smile and he arches his eyebrows. "Glad to know you don't like the thought of me having a girlfriend."

I open my mouth, but nothing comes out. Heat crawls up my neck and into my cheeks.

He softly chuckles. "It's okay, gorgeous. I like you too." He winks and pecks me on the lips. Then he turns and grabs a packet of hamburgers out of the fridge.

Happiness soars through me. I'm too shocked and excited to move.

Dax Carrington just kissed me.

He did, right?

I didn't imagine that?

"Ugh. She has it bad," Avery scoffs, snapping me out of my bliss.

Embarrassment floods me. I'd love for Avery and me to be friends, but it's hard to see how we will ever be. For some reason, she's got it out for me. Well, except when she's invading my space.

"Ignore her," Dax orders and hands me a tomato. "Mind slicing a few?"

Relieved to have something to do, I eagerly grab it and another one off the side of the grill. "Sure."

"There're knives in the drawer," he directs, pointing at the counter.

I make my way to the outdoor kitchen and pull open the drawer. A dozen very expensive knives gleam in the sunlight.

I select one, then concentrate on the tomatoes, enjoying the summer heat and music.

Dax brings an onion over and says, "Can you grab another knife for me?"

I reach for one inside the drawer, then hand it to him and motion toward the onion. "You're brave."

Arrogance fills his expression. "I never cry."

"How is that possible?" I question.

"It's all in the preparation."

"Oh?"

He takes his knife, slits the onion in half, then picks it up. He peels a layer of skin off, claiming, "Yep. First, you soak it in cold water. It slows down the production of chemicals. You can freeze it if you prefer, but I never remember to take it out in time to defrost."

"Wow. I'm going to have to remember this trick. I cry long after the onion's cut," I admit.

"Again, we have peons on payroll to do all this." Avery huffs, stepping next to us and finishing her drink. She tosses the bottle into a trash can and grabs another.

"Such a snob," Dax seethes.

Avery chirps, "At least I'm being real, big brother." She tilts her head and gives him a knowing look.

"Leave them alone," Cooper adds, joining us.

She glares at him. "Why are you on his side all of a sudden?"

"Just cool it, Avery," Cooper demands, then grabs a slice of tomato and pops it in his mouth.

"Where's the flipper?" Bobby calls out.

Dax gives Avery another nasty look and opens a cabinet. A dozen grill utensils are hanging on the door. He selects one and takes it to Bobby.

"Where are you from?" Cooper asks.

"West Virginia," I reply, deciding I like Cooper. He's a cross between Avery and Dax and seems more like his brother than his sister. And that is welcomed. Avery's rubbing me the wrong way.

"You like the mountains?" he questions.

I nod. "Yeah. Especially the lakes in summer."

"Have you been on our lake?"

I shake my head. "Not yet. We arrived late yesterday."

His face lights up. "We'll have to take you out on the boats before summer ends. Tomorrow should be a good day to sail. Why don't we plan on it?"

"I'd love to go, but I need to finish unpacking."

"How long will that take?"

I shrug. "Not sure. My room and my dad's are all that's left. I might be able to do it tonight when I get home."

He asks, "Do you have a lot of stuff?"

I ponder his question. "Not really."

"Then you have to agree to come! We don't always have perfect sailing weather."

I softly laugh. "You're making it hard for me to say no."

His expression grows kinder, and I decide I like him even more. He says, "Good. It's a sin to miss out on a good sailing day."

I cave. "Okay. What time are you leaving?"

"I can go later in the day if you want."

Dax slides his arm around my waist. "Didn't remember inviting you on our sailing trip."

Cooper's face falls. "Don't be a dick."

"For speaking the truth?" Dax states.

I turn to him in surprise and pin my eyebrows together.

"What's that look for?" he questions.

I point out, "I've never met siblings who are so mean to each other."

"Welcome to the Carrington's," Bobby sings.

A satisfied sound comes from Avery.

I ignore them and stare at Dax. Besides him, Cooper's been the only other one who's truly been nice to me. So I ask, "Why can't Cooper come with us?"

Dax stares at me for a moment, then sighs. He shakes his head and turns to his brother. "Fine. You can come."

"Well, don't do me any favors."

"Then stay home."

"No. All of us can go," I interject, appreciating Cooper's love of sailing and excitement around it.

"And she's a do-gooder," Avery mutters.

"Shut up," Dax spits at her.

I ignore her. "So it's settled, then? The three of us will go tomorrow once I finish unpacking?"

"And me," Bobby interjects.

"Plus me. You wouldn't want to exclude us, would you, Ivy?" Avery whines.

My gut dives, but I force myself to smile. "No. Of course I wouldn't."

"Great. Have you sailed before?" she asks.

"No," I admit.

"Sorry. That was a dumb question." Her lips turn into a thin line.

My chest tightens.

"Snob," Dax and Cooper say at the same time.

Bobby drops a platter of burgers on the counter. "Time to eat."

Cooper grabs a bun and cheeseburger and puts it on a plate. "Ivy, what do you want on yours?"

"She can make her own food. You shouldn't be waiting on her anyway. So inappropriate," Avery scolds.

"Inappropriate?" Cooper snarls.

"Please. Her dad's on payroll."

"Jesus, Avery. Knock it off!" Dax warns.

Heat floods my face. I shouldn't be embarrassed. My father does work for their family.

"Does your face always turn red so easily?" Bobby asks.

"Bobby!" Dax threatens.

"What? She looks like the tomato she just cut up," he claims.

My face turns even hotter, and I scold myself for reacting, but I can't help it. Since I was little, I've shown my embarrassment through my cheeks.

Why am I embarrassed about my father working here?

I'm not.

I don't belong here.

I blurt out, "Maybe I should go home and finish unpacking."

"Don't be silly. Let's go eat at my place away from these idiots," Dax suggests.

"You don't have to run away. I merely stated the truth. Didn't mean to offend," Avery claims.

Dax seethes, "Sure you did."

"No, I did not," she declares and stares at me. "Ivy, you didn't take offense, did you?"

My stomach flips. I did, but I'm not admitting that to her.

Dax interjects, "Of course she did."

"Why? She's not proud of her father working for us?" Avery suggests.

"That's not true!" I protest. My insides shake.

She adds, "We usually don't keep people around who aren't proud to be associated with the Carringtons."

My lungs tighten. My father's had a bad streak of employment since my mom disappeared. I don't need to ruin this for him. I blurt, "I never said that!"

Dax slides his arm around me. "Of course you didn't. Don't listen to her."

"I didn't," I mumble to him.

He tugs me tighter against him and picks up a plate of burgers, announcing, "Pool time's over."

"You're such a downer," Avery whines.

Bobby adds, "Pussy. Don't tap out."

But Dax ignores them, leading me toward the golf cart.

I grab my wrap off the lounger, more than ready to go. And I curse myself for putting my dad's job at risk.

We get to the golf cart, and Dax drives off in a different direction.

"Where are we going?" I question.

"My place."

"I think it's best if you take me home."

He glances at me. "Why would that be best?"

My stomach flips faster. "Today's been fun, but I don't need to do anything to get my dad fired. I think it's best if we don't hang out anymore."

Dax stops the cart. "Ivy, don't be ridiculous. Avery's a bitch. Don't let her get into your head."

"My father works really hard."

"No one is saying otherwise."

"He doesn't deserve to lose his job because of me."

Dax slides his hand on my cheek. "He's not losing his job, Ivy."

I blink hard, trying not to cry, upset that I'm so emotional.

Concern floods Dax's expression. "Ivy, you don't have to worry about this. I promise you that hanging out with my stupid siblings and me isn't going to ever jeopardize your father's career here."

I stare at him, blink, and a tear drops.

He swipes at it. "You're overreacting."

I sniffle and turn, then pull it together, feeling stupid once again.

"I promise," Dax repeats.

I stare at him with my thoughts racing about my father's past employment troubles and how I can't deny my attraction to Dax.

This isn't good. My father works for him.

He holds my face firmly. His tone is just as stern. "Ivy, don't let Avery win."

"Meaning?"

He slowly licks his lips, studying mine.

My heart races faster.

He meets my eyes. "Meaning she's a snob. She's always

going to be. And if I could eliminate her from my world, I would, but I can't. So I apologize now, but you'll have to deal with her. You know why?"

I barely get out, "Why?"

He glances at my lips, then before I know it, his mouth is pressed to mine, his warm tongue slides into my mouth, and every ounce of breath I have is stolen in a rush of adrenaline-filled bliss.

He kisses me like he owns me. Hungry. Consuming. Unlike any kiss I've ever experienced.

He slowly retreats, locking his gaze to mine, admitting, "Because I like you. And I want you as mine."

Dax 4

HATE TO PULL AWAY FROM HER

Dax

Ivy's lips part. Her breathing turns shallow. She stares at me like she can't believe I told her I want her.

She's playing right into my hands and doesn't even know it.

My sister and Bobby didn't disappoint me. I knew it would be an interesting encounter, and they lived up to their true selves. In the process, it drove Ivy right into my arms.

"Did I say something wrong?" I ask, tucking a lock of her dark hair behind her ear.

She slowly licks her lips, and I force myself not to kiss her again. The girl definitely kisses better than I anticipated. I assumed I'd have to train her, but her mouth molded to mine like it was meant to be.

It was hard to pull away from her, but if I don't play my cards right, I'll screw this up.

There's no way in hell I'm messing up my new pet project.

"Well?" I push.

She shakes her head. "No."

I wiggle my eyebrows. "So you want me too, then?"

She softly laughs.

"Admit it," I goad, taking a small nibble on her ear.

She turns her head so our gazes lock and whispers, "Okay."

I freeze. "Okay, what?"

A vine of heat crawls across her cheeks. I stroke my finger over it. Her lips curve, and she admits, "Okay, I want you too."

So fucking easy.

Still, I'm giddy. It's been a long time since anyone caught my interest the way Ivy has. This is just the beginning of the game, and I couldn't have played it any better.

I glance at her lips until she's practically drooling for me to kiss her again. Instead of giving it to her, I turn away and put the golf cart into gear. I snake across the lawn and park in front of my place.

"You live in a cottage?" she asks.

I nod. "Sure do."

"I figured you'd live in the main house."

I glance at the looming building in the distance. It looks like a castle in some ways. The 30,000 plus square feet spread across the horizon. To most people, it's impressive. To me, it's nothing but a prison. I mutter, "Got out of there as soon as possible."

"Why? It looks like an amazing place to live," Ivy gushes in awe.

"It's not as awesome as you'd think it would be," I admit.

Ivy's expression falls. She puts her hand on my thigh and says, "I'm sorry. Did something bad happen there?"

I almost laugh. I could list hundreds of bad things that took place in my parents' fortress. But I don't air our dirty laundry.

It wouldn't be becoming of a Carrington. Plus, I'm not a pussy. I don't cry over the past. And eventually, I get revenge. One day, everyone in my family will feel my wrath. Until then, I'm biding my time.

"Dax?" Ivy asks with a concerned voice.

She's so fucking innocent. If I told her the basics, she'd probably freak out. She'd never look at me the same either.

Maybe she wouldn't.

What am I saying? Of course she would.

Best to keep my mouth shut.

I get out of the golf cart and answer, "Just family bullshit. Let's eat. I'm starving. How about you?" I grab the plate of burgers from her.

She steps away from the cart and nods. "Yeah, I'm hungry."

"Great. Welcome to my abode." I grin and open the door.

She hesitates but steps into the cottage.

I'm tempted to push her down to her knees and then have her suck me dry until I'm spent. But I remind myself it's too soon.

"Not like the main house, but it's my own space," I state.

She turns in a circle and takes it all in. "I like it."

"Good." I stare at her a moment, wishing I could suck on her lips until they swell.

She shifts on her feet and then says, "Should we eat?"

I'll eat you.

I point to the table. "Sure. Make yourself at home."

She slides into a chair, and I plop on the one next to her. I hold a burger up to her mouth. "Take a bite."

She doesn't hesitate and sinks her teeth into it. A bit of ketchup lines her mouth, and I swipe at it while she chews.

I suck it off my finger and grab the other burger. I take a bite and groan.

She laughs.

"So good," I say through a mouthful of meat.

"Mm-hmm," she agrees, then takes another bite.

I rise and grab two sodas from the fridge. I put them on the table and then sit back down.

She takes a sip, swallows, and declares, "Cooper seems nice."

I grunt. "Don't let him fool you."

She arches her eyebrows. "Oh?"

My brother's not as toxic as Avery, but I don't trust him either. If he had the chance, he'd swoop right into what's my given birthright and steal it from me. But I can't exactly explain that to Ivy. So I answer, "Trust me on this."

"What does he do that's so bad?"

I shake my head. "Nothing I want to discuss. Eat your burger before it gets cold."

She hesitates, then obeys, which makes me happy. I don't like to have to convince my pet projects about my siblings this early in the game. All Ivy needs to know is I'm the only one she can fully trust.

So I add, "My brother is more like Avery than you know. That's all I'm going to say. And you deserve a real chance here."

Ivy freezes, her eyes turning to slits.

I wait for her to gather her thoughts. The seeds of doubt about anyone but me need to be planted before they can grow. I'm more than happy to spread them.

She says, "What do you mean a real chance?"

Play the part, I remind myself.

I sigh, lean back, and put my hand on her back. I slowly rub it and, with a concerned voice, say, "Nothing you need to worry about. I'll protect you from anything they could ever do to you."

Fear laces with bravery in her expression. She sits up straighter. "What would they do to me?"

I lean closer and cup her cheeks in my palms. "Nothing. I won't ever allow it."

She swallows hard.

"I shouldn't have said anything. I don't want you to worry about any of this."

"Dax—"

I put my fingers over her lips. "I'll always protect you, Ivy. Understand?"

Confusion fills her face. She furrows her brows and parts her lips, but nothing comes out.

"Dax! I'm not taking no for—"

My gut dives.

Not now.

Ivy spins, and the color in her face drains.

"Cindy, what are you doing here?" I bellow, cursing myself for giving her access to the estate. She's wearing a bikini top that barely covers her nipples and a thong that is just as skimpy in the front as it is in the back.

I used to love that bikini. Now, I hate it.

I make a note to revoke her access to the estate.

She's high on something, which isn't new. She struts toward us, then leans down and slides her hands on Ivy's face. She slurs, "Who do we have here? New toy for us, Dax?"

Shit, shit, shit. I don't need her destroying everything I've built today.

Ivy flinches, but there's nowhere for her to go.

I rise and tug Cindy away from her. "I don't know what you're talking about, but you're high."

She giggles and tosses her arms around me. "So? Since when aren't you?"

And this just gets worse.

"You need to go. Let me get our driver to take you home," I offer. Normally, I wouldn't. It's Cindy's choice to drive high as a kite. If she dies, what the fuck do I care? The world won't be a worse place without her.

She grabs my cock. Her mouth twists, and she slurs, "Don't be silly. I'm here to pay homage. It looks like I have more than one person to take care of, but you know me, Dax. I'm always up for your challenges." She giggles and looks at Ivy.

My chest tightens. I don't need this kind of talk right now. I move her toward the door. "You're not making sense, Cindy. Go home. I've told you we're over. Let's not keep going through this."

Cindy's eyes widen, blazing with horror, as if I just told her that her beloved mother died or something. She whines, "Stop playing games, Dax."

I firmly assert, "This isn't a game, Cindy. Time to go home. Sober up. I'll see you when school starts, but don't come back here."

Her expression drops. She clings to my neck tighter and presses her fake tits against me. Her voice lowers. "You don't mean that."

"I do."

She shakes her head. "No, no, no! You told me no one sucks your dick like I do."

My pulse skyrockets. "That's a lie," I deny quickly.

"It's not!"

Ivy rises and clears her throat. "I'm going to go home."

I spin toward her, but Cindy's still locked against me. I order, "No. You stay. She's leaving."

"Not until I suck your cock like I did last night, big boy," Cindy claims.

My insides shake with anger. I do not need this after all the progress I've made.

Ivy high-tails it to the door.

"Ivy, wait," I call out.

"It's okay. I'll talk to you later. Thanks for the burger," she says and disappears past the frame.

"Wait! Come back! I want to play with you too! Dax can handle both of us," Cindy shouts.

"Enough!" I bark, pissed off she's ruined my perfect start with Ivy. I push her off me, and she stumbles and falls to the floor.

I don't care. I lunge out of the cottage and after Ivy. She's already halfway across the lawn, and stupid me doesn't take my golf cart. By the time I catch up, she's in view of her place.

"Ivy," I yell and grab her arm.

She spins on me, seething. "Go take care of your girlfriend, Dax."

"She's not my girlfriend!"

"She seems to think so!" Ivy cries out, her blues full of fire.

"She's not!" I try to pull her into my arms, but she wiggles out of them.

"Don't you dare touch me when you were with her last night!"

"I wasn't," I lie.

"Bullshit!"

"I'm telling you the truth!"

Ivy shakes her head, and anger spews from her lips, "No, you aren't! I'm not stupid, Dax. A girl isn't going to claim those things if she doesn't do them!"

I laugh, but it's more from the nervousness of losing Ivy forever. I declare, "You don't know Cindy very well."

"Yeah, but you do!" Ivy spouts.

I run my hand through my hair. "Ivy, I told you I'm not with her anymore."

"You left off the important part!"

"What's that?" I ask.

Ivy sarcastically laughs. "The 'since last night' part!"

I groan. "You're not listening."

"Oh, I'm listening just fine, Dax!" She turns and trots toward her house.

"Ivy!" I call after her, close on her heels.

"Leave me alone, Dax!" she cries out.

We get to the porch, and I grab her. I spin her into me. "Stop! Let me explain!"

"There's nothing to explain! I have a very clear picture of what's going on," she claims.

"You don't!"

"I do!"

"Ivy, what's going on here?" John interjects, stepping out of the house.

Ivy stares at me, her face red and her breath short.

"Ivy?" John repeats, scowling at me.

She shakes her head. "Nothing, Dad. I was just coming home to finish unpacking."

I stay frozen. "Ivy—"

"I think it's time for you to go home now, Dax," John states.

I debate about how to play this out and whether I should fight with him right now or not.

"Son, I'm not asking," he asserts.

My blood pumps harder. I reluctantly release Ivy and step back. I lower my voice and claim, "You're not being fair. I can explain everything."

She stays quiet, blinking hard.

"Ivy, go into the house," John directs.

She hesitates a moment, then obeys him.

He waits until she disappears inside and then he steps in front of me. "Your father warned me about you."

My gut sinks.

I should have known.

Time to change the game. If you can't win with one strategy, you have to switch things up. If I can't win John over, I'll make him hate me. It'll drive him nuts to know I'm with his daughter.

"Yeah? What boat of lies did he tell you about me?" I snarl.

John gives me a knowing look. He replies, "Why would your father tell me lies? A father doesn't want to speak poorly of his son."

"Mine does," I claim.

"So I should feel sorry for you?" John asks.

Anger fills me. My father screws up too many things in my life. He'll do whatever he needs to in order to take me down.

"No, sir," I seethe.

John looks around us and steps closer. He lowers his voice, warning, "I'll only tell you this once. I don't like you. I'm never going to like you. So don't come near my daughter ever again. Are we clear?"

Every bit of my rage mixes with how much I love a good challenge. John just gave me the best one he could.

I step closer. "Do you think you're the first man to warn me to stay away from his daughter?"

His eyes turn to slits.

I slowly pat him on the shoulder. "You've got the wrong information about me. But I'll be clear about my intentions. I like your daughter. And I'm not going to disappear out of her life. And as long as you're working for the Carringtons, you'll deal with me. Do you know why?"

He sniffs hard and spits on the ground. It lands next to my foot. He aims his sharp disgust back on me. He snarls, "Why's that?"

There are tons of times I could tell the world about who I really am and what power I hold. But I don't. I never need to.

I'm a Carrington, and that's good enough. But right now, it's a beautiful piece of information that's going to knock John on his ass.

I glance around us to make sure we're still alone. Then I drop the bomb. "You think my father's in charge, but I can assure you that he's not."

"Yeah? Why isn't he?" John snarls.

I can't contain my grin. "Because he didn't inherit all that you see from my grandfather. You know who did, John?"

The color drains from his face as I give him a moment to process.

I continue, "Ah, that's right. You work for me. My father is only a placeholder until I graduate. Then, the trust fully transfers the estate to me. So I suggest you decide if you want your cushy job here or not. This is my property. And I like your daughter. So you don't have a say about whether or not I'll see her. That'll be up to her. Understand?"

John regains his composure and steps back. He grinds his molars and then states, "Then it won't be a problem. My daughter has already made her decision. She wants nothing to do with you."

An uncontrollable laugh fills the air, and the more I try to stop it, the harder it rolls out of me.

"Want to tell me what's so funny?" John questions.

My laughter cuts off, and I answer, "Your daughter will be back in my arms by the end of tomorrow. You'll see. But so you know, I don't intend to be anything but good to her."

I'll leave that for the others, I think, then pat him on the shoulder. "Have a nice night, John."

I take my time walking across the estate and to my cottage. When I get there, Cindy's naked on my couch. Normally, I'd let her fuck me, but she's too used up.

I decide I don't want to deal with her. I pick up my phone and call security.

"Dax," Steven answers.

"I need you to remove Cindy from the premises and revoke her access. She's in my cottage," I order, then hang up and walk to the lake. For hours, I sit on the dock, thinking about my next moves and how I'm going to get back into Ivy's good graces.

Ivy 5

MAYBE HE WAS RIGHT

Ivy

Rage, hurt, and fear fill me. I stare out the window at Dad and Dax having a heated exchange.

My dad's not going to be happy with me.

Wait. Why am I blaming myself for this? I haven't done anything.

He's not going to want me to see Dax again.

What am I talking about? Of course I shouldn't see him again.

I can't believe that girl. She was drunk, but it's clear she and Dax have a thing going on.

She was with him yesterday, and he kissed me today.

My chest tightens. I hold back tears.

Why did I let myself start to fall for him?

I should have known better.

Dax Carrington's the most handsome man I've ever met. He's also strong, powerful, and rich. I'm a girl from West

Virginia who needs to remember my place. I don't belong here and shouldn't have thought I could fit in with these people.

My father warned me. He told me that rich people are selfish and you have to be careful around them. I didn't want to believe him. I still don't want to believe him. Yet, maybe he was right.

Dax spins and saunters across the yard. My father watches him go, then turns and makes his way toward our cottage.

My insides quiver harder. I don't want to get into it with Dad, but I know it's coming.

I move from the window and go into my room to try and escape my fate.

It's pointless.

My father's footsteps pound on the wooden floor, and he looms in my doorway, seething. "Ivy."

I close my eyes for a brief moment and then open them. "Don't start, Dad."

"You can't see him again," he directs.

"I don't want to see him again," I lie.

"No?" he questions, arching his eyebrows like he knows me better than I know myself.

I shake my head, adding, "No. There's no reason to see him. Why were you fighting with him?"

"Don't worry about it."

I put my hand on my hip. "Don't tell me not to worry."

Dad's anger bubbles. His scowl intensifies. He warns, "I could lose my job, so stay away from him, Ivy."

Every fear I have rises within me, but then I remember Dax telling me that he would never put my dad's job in jeopardy. But that was when I was starting to trust him. "I'm sorry. I would never jeopardize your job on purpose, you know that, right?"

My dad holds his hand in front of him and releases a

stressful breath. "I'm sorry. I shouldn't have said that, Ivy. This isn't your fault. Don't worry. Everything's fine. But I want you to stay away from Dax Carrington. Do you hear me?"

I decide it's best to agree. Besides, I don't want any part of Dax. If he's going to play me and that other girl, I don't need to be around him again. "Okay."

My father stares at me for a moment with a mix of pity and anxiety in his expression.

"Please don't look at me like that," I beg.

His voice softens. "Ivy, we have to remember who we are and who they are."

After everything that happened today, I should agree with my father, but I still don't understand why we have to be so different. I admit, "I don't know why it has to be like that. It's just money."

My father scrubs his hands over his face, sighing. "Ivy, it's hard to explain. You'll understand when you're older, but this is how the world works. We aren't their kind, and they're not ours. Don't let that boy fool you," he warns, his gaze drilling into mine.

My cheeks heat. I swallow hard. I hate how my dad knows that I was starting to fall for Dax. He doesn't even have to say anything else.

I lift my chin and announce, "I won't see him again."

My father takes a deep breath and crosses his arms. "What happened between you two?"

Embarrassment fills me. The last thing I want to do is talk to Dad about it. I mutter, "Nothing."

"If he comes near you, I want to know."

"Why, so you can lose your job?"

Tense silence fills the air. My father grinds his molars.

I panic. "Dad, I don't want you to lose your job." Memories of how bad it was in West Virginia when he didn't have one and how we were struggling, plague me. Plus, my father was so excited to get hired by Dax's dad. He claimed this position was his dream job.

Dad shakes his head. "That's for me to worry about, but I'm not going to get fired."

"How do you know?" I question, then wish I could get Dax's voice out of my head, promising me that he would never jeopardize my dad's job. But now, I don't know what to believe. If he can kiss me after having sexual encounters with that girl the day before, how can I ever trust him again?

And what did he and Cindy do with others involved?

The thought makes me feel ill.

Dad responds, "Because I'm not, and that's not for you to worry about. Now, are you hungry?"

I shake my head. "No, I just ate a cheeseburger. Do you want me to make you something?"

"No, I can make dinner. Why don't you unpack your room?" He points to the boxes.

I glance at them, not wanting to unpack, already tired of the moving process. Part of me wants to run back to West Virginia. Yet, I don't want to lose my opportunity to go to Clifton University, which has one of the best botany programs in the country.

Dad adds, "They won't unpack themselves."

"On it," I claim.

My father leaves the room and I choose a box. I open it, and for the rest of the evening, I slowly make my way through every piece of cardboard until nothing is left to unpack.

I break down the boxes and take them out to the front room. A pile of broken-down cardboard is near the front door. Guilt fills me. I blurt out, "Dad, I was going to unpack your room."

He shrugs. "I don't have that much."

"Yeah, but you've been working all day."

His lips curve. "I'm not decrepit, you know. I can work and come home and unpack."

I tilt my head. "Haha, very funny. Are you sure you're not decrepit?"

He grins. "Not yet. Don't need to go get those diapers yet."

I laugh. We have a running joke about my dad with adult diapers. One time, I filled out a form where they sent samples. He couldn't figure out who did it and why he was getting them. One day, he caught me filling out a form to get a sample from another brand. Since then, it's been an inside joke between us.

He glances at his watch. "It's getting late. Let's hit the hay."

I'm not tired, but there's nothing else to do, so I don't argue. I hug him and kiss him on the cheek, and he tightens his hold around me. He lingers for a minute, then finally releases me.

I brush my teeth and wash my face, then shut the door to my bedroom. I put on a nightgown and slide under the covers.

I don't know what to do about Dax. I try not to think about him, but I can't get him out of my head. I toss and turn most of the night. I finally fall asleep until I feel hands over my mouth and the weight of a body over me.

My heart beats faster than ever before, and I try to move, but the large frame on top of mine is too heavy to push away. Then I realize the smell of Dax fills the air.

"Quiet, Ivy," he orders.

My eyes widen. Excitement fills me. It's not fear, except for a small part. It's mostly excitement.

Dammit, why do I still like him?

I get over my confusion and try to fight him again.

"Ivy, stop it. I don't want to wake your dad up," he scolds.

I freeze. My dad will kill Dax if he finds him here—there's

no doubt about it—and then he'll definitely lose his job. So I stare into Dax's clear eyes that are only inches from mine.

He keeps his hand over my mouth and states, "Come with me."

More confusion fills me. I can't talk. His hand never moves. His intoxicating scent keeps flaring through me, making my body ache for something I know I shouldn't want with Dax. He's a slimeball, and I need to remind myself at all times I've gotten insight into the real Dax Carrington.

"I am going to remove my hand from your mouth. I need you to be a good girl and stay quiet. Then we can talk about earlier, okay?"

I glare at him. His lip curves into an arrogant smirk I want to wipe off his face and kiss at the same time. Then I remember what it's like to feel his lips on mine and his tongue swirling in my mouth.

"Oh, I see you're going to be stubborn," he says, as if this is a joke.

I huff a blast of air through my nose.

He warns, "Remember, if I lift my hand and your dad wakes up because you're loud, he won't be happy with either of us."

I want to tell him that I haven't done anything. I'm just lying in bed, doing what I'm supposed to. He's the one who somehow got into my room.

New panic fills me.

How did he get into my room?

Does he have a key?

Yes, he probably does since his dad owns this place.

A tickle of summer breeze comes through the curtains, and I glance at the window. My question gets answered as I realize that's how he got in.

His hot breath puffs against my ear when he murmurs, "Let's go to the lake and talk. There's so much you don't understand. And I need you to know the truth, Ivy. What you heard isn't the truth. Cindy's a liar."

My heart pounds harder. I want it to be true. But she was adamant, even though drunk. And aren't drunken words sober thoughts?

Plus, if I add everything Avery and Bobby talked about, there seems to be more to Dax than he let on. Things I want no part of...things that are beyond the scope of my knowledge or my experiences.

Besides, I can't get the thought of Dax doing things with Cindy out of my mind.

He adds, "I know you're upset with me, but there's something between us. You felt it just like I did. So you have to give me a chance to explain."

My butterflies take off.

He felt it too?

What am I thinking?

I remind myself not to be a dumb girl.

"Ivy," he begs.

I blink hard, not sure what to do. He stares at me, then moves his hand off my mouth. His lips quickly press against mine.

I push against his chest, but it doesn't help. He doesn't give me a big kiss. It's small and quick, but it's a fresh reminder of what it's like for Dax Carrington's mouth to be against mine.

He keeps his lips close to mine and murmurs, "Come to the lake with me. Please."

There's a desperation in his voice I've not heard before. I kid myself and say I don't want to wake my father up, but it's more than that.

I want to be with Dax.

I want to hear what he has to say.

I want to believe that Cindy's a liar and she made all this up.

And I want to know that he's good inside—how I thought he was when I met him.

Then all the nice, kind things he did for me all day swirl through my head for the millionth time.

"Please," he pleads again.

I cave. "Fine."

A tiny smile erupts on his lips. He gives me another peck, then rolls off me, grabs my hand, and helps me to my feet. His eyes trail down my body, and I realize I'm in my nightgown with no bra on. I fold my arms over my chest.

His eyes turn to burning flames, and he slowly lifts them from my hands to my gaze, stating in a suggestive tone, "I'll let you get changed, unless you don't want to?"

My butterflies escape in furious flutters. They shouldn't. I need to remind myself I'm mad at him. What he's done is disgusting. Unless, of course, Cindy really was lying.

He turns and stares out the window.

I quickly put on a pair of shorts, a bra, and a tank top, then turn back toward him.

He motions for me to come closer.

I meet him at the window.

He teases, "Sorry, gorgeous. I don't think the front door's a good option tonight. Do you?"

I try not to smile, but my lips twitch. I shake my head.

"Alrighty, then." He slides out the window and then reaches in for me. I let him help me out, and seds grabs my hand. He pulls me across the lawn, far away from the cottage, until we get to the golf cart.

He orders, "Get on, gorgeous."

I should tell him not to call me that, but every part of me likes it. I obey him, and he sits next to me.

We don't speak, driving through the woods until we reach the lake. The moon is full, creating a sparkle in the water. Trees surround the lake, and sailboats bob gently at their docks.

It's beautiful. It reminds me of when I snuck out of the house to hang out with my friends at a lake in West Virginia. A small part of me aches for home.

Dax gets off the golf cart and comes around to my side. I step out. He puts his hand around my waist, leading me to a little cove. We sit down on the grass, and he picks up my hand.

I should take it away, but I don't. It's warm, and I love everything about Dax touching me. I once again wish I didn't.

I blurt out, "I'm not stupid."

His face falls. He pulls my hand toward his lips and kisses my knuckles.

Tingles race down my spine.

He replies, "I know you're not stupid. It's one of the reasons I like you."

I bite on my lip, staying quiet. I don't know where to start, but I realize it's not for me to begin. It's his girlfriend who told me the truth. He's the one who slept with Cindy the night before and then kissed me the day after. So I remind myself I'm mad, and I glare at him.

He puts his hand on my cheek. "I understand why you're upset with me, but I promise you, Cindy lies."

I tilt my head. "She didn't seem to be lying, Dax. She seemed to know a lot of things about you and was more than open about things you have done with her and others," I say, my stomach flipping with sickness at the thought.

He shakes his head. "It's not true. I broke up with her a long time ago."

"Well, she knows a lot about you," I repeat, mad and upset, still hurting about the thought of them being together, even if it was before me.

"She doesn't," he claims.

I proclaim, "I don't kiss guys who are with other women."

He sighs, scoots closer, and puts his arm around my shoulders, pulling me into him. "Ivy, I'm telling you, I'm not with her. I was a while ago, but that ended early this summer."

I stare at the grass, my heart beating faster, unsure what to think. I want to believe him, but I don't want to be stupid.

"I promise you, I ended it with her at the beginning of summer. She doesn't take no for an answer," he insists.

"Why was she in your house if it's over? Does she have a key?"

"Bobby likes her friend Marcey. So she tags along a lot. But I've not done anything with her in months. I swear."

I remain motionless, not wanting to be one of those girls who believes what a guy tells them when it's not true, but I want so desperately to believe Dax.

He gently turns my chin toward him. "Ivy, you have to believe me. I didn't realize she still had access to the estate or my place. I only realized it tonight. But I called security and had it revoked. She'll never be here again without our permission, I promise."

Our permission, as if Dax and I are already a couple or mean something to each other.

"I don't know what else to do or say to you. I'm telling you the truth," he asserts, so convincingly it's hard not to believe him.

But there's another issue to address before I can even think about whether I'll believe him and give him a second chance.

Is that what this is?

He wants a second chance?

It is.

The realization sinks deep into me, and adrenaline fills me. I hate that I'm so happy he wants to earn me back.

Was I even his?

No. It was only a day.

Still...

"What's that, gorgeous?" he asks, concern filling his expression.

Anxiety rolls in a ball in my stomach, getting bigger and bigger.

"Tell me," he urges.

"What did you say to my dad?"

His face falls. "Your dad doesn't want me to see you anymore. I told him I'm going to anyway. That is if you forgive me for something I didn't do."

I swallow hard, and my mouth turns dry. It's not fair if I blame Dax for something he didn't do, and I don't have proof Cindy's telling the truth. He seems adamant she's lying. And in fairness, I didn't take Dax to be a liar. He was nothing but good to me all day.

"It's not fair for you to think this of me," he says, as if he can read my thoughts.

I sigh. "Okay, say I believe you about Cindy. Are you going to harm my dad and talk to your father about firing him?"

Dax's eyes widen. "No. Why would I do that? I promised you that your dad would never lose his job because of us. Even if you tell me right now that you never want to see me again, I wouldn't do that. Do I seem like I'm that type of person to you?" A look of hurt flashes across his features.

Relief fills me, but his expression hurts my heart. It's the same relief I felt earlier when he promised me my dad's job would always be safe.

His voice turns more adamant. "Ivy, I never want to have this conversation again. Your father's job has nothing to do with our relationship. I'm not that type of person. Do you understand?"

I nod.

"I want to hear it from your lips. Tell me you understand that I'm not that type of person," he demands.

I clear my throat. "I believe you, Dax. And thank you."

"Why are you thanking me?"

I shrug. "I don't know."

"Well, don't thank me. Just tell me we can start again. I've not been with Cindy, I promise you. I'm not interested in her. I'm interested in you."

"Why?" I blurt out, voicing the question that's run through my soul all day.

Surprise fills his expression. "What do you mean why?

Nerves fill me, but I'm already going down this path, so I might as well finish it.

I declare, "I'm a girl from West Virginia. I don't know anything about the things you know about. I don't come from money, and I don't have any power. You're somebody. I'm a nobody, Dax. So why are you interested in me?" My voice shakes with emotion, and I will myself not to cry.

He pulls me closer and puts his other hand on my cheek. Then he slides it to the back of my head and puts his face right in front of mine, claiming, "You're everything I've been looking for."

They're words that are better than anything he could have said, and all I want to do is believe him.

I open my mouth to speak, but he doesn't let me. He kisses me with the same hunger I feel for him, and I'm soon falling back into the web of everything that's Dax Carrington.

Dax 6

HIGH ON LIFE

DAX

"So tomorrow, I'll see you at ten o'clock," I murmur.

She nods. "Okay."

I give her another kiss, until she's kissing me like I'm her everything, and then I pull back. It's part of my strategy. I need to make her want me but not always get me. Not yet, at least, even though my cock's been hard as a fucking brick all night.

She glances at my lips again.

I continue holding back. "You better get back inside before your dad wakes up."

She breathlessly agrees. "Yeah, okay."

I help her through the window, then I race back to the golf cart, get on it, and return to my house.

The sun will rise soon, and there's no way I'm sleeping. I don't need to. I'm high on life right now.

It wasn't even that difficult to convince Ivy that Cindy's a liar, and I had to stop myself from laughing.

Ivy's super naive. Like every girl around here, she's already fallen for me. It won't be long before she'll do anything to please me.

And there's no doubt she'll soon be miserable living here. The things the others will do to her will break her in two. And it's going to be joyous to watch.

As the sun rises and the morning progresses, I stay busy preparing for our day. I order the staff to bring me a cooler full of drinks and food for the boat. I select my favorite sailboat. It's not huge; it's more quaint. It has everything I need in it. A small kitchen, a bathroom, and most of all a bed. I debate whether I should take Ivy today or down the road, but I decide to keep my options open.

I return to my golf cart to pick up Ivy, and my phone buzzes. I glance down at the text.

Ivy: I'll meet you at the lake.

Me: No, I'm coming to get you.

Ivy: I think it's best if I meet you there.

I freeze, but it doesn't take long for me to figure out why.
My adrenaline pumps up.
Time to lay the guilt on her.
I text her back.

Me: Is your dad there?

Ivy: He's within eyesight.

Me: I'm not going to hide us from him. And you're eighteen. You can see me if you want to. Plus, it's your dad. I want him to like me. So he needs to get over this and give me a chance.

Ivy: That's not a good idea right now, Dax.

Me: Are you embarrassed by me?

Ivy: Of course not. But this is complicated. I need to deal with my dad on my own terms. That will take some time.

I love it when I get to create a guilty conscience. So, I fire off a new text.

Me: So you are embarrassed by me. Am I not good enough for you?

Ivy: Dax, I'm not saying that.

I go quiet on her, just to add to the tension. It works. She sends another text.

Ivy: Please don't be mad at me. I just need to talk to my dad, and I haven't had time to do that. It has nothing to do with you or how I feel about you. And I'm not embarrassed by you.

I decide fewer words will keep her a bit anxious, which is how I want her. I learned a long time ago to put girls in positions where they need to please me and make me happy. Nothing does that better than a touch of planted guilt and anxiety.

Me: Okay.

Ivy: I'll see you in a few minutes.

Me: Okay.

Ivy: Dax, don't be mad at me.

Me: I'll see you on the boat.

I get on the golf cart, and I drive down to the docks. Alan, a man who works in our kitchen, is on the boat.

I question, "Got everything loaded?"

He nods. "All set up, sir. Do you need anything else?"

I shake my head. "No, I'm good. You're dismissed."

He leaves, and I step on the boat, glancing at everything, making sure it's perfect. I don't know why I do. Alan always makes sure everything is to my standards. But after yesterday, I can't let anything go wrong.

"Dax?" I hear Ivy call out.

I step out of the bedroom. My heart beats faster. This girl really does turn me on. Part of me wishes she didn't, but I'm here to do what I need to do.

Destroy all the good within her.

And I'm going to enjoy all of her while doing it.

I jump off the boat, tug her into me, and slide my hands through her hair. I kiss her, then retreat.

Her face flushes like it always does. She shyly says, "Hi. Did you get any sleep?"

"No."

She arches her eyebrows. "No? Aren't you exhausted?"

I grin. "Nope." Then I intentionally let my expression fall. "Are you sure you're not embarrassed by me?"

Guilt flashes in her eyes. "I swear I'm not. I just... I need to talk to my dad on my own terms, and he was at work when I woke up. He only came home for a quick minute."

"Okay. But just so you know, I won't hide with you forever."

Anxiety fills her expression, and it is just what I want. I don't want her relaxed. Not about this. Not about us.

Her current emotional state works perfectly into my plan. She must always feel a little bit of stress unless it's to my advantage for her not to.

"Come on, let's go," I order, then jump into the boat and reach for her. She takes my hand and lets me help her aboard. I show her around quickly, take the ropes off the dock, get behind the wheel, and steer the boat toward the center of the bay.

"It's so beautiful here," she chirps.

"You're in for a treat. It's the perfect day for sailing," I declare, and an energy fills me that I always feel when I'm on the water. I breathe in a deep breath and glance around.

Ivy smiles. "You look like you're in your element."

"I am. Sailing is the thing I love to do more than anything."

"I can see why," she says, glancing around.

I sit down and pat the seat next to me. "Come on, sunshine. I'm going to speed things up here till we get out."

There's a small breeze blowing through the bay. She sits down, and I hit the throttle. We coast away from the docks. And then I turn the motor off and declare, "Time to get up and help me with the sail. Come on."

I show her what to do, and the sail's at full mast in a few minutes. The wind provides just the right amount of speed. It's not cold or rough but has enough power to get us where we're going.

"Wow, it feels like we're floating."

She's adorable.

Stop it.

I grunt. "We are floating, we're on water."

"Oh, yeah. But you know what I mean. Like we're soaring across it." Ivy beams.

I tease, "Isn't that how you always feel when you're with me though? Like you're soaring?"

Red creeps up her cheeks.

"Ha ha, funny," she snarks.

But I know it's true. At least I'm going to make her feel that way. And then I'm going to make her feel like everything's all wrong and that she's going to lose me. She'll never know whether to be happy or paranoid. *And I'm an expert at making people paranoid*, I remind myself. It gives me great satisfaction and makes me giddy to think of her living in a confused state, doing whatever I want her to do, and being at my mercy.

We sail for a good hour and come to an island. I anchor the boat a hundred yards away from the shore.

"Wow, this is beautiful," Ivy claims.

"Yeah, I like it. It's quiet out here. Not a lot of people know about it."

She smiles. "Well, it's really nice."

"You hungry?" I ask. Her stomach growls, and I laugh. "I guess that's my answer."

"I haven't eaten since I had that cheeseburger."

"Me either. But I've got lots of food for us, so let's dig in."

I go into the kitchen and pull out a tray of sandwiches. I hand it to her, pick up a fruit platter, and grab a bag of chips. We take it to the table outside.

I reach into the cabinet and remove two flutes. Then I open a bottle of champagne.

"Oh, I don't drink," she reminds me.

"You don't want a glass of champagne with me?" I ask, staring at her as if that's the craziest thing I've ever heard. I add, "It's just a glass to celebrate us."

She glances at the bottle and then at me.

"It is just a drink, but you don't have to have it if you don't want to. I can put it away. It's a bottle I saved for a special occasion. I wanted to share it with you, but we don't have to drink it." I stare at her like a puppy dog. It's another look I've perfected.

It's time she stepped into my world.

My reality includes intoxication.

She caves. "Okay. That's sweet of you. I guess a glass won't hurt."

"You really never had a drink before?" I ask.

She shrugs. "I've sipped my dad's beer, but not really."

"You not curious about what it tastes like?"

She shrugs again. "Everybody I knew in West Virginia who drank always got into trouble."

"What kind?" I question.

"Stupid stuff, but I don't want those kinds of problems."

I can't blame her. Everybody I know who drinks has problems from it too. They always get in trouble because they're drunk. Hell, I'm always getting in trouble because I'm under the influence of some sort. But I don't know why anybody wouldn't drink. Once again, that's pretty boring. And I'm going to turn her into as big of an alcoholic as the rest of the women around these parts.

"Okay, well, this is a really good bottle of champagne. Promise you I won't do anything stupid or let you do anything stupid either," I tease.

She laughs.

I add, "Besides, it is a really special occasion."

"What's the occasion?" she cautiously asks, giving me her doe eyes.

My dick hardens. I fill two flutes, hand one to her, then slide next to her. I grab my glass and hold it next to hers. Then I move my face so that she can feel my breath upon her lips.

I reply, "You and me. Meaning you. Somebody real. Somebody I'm *finally* interested in. It's a good enough reason, right?"

She glows, beaming at me as if I just told her she won the lottery and will no longer be in the depths of poverty. She blinks a few times. I wonder if she might actually cry.

She agrees. "Yeah. That sounds like a good reason. And I'm glad I met you too. You're the most interesting person I've met."

Of course I am.

I peck her on the lips. "To us. Cheers."

"Cheers," she chirps with admiration in her gaze.

We clink glasses, and she takes a small sip while I take a large mouthful.

"What do you think?" I ask.

"It's really good."

"Good, drink up. We've got the whole bottle." I lean closer to her. "But don't worry, baby girl. I'll take care of you if you get a bit tipsy," I tease, wiggling my eyebrows.

She nervously laughs, and I wonder if she's ever going to not be nervous around me. But I like it, and I'm going to use that to my advantage as well.

We each make a plate of food and talk for a few moments. We're halfway done with our sandwiches, and I notice again how she doesn't worry about carbs, which is refreshing for me. Then I refill her flute.

"I probably shouldn't," she says.

"Why? Are you dizzy or something?" I ask.

She pauses, then shakes her head and giggles. "No, but I don't know. I'm not used to alcohol."

"Don't worry. You're fine. Plus, this bottle is too good to waste," I assert.

She takes a sip.

I fill mine, take a gulp, then set it down.

She blurts out, "Did you and Cindy used to have orgies?"

I freeze, arching my eyebrows in shock. I didn't expect that to ever come out of her mouth.

Maybe she isn't as innocent as I thought?

"S-sorry, I-I just..." she stutters.

"You just what?"

"She said a lot of stuff yesterday, and it got me thinking. I've just been wondering, and I should have asked you last night, but I didn't and—"

I put my finger over her lips.

She nervously stares at me.

"No, we haven't. I told you, Cindy's a liar."

But I'm the liar. I've had tons of orgies with Cindy. Anything you can think of, we've done. But it's not just Cindy. Lots of women have done whatever I've wanted.

Relief fills Ivy's expression. She's so damn cute, I want to kiss her again. My cock's harder than a rock, and I need some relief. Today's going well, so it's time for her to pay the piper. Once I make her feel guilty again, she'll be more than willing to make it up to me.

I drop my voice, whining, "I feel like you think really badly of me, as if I have some immoral things about me. I'm unsure what to do so that you don't think that, because that's not who I am."

Worry filters over her features. She claims, "I didn't mean that, Dax."

"Are you sure? I wonder if you think I'm not good enough for you. I mean, I guess I can understand why if you think I'm just a male whore, but—"

"I didn't say that."

"Well, you're making me feel like one," I say, to lay it on thick.

"Dax, no. I swear I don't think that. I just want to clarify what Cindy said, that's all," she insists.

I stay quiet and tap my champagne flute, staring at it.

She slides her hand over my cheek. "Dax, please. Please believe me."

I slowly turn to her. "I want you to trust me, Ivy. I don't want you to think things about me that aren't true. And, well, never mind," I say, looking away.

"No, tell me," she urges.

I continue to stare at the shoreline. I have this game down so well, she's never going to stand a chance. And she reacts exactly how I expect her to.

She puts her hand on my thigh, and it's not very far from my cock. It takes all I have not to grab her and take her down to the bedroom.

She pleads, "Dax, please. I'm sorry. I didn't mean to make you feel this way."

"We should get something straight," I assert.

"What?" She wrinkles her forehead.

I hesitate, then state, "You have to understand, I'm a Carrington."

"I know you are," she says.

I continue, "But you don't know. You have no idea what it means to be a Carrington every day. It's not all fun and games. In fact, most of it is horrible." I look away again and take a long sip of my champagne.

She cautiously asks, "Why would it be bad?"

I sigh. "Nothing. Forget I said anything."

"Dax, please tell me what you meant," she begs, playing right into my hand.

I wait a moment and turn back. "It means that people are going to lie about me, Ivy. They have it out for me. I know it seems like having my life would be easy, and I'll admit certain parts are nice. I have money. My family is well-known. But with that comes a target on your back. And there are a lot of people who've tried to harm me. They lie about me, and they say things that aren't true. Cindy's no different. It's why I broke up with her. It's why I've broken up with all of them."

Ivy gives me a look filled with pity, making me giddy.

I add, "There are a lot of girls who make shit up about me. They all want money or power. I've even had girls claim they were pregnant before, and we had never even slept together."

Horror fills Ivy's face.

Jesus, this is easier than I anticipated.

"Dax, that's horrible," she bursts out.

I nod and keep a sad expression. "Yeah, it is. I've had to get DNA tests. And do you know what that's like when your parents don't even believe you?"

Her shock intensifies. She asks, "Why wouldn't your parents believe you?"

I clench my jaw and stare at my champagne once more. My anger is real this time. I tell her the truth. "Because my father hates me. My mother doesn't like me much either."

"What? Why would they hate you? Surely they don't."

I finish the rest of my champagne. "It's complicated."

"Well, why don't you try me? Maybe it'll help to talk about it," she says, with hope in her eyes.

I sigh, reach for her hair, and push a lock behind her ear. "Can we change the subject? Maybe a different time we can talk about this."

She hesitates, then nods. "Okay, if that's what you want."

"It is what I want. I want to know more about you."

"What do you want to know?"

"Can I ask you anything?" I question.

Anxiety fills her eyes, but she agrees. "Okay."

"Good. I don't think we should have secrets between us. Do you?"

"No, but you just told me you didn't want to tell me about your parents," she points out.

"I'll tell you. I just... Well, it's kind of like your dad. I need time to put the words together and figure out how to voice it to you. Does that make sense, gorgeous?"

She ponders my statement, then nods, and a soft smile forms on her lips. "I guess I understand."

"Good. So, do I get to ask you some questions to get to know you better?"

"Sure."

Excitement fills me. I ask, "Why are you single? A girl like you should have been taken by now."

She laughs. "I don't know. Why are you single? You should be taken by now too."

"Ah. Ivy, Ivy, Ivy. I don't go for just anyone. I need somebody interesting. Someone beautiful, but not like the girls around here because they're not. They're only fake. I need somebody real. Someone just like you." I stroke her thigh, resisting the urge to slide my fingers under her shorts.

She looks like she's swooning.

Dammit, this girl is making me hard.

Play the game.

While she's in that state, I inquire, "So, are you telling me you're a virgin, then?"

Her eyes widen, and her face turns fire-engine red. "Why do you assume that?"

I stare at her, watching her turn maroon, then answer, "Ah, so you like to have sex?"

She stares at me as if she's scared.

"I'm just teasing," I claim, but I'm not.

A relieved breath leaves her lips. She doesn't know she did it, but it's obvious.

I scoot closer and stroke her thigh. "I'm not going to lie, Ivy, I'm into you. I've never been attracted to anyone the way I'm attracted to you. Does that make you uncomfortable?" I say, knowing damn well it does.

She stares at me and admits by putting her two fingers close together. "Maybe just a little?"

I push, "So you are or aren't a virgin?"

She takes a deep breath.

"You won't tell me?"

She releases her anxiety-laden lungs and finally nods. "Okay. I am." The maroon in her cheeks turns purple.

Fuck, yes.

She doesn't have any bad habits for me to break.

I kiss her on the neck and add, "Then I'm going to be clear. I'm not a male whore, but I'm a man. And I'm into you. Every part of you. And I want all of you, Ivy Ford."

A few tense moments pass and then she giggles.

"What's so funny?"

She beams at me. "You. Are you always this serious?"

"Only about things I'm interested in. And you are the only person I've felt this way about," I reply.

She stares at me, then giggles some more.

And I realize it's time to refill her flute of champagne.

Ivy 7

TIME FOR A SWIM

Butterflies flutter in a rage in my gut. There's never anyone I've wanted to be my first. The boys in West Virginia weren't anything like Dax.

He wants to sleep with me.

I finish my glass of champagne, buzzing with happiness.

It's going to be hard to resist Dax.

Why should I?

This is the champagne talking.

I wonder again how Dax can be so into me, but I love it.

He gives me a lewd look, and I clench my thighs, forgetting his hand is between them.

He glances down, and heat annihilates every part of my body.

"Are you hot, or is it just me?" I ask breathlessly.

Dax opens another bottle of champagne and refills our

flutes. "It can be time for a swim or time for you to get those clothes off." He tosses me a wicked grin.

I giggle and try to stand but almost fall.

He grabs me. "Whoa. Got to get your sea legs."

"Maybe I shouldn't drink any more champagne."

"Take a break. Drink some more if you want, or don't drink it at all," he directs. Then he grabs a bottle of water off the table. He puts it to my lips, ordering, "Take a few sips."

I obey him as he stares at me, and tingles race all over my cells. His scent flares in the breeze, swirling around me, intoxicating me further.

"You smell so good," I blurt out, then giggle again. "Sorry, I'm saying stupid stuff."

"No, you're not. You can talk all day about how good I smell if that's what you think," he says, then leans into my neck and deeply inhales. He gently bites down on my flesh, and I jump.

He chuckles, then in his deep voice, states, "Sorry, gorgeous. You smell so good, I want to eat you."

I laugh again. No one's ever said the things Dax says to me. But I've never been with anyone half as sophisticated as him, and I have to pinch myself. I still can't believe I'm on this boat with a man who's as sweet, nice, and beautiful as him. Plus, he says what's on his mind, which I like. He doesn't seem to be into playing games.

He lets his hand drop to my ass, and he gently squeezes, suggesting, "Let's go for a swim."

There's something in that suggestion that makes my butterflies flutter faster.

"Ivy?"

I come back from my wayward thoughts. "Okay. Is it deep?"

"Yeah. Why? I thought you could swim."

"I'm just feeling a little light-headed," I admit, cursing

myself for drinking. I shouldn't have, but then again, it was delicious. And I am eighteen. It's not like I'm in high school anymore.

Dax grins. "Don't worry, gorgeous. I'll make sure you don't drown. And I've got a floaty out there." He points to an over-sized blue piece of foam.

I glance at it, then tease, "A floaty? Is that what you call it?"

He shrugs. "Some people call it a lily pad. I say floaty. The last one in is a rotten egg!" He tugs his shirt off, displaying his chiseled chest. Then, he dives over the side of the boat.

Water splashes in the air. He pops out of the water. "Are you coming in, Ivy?"

"Sure." I move my hands to the bottom of my tank top and slowly pull it off, suddenly feeling sexy and a bit naughty, which is something I've never felt before.

He whistles. "Damn, you're giving me a hard-on."

I giggle again, but I'm getting used to Dax's crazy statements and compliments. For some reason, I can't stop thinking about what his dick would feel like, and I know I need to stop that. I remove my shorts, jump in, and pop up next to him.

He holds on to the pad with one arm, then slides his other around my waist.

I curl my legs around his hips. "Hi!"

He chuckles, praising, "Thank God you get your hair wet."

"Why do you say that?"

He grunts. "The girls around here don't get their hair wet."

"No?"

He shakes his head. "No way."

"Well, they're missing out," I claim, then duck under the water.

He grabs me and kisses me as soon as my face breaks the surface.

I catch my breath and then kiss him back.

He retreats and then boosts himself up on the lily pad. He holds his hand out and helps me onto it.

We lie down side by side. He slides his arm under my back, tugs me into him, then faces me. His other hand traces the curve of my waist and over my hip, and my insides quiver with excitement. "Isn't this nice, Ivy?"

"Yes," I breathe.

"Great day, right?"

"Mm-hmm," I agree, staring at his lips, almost drooling for him to kiss me again. He leans closer but doesn't give it to me.

"When will you tell your dad about us?"

I open my mouth to speak, but nothing comes out.

Dax's disapproval fills his sharp features once more. "I need you to be honest with him, Ivy. I'm not going to hide us. Okay?"

I sigh. "Why are you bringing this up again? Let's just have a good day. I told you I'll talk to him."

"You promise me? I don't want to be hidden," he repeats.

Part of me likes that he doesn't want us hidden, but I know Dad won't be happy. However, Dax is right. We can't hide from my father. So I vow, "I promise you, I'll do it soon. Okay?"

He seems appeased by my answer. He finally kisses me, and it doesn't take long before he rolls on top of me, and my limbs wrap around his warm, hard frame. But then, the sound of a boat motor fills the air, and he retreats.

He mutters, "Fucking A."

"What?" I ask, as a boat steers toward us, then it slows.

"Dax," Bobby calls out.

My heart sinks as three women's heads pop up. Avery, a girl I've never seen, and Cindy appear.

Oh God, not now, I think. Things are perfect between Dax and me right now. I don't need her or Avery causing trouble. Bobby either.

Dax stays on top of me and shouts, "Go away."

"Ooh, she didn't take long." Avery smirks.

I groan. "Is she always so annoying?"

Dax grunts and looks at me. "Yes. Get used to it." He rolls off me and says, "Come on, baby girl. They're not going to rain on our parade."

I glance at the boat again, and Cindy drills her glare right at me.

"Ignore her," Dax orders.

I hold Cindy's gaze, not wanting to be the first to flinch, but my mouth's dry and I can barely swallow.

Dax suggests, "Maybe we should go."

I turn my head toward him. "No, we don't need to go."

"Why? There are other islands. We don't need to be around them," he states.

He's right, but something tells me I need to deal with Cindy now. It's not like I won't see her. She's obviously part of their group. So I lift my chin and shake my head. "No, we're going to stay."

He stares at me.

I add, "Besides, you'll protect me. Right?"

He grins. "Yeah, gorgeous. I'll always protect you." He leans in and gives me another kiss.

"Jesus, get a fucking room," Bobby shouts.

Dax slaps my ass, and I giggle. Maybe it's the alcohol that's making me so easy with this situation. I normally wouldn't be. And I've never really been comfortable with public displays of affection. Not that anyone's given me too much, but maybe it had more to do with the boys I was with. But Dax, well, he's someone I'm proud to have stand next to me.

Bobby drops the anchor, and it makes a big splash. The others get in the water, the women each going down the ladder so they don't get their hair wet, just like Dax said. It only takes a few minutes before everyone's on the lily pad with us, and my make-out session with Dax has ended.

"I'm Marcey," the other girl says, and I can't tell if she's being kind or doesn't like me.

"She's my best friend." Cindy smirks, and my heart drops, knowing full well Marcey doesn't like me.

"Ignore her. It's nice to meet you," Marcey says, which makes me feel guilty.

Maybe I shouldn't judge her before I get to know her?

"Ivy, looking good," Bobby says, giving me a lustful once-over.

"Don't," Dax warns him.

"What? Let's not pretend you're a saint, now," Bobby sneers.

"Ignore them," Dax tells me again.

"It's fine," I say, then put my hand on his thigh and look back at Cindy. It's time she learns it's over between them. Dax told me how many times he's told her it is. Maybe she needs to see him with somebody else to finally realize it.

She actually sounds obsessed with him, which makes me a tad uneasy. When I woke up this morning and thought about the situation, I wondered if she's crazy and if I need to worry about her. But Dax promised me last night he would always protect me. And strangely enough, right now, she doesn't bother me. Dax's arm is around me, not her. Plus, it could be the alcohol that's giving me courage.

"I'm ready for more champagne. How about you, babe?" Dax asks me.

"She doesn't drink, remember?" Avery says in a snotty voice.

I glare darts at her and then smile at Dax. "That'd be great, thanks." I shouldn't have anymore. My head's already fuzzy, but I'm done letting these people make fun of me and think they know me.

Dax kisses me on the lips, then jumps off the pad. He swims to the boat and comes back with a Styrofoam cooler. He puts that on top of the float, opens it up, and hands everyone flutes. Then he opens several bottles of champagne and fills them all.

I've lost track of how many glasses I've drunk and take another sip. It's just as good as every other sip I've had.

Cindy turns to me and offers, "I think we got off on the wrong foot."

"Oh, do you?" I ask, wary of her sudden nicety.

"Are you going to be nasty to me?" she accuses, and I realize that maybe I was, and that's not like me. So, I release a breath and apologize.

"No, I'm not. I'm sorry if it came out that way. I'm Ivy." I hold my hand out.

She gives me a dainty handshake like Avery did, which I don't understand. My dad taught me how to really shake a hand. When people don't know how to, it bugs me.

Her lips twitch. "Yeah, great to meet you too. You're from West Virginia, I hear."

Something tells me she's making fun of me, but I don't want to not give her the benefit of the doubt again, so I nod. "Yep."

"Mountain girl, right?" she adds, her lips twisting into a smirk.

My defenses come out. "Yeah. Something wrong with that?"

"No, just, you don't look quite as hillbilly as I expected."

Embarrassment floods me. Of course she'd think that.

"Cindy, that's rude. You can't say that these days," Marcey scolds.

"I can't?" Cindy questions.

Marcey shakes her head. "No. You have to call her a hick, not a hillbilly," she states, then looks at me and smiles, quickly adding, "But I wouldn't call you that."

Sure you wouldn't, I think.

"You should be ashamed of yourself, Cindy," Bobby reprimands, making me wonder if he likes me.

Avery interjects, "Let's move on from all this hillbilly versus hick nonsense. Who wants to play spin the bottle?"

Dax groans. "Not me."

"Don't be a pussy," Bobby chides.

Dax slides his arm protectively around me and claims, "There's nobody here I want to play spin the bottle with except Ivy."

"Oh, is she too innocent to play? She's probably still a virgin, isn't she?" Avery states.

"I am not," I blurt out, then remember Dax knows the truth. I guiltily look at him, and he squeezes my hip.

"Then why won't you play?" Avery asks, locking her gaze with mine in a challenging stare.

"I didn't say I wouldn't."

"No? So Dax doesn't speak for you?" she questions.

"Of course he doesn't speak for me. Besides, Dax isn't that type of person. Are you, Dax?" I say.

"No, but—"

"But, what?" Cindy chirps.

"Shut up, Cindy. I've had enough of you," he seethes, then turns toward me. "We don't have to play."

"It's fine. We can play," I state, getting a burst of courage.

He hesitates, then asks, "Are you sure you want to play this game? I don't think we should."

I glance around the group, but a new determination fills me. These people aren't better than me, and I'm not scared of them. After all, it's just spin the bottle. How bad could it be? I have to kiss Bobby? Dax has to kiss Cindy or Marcey? It won't mean anything. So I claim, "Why don't we just play if they want to?"

Dax arches his eyebrows, repeating, "You sure, Ivy?"

"She said she wants to play, let her play," Cindy orders.

I don't take my eyes off Dax. "Yeah."

My stomach flip-flops.

What am I getting myself into?

I've never played spin the bottle. Sure, I've heard about it. I've seen it on TV shows and movies, but nobody I hung out with ever played it.

"Great, let's start," Bobby declares and takes the empty champagne bottle. He orders us around until we're sitting in a circle, then questions, "Who's first?"

"I'll go first," Avery volunteers and picks up the bottle. She moves it in the center and spins it.

It stops in front of Cindy.

My heart beats faster. I blurt out, "Looks like you have to spin again."

She looks at me and laughs. "Oh, aren't you naive, little girl?"

"Don't call her that," Dax warns, putting his hand on my thigh.

Avery smirks. "Watch and learn, Ivy. This is how you play spin the bottle in the real world." She seductively crawls across Marcey and slides her hand into Cindy's hair, then straddles her and slowly takes her tongue and licks Cindy's lips.

My pulse races, beating hard in my neck, and I stare at them, trying to keep my mouth shut, but I can't. My lips part as my jaw drops, watching Avery slowly slide her tongue into Cindy's mouth until they're making out and she's grinding her hips hard against Cindy's body.

"That's enough," Dax says.

Avery kisses Cindy for another moment, then turns and looks at Dax with a satisfied smile. "What's wrong, Dax? Are you suddenly becoming a saint?"

"Enough. You're boring us," he declares.

I can't help but wonder why everybody claims that Dax is into these things. He's repeatedly assured me that he's not, and every time they try to accuse him of it, he holds his ground. I wonder, again, if I'm being a stupid girl by believing him. But then I tell myself my doubt is from the champagne.

He moves his hand a little higher on my thigh, and the throbbing in my lower body intensifies, wiping out all the thoughts about how I shouldn't believe him.

"Did that turn you on?" Bobby asks, and I realize he's directing it at me.

I nervously stutter, "Wh-what?"

"Avery and Cindy. Did that turn you on?" he repeats.

"Bobby," Dax says, a threat in his tone.

"What? It's an innocent question. She's obviously never seen two girls make out before," Bobby asserts, which I can't deny.

"Or is she a prude and homophobic?" Marcey pipes in.

"I'm not a homophobe," I claim.

"No? Okay, then. Spin the bottle, Cindy," Bobby demands.

She obeys, and my gut drops when it points at me.

Marcey challenges, "If you're not a homophobe, then prove it."

"Okay, game over," Dax says.

Cindy smirks. "See, she's not like us."

I reply, "I didn't claim I was like you."

"Right. You're a homophobe," Marcey repeats.

"I'm not a homophobe," I adamantly state.

Avery pushes, "Then what are you scared of?"

"Okay, this has gone too far," Dax claims.

"No, it's fine," I offer, and I realize that the alcohol really is leading me. There's no way I'd ever agree to this. Not because I'm homophobic, but I'm just not into women.

Cindy doesn't hesitate. Before I know it, she's in front of me. Her alcohol-laced breath mixes with mine. She takes her finger and moves it from my shoulder, down over my boob so it grazes my nipple.

I jerk back so hard I fall off the raft and into the water. When I come up, everyone's laughing.

Dax is the only one with concern on his face. He jumps in and tugs me close to him. "We've had enough. Let's go, Ivy."

"Yep. Let the homophobe go," Marcey calls out.

"Ignore them," he orders.

My insides quiver.

What was I doing?

That's not me.

Why was I even going to let her do that?

My head's suddenly spinning.

Dax swims me over to the boat ladder. "Get up, gorgeous."

"I'm not a homophobe," I tell him.

He nods. "I know. It's okay. Just don't listen to them. They're idiots."

"Homophobe!" Marcey calls out, and my bottom lip quivers.

Dax slides his hand behind my head and puts his lips next to mine, declaring, "You're going to have to get a bit tougher. You can't let them get to you, gorgeous. I've told you this once. I'll keep telling you, but you need to understand. Just block them out."

I stare at him for a moment and lean closer for him to kiss me, but he pushes my butt up. "Time to get up. Let's get out of here."

Disappointment fills me, but he's right.

I put my foot on the ladder and climb out, but I'm too drunk. He pushes me up as the others laugh.

He follows and leads me to the captain's chair. He helps me sit, pulls up the anchor, and puts down the sails.

I avoid looking at anyone and try to get my head to stop swirling and drown out the insults.

He sits next to me, starts the engine, and takes off while Marcey screams, "Homophobe!"

Dax 8

YOU'RE ALL WET

Dax

Ivy's drunk. I thought she was just tipsy, but she's definitely past that point.

We get off the boat, and she stumbles across the dock. I grab her before she falls into the water and lead her to the golf cart. It takes me two seconds to decide to take her to my place.

She settles against my body but suddenly moves her head off my shoulder. She glances around and frets, "Where are we going?"

I tighten my arm around her. "I think we should go to my place. You're in no shape to go back to yours."

More anxiety appears in her expression. She claims, "My dad can't see me like this. I think I drank too much."

"Don't worry about it, babe. I'll take care of you. Everything is fine. Your dad won't know you've been drinking."

"He will," she whines.

"But you're eighteen," I reiterate, wanting to plant the seed that she can do what she wants. She may not be twenty-one, but she's past the point of needing her dad's approval, and I need to ensure she gets far away from that ideology.

"But my dad is strict."

I tug her closer to me. "Don't worry. I've got you."

She calms and gingerly smiles at me. "Thanks, Dax."

I give her a quick kiss on the lips. "No problem, gorgeous. Hold tight. We'll be there soon."

She puts her head back on my shoulder, and before I get to my place, she's passed out.

I groan. The last thing I wanted to do was take care of a drunk. I need to wake her up. My dick's still hard. And today was perfect. It had just enough shock factor to make her feel bad and cling closer to me.

Plus, I had her drink alcohol for a reason. I know she wants me, and I wanted to loosen her up. She confirmed my suspicion that she has no experience, and I already knew she wasn't like the other girls around here. So I figured she'd need some liquid courage to let me do what I want with her.

"Ivy, wake up," I order, stroking her head.

She blinks a few times, then closes her eyes again.

"Sweetheart, wake up," I repeat several times.

She finally becomes coherent and leans away from me. She glances around. "Oh, did I fall asleep?"

I chuckle. "Yeah. You're okay though. Come on, let's get some water and food in you."

She glances toward her cottage, then frets, "My dad didn't see us, did he?"

I sternly answer, "No. But like I said, he needs to know that we're together."

"I meant because I've been drinking, that's all," she quickly states.

A bit of relief fills me. The last thing I'm going to do is hide our relationship from her father. Nothing is better than a good girl displeasing her daddy. And I'm up for the task of making that happen.

So I'm glad she's come around and isn't fighting me telling him. But I'm still going to use it as a guilt trip when I want.

I get off the golf cart and go around to the other side. I help her on her feet, steer her inside the house, and lock my door. I don't think anyone's coming over, but I'm not taking any chances after yesterday.

It makes me nervous Cindy was there today. Once the boat docks, she'll be back on the estate with the others.

I bypass the kitchen and lead Ivy into the bedroom. I pull back the covers and tug the string on her bikini top. It falls to the ground.

She covers her chest in surprise. "What are you doing?"

"You're all wet, babe." I take my hands and push her bathing suit bottoms down to the ground. They fall at her feet, and I resist looking down.

Her eyes widen further. She moves one hand down to her pussy.

I slide my hand behind her hair and pull her close to me, then put my arm around her and cup her ass, asserting, "Everything's fine. Your suit's wet. You drank a little too much. Just get in bed. Okay?"

She stares at me for a moment.

"I won't touch you if you don't want me to," I lie, knowing the time has come for me to manipulate her into doing exactly what I want.

I've done it millions of times. I'm an expert at it. But something about Ivy makes me want to do it more than I've ever wanted to before.

I've deflowered virgins, but they weren't like Ivy. All I've thought about since I laid eyes on her was getting her in my bed, but now that I've confirmed she's a virgin, it's driven my obsession to a new high.

And my ego needs to hear her say she wants me to touch her and do things to her no one else has.

She blows a hot breath out to move a wisp of her hair away from her mouth and agrees. "Okay."

I kiss her and squeeze her ass again. "Good girl. I'm going to go get you some food and water."

She softly smiles. "Thanks, Dax."

"Anything for my girl," I say, then wait until she gets into bed. I tuck her in, kiss her forehead, and go to the kitchen. I make a plate of cheese and crackers and grab a couple bottles of water. Then I take it into the bedroom.

My heart almost stops when I walk into the room.

She's curled up into the pillow I sleep on, somehow looking more gorgeous than ever.

She's an angel under my sheets.

Jesus, she's special.

What the fuck am I saying?

Special enough to break, I remind myself.

She smiles at me, and a weird flutter fills my stomach.

I can't help but study her. Her curves that no one around here has, her puffy lips, and those damn innocent, naive eyes that look at me in adoration, even in her intoxication, are all constantly driving me nuts.

She sits up, and the covers slip. She grabs them and pulls them up over her tits.

Those fucking C cups.

I hold in my groan and set the tray down on the table. I pick up another pillow and put it against the headboard for her to lean against.

"Thanks," she says.

"No problem." I drop my swim trunks, and she stares at me, once more in shock, her eyes darting all over my body, unsure where to go.

"You like what you see, Ivy?" I ask, giving her a lewd look.

Her face turns scarlet red within seconds. She stutters, "I-I-I..." Then her eyes dart to my erection again. She swallows hard.

I chuckle. "It's okay." I slide under the covers and sit against the headboard, reminding myself to stay the course.

Need to sober her up a bit.

I select a cracker, place cheese on top, and hold it to her mouth. "Eat this, sweetie."

She slowly does, and I shove one in my mouth, suddenly famished.

But I'm really starving for her, not these damn crackers with cheese.

My cock throbs for the millionth time today.

Sober her up a little bit, I remind myself again. There's no way I'm ever letting her claim that I took advantage of her.

No. She's going to beg me just like all the other women do. So I feed her water and more crackers and cheese. When the bottle's finished, she seems a lot better. I ask, "How do you feel?"

She beams at me. "Good."

The blanket's fallen several inches, barely resting on her tits. I tug it on my side so it drops to her waist.

It takes her a minute to realize it. She glances down, staring at her breasts, and then slowly back at me.

I admit, "You have the most beautiful breasts I've ever seen."

She arches her eyebrows but doesn't cover herself up again, which I take as a win. She questions, "How's that possible?

Everybody around here has perfect ones, which are much bigger than mine."

I take my finger and swirl it on one of her tits until her nipple turns rock hard.

She shakily inhales a deep breath.

I murmur, "I don't like fake ones. I like the real thing. And I'll tell you a secret if you want to know."

She inhales again, bites her lip for a minute, then asks, "What's that?"

I move to her other tit, making it just as hard, and confess, "I've never dated anyone who doesn't have fake boobs."

She burst out in a laugh. "How's that possible?"

I shrug. "You've seen what it's like around here. They all get them around fourteen."

Once again, she looks like a deer in headlights. "Are you serious?"

I nod. "Absolutely." Then I cup more of my hand around her breast, moving my thumb over her nipple. I add, "You really do have beautiful breasts. I want to kiss them. Can I kiss them?"

Nervousness fills her expression. I wait and wait, fascinated by her tits, as if I've never seen or touched one before.

She finally says, "Okay," snapping me out of my trance.

I move close to her breasts, then look up.

She stares at me, frozen.

"Has anyone kissed them before?"

She bites on her lip again, her face turning maroon, and shakes her head.

Fuck yeah.

One thing I love is a virgin. But what I love more is a virgin who's never done anything. And it's clear Ivy hasn't. I declare, "Good, because you're mine. I'm glad to know no one else has touched these gorgeous tits. Have they touched you anywhere else?" I slip my hand down her stomach right above her pussy lips.

She inhales sharply. "No."

"But you're okay with me touching you, right? You want me to?" I goad, teasing her slit.

She doesn't say anything. She keeps inhaling sharp, short breaths, her gaze drilled into mine.

I kiss her, sliding my tongue against hers.

She returns my affection the moment our mouths meet.

I slide my finger through her pussy lips, and she moans.

Jesus fucking Christ.

She's fucking wet and perfect.

I kiss her chin and her neck, moving down to those fucking perfect C cups I've been dying to get my mouth around.

I kiss both of them with butterfly kisses, loving how her chest rises and falls faster and the little sounds flying out of her. Then I decide it's game over.

I slide my finger inside her and suck on her breast, swirling my tongue around her tit and groaning.

"Oh Lord," she whimpers.

I pump and swirl my finger inside her slowly, then move my thumb over her clit. I reposition my face to her other breast, giving it the same attention I did the other one. Then I increase the pressure and suck harder.

"Oh...oh..." she barely gets out and grinds her hips into my hand.

I move the pillow from behind her, ordering, "Slide down."

She doesn't hesitate and obeys until she's fully on her back.

I kiss her as a reward, but then I leave her wanting more, pulling away, returning to her tits, and finally realizing what I've been missing all these years.

They're soft and palatable. They're not hard except for those pink nipples I suck and bite until they're red.

She whimpers louder.

I grunt. "Fuck, you have me so hard, baby girl." I move my hand from her pussy to my cock. I pump it a few times, then reach for her hand and curl her fingers around my erection. I study her.

She swallows hard.

"Have you felt anyone's dick before?"

"No," she replies, her voice cracking.

I squeeze her hand. "Good. My cock is yours. You can play with it. Use it for your pleasure. You can even kiss it. Do you want to kiss it, Ivy?" I give her a challenging stare mixed with my puppy dog eyes.

She opens her mouth, but nothing comes out.

"Don't be shy. Feel me," I demand.

Her thumb slowly moves across the tip.

I groan and close my eyes. "Baby girl, you don't know what you do to me."

She puts her lips against the curve of my neck, and electricity zaps down my spine.

My cock hardens further. I pin my gaze on hers and ask, "Do you like what you do to me?"

She nods, admitting, "Yeah, I just don't understand."

"What don't you understand?"

"Why me? There are so many other girls in this town. So why me?"

I chuckle. There are so many reasons I could give her. I could tell her the truth about how she's naive, unspoiled, easily manipulated, and so goddamn beautiful I can't stop thinking about her. Or I could confess about how the moment I saw her, I became obsessed with turning her into my play toy.

Instead, I tell only half the truth. "You've seen those girls, Ivy. There's nothing special about them. They're fake. They're mean. They're not who I want to be with. And I told you before, you're real. You're beautiful. You have curves and real boobs, for God's sake. And this pussy..." I put my hand back on it, circling her clit.

She inhales a deep breath again, holding it, waiting to exhale.

I continue. "I want to kiss it. Tell me I can kiss it, Ivy."

She doesn't answer for a moment. She looks so scared I think she might tell me no. But then she surprises me. In her hoarse voice, she barely gets out, "Okay. You can kiss it, Dax."

"That's my good slut. You make me so happy. You know that?"

She scrunches her forehead. "Slut?"

I lean closer and pinch her clit, murmuring, "Yeah, my slut. Every man wants a slut, Ivy. They don't want a tease. They want a woman who knows she's a woman, not a prude. So you want to be my slut, right?"

She holds her breath, and tense silence follows.

I slowly start to roll off her. "Sorry. I guess you're not ready for me. Or maybe you're a prude and don't go after who you want in life...someone who is dying for you and wants to give you the world."

She grabs my arm. "Wait."

Bingo!

I freeze and turn. "It's okay, you don't—"

She tugs my head toward her and presses her lips to mine.

I mumble against her lips, "That's my good slut."

She stills again.

"You and your hungry pussy are mine, Ivy. Your sexy-ass C cups and teasing lips are all mine. Understand, my sexy little slut?"

Her mouth curves up.

"Ah. My slut likes it when I talk dirty," I claim.

She giggles. A light fills her eyes. "I do?"

And this is why I gave her alcohol.

I pat myself on the back, then praise her some more. "Yeah, my dirty whore. And you make me so happy that if I don't make you feel the best you ever have before, I'm going to die. You're going to be the cause of my death, my pussy-dripping slut."

She beams brighter, but anxiety swirls in her light. I can tell she still isn't totally on board with my pet names, but she will be soon. It's all about training her, and I'm an expert at turning naive girls into wanting me at all hours of the day.

I circle my finger around her clit again and suck on her tit some more until she's moaning. I retreat and ask, "How often do you play with yourself?"

She tenses, staring at me as if caught in an act.

"It's okay, my little whore. Tell me. I can't stop thinking about you pleasuring yourself. It makes me so damn hard." I squeeze her hand that's holding my cock.

"I-I h-haven't," she stutters out.

I can't help it and groan out loud. I shouldn't, but it's better than I fucking thought. I admit, "That's so fucking hot."

She timidly asks, "It is?"

I don't answer her, wanting to be sure she's telling the truth and finding it hard to believe. "You've never made your-self come?"

"No," she says, her face again filling with embarrassment.

I kiss her lips, move my mouth to her ear, lick her lobe, and whisper, "I guess this is good then, baby girl. I'm the one who will show you how good I can make you feel. Just relax. Okay?"

"Mm-hmm," she says, squirming slightly underneath me.

I move my body down, hating the fact that she has to let go of my cock. I put my face right into her pussy, slowly licking it, staring at her, watching the way her mouth opens and her breathing becomes labored.

How long has it been since I did anything with anyone inexperienced?

I rack my brain.

Too fucking long. All the girls around here are only virgins until they are twelve, maybe thirteen.

Ivy's eyes turn glassy. And I know it's not the alcohol. I'm an expert at licking, sucking, and fucking. But Jesus, her pussy tastes good, and it's pinker than I thought it would be.

I get her to the point she's going to come and then I stop and look up.

She gapes at me, waiting, her hands clenched in my hair.

I demand, "Tell me to make you come."

Her eyes widen. She shuts her mouth and swallows hard, then licks her lips.

"Tell me to make you come," I repeat.

She mutters, and her voice cracks, "Make me come."

"Tell me you're my slut and to make you come," I order.

She stares at me again.

"Baby girl, tell me. I need to know you want this," I confess, then add, "It pleases me. And you want to please me, right?"

She nods.

"Good. Then be my good wet whore and tell me you want to come."

"Didn't I already?" she asks, her maroon cheeks turning purple.

Jesus, she doesn't even know what a fucking orgasm is?

How the fuck did I get so lucky?

I can't help but grin. "No, sexy slut. You haven't. Now be a good girl and tell me you're my slut and want to come. And use my name."

Her voice cracks even worse. "I-I'm your slut. Make me come, Dax."

Pre-cum seeps out of my cock, and my balls throb. It's

something else that never happens. It takes me a long time for anything to leak out of me these days.

"Good little slut," I mutter, then go back down on her, working her pussy hard until she's crying out and shaking underneath me, writhing from the pleasure.

I extend her orgasm for as long as possible. And when I finally come up for air, she's spent. Sweat covers her quivering body.

It's one of the most beautiful things I've ever seen.

I slide up against her, sticking my tongue in her mouth, stealing more of her breath. When I retreat, I keep close to her. "Do you smell that?"

"What?" she asks.

"Your hungry pussy. Do you smell how good it is? Did you taste your delicious, wet cunt?" I press.

Shock fills her face again.

"Don't you understand how good your slutty-self is, baby girl?"

She stays quiet with a fire in her eyes I've not seen before.

"Admit you love the taste of yourself and your scent on my breath. Otherwise, I won't feel comfortable pleasing you again," I threaten.

She blurts out, "I do."

"Good." I kiss her again, retreat, and direct, "Now, I need these lips on my cock. Do you understand me?"

Fear overtakes her features.

I put on my hurt expression. "You don't want to? You don't like me?"

She shakes her head. "No, of course I like you."

"Then you want to be my good sexy slut and suck my cock, right? You want to lick it, taste it?" I push, using the same words I've used with I don't know how many women.

But then again, they weren't women. They were girls. Ivy

may only be eighteen, but she seems more of a woman than anyone I've ever had, even though she's inexperienced.

I wait for her, and she finally nods, confessing, "Yeah, I do."

Giddiness flows through me. "You've been thinking about me and my cock, haven't you, my little whore?"

Her lips twitch, and I realize that she's into this. She's going to get wet every time I call her slut or whore going forward.

Her blush reappears, and she softly admits, "Yeah, I have."

Adrenaline pumps through my veins. I reply, "Good, baby girl. That's because we're meant to be together. Now, slide down and show me what you want to do to me with those slutty lips of yours."

Ivy 9
I NEED YOUR MOUTH ON ME

Ivy

So much adrenaline rushes through me that I've never felt so high. It's an incredible feeling, and I wonder how I've missed out on this all this time. How it's possible that I've never let anyone touch me like this, or how Dax can make me feel so good.

Normally, I fight guys off. Sure, they've tried things while on dates. I even had a boyfriend for a while, but we didn't get past kissing. Anytime he tried anything, I shut him down. But with Dax, I don't want to stop. I want to do everything with him.

My conscience gets to me momentarily, and I wonder if I'm moving too fast.

"What's wrong?" Dax asks, stroking my head.

"I don't want you to think bad of me," I say quietly.

"Why would I think bad of you?"

"I don't want to be a real slut," I blurt out.

Amusement fills his expression. "Why? You're *my* slut."

I tilt my head, but my lips twitch. I shouldn't let him call me his slut or whore, but my pussy aches every time he does.

It's like Dax knows me better than I know myself. He leans closer, and his deep voice is teasing when he says, "I just went down on you. You haven't done anything to me. I've still got blue balls."

Guilt fills me. That makes me sound greedy.

Am I?

"So you want to be a prude instead?" he asks.

"No, but... I don't know." I'm so confused.

His face falls. "Is this really about me being a manwhore?"

Once again, I feel bad. I can't stand it when he looks so upset. I don't know why I keep making him feel that way, so I assure him, "No, that's not what I'm saying."

"Then what are you saying? I like you. You like me. What's wrong with us being together?"

I ponder his question, my brain fuzzy from champagne, high from my first-ever orgasm, and dizzy from the emotions Dax brings out in me.

In a disappointed voice, he asks, "So you think there's something wrong with us being together?"

"No! I swear it's not that," I insist.

A bit of anger taints his tone. "If it's not that, then what is it? Me? Maybe you think I'm not good enough for you." More hurt fills that statement, and that pains my heart.

"I could never be embarrassed by you or think that you aren't good enough for me. You're amazing." It surprises me how easily I tell him what I'm always feeling, but one thing about Dax is he never holds back. So maybe it makes it easier for me not to.

Plus, he doesn't want any secrets between us. I want to honor that request.

My heart beats faster, thinking that I've only known Dax for a day, but I feel so close to him. This is right between us. I know it in my heart.

He rolls off me and lies on his back next to me. He stares at the ceiling, his jaw clenched, and I can tell he's hurt and not happy.

I don't want him to think I don't want him as much as he wants me, so I do something I've never done before. I roll on top of him.

He keeps his eyes pinned to the ceiling.

I force him to look at me. Then I assert, "I could never think you aren't good enough for me. Do you understand?"

His expression doesn't change, and I hate that I've put that thought into his head. I don't know how I did it, but I have. He remains silent.

I decide to kiss him.

He doesn't kiss me back at first, but then he slowly does until one of his hands is back on my ass and the other reaches up and tweaks my nipple, which is already sore and sensitive.

It gives me another rush of adrenaline. I wonder again how he can make me feel so alive.

His cock grows even more erect, pushing against my pussy, and I'm tempted to slide on top of it. It's another surprising thought.

He mumbles in a desperate tone, "I need your mouth on me, Ivy. Please. You don't understand how much I need it."

How is it that he needs me?

I still can't believe he's chosen me out of all the other girls around here. I'm simple compared to them. He claims that's what he wants. And maybe it's true that you always want what you can't have, and I'm the first girl that he's ever been able to meet who is different.

Maybe that does make me special.

As if he can read my thoughts, he says, "No one's special like you, Ivy, and I just... Well, I need you. I do, baby girl. You don't understand. I'm hurting without you down there. I need to see what it's like for you to be consumed by me."

My heart beats faster. I find some courage and try to look sexy. I bat my eyes, cooing, "Are you sure you can handle it?" Then I giggle. I don't know what I'm saying. I don't even know what I'm doing, but I'm going for it.

His lips twitch. "I don't know. Why don't you show me?" He puts his hand on my head and gives me a little push.

I take a deep breath, kiss his chest, and make my way down his torso, pressing my lips against every one of his cut abs.

Everything about Dax Carrington is perfect. His body, kisses, attention, and how he protects and holds me make me feel like the only girl in the world. All he has to do is look at me and I feel that way. So there's nothing I want to do more than please him.

Even if I'm clueless about how to do it, I'm on a mission.

My face hovers above his cock. He's shaved, which surprises me. I assumed there'd be pubic hair there, and I like that there's not.

My insides quiver while I stare at his huge cock. At least, I think it's huge. But then again, I don't know what's normal. And I wonder how I'm going to fit it in my mouth.

"Just start with a lick, gorgeous," he suggests.

Nervously, I obey him. I don't know what else I'm supposed to do. I start at the base and work my way up.

He groans softly, gently caressing my head. Then he praises, "That's it, baby girl. Keep doing that. Get all of it wet before it goes into your slutty mouth."

My insides once again throb, and I wonder why his dirty talk that should offend me, doesn't.

I make my way around his cock until it's dripping wet with my spit.

Then he directs, "Now put me in your mouth."

My butterflies flutter faster. I take another breath, stare at his huge dick, and think about the size of my mouth compared to it.

"It's okay, my sexy whore. Just try it," he urges, then adds, "I need to be in your mouth, baby girl. I'm desperate for you."

Everything about that statement sends a surge of adrenaline through me.

Dax Carrington is desperate for *me*, not Cindy, Marcey, or any other girls around here.

Me.

Pride sweeps through me. Maybe it's the alcohol. I'm normally not a prideful person. But I carefully move my mouth over the head of his cock, and he groans, then pushes me down farther until it's in the back of my throat.

There are still several inches to go. I go rigid and start to panic.

He orders, "Open up the back of your throat, my little slut." He pushes me farther, and I gag.

He pulls me back.

"I'm sorry," I fret, and my eyes water as I try to catch my breath.

He sternly states, "You have to learn to open your throat. But don't worry. You will. You know why, Ivy?"

I clear my throat. "No. Why?"

He gives me a heated look, slides his hand over my sensitive tit, and pinches my nipple. My pussy throbs, and he states, "You're my slut, Ivy. Mine. And we're perfect together."

My heart soars.

Yes! We are!

His statement makes me want to please him more.

He pins his challenging stare on mine, questioning, "Now, are you ready to try again?"

"Yes," I admit, eager to please him.

His lips curl. "Good girl. When you finish, I'm going to play with that wet cunt of yours some more. Now, proceed."

Normally, any man saying the c-word or ordering me around would piss me off, but everything about Dax doing it turns me on. And my lower body turns hotter at the thought of him touching me down there again.

I return to his cock, determined to be good for him, to please him like he's pleased me, and to make him happy.

This time, I get all of him into my mouth, and he slides all ten of his fingers through my hair and starts moving my head up and down, guiding me while groaning, "Fuck, you're fucking good at this."

Pride swells within me until a loud banging noise pulls me out of my trance. My father's voice booms, "Ivy, get out here."

I freeze. My heart beats faster, and my pulse pounds in my neck. I gape at Dax.

He doesn't even look scared, only annoyed, making him even more attractive to me.

My father shouts, "Ivy, I know you're in there!"

I attempt to roll off Dax, but he shoves me back on his cock, ordering, "Ignore him."

"Ivy," my father cries out, pounding harder on the door.

Dax pushes me faster, and my eyes water so much, tears drip down my cheeks. His erection hardens even more while my father continues to bark my name and bang on the door.

"Fuck, you're amazing, my little slut," Dax praises, keeping me positioned over him at the same pace.

Dad rages. "I'm going to knock this fucking door down if you don't come out here right now."

My father never curses in front of me. It's another shock to my system, but I don't have time to process anything.

Dax just keeps me locked on his cock, moving my head up and down and commending, "That's it. That's it, baby girl. Come on, my sexy whore, don't let me down."

Everything's confusing, scary, and laced with adrenaline. I don't understand why, and my father's angry voice becomes louder. It's beyond petrifying, but Dax's salty cum drips onto my tongue, and his shaft swells in my mouth.

"Touch yourself," Dax demands.

"Ivy!" my father explodes.

"Hand on your pussy, my good little slut," Dax grunts out.

I move one hand to my upper thigh. Juices slide down my skin, and I touch my pussy.

"Give me your hand," Dax orders, and his scent and taste overwhelm me.

I move my hand to his torso.

"Goddamnit, you bastard! Let me in!" Dad fumes.

Dax takes my fingers and sucks on them, then groans. "Fuck, baby girl, you're the best-tasting slut ever," he grits through his teeth, keeping me locked on his dick.

My pussy throbs harder. He reaches down and pinches my nipple, and I moan.

And I can't understand any of this. Everything spins, probably from the champagne. Adrenaline pounds through me, and the more my father yells and bangs on the door, the more Dax groans in pleasure and hardens in my mouth.

All I want is more of his salty taste. I want to make him come and please him better than anyone else ever has.

"Ivy!"

"I need you, baby girl. I do. Keep going. Don't stop. Don't you dare let him stop us from being together," Dax pants.

My head spins faster, but I couldn't get Dax's cock out of my mouth if I tried. He has me pinned, in control of his pleasure, and waterfalls of tears streaming down my cheeks.

I love everything about it.

Glass shatters, and a rock lands near my foot. Dax muffles my cry and then releases me.

I roll off him.

Dax shouts, "What the hell, John!"

I dive off the bed and scramble for my bikini, ready to run out but can't.

From the corner of the bed, I see my father's silhouette. My excitement disappears, and fear overpowers everything else.

He seethes, "My daughter's in here. I know she is."

I stay quiet, squeezing my eyes shut, wishing my heart would stop beating so hard.

Dax accuses, "You just broke my window. Are you crazy?"

My father's anger intensifies. "I want my daughter, now. Where is she?"

"She's not with me," Dax lies, and I'm thankful for it. I know he doesn't want to hide us from my father, but I do not want my father to know I'm here in Dax's bed.

Still, I peek around the corner of the bedpost.

Dax steps closer to my father, fully nude. The tension in the air builds.

My father busts out another pane of glass, and it falls toward Dax's feet.

I'm more scared than I've ever been. I've never seen my father so angry. I don't know why he hates Dax so much. He doesn't even know what our fight was about earlier yesterday, but he has it out for him.

"You're crazy," Dax repeats.

"I want my daughter," my father snarls.

"I told you she's not here. You just broke my window. That's coming out of your wage, old man."

"I know my daughter's in here," my father declares.

Dax puts his hand on his hip. "She's not, and you just interrupted me from my nap."

Dad barks, "Nap my ass. I know Ivy's here. The other kids on the boat told me she was with you."

"Yeah, I dropped her off at your house," Dax lies again.

"She's not at my house," my father states.

"Well, that's not my problem. Is it? I was sleeping, and you woke me up by throwing a rock through my window. I should fire you now."

My pulse races faster. I put my hand over my belly, feeling ill.

Dax promised he would never fire my dad.

That was before Dad threw a rock through his window.

This is all my fault.

"How dare you bring my daughter here! I told you to stay away from her."

"Look around the room, John. Ivy's not here. Now, get off my property. If you don't stay at least 500 feet away from my house, I'm firing you. Do you understand?" Dax threatens.

My fears escalate.

"I want my daughter," my father repeats.

"I told you she's not here."

The walkie-talkie on my father's waist starts blaring.

More tension mounts.

Dax snarls, "Are you going to do your job and find out what's happening?"

More silence follows, and I keep low, with my eyes closed, praying my father doesn't see me.

The beeping gets louder. A man's voice calls out over the walkie-talkie, "John, we have a situation."

Dad finally picks up the walkie-talkie, presses the button, and replies, "What's going on?"

"Something's wrong with the heating in the greenhouse. You need to get down here and fix it. Everything's wilting. It's two times the normal temperature range."

I peek around the corner of the bed.

My father shakes his head and shuts his eyes.

Dax orders, "Do your job, John. Ivy isn't here."

My father gives him another dirty look. Then he says into the walkie-talkie, "I'm on my way." He hooks it back onto his belt and warns Dax, "You're to stay away from my daughter."

Dax doesn't flinch. He points at Dad, stating, "Don't come within 500 feet of my house again. Or I will fire you. Am I clear?" Dax threatens.

I close my eyes, my head spinning faster.

I caused this.

My father's going to get fired.

No, Dax told me he would never do that.

But Dad's actions are out of control.

"Stay away from Ivy," my father warns again and finally leaves.

When he's out of sight, Dax turns, declaring, "Your father is crazy."

I rise off the floor and finish putting my bikini on. Then I beg Dax, "I'll pay for the window. Please don't fire him."

Dax tugs me into him. "Shh. Your father's not getting fired. But he's crazy. You saw that, right?"

I nod into his chest. "Yes. I'm sorry. He's overprotective of me. Please don't fire him," I repeat, even though Dax just told me he's not going to.

He tightens his hold on me. "You need to trust me, Ivy. I've told you that will never happen, so calm down."

I pull my head back. "How can you be so calm after this? Your window is broken."

He slowly looks behind him at the window, then back at me, and shrugs. "So what? It's a piece of glass. I'll have someone fix it by the end of the day."

I gape at him.

He adds, "Your father's going to have to do way more than break my window to keep me away from you."

I slowly smile.

Dax still wants me.

"There's that smile I love." He leans down and kisses me, then states, "I better take you back to your place while your father's gone. But, Ivy, you'll have to stick with the story that you were home, okay?"

I nod. "All right. I'll tell him I was home for a bit, then went for a walk."

Dax smiles in approval and squeezes my ass. "Good girl." Then he stills, staring at me for a moment.

Nerves fill my belly. "What's that look for?"

He assesses me one more time and leans into my ear. He murmurs, "I loved your mouth on me."

Through all the stress, I laugh.

Dax tugs me close and claims, "I mean it. And I can't wait for you to do it again, my filthy whore."

I KNOW YOU'RE WITH HIM

Ivy

Dax gives me a final kiss and drives off in his golf cart. I step inside and close the door. I immediately get a text.

> Dax: Take a cold shower, Ivy. You need to sober up a little more. And erase this message in case your father reads it.

My heart beats faster. I close my eyes, leaning against the door. I can't believe my father did that. If he finds out I've been drinking, he's going to be even angrier, but I've never seen him like this. Even when my mom disappeared, he controlled his rage. But this is another level.

I reply.

> Me: Okay. Thanks.

I erase his message. I go into the bathroom, lock the door, and strip out of my bikini. Then, I study myself in the mirror.

My glassy eyes aren't going to help convince my father I haven't been doing things he doesn't approve of, even though I've never drunk before. I assume I look better than earlier, but my head's still a little woozy.

I open the medicine cabinet and pull out a bottle of drops, putting several in each eye. I look better than I'm sure I did, but not totally sober.

The more I gaze at my naked reflection, the more my anxiety builds.

What was my father thinking?

Dax said he wouldn't fire him, but what Dad did was extreme. How could Dax not fire him?

It confirms what kind of person Dax is, because if I were in his position, I can't say I wouldn't let my father go.

I tear my gaze off myself, turn the water on, and let it run for a while, returning to my reflection.

Did I really just do all that with Dax?

I bite on my lip and take a deep breath.

Dax's deep voice rings in my mind.

Slut.

Whore.

My expression falls.

Why did I agree that was okay?

I hear echoes of Marcey screaming *Prude! Homophobe!*

I am not! I reassure myself.

They want a woman who knows she's a woman, not a prude. So you want to be my slut, right, Ivy? Dax's voice reappears.

My insides quiver. I put my hand over my belly and lift my chin.

Dax is right. That's better than being a prude, isn't it?

I decide there's nothing wrong with Dax calling me his slut and whore. After all, he called me *his*, not just a slut or whore.

I check the water. It's warm, so I force myself to make it colder. I stand under the water as long as I can, washing my hair, conditioning it, and quickly using my loofah all over my body. I finish rinsing and turn the freezing water off.

I dry my body and brush my hair and teeth. I can't help but gaze at my reflection once more. I feel different. I don't know how, but everything Dax and I did makes me feel so much more alive.

I close my eyes and smile, thinking about how he made me feel and how much I loved trying to please him. But then my father's voice barking my name interrupts my dirty thoughts, and confusion sets in again.

Why was I still okay doing that with Dax while Dad was banging on the door?

We could have gotten caught.

Something must be wrong with me.

But Dax was into it too. I'm sure he was.

I must be the only person in the world who doesn't get turned off by the possibility of getting caught.

If only my father hadn't thrown that rock through the window.

My stomach curls. I sigh and open the bathroom door. I turn off the light, go into my room, and put on a pair of shorts and a tank top. I glance at the clock.

My father will be home soon, I assume.

What's he going to say to me?

I have to stick to our lies.

My stomach dives. My father and I don't have lies between us. No secrets. I'm not one of those kids who would sneak out or not tell him what I'm doing. Plus, I never had anything going on in my life that he disapproved of.

But I don't want to hide Dax. He's adamant that we're open to my father about us, which I admire. It shows Dax isn't a coward, which my father should appreciate since he hates cowards.

But I don't know how I can ever tell him about Dax and me. My father hates Dax, and I curse Avery, Marcey, Cindy, and Bobby for telling him we were together.

I have to get my story straight before he comes home.

I rehearse my story over and over, until I feel like I'm going to drive myself nuts. I glance at the clock again and decide to start dinner. So I go into the kitchen and open the pantry.

I pull out some noodles and marinara sauce to make my father's favorite meal. I open the freezer, pull out a loaf of garlic bread, and find a cookie tray. I pull it out of the package, lay the pieces across it, and then preheat the oven.

I add water and olive oil to the pot, then set it on the stove. I turn the burner on. Then, I remove a saucepan from the cabinet, open the jar, dump it in, and set the lid on top. I put the setting on low so it doesn't burn.

Where is Dad?

I pace, then finally sit down at the kitchen table, shifting my thoughts to Dax.

Every now and then, my father's face and his angry voice appear, but then I think of how Dax tasted and how I got all of him in my mouth. Pride fills me. I really didn't think I could.

Something about that makes me feel like I'm just as good as those other girls.

I need to stop comparing myself to them.

He told me he's not into them, but I'm no dummy. I know he's been with others, so he must've been interested at some point.

Cindy's face appears in my mind, and my stomach churns.

I try to force myself to not think of her, but the lingering question won't turn off.

Did I please him more than she did?

Or does Dax regret me and want to go back to her?

I can't expect a man like Dax not to have had any experience. I vow not to hold that against him.

Please let him like me more, I silently plead to the universe.

The water boils over the pot, pulling me out of my worries. I move it off the burner, lower the temperature, wipe up the water, then add the noodles. I stir them to make sure they don't stick together, then put the pot back on the burner.

I stir the sauce, put the lid back on, and stick the bread in the oven.

I set a five-minute timer and then pace again. It's getting dark out. It's now eight thirty. My father should have been home by now, but with what the man on the walkie-talkie said was going on, he could be gone longer. Yet, with every second that passes, I'm just extending the anxiety about the conversation I know looms in front of me.

How will Dad act?

Will he have calmed down?

The meal finishes cooking. I take everything off the stove and the bread out of the oven. The scent of garlic flares in my nose, and my stomach growls.

Where is Dad?

I go to the door and open it right as he's reaching for the handle. His eyes turn to slits. He booms, "Ivy."

My insides quiver. I try to appear clueless, asking, "Dad, where have you been? I have dinner ready."

He scowls. "Don't act like you weren't there."

My chest tightens. I pray I look innocent. I've never been a good liar. I question, "Where?"

"Don't you dare lie to me, Ivy. I'm no fool," he warns.

I reach for his arm. "Dad, I'm confused. What's going on?"

He tenses for a moment, and my heart feels like it'll beat out of my chest.

It reminds me that I need to be careful. I don't need my father having another heart attack. And I definitely wouldn't want that to be my fault.

He steps closer, accusing, "I told you to stay away from him, Ivy."

"Who?" I stupidly ask.

"That boy, Dax. I know you were with him. Don't lie about it," he seethes.

My eyes widen as I try to look innocent. My mind races with what direction to take this, and I remember what I rehearsed. I recover and admit, "Yeah, he took me on his sailboat."

"I was clear you weren't to see him!"

Anger fills me. "Dad, it's not fair for you to tell me not to hang out with him. He's been a good friend to me."

Dad's head jerks backward. "You ran away from him last night. He obviously did something that offended you."

I shake my head. "No, one of his friends lied about something. So we got into an argument. That happens between friends. But he apologized even though it wasn't his fault."

My father grunts. "Don't be naive, Ivy."

My rage grows. "Dax apologized last night, but I was too stubborn to understand what happened."

"Which was what?" Dad snarls.

My pulse skyrockets. I square my shoulders and lift my chin. "It was nothing. Like I said, a stupid misunderstanding due to someone else lying."

"Why would they do that?"

"Some of the kids around here...well..." My voice trails off.

My father waits.

When I don't speak, he says, "Go on. Some of the kids around here what?"

My voice cracks, so I clear my throat and answer, "They're not very nice."

Dad sarcastically laughs.

"What's so funny?" I question.

"No shit, they aren't nice. I told you they wouldn't be."

I tilt my head and soften my tone asking, "Since when do you curse around me?"

My father's expression doesn't change, but his face grows slightly redder.

I hate it. I'm the cause of his disappointment and anger.

Dad repeats, "I told you not to hang out with him."

"Dax is my friend. We went out on his boat. What's the big deal?"

"I told you to stay away from him!"

"What do you want me to do? Sit in this house all day and do nothing?"

Rage contorts his features and he nods. "I don't care what you do, Ivy, as long as you stay away from him. That boy's bad news."

"How is he bad news? What exactly has he done for you to speak so horribly of him?" I question, defending Dax.

My father takes a step back and studies me.

It makes me feel powerless and small. I've never felt like that with my father before. Not once. We've always been close. In fact, I don't ever remember him being disappointed in me.

His voice lowers. "Ah, I see."

"You see what?"

"I see you've chosen your side."

"What are you talking about?"

My father scoffs and points at me. "You've let that boy trick you even though I've warned you about these people."

"That's not fair!" I exclaim.

"They aren't our kind, Ivy."

My tone turns incredulous. "Why? Because they have money, and we don't?"

"Partly."

I scoff. "Who cares if we don't have money? Dax doesn't seem to care. Why do you?"

My father's eyes turn to fire-filled slits.

I decide I'm over this conversation and Dax is right. I'm eighteen. I don't have to listen to Dad. And I'm not going to back down about hanging out with Dax.

So I motion toward the table, pointing out, "I made us dinner. Sit down. You have to be starving."

My father stays planted in the doorway.

I blurt out, "Why are you so late anyway?"

A new look of disgust fills his expression. He answers, "There was an issue with the greenhouses, but you already know that, don't you?"

I jerk my head back, and I'm proud of myself for playing my role. I lie some more, and it rolls out easier than at the start of this conversation. I reply, "How would I know what's going on?"

Dad barks, "You were with him when I threw the rock through the window."

Shock fills my body even though I already know the truth. I can't believe my father's acting like his actions are okay.

"You threw a rock through his window? What the heck, Dad!"

He keeps his scowl pinned on me. It makes me feel like the smallest person on Earth.

He adamantly states, "I know you were with him."

"I told you I went boating! He dropped me off, and I went for a walk. I didn't feel like sitting here twiddling my thumbs."

His raised brow tells me he doesn't believe me.

My mouth turns dry. Panic sets in, and I add, "I'm allowed to hang out with new friends, Dad."

He crosses his arms, declaring, "I expect you to listen and obey me because I know what's best for you. I'm the one who loves you and has your best interests at heart."

"You're paranoid. No one has bad intentions toward me," I lie again. Avery, Cindy, Marcey, and even Bobby have it out for me. Yet, I'm not admitting that to my dad.

Besides, Dax is going to protect me. He promised he would. He has already shown me he will. And somehow, his protection makes me feel invincible toward them.

"You're naive, Ivy. That boy is no good. His own father warned me about him," Dad declares.

I glare at him, spouting, "Then what's wrong with his father? That's a horrible statement to go around saying about your son."

"He's making sure you stay safe," Dad states.

"That's disgusting! Dax doesn't deserve that!"

Dad grunts.

Once again, I'm over this discussion. I go to the table and pull out a chair. I sit down and put spaghetti on my plate. I look up, informing him, "You can eat or not. I made a nice meal for us. But all you want to do is accuse me of things. And I don't know what this whole rock business is about, but it sounds like you went crazy. Do I even want to know the entire story?"

There's a moment where my dad's face falls, as if he's embarrassed, but he quickly recovers. His stubbornness won't go away. He looks at the table, saying, "I appreciate you making dinner, but I'm not hungry. Actually, if I'm being honest, I can't sit across from you tonight, Ivy."

My body starts to tremble and I blink back tears. "What do you mean you can't eat dinner with me? I'm your daughter."

He sniffs hard and shakes his head, answering, "You're lying to me."

"I'm not!"

He points at me. "You're choosing that boy over your own flesh and blood."

"I'm not choosing anyone! And I shouldn't have to! You're misinformed and being unreasonable!"

Dad comes over, puts his hand on the table, and leans over. He kisses me on the forehead, then pins his dark gaze to mine.

The more he stares, the more uncomfortable I get. And the feeling that something bad is going to happen grows.

My father opens his mouth and shuts it.

I wait.

He grabs my chin and angles my face higher toward the ceiling so his eyes look directly into mine. He lowers his voice. "I don't know what's happening with you, Ivy. You've never defied me before."

"I'm not trying to hurt you. But I have the right to make new friends," I claim.

"I love you, Ivy, I do, but you..."

My insides quiver harder. I blink hard.

"You're making bad decisions. And I'm afraid they'll affect your life forever. I don't know how, but I see it, and I won't stand by and let it happen."

I seethe, "By throwing a rock through Dax's window?"

Pity fills my father's face. "You've always made good decisions, Ivy. This is not the time to start making bad ones."

"I am not making bad decisions. You're creating scenarios that aren't true," I declare.

Dad shakes his head and then studies me another moment. He asks, "Have you been drinking today?"

My pulse pounds so hard at my neck, I'm sure he can see it. "Of course not! You know I don't drink."

His scowl intensifies.

My insides feel like they're crumbling.

How does he know what I've done?

Did the others tell him? Like they told him I was with Dax?

He adds, "I really hope you don't become an alcoholic."

"What? I'm not going to become an alcoholic!"

"I hope not. Children who drink—"

"I'm not a child, I'm eighteen!" I explode.

He takes a deep breath.

I add, "I've graduated high school. I'm going to college in two weeks."

He steps back and scratches his head. He replies, "Yeah, you are, but that doesn't mean you know everything, Ivy."

"I didn't say I know everything. But neither do you since you're wrong about Dax!"

Tense silence builds between us.

My father warns, "The decisions you make now can come back and bite you in the ass, Ivy. You need to look out for yourself. You can't trust people so easily."

"What does that mean? I'm not a fool!" I snap.

"It means that that boy is bad business. You don't know what he's capable of."

"He's been nothing but kind to me!"

My father closes his eyes and shakes his head in disappointment.

I hate it. I want to wipe that expression off his face, but I don't know how. And I won't not stick up for Dax. It's not right. He's been perfect with me, except for that stupid Cindy incident, and that wasn't his fault. He's done everything to make up for it too.

Dad pleads, "I'm begging you to think about things and make good decisions."

I don't say anything. I'm tired of having to defend myself and Dax.

More tension builds.

I finally state, "Sit down and eat before it gets cold."

My father glances at the spaghetti, then shakes his head. "No. Like I said, I'm not hungry. I'm going to bed. I hope you make better decisions tomorrow." He turns and leaves the room.

I stare at my spaghetti, no longer hungry, wondering how I'll make things right between us.

My father's hatred for Dax runs deeper than I thought. How will I ever convince him that Dax isn't a bad person?

$\mathcal{D}ax$ 11

I'M GOING CRAZY NOT SEEING YOU

Dax

One Week Later

John has Ivy on a tight leash. It's been a week since I've seen her, and I'm going crazy. I've caught glimpses of her across the estate, but that's it. Every time I text her, she gives me the same excuse that her father won't let her out of his sight. She claims she's trying to keep the peace and keep him calm.

This morning is no different.

Me: I'm seeing you today, and that's it.

Ivy: My father has my day planned out. I can't.

Me: You're not a child, Ivy.

Ivy: I know I'm not, but it's complicated.

Me: No, it's not. Your father's trying to be a tyrant, just like mine. Stand up to him. I'm losing patience with this situation.

Ivy: It's not that simple.

Me: Maybe you don't want to be with me.

Ivy: That's not true! Don't say that!

Me: Then stand up to him.

Ivy: I need to keep him calm. I don't want him to get fired.

Me: How many times do I have to tell you that won't happen? When are you going to trust me?

Ivy: Dax, please. I'm doing the best I can.

I pick up the phone and call her.

She quietly answers, and her voice alone makes my cock harder. "Hey."

I don't beat around the bush. "I'm coming to get you right now."

"You can't. I told you that," she argues.

"Ivy, how are we supposed to be together if you never see me? It's been a week."

"I know, and it's killing me," she whines, which only makes my chest tighten.

"I'm going crazy not seeing you," I tell her, which isn't a lie. I am.

I spend all day pacing, trying to figure out how to get her away from her father and see me. Part of me wants to fire him, but then she'd be off the estate, which wouldn't help my cause.

I've never wanted anyone as much as I want her, and my

obsession is growing. And I should be moving forward in my game, not backward.

She coos, "Dax, I miss you."

"I miss you too. That's why I'm coming to get you," I repeat.

"Please. You're not listening."

"Ivy, all I know is that you say you want to be with me, but you're not making any effort," I accuse.

"Really? Is that what you think? I've been fighting with my father all week," she admits, her voice shaking. Then I hear a sniffle.

My heart sinks and then I wonder what the fuck is happening to me. I've never been soft for anyone. I don't care if girls cry. But I lower my tone. "Ivy, this hurts. I miss you."

"I miss you too. I'm working on it, I promise."

I sigh.

She adds, "You can't come here right now, Dax. I can't get my father anymore upset. His heart..."

My ears perk up. I ask, "What about his heart?"

She hesitates, then relays, "He was having palpitations the other day. He didn't want me to know. I don't want to be the cause of him having another heart attack."

So, John has a heart issue.

Hmm.

I put that in the back of my mind for later if needed. Then I decide the best thing to do is to let it be for now. So I cave. "Okay, gorgeous. But I need to see you soon."

"Yeah. I need to see you too, Dax."

My pulse increases. I realize I'm way too pleased she feels this way. But I question, "You do?"

"Of course. I'm going crazy without you," she admits.

I can't help my grin growing larger. "Good. I feel the same. Keep working on it," I tell her and hang up.

I have a week before school starts, and I don't want to waste more time. So, for hours, I pace my cottage like I've done every other day this week.

Then it hits me. I know what needs to happen. I spend another hour researching options on my computer.

"Yes!" I shout, pumping my arm in the air when I finally find the perfect solution. I go outside, get on my golf cart, and drive to the main house.

I let myself in, ignore the staff trying to stop me, and go into my father's office.

He looks up. "Dax?"

"Everett," I reply.

My father's real name is Dax Everett Carrington, the fourth. I'm the fifth. So he goes by his middle name, which I'm happy about. I can't stand that I have his name, but at least he gets called something different.

His eyes turn to slits. "I told you not to call me by my first name. I'm your father."

I ignore him and take a seat, not looking for small talk. I announce, "There's a botany conference in New York. I need you to send John Ford to it."

He puts his pen down, sits back in his chair, and presses his fingers together, staring at me.

I remind him, "It's my right to make this decision, and you're to do it."

My father grinds his molars. He hates it when I order him around about the business.

I typically let him run things because there are trust stipulations in place. My mother's father hated my dad. He didn't want him to have the family business either.

But my father worked his way up and learned everything he could. So when my grandfather died, he was just as surprised as I was to learn he left the business to me and my siblings.

I was the one who was supposed to be in charge unless I couldn't take over after I graduated from college, then it would fall to my brother. My grandfather didn't believe women should be in business, so Avery doesn't even have that option, thank goodness. She'd run it into the ground. And I'm still way smarter than my brother, so I won't let our family fortune go down the tubes.

Until I graduate, my father gets to run things. And his days of power are coming to an end. I remind him any chance I get.

He gives me a disapproving look.

It's in vain. I have the right to veto things and make decisions. There's no way this isn't happening.

"Why?" he questions.

"It doesn't matter why," I claim.

He argues, disdain clear in his tone, "You know I have to document everything for the trust or I can be sued."

It's another caveat my grandfather put in the trust.

My father hates it.

I love it.

"The week-long conference in New York is about hybrids, and there's some cutting-edge research. It makes sense for John to go. The staff is in place to care for everything while he's gone. So this is good for the business. Now document it and tell him to pack up," I order, getting up and leaving. I don't need to say anything more. I know my father will do it. He has to. He has no choice.

I get back on my golf cart, proud of myself, feeling elated that I figured it out, and I text Ivy.

> Me: I figured out how we can see each other, my little wet slut.

A moment passes, and she doesn't respond.

Me: Are you squeezing that sexy pussy of yours together thinking about me?

Ivy: Dax! (Laughing emoji)

Me: Get ready for lots of time with me.

Ivy: How?

Me: You'll find out soon enough.

I put my phone back in my pocket and take off across the estate. It'll be a few hours until things are set in motion. So I go down to the docks and take one of the boats out.

I spend two hours riding around the lake. I'm halfway back to the dock when I get another text.

Ivy: I have to go to New York with my father for a week.

Panic hits me.

Me: No, you're not. I set that up so you and I can hang out and be together.

Ivy: He's insisting I go.

Me: You're eighteen. Tell him you're not going.

Ivy: It's not that simple.

Me: How is it not simple? You're an adult.

I scrub my hands over my face in frustration. How many times do I have to remind her?

Ivy: I don't have a relationship with my father like you have with yours. I don't get to make rules.

Me: Okay, then. I'll figure this out too.

Ivy: How?

I don't reply to her. I rack my brain as I return to my cottage and get in my car. I rev the engine of my Porsche and take off through the estate.

I exit the gates and drive over to Clifton University. I park in the fire zone, stroll inside, bypass the newest secretary, and knock on the door of Professor William Dyer's office.

"Sir, you can't go in there," she says.

I look at her. "You're new, aren't you?"

The fifty-something-year-old redhead with orange lipstick and blue glasses nods. She gives me a disapproving look that reminds me of my father. Her voice has an air of false authority as she replies, "Yes, I am, and you can't just walk past me and knock on his door. He's in a meeting."

I cross my arms, grinning at her. It's an arrogant look. I know it is, but I can't help it.

"Sir, why are you looking at me like that?" she asks.

I smirk for a moment, then drop the mic on her. "Let me introduce myself to you. I'm Dax Carrington. I'm assuming you know who I am?"

Her mouth falls open and she quickly recovers. She swallows hard. "I'm sorry, sir."

"Yeah, that's what I thought. Don't let it happen again," I warn, then open the door and walk into the office.

Professor Dyer's there with a man I don't know. He looks up. "Dax. Everything okay?"

"I need to speak with you now," I assert and sit in the chair next to the stranger.

Professor Dyer clears his throat and turns to the man. "Sorry. We'll have to talk another time on this, Max. Okay?"

Max nods, obviously aware of who I am, and starts to leave the room.

I call out, "Shut the door on your way out."

He obeys.

Once we're alone, Professor Dyer focuses his attention on me. "Dax, long time no see."

I nod. "Yeah, it's been what...?"

He ponders my question.

I snap my fingers, declaring, "Since February, when we played around with... What was her name?" For some reason I can't remember the girl's face, but I remember her mole.

"Lacey," Professor Dyer says in a darker voice.

We've played the game too many times in the past. It's gotten so easy to get coeds into our beds, making them do things they never considered before. We capture them on video in orgies or just with us. We set them up in compromising positions doing things they shouldn't do. It may involve stealing, committing arson, or anything else that can have lifelong consequences.

And Dyer's fun. His imagination is just as twisted as mine at times.

Once they do what we want, we figure out how to hold it over their heads. We've gotten our way on so many different things, and Dyer's always up for a challenge.

"Oh, yeah. Lacey," I state.

"I kind of miss her pussy," he declares.

I grunt. "Really? All I remember is that mole on her ass."

"Oh, her ass. She loved our cocks up there, didn't she?" he reminisces.

Lots of coeds love that. I shrug. "Did she?"

"How do you not remember this?" he questions.

Once again, my arrogance shines through. "Guess it's because I get so much ass I can't remember one girl. Maybe you should try it."

He chuckles. "Touché. So, what can I do for you today? Do we have a new project?"

"*We* do *not* have a new project," I assert, wanting him to understand he's not to do anything with Ivy. She's mine and staying mine unless I decide otherwise and call the shots.

He arches his eyebrows. "Oh?"

"Yeah. There's a girl named Ivy Ford who's starting here. I need you to call an orientation for new students and a special project to start tomorrow."

"Tomorrow?" he questions.

"Yes, tomorrow. Is there a problem with that?"

He shakes his head. "No. Of course not. But what are we looking at here?"

"*We* aren't looking at anything. You're going to call the orientation. She's not going to show up, and you're going to pass her. Do you understand?"

He nods. "So I have a fake orientation for one student. No problem."

"Nah. Call the others."

"Why?"

I grin. "Just to ruin the end of their summer."

He chuckles. "Fine. Sounds like a great plan for my newest teaching assistant. It's about time she asked me for some extra credit anyway." His face darkens with excitement.

"Whatever. Just make sure Ivy gets notified right away," I direct.

He whines, "So, I don't get to have any fun with this one?"

"No, you don't. Not unless I let you in on it in the future. Understand?" I declare, waving the carrot in front of him.

That's the thing with Professor Dyer. You always want to wave the carrot so he thinks he might have a chance. Manipulating him is also part of my game, and I can almost see him salivating.

He nods. "Sure. What's she look like?"

I find a photo on my phone that I took of Ivy when we were on the boat. She's in her bikini. I hold it toward him.

He tries to grab my phone, but I don't let him have it. He doesn't need to see her any closer. He whistles. "She's not from around here, is she?"

"West Virginia," I admit.

"Are those real boobs? What are they? C cups?"

I chuckle. "Yeah, they fit perfectly in my mouth." I grin bigger, remembering how Ivy felt against my body.

Fuck, that girl could suck my dick.

It's one of the things I've not been able to stop thinking about, and I curse myself for not having a 69 with her, instead of going down on her first. That would've made sure that I came that day.

Fucking John Ford. I'll make him pay, I vow for the millionth time this week.

My cock still has blue balls from her not finishing me off.

"So, what's your game plan on this? What's the end goal?" Dyer asks.

I shake my head. "None of your fucking business. Now call the orientation and make sure you send an email to her. I need it done now." I rise and move toward the door.

"Done," he calls out, then adds, "But you know I like it better when I get to play too, Dax."

I spin back toward him. "Don't worry. I'll find some pet

projects for you. School starts in a week, and there's always a lot to go around."

He taps his pen on his desk. "Yeah. But I kind of like what you just showed me."

I lunge across the room, slam my hand on his desk, and grab him by the collar. In my firmest voice, I seethe, "She's off-limits to you. Do you understand me?"

He holds his hands out to the side. "Easy, Dax! I got it."

"Send the email now," I order again and leave the room.

I whistle down the hall, geeking out that I solved the problem and figured out how to spend an entire week with Ivy without her asshole dad around. Everything I'll create during these next seven days to manipulate her flies through my mind.

By the time I get to my car, I'm feeling as high as if I just orgasmed. I pick up the phone and call Ivy.

She answers in that breathless voice that drives me wild. "Dax?"

I keep my tone low. "What are you doing, my little slut?"

She sighs, fretting, "I'm packing."

"Stop packing."

"I can't. I told you."

I chuckle. "Ye of little faith."

She goes silent.

I wait for her to speak.

She finally asks, "What does that mean, Dax?"

I order, "Check your email."

"Why?"

"Just do it."

I wait a few moments until she says, "Orientation?"

"Yeah, but you're not going."

"I'm confused."

I chuckle again. "Don't be. All you need to know is I just

created a week for us to be together. Your father will have no choice but to let you stay home. And he won't be breathing down our necks. So what do you think about that?"

Silence fills the line, and I start to get nervous.

Does she not want it?

But then the excitement rings in her voice, and she praises, "I can't believe you figured this out."

"Don't worry, baby girl. I told you, you have to trust me. When are you going to trust me, by the way?"

"I do trust you."

"Okay. Then know from now on, any problem that arises, I will fix."

"Just like that, huh?" she asks.

I confidently reply, "Yeah. That's what I do."

Humor laces her voice. "Good to know."

I demand, "Now, go tell your father you're staying here. I'm coming over to get you the minute he leaves."

I hang up the phone, happier than I've felt in at least a week, knowing everything in Ivy Ford's life is about to change —starting today.

Ivy 12

WE RUN THIS TOWN

Ivy

"Ivy," my father says before he walks out the door.

"Yeah?" Things have been tense between us the entire week. He gives me a worried expression. "What is it?" I ask.

"I don't like you staying here by yourself. Please don't see that boy while I'm gone," he begs.

I sigh. "Dad, I'm starting college. You saw the email from my professor. I have an orientation project."

He doesn't speak.

I add, "You don't want me to lose my ability to go there, do you? I'm sure the Carringtons aren't going to pay for me to go if I flunk out before school even starts." The guilt I can't escape grows.

I feel horrible lying to my father, but he's made sure I've stayed away from Dax all week. A few times, I caught him having chest pains, so I've abided by his rules so I don't agitate him in any way.

He sighs. "No, I don't want you to lose your education. It's another reason you should stay away from Dax."

I close my eyes and shake my head. "Dad, can you just stop?" I open my eyes and step forward. I hug him, continuing, "Have a safe trip. Try to enjoy yourself."

He reluctantly hugs me back.

I squeeze him tighter, and he finally caves, giving me a hug like I'm used to.

I retreat and grin, chirping, "That's more like it. Now, get out of here. I have to be at school within the next hour."

He hesitates but finally leaves. I watch his truck until I can't see it anymore, then pick up my phone. Before I can text Dax, he sends me one.

> Dax: I'm on my way over, you little slut.

My butterflies take off. I'm still confused about how I'm okay with him calling me that, but I'm not going to think about it anymore.

I get an entire week with Dax.

My insides tremble with excitement. I go to the mirror and double-check my reflection. I put on a little bit more lip gloss and brush my hair.

I've never been one to wear much makeup, and I debate if I should start. Everyone Dax is around is sophisticated, so I decide I need to step up my game. I don't want to lose him.

No, I won't. He told me he likes me how I am.

Yes, I will. These girls are competition whether I want them to be or not.

During the last week, I've studied magazine articles on

how to give yourself inexpensive makeovers. I decide I'll do it sometime this week. I don't want Dax to get bored of me.

Within minutes, he pulls up in a Porsche.

I walk outside, saying, "I figured you'd come over in your golf cart."

He gets out, picks me up, and twirls me, giving me a hug tighter than my dad gave me, which feels amazing.

I shriek, "Dax, what are you doing?"

He plants me on my feet, slides his hands on my cheeks, and kisses me. He murmurs against my lips, "You have no idea how much I missed you."

I beam up at him. "I missed you too."

"Really? How much?" he questions, giving me a mischievous look.

I giggle again. "A lot. More than I can explain."

He moves his hand down my back and cups my ass. It ignites the tingles I felt in his bedroom.

I repeat, "I missed you. I really did."

His grin widens. "Good. I have a surprise for you."

"Oh?" I question, my heart fluttering.

"Yep." He takes my hand and pulls me toward the passenger side of the car. He opens the door of his Porsche and orders, "Get in."

I obey.

He bends down and puts his hand between my legs so his middle finger is touching the slit of my pussy.

I inhale sharply.

A dark look enters his expression.

My adrenaline spikes.

He states, "I think it's time for you to experience what it's like to be a Carrington."

My lips twitch. "A Carrington? But I'm a Ford."

He grunts. "Well, if I have my way, you're going to be a Carrington one day."

I tilt my head. "You can't say that. You just met me."

His face falls. "Ivy, I'm a man who knows what I want, and I want you."

Every part of me hopes that's true—that this is my love story. Dax and I will end up together forever, and my father will love him too.

I'm screwed if it's not. If I can't have Dax, who would I ever have that could ever come close?

He pecks me on the lips, straightens up, then shuts the door. He goes around to the other side and slides in. Then he puts his hand between my thighs.

"Where are we going?" I question.

"It's a surprise." He revs the engine, and my pulse picks up. I've always wanted to ride in a fancy car. I never have. There aren't many of them in the small town in West Virginia where I'm from. Most guys have trucks if they're doing well.

Dax zooms through the estate, and I squeal when he goes faster toward the closed gate.

I blurt out, "Dax, the gate!"

"Don't worry, baby girl," he assures, and the gates open just in time for him to fly through.

Endorphins fill my cells. "You're crazy!" I declare, but I'm smiling.

"Is that what you think? I'm crazy?" he asks, putting on a pair of aviator sunglasses.

I giggle.

"I'm crazy but not sexy?" he teases.

My face heats. I admit, "You're both. Are you an adrenaline junkie?"

He shrugs, speeding up even more and veering left on a curve. "You could say that."

"Aren't you scared that you'll get hurt doing something like that?"

He plants his gaze on me. "Are you back to being a prude, Ivy?"

My heart sinks. "I'm not a prude," I mumble and then fidget with my fingers in my lap. The last thing I want is for him or anyone around here to think that. Sure, I may be inexperienced, but it's not that I think bad about having fun or sex.

Maybe I am a prude.

I'm not.

But maybe I am.

"I was just teasing," Dax states, grabbing my hand and kissing it. He adds, "Come on, my little whore. Don't look so down."

"Ha ha, funny."

"Just sit back and relax. I assure you we're going to have an amazing day."

Once again, happiness surges through me.

He orders, "Open the glove box."

I reach for it and unlatch the lock. The only thing in it is a white box with a fancy pink bow around it. My butterflies increase, and I glance at Dax.

He chuckles. "Well, open it."

"It's for me?"

"Of course it's for you. You're my little sexy slut. Who else would it be for?"

Cindy.

What am I thinking?

I pull the box out.

He leans close to my head. "Open it up, you naughty whore."

More excitement fills me. The only gift I've ever gotten from a boy was chocolate on Valentine's Day. I glance at the box, but there's no way chocolates are inside. I confess, "It's so fancy and pretty, I feel bad opening it."

He groans. "Ivy, more pretty boxes will come when you're with me. Now, open it up."

I gingerly pull the bow and open the lid. A pair of Gucci sunglasses are nestled inside. I pull them out and gape at them.

"Do you like them?" he asks.

"Dax, they're beautiful." But I feel guilty. I know what these glasses cost. I've seen them in magazines, and there's no way I could ever afford anything so nice.

"Try them on," he orders.

I eagerly put them on my face, and he flips down the visor with the mirror.

I glance at myself.

He whistles. "You're stylin'."

"This is too much, Dax."

He groans. "Ivy, don't be like that."

"Like what?"

"Like a poor girl who can't accept a gift."

My gut once again dives. I stay quiet, not sure how to respond to that.

"Hey, did you wake up on the wrong side of the bed today?" he questions.

I stutter, "Wh-what do you mean?"

"Because you're taking a lot of things I say very seriously. I thought we were going to be carefree and fun. Your dad's gone, and we finally get to be together."

"Yes," I agree.

"Then why are you so uptight today, baby girl?"

"Am I?"

He nods. "Yeah. Stop taking everything so seriously."

I exhale a stress-filled breath and realize he's right. I nod.

"I'm sorry. I'm just really happy to be here with you. And these sunglasses are beautiful. Thank you!"

He picks up my hand, kisses it again, then replies, "You're welcome. Nothing but the best for my little slut." He wiggles his eyebrows.

I laugh.

He turns up the music, speeds through the town, then parks the Porsche in a fire lane.

"I don't think you can park here," I state.

He shakes his head as if in disapproval. "You have a lot to learn, Ivy Ford."

"I do?"

"Yeah. I'm a Carrington. We run this town."

"That's a little arrogant, Dax," I blurt out.

"Touché. It is, but you know what? It's true. And you're now going to get the perks of that. Come on, let's go." He jumps out of the car and comes around to my side. He opens the door and pulls me out.

"Where are we going?" I question.

"We're going to get you clothes."

"Why? I have plenty," I say.

He shakes his head again and keeps leading me toward a store. A security guard stands outside near a red rope.

Why would a store try to keep people out?

Dax leans into my ear and murmurs, "You're my girl, Ivy. You're going to have the best, just like I do. Understand?"

"But you don't have to do that," I assert, not sure why I'm fighting him on this. It's every girl's dream, after all.

Arrogance fills his expression, and my pussy throbs. Something about that look on his face makes my knees weak.

"I know I don't have to do it. That's why I'm doing it," Dax declares, nodding to the security guard who opens the door. He leads me past him and into the boutique.

"Wow," I blurt out, amazed at how high-end everything looks.

Dax laughs. "Baby girl, anything you want in here is yours. Sky's the limit, okay?"

I arch my eyebrows.

He holds a leather miniskirt up to me. "You'd look hot as fuck in this."

I glance at it. It's nothing I'd ever normally choose.

"Where would I wear that?" I question.

"Tonight, when I take you to dinner."

I bite on my lip, my face crawling with heat. "You're taking me to dinner?"

"Yeah. I'm taking you to a five-star restaurant with a four-month waitlist, but not for me or you. Is that okay?"

Is he for real?

"I feel like Cinderella right now," I blurt out, then realize what I said. I put my hand over my face, groaning, "Oh my gosh. I'm sorry."

Dax chuckles. "Come on. Let's see what else they have."

He guides me farther into the store. Saleswomen gather around us. They seem to know Dax.

They fret and fuss over me, but it's clear Dax is in charge. He has style, and he knows what he wants on me.

Everything he chooses is skimpy, which is a tad uncomfortable for me. I'm not used to wearing things so expensive or revealing.

Dax must sense it. He leans into my ear. "This is what people wear around here, baby girl. Don't be scared of it." He gives me a challenging stare.

I take a deep breath and smile. "It's very sweet of you to want to buy me a new wardrobe."

He grins, then loudly states, "That's my little whore."

I glance at the saleswomen, my face heating.

Dax chuckles, then tugs me into a dressing room full of clothes and keeps his voice loud so I'm sure everybody else hears, demanding, "Strip."

I tilt my head. "Funny." I give him a peck on the lips. "I'll put something on and come out."

He shakes his head and crosses his arms. "No, that's not how this works. Strip."

My heart beats faster. My mouth turns dry. I swallow hard.

He doesn't lower his voice. He takes his finger and drags it down my cheek. He traces my jawline, moving down my neck and onto my cleavage. His fingers touch my belly button before he cups my pussy.

Tingles explode under his touch.

He adds, "Did you forget I've seen all of you, or do I have to remind you where my tongue's been?"

A mix of embarrassment from him being so loud and a deep need fills me. I squeeze my legs together, and he notices. It's all over his face, and I scold myself for making it so easy for him to tell what's on my mind.

He unbuttons my jean shorts and slides his fingers on my hips, shoving them and my panties to the ground. Not once does he take his domineering stare off me. He demands, "Now, show me those perfect fucking C cups."

I take a deep breath, still uncomfortable that I'm in public and people know what's happening in the dressing room. I plead in a whisper, "Dax."

He leans in my ear and murmurs, "Did you forget I'm a Carrington? We own this place, baby girl. Now, be a good little whore and show me those tits. But don't just show them to me. Take your top off in the sexiest way you can."

I gape at him for a moment. One thing I'm not is sexy, nor have I ever practiced sexy moves.

He comes close to my lips. "What's wrong? You don't want to please me?"

There's nothing more I want to do than please him. I barely get out, "Of course I do."

"Well, this is what pleases me." He drags his fingers over my slit, continuing, "My dirty little slut acting sexy for me. You still want to be mine, right?"

My heart races.

His face falls. His puppy dog gaze falls on me. "No?"

I take a deep breath and nod. "Of course I want to be yours." I bite on my lip.

"It's cute when you do that," he states.

"Do what?" I question.

"You bite on that puffy lip of yours. You know what I think about when you do that?"

I shake my head.

"Your lips, sucking my big cock," he roars.

My cheeks grow hotter. I glance at the door, but the same adrenaline that filled me when my father was banging on his door mixes with my fear.

"If you think I haven't thought about how you took all of me inside that pretty, slutty mouth of yours, you're wrong. I can't stop thinking about it. In fact, I'm obsessed with it. You have no idea how good you are at it either," he claims, in a voice loud enough for the entire store to hear him.

So much heat fills my face that I might start sweating.

He drags his knuckles down my cheek. "What's wrong? You don't like me complimenting you or telling you how much I enjoy you? Should I not do that?"

I ponder his question.

Stop being silly. I want to know what he likes and doesn't like.

Act like the woman Dax Carrington deserves.

One who makes him happy.

"Yes, I like to know what makes you happy," I quietly reveal.

Satisfaction appears in his expression. He steps back and snaps his fingers. Then he swirls his finger in a circle with a dirty grin, ordering, "Strip, my little slut. Show me what you got."

I take another nervous breath, put my hands on the bottom of my tank top, and slowly pull it over my head. Then I shake my hair so it swings all over my back.

Dax's grin grows. He praises, "You fucking whore. That's it. Now, let me see those pink titties."

I reach behind me, unhook my bra, and hold the top, letting the straps fall off my shoulders. I slowly take my arms out one by one, then slowly hold it out and dangle it in front of him.

He groans and holds his hand over his heart. "Fuck. You're so fucking hot."

Excitement surges through me.

Yes, I can do this, I tell myself.

It's as if he once again reads my thoughts. He licks his lips, steps forward, and slides his finger past my slit, right on top of my hole but doesn't slide it inside. He again keeps his voice at the same loud volume, stating, "I wish everybody could see you like this. You don't know how fucking sexy you and your wet cunt are, do you?"

I stay quiet.

He chuckles. "Yeah, you and your wet cunt are my little whore. Now, turn around. Put your hands on the mirror and spread your legs."

Dax 13

YOU DON'T WANT TO PLAY?

Dax

Fear fills Ivy's expression. I know I'm embarrassing her. She's fully aware everyone can hear me, but my little slut wants to please me.

She's more trainable than I anticipated. I assumed I'd have to wait months for this progress.

I circle my finger in the air, repeating, "Hands on the mirror."

She swallows hard.

"You don't want to play?" I challenge.

She furrows her eyebrows. "Is that what we're doing? We're playing a game?"

I step forward and tug her into me. I kiss her like my life depends on it. I slide my tongue in her mouth so fast she loses her breath. It only takes a moment before she returns my affection with fervor.

I retreat, leaving her wanting more, and hold her ass cheek firmly. "You have no idea what you're doing to me, baby girl. Do you feel this?" I pull her even closer so my cock's throbbing against her stomach.

She takes a shaky breath.

Fucking A.

I've had blue balls since she left my house. Hell, I've had them since the moment I first laid eyes on her. There's been no relief since Cindy got me off that last time. And that was only because I was thinking of Ivy.

Her little naive expressions are making my situation worse. I'm obsessed with her. The only thing diverting me from focusing on my hard dick is the high I have from figuring out how to get her dad out of town for a week and for her to stay.

Her blush deepens. She whispers, "Yeah."

"This is what you do to me. Now, don't ask questions. Be a good little whore. Turn around and put your hands on the glass."

She takes a deep breath and slowly obeys, putting her hands on the mirror.

I take my foot and move her feet wider. Then I instruct, "Good slut. Now, step back and slowly move your hands to your ankles."

She gives me a nervous glance in the mirror.

I murmur, "Sorry. I forgot you're not as experienced as the other girls around here. Forget about this."

"What? N-no! T-tell me again to do it," she stutters.

Endorphins flood through me. It won't be hard manipulating her to do things by reminding her she's not like the other girls.

I say louder, "Take a step back. Move your hands slowly to your ankles."

Her fingers tremble. She slowly slides them down the front of her thighs.

I make a note to take her for a manicure. The hot pink polish isn't doing it for me.

I need her in whore red.

She stops when she gets to her ankles.

"That's my good slut. Now, wrap your fingers around your ankles and stick your sexy ass higher in the air," I instruct.

Her eyes once again meet mine in the glass.

I crouch down and stroke the back of her thighs, muttering, "Too much for you?"

Determination fills her gaze. She shakes her head, then grips her ankles.

Giddiness fills me. I take my fingers and slowly trail them up the back of her legs.

She shivers.

I put my face near her ass, deeply inhale, and groan. "Fuu-uck, you little cunt. Your ass smells as good as your pussy."

She bites on her lip, confusion mixing with need.

I've seen it before in others. She's into this, she just doesn't know it, which only elates me further.

It's always better when I don't have to totally convince a girl to like what I want her to do.

Her words come out nervous when she says, "Wh-what are you doing, Dax?"

"I'm smelling what's mine," I say just as loud as before.

She stays quiet, but her breath turns ragged. A slight fog forms on the mirror.

I continue stroking her until a drop of juice runs down her thigh. I loudly boast, "My sexy slut pleases me so much. Tell me, Ivy, do you want me to lick your ass or your pussy?"

Her cheeks burst into flames. She gapes at me.

I circle my finger around her pink forbidden zone.

She clenches her ass cheeks.

I continue, "I don't like it when you're a tease, my little whore."

"I-I'm not," she declares.

"No?"

"No."

"So you want me?"

She nods. "Yes."

I pull a handkerchief out of my pocket, wad it into a ball, then put it in front of her mouth. "Open wide."

She swallows hard.

I murmur, "You're gonna get loud. Do you want the entire store to hear?"

She takes a few ragged breaths, with more fear and excitement on her face.

And she's debating. It's so clearly written in her expression that she's analyzing what's going on and trying to figure out what I'm going to do.

I repeat, "Open up. I'm going to make you feel good, baby girl."

She stares at me.

"That's what you want, right? Me to make you feel good?" I goad.

She stays quiet.

"Answer me," I demand.

Her voice cracks. "Yes."

"Then open up, because I'm going to make you feel so good the entire block's going to hear you," I assert.

She licks her lips, takes a deep breath, then opens her mouth.

My pulse skyrockets. There's nothing worse than a prude who won't let me shove whatever I want into their mouth. But my Ivy isn't a prude, and I'm confident I won't have any problem eliminating any hesitations she has about whatever it is I want to do.

I shove the cloth into her mouth, then declare, "I'm taking what's mine, you sexy whore."

Fire burns in her eyes, mixing with her scared-little-girl expression.

My dick throbs, reminding me of the pain she's caused me all week. She chose her father instead of me, and that's never happening again.

I announce, "You're going to take all of me, Ivy. This will only hurt your virgin pussy for a minute. Then your greedy cunt's going to feel like it's Christmas and Santa left his entire sleigh of presents under the tree."

She swallows hard.

I lean close to her ear. "Do you know why I brought you here for this?"

She shuts her eyes, as if debating whether to keep going or not.

"Look at me."

She pins her confused gaze on me once again.

"I want you to watch and remember this moment. I never want you to forget how sexy you look or how much you love taking all of me deep inside you."

Her cheeks turn maroon.

I add, "I want you to always remember how everyone else outside of this room wishes they were us, in here, connected in a way they'll never understand but always crave."

She blinks hard.

I stroke her cheek, declaring, "That's what we have, baby girl. A connection no one else in this entire world will ever have. You feel it, don't you?"

She swallows and nods.

Anticipation fills my belly. "You're making me so happy.

Now, stare at the sexy slut in the mirror and be proud of you...of us. I know you can take every ounce of me like the woman you are...the woman you crave to be."

A tear slides down her cheek.

I brush it off and ask, "You want me, right, baby girl?"

She hesitates, then nods. A muffled, "Mm-hmm," noise comes out of her.

The high that hits me resembles the one I have when I snort coke.

But it's better.

I kiss her cheek, put my hand over her mouth, and remind her, "You study your gorgeous self the entire time, understand?"

She nods.

I debate about ramming my cock into her ass but decide that'll come later. Right now, I'm going to let her tight cunt suck up my cock.

I move my hand around her waist, position it on her clit, and rub her. My other hand holds her hip to my pelvis, and I move the tip of my cock to her hole.

I circle her clit faster, and sweat bursts out on her skin. Her knees wobble, and she whimpers louder.

"Fuck, your pussy's wet, you little slutty tease," I boom, so the entire store can hear us.

She glances at me in the mirror.

"You want me inside your dirty cunt, don't you?" I growl.

She blinks, barely able to stand.

I take all my fingers, rotate them quickly on her clit, and her eyes roll. Her knees give out, and she places her hands on the floor to avoid falling.

I tug her hips up and push my cock all the way into her, and the gates of heaven open up. She's tighter than I thought, and I don't pause to let her get used to me, slowly moving back and forth inside her.

A noise like a wounded animal fills the air for several seconds. I work her clit harder, and her eyes flutter shut.

"Open your eyes and look in the mirror," I shout.

They fling open, then roll again.

I've never witnessed anyone's body convulse as hard as Ivy's. Maybe I've never fucked anyone as hard. Who knows. But my groan fills the air. It all turns me into a wild animal, pounding into her faster, declaring, "Fuuuck, you're a perfect little slut. Look at you taking all of me on your first try, baby girl."

She can barely focus on anything. Her glassy eyes roll at times, dripping with tears, and the muffled whimpering sounds keep getting louder.

And it's time for that to end. I release her clit and tug the cloth out of her mouth.

"Tell me you're my slut," I order.

"I-I..."

"I want to hear it," I say, tugging her hips harder against me.

"Dax!" she screams, so loud I'm sure the entire town hears her. Her body explodes into another long convulsion.

"Fuck! You fucking little cunt whore!" I bellow. I pull out of her, slide my finger into her pussy, then remove it. I thrust back into her hard.

"Dax!" she cries out.

I push my fingers into her mouth, ordering, "Suck like you're sucking my cock."

She obeys, driving me closer to my final high.

"Look at yourself," I demand.

She glances in the mirror.

"Fuck. Baby girl. You love the taste of yourself, don't you?" I say to embarrass her further.

She glances at me and continues shaking and sucking.

I pull my fingers out. "Admit you love tasting yourself after I've been inside you."

"I do," she breathes.

I move my hand to her ass.

She breathes harder through her nose.

"Dirty whores like to come. Do you like to come, my dirty little whore?" I question, inching past her forbidden zone but just barely.

Her mouth forms an O, and her eyes widen.

"You'd better nod, baby girl, or I'm not going to give you anymore orgasms," I threaten.

She obeys.

"Tell me you're my dirty slut," I roar, pushing deeper.

Her eyes roll again, and she cries out, her body giving out, forcing me to have to hold her up with my forearm.

"Tell me!"

"I-I'm your dirty slut," she chokes.

"Louder!"

"I'm your dirty slut!"

Fuck I'm going to come.

I pull out, slide my other hand around her neck, tug her up, then spin her around. I press her back to the glass.

Tears stain her red cheeks. Lust, exhaustion, and a desire that I've never seen create a wild statement in her eyes. It takes me a minute to realize what it is.

She's insatiable.

Jesus.

"You like what I give you, baby girl?" I taunt.

Her lips part and hot breath hits my mouth.

I add, "You love my cock in your tight pussy, don't you?"

She tries to catch her breath.

"Well?" I murmur.

"Yes," she whispers.

"Are you on birth control?" I ask.

Fear fills her expression. She shakes her head.

A feeling of disappointment hits me. I'm aching to fill her with my cum. I want to make her stand in front of the mirror and watch it drip down her legs afterward.

I don't need to get her pregnant.

I'll take care of this problem later.

I push her shoulders toward the ground and order, "Then get on your knees and suck me like a good little whore."

When she's on her knees, I step closer, grab her hair with one hand, and shove my cock into her mouth.

She briefly chokes, then recovers. She quickly resumes the intensity of our last encounter when she almost got me off.

This time, she's not leaving me with blue balls.

I'm past my breaking point. I move her as fast as I can, with an out-of-control need pulsing through my veins.

"Look at me," I demand through gritted teeth, slamming my hand on the glass to support myself.

She moves her watery gaze up, her mouth full of me.

It's all it takes. I can't handle it anymore. This girl excites me too much. So I stop trying to make it last longer and explode into her.

She gags, but I don't leave her mouth. My cum seeps past her lips and keeps pumping out of my cock.

"Don't fail me, Ivy," I threaten.

It takes her a minute, but she grips my hips, sinking her hot pink nails into my skin.

She needs whore red, I remind myself.

"Suck me," I seethe, wanting to ride out my high as long as possible.

To my surprise, she begins to suck me again while continuing to stare at me with her big doe eyes.

It's more than I bargained for and nothing I've ever felt before. I violently convulse, shouting, "Jesus Christ, you fucking slutty wet whore!" I keep a firm hold on her head and don't let her pull away.

And Ivy's a delicious surprise. She sucks me off, gazing at me. It normally takes me months of training whatever girl I'm playing with to take all of me.

Normally, I don't want them looking at me. Something about Ivy's innocent, wild gaze drives me higher until I think I might explode from endorphin overload.

She sucks, and sucks, and sucks until I'm spent and there's nothing left but my limp dick.

Jesus. I'm normally still semihard.

I breathe hard, holding myself up by pressing against the glass and staring down at her.

She wipes her mouth with the back of her hand, searching for my approval.

I don't give it to her. I command, "Say thank you."

Her forehead wrinkles.

"You don't want to thank me for making you come more than I did?" I challenge.

Guilt fills her expression. "I-I'm sorry."

"I didn't ask for an apology. I told you to say thank you so I know my little slut liked what I did to her. If you don't, then I won't know what to do to you in the future."

Her lips twitch. "Thank you."

I reach under her armpits and pull her to her feet. I spin her so she faces the mirror and palm her ass. "Next time we come here, I'm fucking you in the ass."

Horror fills her expression.

"You don't think I know exactly how to make you feel good?"

She opens her mouth to speak, but nothing comes out.

"No? You don't have faith in me?"

"I-I didn't say that."

"But you don't want all of me?" I question with a semi-glare.

Her lip quivers. "Of course I want you, Dax."

"But you don't want all of me?"

She stays quiet.

I step back, pull up my pants, and state in a low tone, "I guess I misjudged us. I thought you wanted me."

She reaches for my arm. "Dax, no! I didn't mean that! I do!"

"Are you sure about that?"

She nods. "Yes."

"Good. Then tell me who you are to me," I push.

She bites on her lip.

I grip her chin and tilt her face up. I hover close to her mouth, murmuring, "Tell me. I need to know you really want me, Ivy. That you're feeling all the emotions I am and aren't using me to gain experience or for who I am."

Shock appears on her expression. She opens her mouth, then shuts it, shaking her head.

"What's that response for?" I question.

Her voice shakes. "Why would you say such a horrible thing?"

I lay it on thick. "That's what women do around here. They use me. I—" I look at the floor, clench my jaw, then slowly meet her gaze again.

"You what?" she pushes, playing right into my palm.

"I can't handle it if you aren't really into me. The others, I can handle. But you? No, not you."

"Dax! Of course I'm really into you!"

"Then I need to hear it, Ivy. Tell me who you are to me," I repeat.

Her chest rises and falls faster. She blurts out, "I'm your slut."

"No. You're not."

Her face falls and her head jerks backward.

I add, "You're my sexy slut."

Her lips twitch.

I demand, "Now, say it louder, like you mean it. Step into your power, baby girl."

Her eyes dart to my mouth, and her voice turns sultry. She confidently declares, "I'm your sexy slut."

I don't say anything. I release her, buckle my belt, and leave the room. I shut the door and stroll across the boutique, feeling everyone's eyes on me.

"We're taking one of everything in the store in a size eight," I declare.

Liza, the manager, nods and smiles, but it's fake. I've fucked her too many times in this building. She forces herself to reply, "Sounds good, Mr. Carrington." She turns and points to three other women. "Zara, Katie, Pamela, pick one of each and package it up."

Liza begins ringing up items. She's halfway through when Ivy steps out of the dressing room.

She timidly steps toward me, her face turning redder.

I slide my arm around her and quietly murmur in her ear, "Stand confident, baby girl."

She releases an anxious breath but squares her shoulders and lifts her chin.

It takes twenty minutes until the transaction is over. They fill my trunk and back seat with bags.

I guide Ivy into her seat, then shut the door. I go up to the security guy and direct, "I want that video footage sent to me within the next fifteen minutes."

He nods.

Giddy, I hop into the car and rev the engine. I pull out into traffic and speed down the road, knowing I just had a huge win.

She might have been winning the game all week by staying away from me, but the game has turned.

It's no longer Ivy and me behind closed doors.

FAKE IT UNTIL YOU MAKE IT

Ivy

Music blares from the radio. Dax drives as recklessly as he did on our way into town.

I just had sex. And the entire store could hear us.

My pulse pounds harder. Since we left the store, my excitement has turned to worry and embarrassment.

Why did Dax want to do that with me there?

Too much confusion fills me.

Dax is incredible. On the other hand, I don't fully understand him or the things he's into.

I'm out of my league.

Fake it until you make it.

I can't lose Dax because of my inexperience.

Don't make a big deal about anything.

I glance out the window at the greenery, perplexed about what happened.

I can't help it. I reach over and turn the music down. I ask, "Why did you do that?"

Surprised, he glances at me. His expression looks as confused as I feel. "Do what?"

I answer, "What we did inside the dressing room. Why did you want everyone to hear?"

"You didn't like it?"

"I didn't say that."

His face falls. "Ah, I see. You regret me. I thought you were into me, Ivy."

"I am into you," I insist.

"Obviously, you aren't. I'm sorry. I thought you enjoyed being with me. I guess you don't want me, and I've been under the wrong impression," he states.

Panic hits me. "Dax, I never said I didn't want you."

"Could have fooled me," he mutters, pulling onto the expressway.

Several minutes pass. My insides quiver. All I want is Dax.

I don't know what I'm doing.

Why did I have to be a prude in West Virginia? I could have had some experience so I'm not so naive.

"I-I don't know about these things. I-I told you I've never done anything like that," I fret.

He sighs and pulls over. Cars race past us. He turns toward me and puts his hand on my cheek, declaring, "Ivy, I am a man. A man who's obsessed with you. You're the only person in this world I want. All I've craved all week is for you and me to be together. I thought that's what you wanted."

His words make me happy. Yet I still don't understand why he thinks I don't want to be with him. I assure him, "It is what I want."

He studies me and asks, "Are you sure about that? You didn't sound very sure a minute ago."

I bite on my lip, pondering his question. Of course I want him. But do I want everyone around us to know what we're doing?

And I've never felt so much pleasure before, but... I didn't imagine my first time would be anything like what we just did.

Dax adds, "This is who I am, Ivy. I don't like things vanilla. I'm sorry. I should have known a girl like you couldn't handle me. You're too wholesome. I'll take you back home and leave you alone." He releases me and pulls back into traffic.

My fear is coming true. I blink hard but can't stop the tears.

He's breaking up with me already?

Don't let him!

Fight for him!

My voice shakes with emotion when I say, "Can we please talk about this?"

He exits the expressway and pulls into a parking lot. He accuses, "You're driving me crazy. You want me. You don't want me. Which one is it, Ivy?"

I open my mouth, but nothing comes out. Am I giving him that impression?

He grabs my hand and kisses it. He claims, "I've never wanted anyone as much as I want you. You're the only person I think about. I can't sleep without you invading my dreams. I can't wake up without going to the window and staring toward your cottage, hoping to see you. And all week, you've not allowed me to see you."

"I did! I tried! I told you, my father—"

"You're eighteen, an adult. You can't let him continue to tell you what to do. If you want to see me, you'll have to stand up to him at some point," he asserts.

I take a deep breath and nod. "I know. I'll do better. Promise. Please! Just be patient with me. He's my father. And I know he'll eventually come around. I'll make sure of it. I promise!"

He deeply exhales and rubs his hand over his face.

"Dax," I desperately beg.

He reaches for my head, tugs me toward him, and kisses me.

I slide my arms around him and kiss him with everything I have.

If I lose him, it'll be my fault.

He slightly pulls back, and I whisper, "I'm handling all this wrong. I don't mean to. I... I just haven't ever been in this situation with my dad. But I'll make it right. I promise. He'll eventually realize he's wrong about you. You'll see."

His lips curve. "Do you really think so?"

"Yes," I confidently say, but I'm unsure how I'll ever change my father's opinion about Dax. Yet I'm going to. I *have* to.

"I don't want to lose you because of him," Dax claims.

I shake my head, blurting out, "You won't. And I don't want to lose you either!"

He softens his tone. "I'm sorry. I didn't mean to upset you. Like I said, you're driving me crazy."

"I'm not trying to," I repeat.

"Shh. I know, baby girl. I know. I just... Want me to be honest with you?"

I nod. "Please!"

He hesitates for a moment, and my anxiety builds. Then he lowers his voice. To my surprise, it's vulnerable, which isn't normal for him. He admits, "I've never met anyone like you. No one's caught my interest the way you have. You're special. I need you."

My heart soars. I smile and confess, "I need you too, Dax."

He strokes my cheek and continues, "This week has been the hardest one of my life. We can't let your father win. And I'm afraid he'll never accept me."

"He will. I know he will," I insist, even though I fear Dax might be right.

"I don't think he will. He hates me. And I don't know why."

I blurt out, "Your father warned him to keep you away from me!"

Dax's face hardens, his expression filling with anger.

I question, "Why would he do that?"

He stares out the window, grinding his molars for a few minutes. Then he declares, "My father hates me."

"Why?"

He shakes his head. "I don't know. I've always wanted to know what I did, but I can't figure it out."

I reach for him and hug him, stating, "That's horrible. I'm so sorry. You deserve better."

Dax pulls away. His face is stony. "It is what it is, Ivy."

"I promise you, I'm going to figure out a way to get my father to see the real you," I vow.

His sad expression reappears. "Okay, Ivy. I'll put my trust in you." His intense stare lingers.

Shyness fills me. I finally question, "Why are you looking at me like that?"

He admits, "I wanted today to be special for you. I wanted to give you the world and ensure you never forgot your first time. *Our* first time."

There's going to be more times.

He's not ditching me.

He leans closer. "Did you see how sexy you are? The power you hold over me?"

No one's ever called me sexy or told me I hold power over them. It flusters me. "I...ummm..."

In a firmer voice, he asserts, "I wanted you to always remember how you looked when you first took me. And I wanted you to have the world because your father's not given that to you. He should have, but he hasn't."

My joy fizzles. "My father's given me enough."

Dax tilts his head. "Has he? You only had three boxes for your bedroom. It doesn't look like he's given you much."

My defenses rise. I insist, "I've always had everything I need. My father's been a great provider."

He holds his hands in the air. "I think this is coming out wrong. I just meant—"

"You meant what?" I interrupt.

"Easy!"

I release an angry breath. I calm my voice. "Then what did you mean by your statement?"

Dax slides his hand on my thigh, and even though his comments upset me, tingles race to my sore pussy. I squeeze my thighs together as he reveals, "I knew he was out of work for a while."

"Lots of people have breaks in employment," I offer.

"Why didn't he work for two years? It seems like that had to have hurt you."

I glance out the window and fidget with my fingers on my lap.

"Don't be mad at me," he says, squeezing my thigh.

I turn back toward him. "You don't know what happened."

"Okay. Why don't you tell me?"

My stomach flips. I turn back toward the window, not wanting to talk about it. I never have before, and I don't see why I need to now.

Dax reminds me, "I thought we weren't going to have secrets between us."

I close my eyes, my chest tightening.

"Okay, I guess you're going to hold secrets from me, and

I'm going to be honest with you. How fair," he accuses and starts the car again.

That sounds unfair. So I turn back and put my hand on his arm. "Wait."

He keeps the car in park with the engine running and slowly looks at me. "I'm listening."

I confess, "I don't like to talk about why my father didn't work. But he did try. It wasn't his fault."

Dax arches his eyebrow. He softens his voice. "Oh? How wasn't it his fault?"

"He's not lazy. Even when he didn't work, it's not like we went hungry. I always had everything I needed, and he did look for work," I ramble.

Dax releases a breath, and it hits me that he's genuinely concerned. "Okay. That's good to hear, because the thought of you starving bothers me."

"I didn't starve," I assure him.

"Okay, well, why didn't he work?"

My stomach dives. I hate what my mother did to us. I try to collect my thoughts, staring at my fingers.

Dax adds, "Please let me in, Ivy. I told you about my father and me. I meant it when I said I didn't want any secrets between us. Please. You can trust me."

He's right. I can trust him.

I lift my chin and pin my gaze on his. "My mom left us."

Sympathy fills his expression. He furrows his forehead. "What do you mean your mom left?"

I swallow hard, admitting what I've never said to anyone. And the sting somehow hurts worse than I thought it could. "She left us. She wanted more than my father could give her."

"Because he wasn't working," Dax says.

My defenses go back up. I shake my head hard. "No, my father was working. He had a great job, but my mom always wanted more. She didn't want to live in West Virginia. So, she met some guy and just took off."

"Oh, Ivy. That must've been really hard for you," Dax says.

"It was," I admit. "And my dad, he..." I swallow and continue, "After my mom left, he was a wreck for a while. I can't blame him. But he had savings. We didn't starve or go without any necessities."

Dax gets out of the car and comes around to my side. He flings open the door and reaches in for me. I get out, and he hugs me tightly as soon as I'm on my toes, murmuring, "I'm sorry, baby girl. You deserve better than that."

"My dad's a good person. He's a really hard worker," I reiterate.

"Shh. I'm sure he's good. And I know he works hard. I'm sorry I said otherwise," Dax states.

I sniffle to stop myself from crying.

"Have you talked to your mom since?"

More rejection fills me. It's raw, and I hate how it never gets better. It's always a scab that becomes an open wound whenever I think about what my mother did.

I answer, "No. She left, and that was it."

Dax tightens his hold on me. "I'm sorry." He pulls back and slides his hand through my hair. "Do you want to know something?"

"What?"

"It's your mom's loss."

I shake my head. "I wish I could believe that."

"It is," he insists and pecks me on the lips. Then he firmly declares, "I'll never leave you, Ivy. Never. Do you understand?"

My heart soars. I don't know how I got so lucky having Dax in my life, but I am.

I blink hard, and a tear rolls down my cheek.

Dax swipes at it and then kisses me like I'm his everything.

The world disappears, and his promise to never leave me swirls around us.

My vulnerability gets the best of me. I retreat from the kiss, asking, "Do you mean that, Dax?"

He locks his gaze to mine, and I've never felt so many emotions. It's security. Adoration. And I even wonder if it's love.

Is it possible to love someone so early on?

Isn't this what they mean by soul mates?

He slides his hand on my face and caresses my cheekbone with his thumb, declaring, "I do, but it'll always be up to you if we're together, Ivy."

"Wh-what do you mean?"

He clenches his jaw, studying me.

My heart races. "Dax?"

He closes his eyes and then opens them. "I told you I'm not vanilla. And you're..."

"Boring," I blurt out, blinking hard at the truth.

He shakes his head. "No. Nothing of the sort. But I like what I like, baby girl. There've been a few times when I've wondered if I'm too much for you. If you'll end up hating me."

"You aren't too much for me! There's nothing about you I don't like," I claim.

He studies me.

"Dax, I mean it."

"You sure? Because I don't want to ever hurt you. And the world I'm in..."

Confused, I ask, "What about it?"

He sighs. "Ivy, I'm a Carrington. A lot goes with that. And I have more experience than you—"

"I'll learn. I will. Whatever you want me to do with you, I will."

Darkness enters his eyes, giving me a slight chill. He steps closer, murmuring, "I don't want to change you. You're perfect as you are, gorgeous."

"I... I don't understand what you mean, then?"

"My world isn't vanilla."

"I don't want mine to be either," I declare, although I don't really know what he means.

He arches his eyebrows. "You don't?"

I swallow hard and shake my head. "No. I want what you want."

His lips curve. "You do?"

"Yes."

"So you trust me, then?" he questions.

"Yes. I trust you."

He grins. "Then you won't leave me? I don't need to worry?"

I laugh. "I thought we were talking about you leaving me."

His face falls. "No, Ivy. Every second, I worry you'll slip through my fingers, and the best thing that ever happened to me will disappear."

Happiness fills me. "I'm the best thing that's ever happened to you?"

"Yeah, my sexy little slut," he affirms.

"You're the best thing that's happened to me," I gush, then kiss him.

He retreats and asks, "Did you like me deep inside of you?"

My butterflies awaken. My cheeks heat, and I answer, "Yes. I loved every second of it."

"Did you like swallowing me?"

"Yes."

His smile twists. He cups my pussy, and his voice turns rough. "Did you like others listening?"

My mouth turns dry. I've not had time to fully process our encounter.

He adds, "The way your tight cunt clenched my cock and your body quivered against mine, I'd say you did."

I softly laugh. Why am I being so shy about this? I admit, "I love every minute of being with you, Dax. And..." I overcome my shyness, forcing myself to confess, "I love how you touch me."

He kisses me.

I return his affection, and once again, the world is gone. It's Dax and me and nothing but bliss.

He pulls back and makes me happier, stating, "On my life, I will never leave you, Ivy Ford. You're mine, and I'm yours."

Dax 15

WHORE-RED

Dax

Ivy and I step inside the salon. The scent of acetone and other chemicals flares in my nostrils.

Necessary evil.

Nancy, the manicurist I bring all my girls to, looks up from her station. She smiles. "Mr. Carrington."

"Nancy. This is Ivy. She needs a pedicure and manicure."

"Sure. Nice to meet you," Nancy says to Ivy.

"You too," Ivy replies.

"Are we doing a French manicure or color today?" Nancy asks, directing her question at me.

"Whore red," I answer.

Ivy stiffens, and I geek out. I don't think I'll ever get tired of her embarrassment.

Nancy beams. "Ah. Great color."

Ivy relaxes.

"Yes, it is. And that's what my Ivy wants. Right, baby girl?" I slide my arm around her and give her a kiss on the forehead.

She gingerly smiles, but her face is flushed. She affirms, "Sure. That sounds great."

I love how she agrees to everything I want. It's almost getting easy.

Nancy points to the back room. "Go sit in chair two, and we'll get started."

I kiss Ivy on the lips and pat her ass. I'll be back soon, okay?"

"You're leaving?"

"I'm going to run a few errands."

She smiles. "All right." She disappears into the next room.

I step in front of the lipstick counter and find the matching color to the nail polish. I add it at the reception desk and announce, "I want this added to my bill."

Quinn, the receptionist, grins. "Great color."

"So I hear," I say and leave the salon. I take a breath of fresh air and get into my Porsche. I drive several blocks and pull up to the medical clinic. I walk past the receptionist.

"He's in with a patient," she yells out.

"So what?" I go down the hall and open the door.

Dr. Collins's hand is on a woman's breast. He asks, "Have you felt any lumps?"

"No, I—" She turns toward me and covers her chest with the paper sheet.

"Oops. Sorry, I didn't realize anything was happening here," I lie.

"You should knock first," she reprimands.

Dr. Collins scowls. "Yeah, you should knock."

"I'm sorry." I pull out my wallet. "I'm Dax Carrington. Here, have some money for your troubles. I need to see Dr. Collins about some urgent issues, so excuse us for a few moments."

She glares at me.

Dr. Collins addresses her, "Can you excuse us for a minute?"

"I've never been so insulted," she states.

"Touché," I offer.

She glares harder at me.

Dr. Collins motions for me to step outside, and I follow. We go into his office. He shuts the door and declares, "Dax, you've got to stop doing this."

"But it's so good for business," I taunt.

He crosses his arms. "What do you need?"

I sit back in the chair and push my fingers together. "I need a birth control shot."

He sighs. "For who this time?"

"Ivy Ford."

He squints, pondering, and says, "I don't know an Ivy Ford."

"Yeah, so what? You don't know half the women I've gotten birth control for. Write the prescription," I order.

His disapproving expression deepens.

I lean closer, threatening, "Do we no longer have a deal?"

He closes his eyes and sighs. He grabs a prescription pad, scribbles on it, and tears it. He hands me the piece of paper. "You have to stop doing this, Dax. I'm going to lose my license."

"No, you won't. Stop being a pussy," I state and rise.

"I'm serious. I can lose my license," he reiterates.

I remind him, "You can also lose your clientele."

His face reddens.

It's all I have to say. Dr. Collins has been under my thumb for a long time. And bribery goes a long way.

He's got lots of quirky fetishes. So once I found out, I set him up with a prostitute. He thought he was on a legitimate date.

Smart me got everything on videotape.

That was years ago. But the last thing he wants for his reputation is for that video to get out. So, for the rest of his career, I own him.

He mutters, "You're a horrible person."

"Your song's getting old. Deal with it," I declare and walk out, whistling.

I get back into my Porsche and go over to the pharmacy.

I pull through the drive-through, and a blonde girl named Melissa smiles. She says through the speaker, "Mr. Carrington, how are you?"

"I'm fine. I need this now," I say, sticking the paper into the box.

She grabs it and looks at it. "Sure. Give me five minutes?"

"Can you make it two?"

"Maybe three?" she offers.

"Thanks."

Within minutes, I have the prescription. I take off, going back to the salon. I call Bobby.

"Yo, what up?" he answers.

"Hey, what are you up to?"

"Getting ready for the party. Just snorted a few lines. What are you doing? Why don't you come over?" he rattles off.

The same old Bobby.

I shouldn't be surprised.

I reply, "Nah, I've got things to do."

"Things? Or that new girl?"

I grunt. Bobby knows me well.

"Ah, you've already deflowered her, haven't you?"

"Shut up, Bobby. I'll see you tonight." I hang up the phone and continue to the salon. I sit in my car for a while with my head against the headrest and eyes closed, thinking about Ivy. I don't know if I've ever enjoyed a girl as much as her. And now that I have the shot, it'll get even better.

My phone rings. I glance at the screen and pick it up. "What do you want, Avery?"

"You took her to the salon?"

"Why? What's it to you?"

"Ugh. She's so...common," Avery whines.

I don't reply. On the outside, Ivy looks common. But is she really?

What am I thinking? Of course she is.

I recover and reply, "That's the fun of it."

"Don't tell me you actually like her, Dax," Avery declares, as if it would be the worst thing in the world if I did.

I open my mouth to tell her I do, but I stop.

Once again, I wonder what the hell I'm thinking.

Ivy's a pawn in a game. That's it.

"You do like her," Avery says in disgust.

"No, I don't. She's a pawn, simple as that," I lie.

The truth is, I like her way more than I should, but I tell myself it's okay. Better I enjoy her than not.

It's about time I got somebody that lit my interest.

"Where are you taking her tonight?" Avery asks.

"Butcher and Sea Chophouse."

Avery scoffs. "Why are you pulling the red carpet out?"

"I'm not."

"Sure you're not."

I stay quiet.

Avery asserts, "You're trying too hard."

I stare at my reflection in the mirror.

Is Avery right?

No.

I retort, "I'm not. Now, make sure you're there." I hang up.

I get out of the Porsche and go into the salon. Ivy's toes are done, and Nancy's finishing her manicure. She puts her hand under the UV light for the final time.

I lean down and kiss Ivy.

She jumps and looks up. Her face lights up. "Dax, I didn't know you were back."

"Did you think I wasn't coming back to get you?" I tease.

She replies, "That would be tragic."

I couldn't agree more. I pick up her free hand and say, "Whore red's your color."

The light in her eyes turns brighter. I can't believe how easy it is to butter her up.

I take a seat for a few minutes until she's done. Then we get back into the car. I hand her the lipstick. "Put this on."

She opens it up and stares at it. "This is really red."

"You don't like it?" I question.

She glances back at it. "I've never worn anything so bold."

"Yeah, well, you should. You have beautiful slutty lips, and I want to see those whore-red marks on my dick before the night's over. Understand?"

Shock fills her expression, and I get giddy again. I love it. I just took her virginity in a dressing room, and she's still acting shy.

I add, "Baby girl, you got to lighten up."

She softly laughs. "I know. I'm just... I'm not used to people talking like you do."

"You don't like how I speak?" I challenge.

She pauses and shakes her head. "No, I like everything about you."

"Good, I like everything about you," I say, leaning over and kissing her. Then I order, "Put it on. I've been dying to see you in it."

She puts the visor down and looks in the mirror. She

applies it perfectly and then turns toward me. "Um, do you think I can pull this color off?"

"Fuck, yes, you little whore," I tell her, then wink.

She nervously laughs again, then looks back at her reflection.

"You look amazing. Stop worrying about it. Step into your power," I tell her, then rev the engine and take off.

It doesn't take long to get back to the estate. I go directly to my house and pull bags out of the trunk. She grabs a few from the back seat. We go inside.

"Let's put them in my closet," I tell her.

"Oh?" She sounds surprised.

"Yeah, you're staying here all week."

Her smile grows until her cheeks have to hurt.

"I am?"

I tug her into me. "Yeah, baby girl. Do you think I'm letting you out of my sight? I didn't send your dad away and pay Professor Dyer to send that fake email to you for nothing."

Her face brightens again. "Thanks, Dax."

"Oh, no, baby girl, thank you," I say. I kiss her quickly and then put a couple pieces of lingerie on the bed. I sit against the headboard, cross my arms, and order, "Strip and put that on."

She glances at it.

"Is there a problem?"

"I've not worn anything like that before," she admits.

Satisfaction fills me. "So what? Show me your sexiest strip-tease. Once you're fully naked, shake your tits in my face and then put that on."

Worry fills her expression.

"You're not turning into a prude on me, are you?" I challenge.

"No. I just..."

"Just what?"

"Um, I don't know how to do a striptease."

I chuckle. "Then it's time to learn. Alexa, turn on 'Pony.'"

Ginuwine's song comes on, and Ivy gives me another uneasy look.

"Come on, you can do it," I encourage.

She remains still.

"I've wanted to see you do this forever. You're so fucking sexy," I add, to give her a little boost of confidence.

But she is sexy. Her little innocent attitude may be the sexiest I've ever seen, but I wonder again if she truly is innocent. The way she sucks my dick and how her cunt felt wrapped around my cock make me think she really does know what she's doing. It's enough to make me at least question it.

Ivy caves, slowly beginning to sway her hips. I make a note to take her to a strip club to really train her.

I encourage her further with little praises here and there until she's naked, then she starts putting on the lingerie.

I call out, "Stop."

She freezes.

"Slow. You're going to do it slow. That's how you tease a man. Do you not know how to tease a man?" I question, just to humiliate her, wanting to keep her in her place.

Sure enough, her cheeks turn to fire. She slowly shakes her head. "No, I told you I haven't done this before." She looks away.

I jump off the bed and slide my fingers through her hair. I kiss her until she's whimpering, out of breath, and her knees wobble. I declare, "I love the fact that you don't know what you're doing, but you actually do know what you're doing. You just don't see what I do. Now, slow it down and put this on."

I step back. She slowly does as I say, sliding into the panties and into the corset.

"Good. Now stay there."

I open the prescription bag and take out the tiny bottle. I fill the syringe.

"What is that?" she questions.

I rise and walk toward her, holding out the needle. Horror fills her expression.

"Dax?"

"This is birth control. I need to be able to come in you, and I don't want you getting pregnant. Do you?"

She glances at the needle, then back at me.

"Ivy, do you want a kid? I mean, right now. I want an entire houseful with you someday, but we don't want any right now, correct?

Her lips twitch. "You want kids with me someday?"

"Sure. I want everything with you," I lie. "But now's not the time. We should get through college first, right?"

She nods. "Yes, I agree."

"Okay. Well, since you weren't the responsible one, I need to be. So bend over, baby."

"I'm not responsible?"

"Well, you weren't on birth control. You're eighteen. You should be on birth control," I insist.

"But I never had sex before."

"Your father should have made sure you were on birth control," I blurt out, just to set another idea in her head that her father's been a bad dad.

She gapes at me. "Why would he do that? I wasn't having sex. Nor would I tell him if I was."

Oh, but he's going to know we are, I maliciously think. Then I assert, "Ivy, if you were my daughter, I'd make sure you were on birth control. You're too hot not to be. Now bend over." I pat her ass.

She glances at the needle and then at me again, questioning, "Are there any side effects to that?"

"No, you'll be fine. Do you want to have a baby, or do you want to take birth control?" I say, getting irritated, not understanding why she's even fighting me. No one ever has before.

She admits, "I don't like to take prescriptions unless I know what the side effects are."

"Is there something you're worried about? Are you allergic to something?"

She shakes her head. "No, but my mom had bad experiences in the past."

"Okay, well, you're not your mom. Do you want this or not?"

She studies it again.

I step closer. "Ivy, do you not want me to come in you?"

She opens her mouth but nothing comes out.

"You don't want me to have all of you? You don't want all of me?" I press.

She finally gives in. "No, Dax. That's what I want."

"All right, baby girl, bend over."

She finally obeys, and I rub an alcohol pad over her skin, then stick the needle into her ass cheek. I push the plunger, making sure all the medication goes in. I pull the needle out and rub her ass. "Good girl," I praise, then kiss her on the cheek. I grin and add, "You're a fantastic slut by the way."

She shakes her head, laughing. "I don't understand why you like that word and whore so much."

"I told you, it's better than being a prude, right?"

She sighs and nods. "Yes."

"There are things that men say to women when no one else is looking or listening. And then, sometimes, when people are around, they say it. This is normal," I insist.

"It is?" she questions.

"Yeah, but you've never been in a real relationship. You've never had a real man, have you?"

She shakes her head again. "No."

"Okay. Then are you telling me you don't like it?"

"I didn't say that."

"Okay, good. Because you're my sexy little slut." I give her a kiss on the lips, then I grab a leather tube top and miniskirt. "I want you to wear this to dinner tonight."

"Yeah?"

"Yeah."

I hit a button, and green lights start blinking on the ceiling.

"What's that?" Ivy asks.

"I had those installed this week."

"What are they?" she nervously questions, then says, "They look like cameras."

I give her a challenging stare. "They are. I want to be able to watch you when you're back at your dad's house and I can't see you."

"I-I don't know about this."

I groan. "I need it, Ivy. Now, turn around and take that lingerie off the way I showed you. Strip for me. And when you do, tell me that you're my dirty whore."

She gapes at me again.

I put my hand over her heart. "I need to see you when you're not here, showing me you're into me." I lewdly drag my eyes down her body and back up. "Fuck, I need to see you, Ivy. You've been driving me crazy all week. I can't handle it when your dad's back and you're not here. Please do this for me," I beg.

"But somebody might see it."

I chuckle. "Baby girl, who's going to see my video? It's you and me. No one else has access to this. This is my place, on my estate. Do you not think that I'd guard this with my life?"

She hesitates but then nods. "Okay. You're right. But what if I look stupid?"

"Don't worry, my little slut. When you're done, I'll show you what I see. I promise you that you don't look stupid. Besides, why would I want to record you if you did?"

She takes an anxious breath, staying quiet.

I take off my clothes and sit back on the bed. She stares at my cock.

I add, "My cock will be on the recording too. I'm going to play with myself while watching you." I put the music back on and order, "Come on, baby girl. Move that sexy ass."

She slowly starts to move again and then finds her rhythm, just like I showed her how.

I palm my cock, confessing, "You make me so fucking hard."

She beams, continuing to strip until there's nothing left on her.

I stretch my arm and curl my finger.

She steps next to me.

I order, "Go back and crawl from the bottom of the bed to me."

She arches her eyebrows, but her lips twitch.

"Ah, my dirty little slut. You're into this as much as I am. Admit it."

She giggles. "Okay, maybe. It is fun."

"Yeah, it is. Now, go back, pick up that bra, throw it how you just did, and when I motion, you crawl from the bottom of the bed up. Understand?"

Her hesitation is gone. She nods. "Okay, Dax." She takes a few steps away, grabs her bra, steps back into position, and makes the same move she did. Then, she slowly goes to the end of the bed, crawling up it and sliding her hands between my thighs.

I groan.

Her face gets near my cock.

I demand, "Now, use those pretty whore-red lips and show me what you got."

She doesn't hesitate and takes all of me into her mouth.

I groan louder, staring at the green blinking lights, higher than a kite, thinking about all the footage I'm getting.

My little slut has a lot to learn—mostly about me.

Ivy 16

DYING FOR A REPLAY

Dax pulls to the curb. The sign above the restaurant reads "Butcher and Sea Chophouse."

The valet comes over and opens my door.

Dax growls, "Don't touch her."

My butterflies take off. I love how protective he is, even if it is slightly extreme.

He races around the car, helps me out, and leads me inside.

The minute the hostess sees him, she chirps, "Mr. Carrington, so good to see you again. We have your table ready. Right this way." She leads us through the dark restaurant to a quiet, luxurious booth.

Dax motions for me to sit down. I slide in, and he settles next to me.

I'm pretty sure the seats are real leather. They're soft, just like my outfit. Candles are lit, and a blingy chandelier hangs over our table.

Dax slips his hand between my thighs and under my barely there skirt.

I freeze. I'm still not used to his public displays of affection.

The hostess smirks at me, then refocuses on Dax, stating, "Thomas will be your server tonight."

Dax squeezes my upper thigh.

The hostess glances at me again.

I square my shoulders and lift my chin, not wanting her to think she intimidates me or I'm embarrassed, because I'm not. I'm proud to be with Dax.

A server appears. "Mr. Carrington, it's good to see you," he greets, holding out his hand.

Dax moves his hand off my thigh, shakes his hand, then resumes his grip on my body. Only this time, it's higher, and he turns his hand so his knuckles graze my slit.

My butterflies explode into flight.

It's only been a few hours since the boutique dressing room, and I'm dying for a repeat.

After I gave Dax a blow job at his cottage, he took a shower.

He wouldn't let me take one. He claimed he wanted to smell his whore all night, emphasizing the word *his*.

Part of me liked that statement, and part of me cringed. But I decided it's a compliment coming from Dax.

He orders, "Thomas, we want a medium-rare tomahawk, almond-encrusted walleye, gouda mac and cheese with bread-crumbs, and chopped salads."

I gape.

He glances at me. "What?"

I laugh. "Do you know the menu by heart?"

He shrugs. "It's the best thing this city has to offer. Why, is there something you don't like?"

I laugh again. "No, it sounds amazing."

The truth is, I've never had a tomahawk or gouda mac and cheese. I don't even know what a chopped salad has in it. I have had almond-encrusted walleye, but I'm not going to tell Dax any of this.

Thomas replies, "Splendid. I'll get your order right in. I assume you want your usual wine?"

"Of course," Dax affirms.

Thomas nods and leaves.

"How do you do that?" I question.

"What?"

"You're always so..." I search for the word, then add, "Authoritative."

He arches an eyebrow. "Authoritative, huh?"

"Yeah."

"And you like that, right?" he asks, moving his knuckles so they penetrate my slit.

I squirm in my seat. My pussy's sore from earlier, but I want more. I admit, "With you? Yes."

Satisfaction appears on his face. "Good."

Thomas reappears with a bottle of wine.

"That was fast," I say, assuming he's only going to serve Dax, but he pours a small amount into a glass and hands it to me.

I glance at Dax, not sure what to do.

"Try it," he encourages.

I move it to my lips, but he grabs the stem. "Hold on." He sets it down, circles the glass on the table so the liquid swirls around the globe, then holds it to my nose. "Inhale deeply, gorgeous."

I obey, offering, "It smells really good."

"Now, take a sip. Hold it in your mouth for a few seconds before you swallow it."

I do as he says. Smoke, cherries, and other flavors I can't even decipher pop in my mouth.

I've never had wine before. My dad only drinks beer. But this tastes divine.

I swallow it, and Dax asks, "What do you think?"

I gush, "It's amazing."

He nods at the server.

Thomas fills both our glasses. He asks, "Is there anything else I can get you two?"

Dax answers, "No."

Thomas leaves, and Dax slides his arm around me. He holds his glass in the air.

I put mine next to his.

"To our first date and many to come," he toasts, then clinks his glass with mine.

I tilt my head. "Wasn't the boat day a date?"

He scoffs. "No, that was just a day at the estate."

"Oh."

He takes a sip, and I follow his lead. Then I lean closer to him, glancing around, and murmuring, "What if I get caught?"

"Caught?" he questions.

"Yeah, I'm not twenty-one."

He gives me an amused look. "You're with me. Anything's possible when you're with me. Nobody's going to say anything to you."

"Really?" I question, still trying to grasp that concept.

"Yep! Now, drink up. This is really expensive wine, but only the best for you."

I take another sip, not used to anyone spending money on me and not wanting to look ungrateful. Dax is so generous. I couldn't ever dream of anyone spoiling me how he has today.

He takes a large mouthful of wine.

"Can I ask you something?" I say.

"Sure."

I collect my thoughts, my anxiety filling my chest.

"What is it?" he questions.

My pulse increases. "Do you think I'll fit in at Clifton University?"

His eyes narrow.

It makes me even more nervous. I blurt out, "Is that a no?"

He studies me another minute and asks, "Do you want the truth?"

"Yeah, of course I want the truth."

He shakes his head. "You're not going to fit in, but don't let it bug you."

My gut dives. I blink hard and look away.

He pinches my chin between his thumb and forefinger and turns my face toward his so I can't avoid him. "You're better than everyone else, Ivy. You're not fake. You're real. So when you ask if you'll fit in, the answer is no. And I meant that as a compliment, so don't even worry about it. Why are you concerned about what everyone else thinks anyway?"

I shouldn't be, and I wish I could say I'm not worried, but I am. I want to be accepted by my classmates.

Isn't that normal?

I open my mouth to speak, but nothing comes out.

Dax adds, "You're giving them too much credit. Besides, I'm the only one whose opinion you should worry about, gorgeous." He gives me his boyish grin.

I don't get to see it very often, but when I do, it lights up my soul. So I agree. "You're right."

Thomas returns and sets a bowl of chopped salad in front of us. He takes two large forks and dishes a heap onto each of our plates, then refills our wineglasses.

"Thank you," I say.

"No problem, ma'am."

He leaves, and I take a bite. It's just as good as the wine. "Mmm. This is divine."

Amusement fills Dax's expression.

"What?" I question.

He gives me a chaste kiss. "You're adorable."

Happiness floods every cell within me.

We both take several mouthfuls of salad and wash it down with more wine.

Dax reveals, "I'm really glad you're not like the other girls. It's a nightmare taking them on a date."

He's caught my attention once again. "Oh? Why's that?"

"Because they wouldn't even be eating the chopped salad. Do you know how annoying it is to go to dinner with someone who won't eat?"

I glance down. It's all vegetables and a tad of olive oil dressing mixed with something else. I'm not sure what, but it can't be that many calories. So I question, "Are you serious?"

"Yep."

I cautiously ask, "Is everyone as skinny as your sister, Marcey, and Cindy?"

He rolls his eyes. "Yeah. They all have fake boobs, starve themselves, and take a lot of drugs and alcohol. See why I'm saying you don't have to fit in around here?"

I can't help but smile. Somehow, he's eased my worries about fitting in. Plus, he's right. I've never been fake, so why should I start to pretend to be someone I'm not?

We eat a couple more bites of salad and then Thomas brings out a tomahawk, the almond-encrusted walleye, and a bubbling dish covered in toasted breadcrumbs.

It all smells delicious.

He leaves, and Dax puts a heaping spoonful of gouda mac and cheese onto my plate.

"This looks amazing," I state.

"It is. Eat it." He spears a piece of tomahawk on his fork and holds it in front of my mouth.

I bite into the meat, and it melts in my mouth. I moan, never having tasted a steak this good.

He chuckles. "Told you it's delicious."

"It is," I agree. I take a bite of mac and cheese, then another.

Dax says, "Yeah, there's no way any woman around here would eat that. It's full of fat and carbs."

I glance at the gooey dish, but this time, I feel guilty.

Maybe I shouldn't eat anymore.

"Yeah, I'm really glad you eat normal food," Dax states again, then takes a bite himself.

I tell myself to stop being silly. I put another forkful in my mouth, and the creamy cheese tastes amazing. I ask, "Do they always bring the food out this fast?"

Dax shrugs. "Depends what I want."

"How do they know what you want?"

"Because when I made my reservation, I told them we needed to be served quickly."

"Oh. Why is that? Are we going somewhere else?"

Dax nods. "Yeah, back to my place. Do you think I can stand it very long with you in this outfit?"

I bite on my smile.

He drags his finger down my bare shoulder. "No way, my little slut. This needs to come off and soon."

I softly laugh, teasing, "You have a one-track mind, don't you?"

He drags his eyes over my body in the lewd way he always does and then answers, "If it's about you? Yeah."

My heart once again soars. Being everything to Dax and having his full attention is the most amazing thing in the world. I wonder how I ever lived without these feelings.

But my bliss is interrupted.

Avery steps next to the table with a lanky guy. He has a few zits, clean-cut dark hair, and thick glasses. He pushes them up on his nose and looks slightly uncomfortable when Dax says, "Matt. Never thought I'd see you in this place."

"He's with me," Avery states, sliding her arm through his.

"Only way he'd ever get in here," Dax claims.

"You should talk, with who you're with," Avery replies.

My gut dives. I seethe, "Why do you have to be so mean all the time?"

"Aw," she says, tilting her head and looking at me with pity, adding, "Can the new girl not handle the truth?"

"Shut up, Avery," Dax orders.

Uncomfortable silence fills the air.

The guy holds out his hand in front of me. "I'm Matt."

"Oh, I'm Ivy." I go to take his hand.

Dax swats at his fingers. "Don't touch my girlfriend."

Girlfriend! I'm Dax's girlfriend.

My heart soars.

Matt flinches and holds his hands in the air. "I was just introducing myself."

I put my hand on Dax's thigh, feeling a bit bad for Matt. I announce, "I'm Ivy. I'm new."

"Obviously, you're new," Avery mutters under her breath.

I shake my head, glaring at her.

Matt gives her an uncomfortable look.

"Are you just getting here?" Dax questions.

"No. We're on our way out to the party. Hopefully, we get there early enough to not have to entertain you two."

"There's a party?" I inquire.

Dax shakes his head. "No, we're not going."

"You're not going? You have to. You're the president," Avery declares.

"President of what?" I ask.

Avery answers, "Alpha Omega Tau. It's Dax's frat. You're not going to try to stop him from being who he is, are you? It's his job to be at that party. In fact, he should be there right now, not here with you."

My chest tightens. "Dax, is that true?" I fret, not wanting to get him in trouble with his frat or change anything about his life. I like Dax for who he is. I would never want him to change anything for me.

Dax turns to me. "It's fine, Ivy." He snaps his head back toward Avery. "We're not going. Enjoy your night not in my presence."

Avery puts on a fake smile and adds sugar to her voice when she says, "Oh, sorry. I forgot it's probably a little too intense for Ivy, isn't it?"

Too intense for me? What is she talking about?

Dax booms, "Shut up, Avery."

Avery rolls her eyes. "Tell me it's not true, Dax. You know it's too intense for her. She can't handle it."

"I can't handle what?" I question.

Matt nervously looks away and then back at me.

I push, "What does she mean, Dax?"

"What I mean is your country-girl, Ms. Goody-two-shoes self can't handle a real party," she spouts.

Anger fills me. I get defensive. "I can handle going to a party, Avery."

"Really? Why don't you prove it?"

"We're not going," Dax says.

I let my insecurities get the best of me, and my voice shakes as I blurt out, "Why? Because you don't think I can handle it either?"

Avery smirks. "You're good enough for him here, but not in front of the people who actually mean something to him."

Dax's eyes widen. "Shut up, Avery!" He focuses on me,

claiming, "I never said that, so don't listen to my annoying sister." He turns back to her, ordering, "Avery, go away."

I blink hard.

"Oh, are you going to cry now?" she taunts.

I hate myself because I feel like I might. And I hate how Avery, Cindy, Marcey, and even Bobby can get under my skin and make me so emotional.

Dax slides his arm protectively around my shoulders, calming me. He declares, "Ivy and I have other things to do tonight. The parties are overrated anyway. They're getting old, Avery. Stale. Like you."

She smirks. "They won't be stale if she comes."

Everything about that statement makes me uncomfortable. I shift in my seat.

"Oh, but wait, you can't handle it," she taunts again.

"Avery," Matt reprimands.

She looks at him and bats her eyes. "Yes, Matt? Is there something you want to say? Maybe you don't want to go either?"

Matt clenches his jaw and stares at her.

"You're such a bitch, Avery," Dax proclaims.

She gives us her fake smile again. "I may be a bitch, but at least I know what I am. At least I'm not pretending to be a Ms. Goody-two-shoes when I'm really not."

"I'm not pretending to be anything," I declare.

She huffs. "Sure you aren't. You're here, your daddy's gone, but as soon as your daddy comes back to the estate, you're not going to have anything to do with my brother, are you?"

My gut flips. How does she know about my dad? I glance at Dax.

He shuts his eyes and shakes his head. He mutters, "Avery, you seriously become bitchier by the second." He opens his eyes and pins a nasty scowl on her. Then he adds, "I'm so glad

Dad can inform you of whatever's happening on the estate. It's a good thing you'll never run it though, huh?"

Her face falls for a moment. Then, she recovers and glares at him. "Too bad it'll only stay in our family for a little while until you run it into the ground."

"You wish," Dax hurls.

Matt clears his throat. "Are you two coming to the party or not?"

Dax looks at him as if he's never seen him before and is bored. It makes me uncomfortable. I wish he wouldn't do it, but maybe there's a reason he doesn't like him.

Matt seems nice though. It makes me wonder what he's doing with Avery. But then again, she's gorgeous and looks perfect, so Matt's probably into her.

Avery suggests, "They're not coming. It's too adultish for her. She needs something more preschool-level."

"Avery, shut up," Dax orders.

I put my hand on his arm. "It's okay. You don't have to yell at her. Why don't we go to the party?"

He turns and stares at me.

I push, "You don't want me to go with you?"

"It's not that. Of course I want you to go, but we had other plans."

"Yeah, because he's embarrassed by you," Avery says.

Dax's gaze burns with hot fire. He snarls, "I am not embarrassed by Ivy. I'm embarrassed by *you*."

She ignores his last comment and declares, "You are totally ashamed of her. You're hiding her from everybody else because you don't want anyone to know that you're dating Little Miss Hillbilly." She turns her smirk on me, continuing, "Don't worry, Ivy. School starts in a week. You'll be off Dax's radar, then."

My heart sinks, and my insides quiver. My mouth turns dry. I stare at the table, blinking hard.

Dax pulls my chin up so I can't avoid him. "Don't listen to her. It's not true."

"Prove it. Take her to the party," Avery demands.

Dax clenches his jaw for a few moments.

I say nothing, too afraid I'll cry and give Avery another win.

"You want to go to the party?" Dax quietly asks me.

I shrug. "If you want to."

"See? She doesn't even want to go. She's embarrassed to show up, as well," Avery claims.

Matt scolds, "Avery, please."

"You sure you want to go, baby girl?" Dax asks.

I take a deep breath and nod. Then, I look at Avery, lifting my chin in confidence. There's no way I'm letting her win and not showing up on Dax's arm. "Yeah, we'll see you there."

SHE'S ANOTHER PAWN IN MY GAME

DAX

Something feels off. My original intention to take Ivy to the Alpha Omega Tau party no longer feels right.

Avery arrived at just the right moment. I should be elated by manipulating Ivy into going.

I'm not.

My sister played her part perfectly, but it feels like Avery has something up her sleeve...something I'm not going to like.

I shouldn't be surprised. She always does. So I should have played this differently than normal. I shouldn't have told her about my dinner at the chophouse.

That dweeb, Matt, better keep his paws off Ivy.

It's a mystery what Avery is doing with him. She has yet to lay her cards down, but she's using him for some reason. She would never be into him, and he's too stupid to realize it.

I'll have to be patient to find out whatever game Avery is

playing. That's the thing about her. She's a master at keeping things hidden, divulging tiny details only as needed. So only time will tell me her end game.

Knowing Avery, she'll reveal it when it's least expected and takes everyone by surprise. And I have to give her credit for her skills. As annoying as she is, she plays the game even better than I do at times.

Then again, I taught her everything she knows. It was my mistake to not realize she'd be even better at it than I am at times. When it works in my favor, I love it. When she outplays me, I detest myself for mentoring her.

We leave dinner and I head toward the party. My gut continues to sink when I pull up to the frat house.

This isn't the right move.

It is. Stick with the plan.

It's clear Avery and I tapped into Ivy's insecurities about fitting in. We've done it a hundred times with different girls and guys. So I don't know why I'm feeling so off about this, but I am.

I'm going soft.

I turn to Ivy. "Are you sure you want to go in there?"

It's a normal question to solidify her downfall. Every step Ivy makes needs to be her choice. As things crumble around her, I'll remind her it was her decision—that she's the reason chaos is falling all around her. Then, I'll manipulate her further, driving her deeper into my destructive web of broken dreams.

My stomach churns. I stare at my little slut.

Tell me to take you back to my place.

Jesus, I'm becoming a pussy.

"Do you not want to be seen with me?" she questions with hurt in her voice.

It's the exact paranoia I want her to develop. I'd normally

be giddy, yet right now, my groan is genuine and full of frustrated fear. "Ivy, get Avery's comments out of your head. She will never stop, so you'll have to get past it. I'd never want to hide you."

Ivy's face softens. "I'm sorry. You're right. I shouldn't let her comments get to me."

"The only person hiding us is you," I add.

She pins her eyebrows together, insisting, "I'm not hiding us."

"You're hiding us with your father."

"That's...that's different," she claims.

"Is it?"

She bites her lip and looks away.

And I'm back on track.

One thing I've learned about guilt is it'll make people do things they never thought they would. Ivy is no different. If anything, her genuine good-girl upbringing only speeds up the trajectory of my game.

She turns toward me with glassy eyes. "I promise you I will tell him about us."

I grab her hand and kiss it, then softly state, "Okay. But don't accuse me of things that aren't true."

"I'm sorry. I didn't mean to. I'm just..." She looks away.

"You're feeling paranoid. Is this normal for you?" I question, planting another seed for her to dwell on now and in the future.

She pauses, then claims, "No. I'm not a paranoid person."

I stroke her hand. "Okay, baby girl. Then stop listening to Avery."

She nods. "All right."

I point out the window. "Do you really want to go into the party?"

She glances at the house. Lights flash, music blares, and college kids dance and party all over the lawn.

She turns and locks her gaze with mine. "Yeah. Besides, you're the president. You need to be there."

Yes, I am the president, and they do what I say. Yet I keep those facts to myself. It's best not to reveal too much to her.

"All right, then. Let's go," I order, then get out and meet Ivy at the front of the Porsche. I grab her hand and lead her into the party.

It's the same scene as every event. Smoke from vaping, cigarettes, and weed hangs in the air. Cocaine lines tables in long rows. Razors and straws sit next to them. Crowds hang close by, waiting for their turn to snort it.

The walls vibrate from the loud music. Everyone's drunk or high on something. Guys play beer pong. A few half-naked coeds that I recognize and a few new freshman faces sit on couches with guys who have paint on their chests.

The house is packed with people, and it all bores me. I had plans for tonight, but now, I don't know. I glance at my whore, and my heart aches. I take long breaths, trying to calm it, wondering if I'm having some kind of attack.

Why am I letting this girl get under my skin? She's just another pawn in my game.

No, she's different.

She's actually special.

Jesus, what the fuck am I thinking?

I continue watching her take in the scene, trying to hide her shock, telling myself she's just another girl.

She's not.

"Look who we have here," Bobby booms, then slaps Ivy on the ass.

She jumps and yelps.

I spin, lunge at him, and grab him by the shirt. "What the fuck are you doing, Bobby?"

He puts his hands in the air, laughing. "Easy. Since when are you so uptight?"

"Don't touch her," I warn, but for the first time in the history of playing our game, I mean it. Every part of me doesn't want him to touch her.

Stop being soft!

Bobby puts his arm around me and pulls me to the side. "Hey, man, why are you so uptight?"

I grind my molars.

His coked-out eyes study me. He adds, "For real. What's going on?"

I shrug out of his grasp. "Nothing's going on."

"You sure? You're not changing your ways on me, are you?" he questions with a challenging stare.

I hesitate.

"Jesus, don't tell me she got under your skin."

"Of course she hasn't. Don't be fucking stupid."

"Good. It would be a shame if you fell for a country girl from West Virginia." He chuckles.

I refrain from sticking up for Ivy.

He's right.

I insist, "There's no chance of that."

He grabs a fifth off the counter and hands me a shot glass. I take it. He pours tequila into both and holds his in the air.

"Salud."

"Salud," I repeat, clink his glass, and we knock back the shots.

"Let's get everyone wasted," he says with a mischievous look.

It's the same old Bobby. Something tells me I shouldn't let

this go on, that I need to take Ivy and get out of here, but I'm trapped.

I turn to leave the room, and my heart almost stops.

She and Matt huddle together, chatting like they're old friends. There's a comfort between them, and I don't like it.

Ivy tilts her head back, laughing.

My gut drops. I clench my fists at my side. What the fuck?

I'm about to go over there and punch Matt when Avery interjects. "Aw, the two dorks are bonding."

I scowl at her. "Why are you with Matt?"

She doesn't respond. She tosses me a knowing look, pursing her lips.

"Time to make the magic work," she chirps and saunters over to where Ivy and Matt are standing.

I follow her, trying to keep my cool.

In a loud voice, she accuses, "Why are you hitting on my date?"

Matt and Ivy both spin.

Red fills Ivy's cheeks. She insists, "I'm not hitting on him. We were just talking."

Avery puts her hand on her hip. "Sure you weren't. I saw you eyeing him at the restaurant as well. I thought you were into my brother."

Ivy's eyes widen. "I am into your brother. Stop talking crazy, Avery."

She sarcastically laughs. "I'm talking crazy? You're hitting on my date and my brother's standing over there. He just took you to one of the nicest restaurants in town, and this is how you repay him?"

"I wasn't hitting on your date!" Ivy exclaims.

I step next to them, and I can't contain the disapproval growing on my face. I pin it on Ivy.

She grabs my arm, fretting, "Dax, I wasn't, I promise. We were just talking. Avery's making stuff up again."

Avery scoffs. "That's convenient. Turn it on me. But I'm not the poor girl using my brother and his generosity and then tossing it in his face, am I?"

My admiration for my sister appears.

Leave it to Avery to spot-on play her role.

It's too soon.

What am I saying?

"I would never do anything of the sort!" Ivy cries out.

I tug her into me, scowling at Matt. I state, "It looks like your date was hitting on Ivy. Keep your nerd-boy away from her, Avery."

"I wasn't hitting on her," Matt insists.

"Sure you weren't," I seethe.

Avery steps next to Matt, sliding her arm through his. She asserts, "That's ridiculous. Why would he hit on her when he's with me? You don't go from escargot to SPAM. Isn't that right, Matt," she coos, batting her eyes at him.

Adoration fills Matt's expression, mixed with shock. He stutters, "Th-that's not nice, Avery. We talked about this."

Her eyes widen. "So you were hitting on her?"

The sucker falls for it. "Absolutely not. You know I only have eyes for you."

My sister puts on her fake, vulnerable expression that she's mastered.

He slides his bony arm around her. He lowers his voice, and red crawls up his cheeks. "You know how I feel about you."

It disgusts me how easily he caves.

He needs to grow some balls.

I allow Avery to play her game for a moment. She softly smiles at Matt, breaks her gaze with him, then glares daggers at Ivy. She seethes, "Stop using my brother."

Ivy gapes at her, shaking her head. Then she tells me, "I'm not using you, Dax."

I tug her into me, lean into her ear, and murmur, "I know you aren't. Stop letting Avery win."

She releases an anxious breath. Then she opens her mouth, but I put my finger over her lips.

I order, "Let's drop it."

She stares at me for a second, and I realize the glassiness in her eyes is more than emotion. She's definitely a little intoxicated from the several glasses of wine I made sure she drank at dinner.

I warn Avery, "Move on."

She purses her lips, and my nerves reappear. I never know what she'll do when she tosses me that look. It's a wild card, and she takes me by surprise most of the time. And Avery's surprises only involve her winning. I just hope she's still on my team where Ivy is concerned.

Bobby holds out a shot. "Time to have some fun. I agree you should ignore Avery." He holds the tequila in front of Ivy.

She glances at it.

I grab it and knock it back.

"Geez, you're a little selfish tonight," Avery mutters.

I ignore her. She's getting on my nerves faster than normal tonight.

Bobby holds another shot in front of Ivy. "Here, take it."

She hesitates again.

I choose my words carefully, encouraging, "It's okay, baby girl. You can handle it."

She reaches for it, takes a sip, and scrunches her face.

Bobby instructs, "You're not supposed to sip it. Take all of it at once."

She glances at me again.

"He's right. Take the whole thing. It goes down better."

She studies her glass, works up the courage, and finally gets it down. Her face scrunches again.

"She can't even take a fucking shot," Avery snarls.

"Avery," Matt mutters.

"Ignore them," Bobby directs, puts his arm around Ivy and me, and moves us through the living room and into a bedroom. He fills our shot glasses again. "Cheers."

Ivy shifts on her feet. "No, thanks. I'm okay."

Bobby leans closer to her. "If you want Avery to take her target off your back, you'll have to show everyone you can handle what she can. Then she can't talk. Drink up."

She bites her lip.

I refrain from speaking.

Bobby pressures, "Come on, don't prove Avery right. I know you have it in you to hang like the rest of us."

Normally, I'd approve of his help getting Ivy drunk. Tonight, something tells me it's wrong. It confuses me further.

Ivy grabs the shot and tosses it back. Her face scrunches like it did the first time. Then, to my surprise, she grabs Bobby's shot and takes his.

"Damn, girl!" Bobby praises.

Once she gets over the initial shock, she says, "There. You happy, now?"

He chuckles. "I guess I can tell Avery she's wrong about you."

"I guess you can," Ivy says, pride in her expression.

I wonder if my little innocent girl has more of a Greenwich attitude than I anticipated.

A smile erupts on her face. She giggles, and it grows so much her eyes tear.

"What's so funny?" I question.

She puts the back of her hand over her mouth and shrugs.

"I don't know." She taps my nose and states, "You're adorable, you know that?"

Giddiness mixes with disapproval. My conflicting emotions frustrate me. I should be elated that the alcohol is hitting her so hard already. So why aren't I?

"I mean it, Dax Carrington. You're the sexiest man alive," she slurs.

"Oh, you are," Bobby agrees sarcastically.

I glare daggers at him and tug Ivy into me. "I think the alcohol is starting to get to you, baby girl. No more."

"Well, aren't you a party pooper," Bobby accuses.

"I mean it, Bobby. No more," I threaten.

His lips twitch.

"I'm only warning you once," I caution.

He narrows his eyes.

Anxiety balls in my chest, but I don't break away from his stare. I don't need Ivy so drunk she can't perform. I only need her loosened up.

He holds his hands up. "Alrighty, boss."

I tell Ivy, "I think we're done with the drinks for now."

Bobby shakes his head in disapproval. "You're getting weak, Dax."

"Oh well," I say, tired of Bobby and his antics.

He's only playing his role. I'm the one changing the game.

And why am I doing that?

I'm trying to figure out my sudden change of heart when Avery comes into the room. Cindy and Marcey stumble in behind her.

"Oh, there's the new girl," Cindy slurs.

"The homophobe," Marcey adds.

"I am not," Ivy spouts.

"Ignore them," I order.

She blows a frustrated breath out.

"I think it's time we—" I start, but Cindy cuts in.

"So, Ivy, it's clear you like Dax," Cindy announces, then giggles.

Ivy gives me her bashful expression, mixed with a new drunken look I've not seen before. I realize I like her much better sober, not because she's done anything wrong but because she's not like these other girls.

I don't want her to be like them.

Then why am I breaking her?

Breaking her doesn't make her like them.

It does in some ways.

Bobby interrupts my thoughts. "You don't like him, or you do?"

"Of course I like him," Ivy answers with no hesitation.

I tug her closer.

Bobby states, "Then kiss him."

Ivy arches her eyebrows. "Kiss him?"

"Yeah. Show us how you kiss him."

"You don't have to kiss me," I say, giving Bobby a look to stop it. Everything inside of me is yelling not to play this game tonight.

Ivy slides her hands around my neck and giggles. "You don't want to kiss me?"

I glance at her. "Of course I want to kiss you."

Before I can say anything else, she presses her lips to mine, sliding her tequila-coated tongue into my mouth.

No matter how much I try to resist, I can't. For a moment, I'm lost. No one else exists. The scent of smoke, the flashing lights, and the music disappear. It's only Ivy and me.

She pulls back, and I'm the breathless one. It takes a minute before I snap back to reality, and I wonder again what the hell's going on with me.

Bobby catches me off guard and pulls Ivy into him. "Now,

that looks pretty good. I need to experience that. Kiss me how you kissed Dax."

I curl my fists at my sides. "Bobby," I warn.

He glances at me. I can't blame him for being confused. This is what we do.

"Why would I kiss you?" Ivy asks.

That's my girl.

All the girls say that.

"To show me how to be a better kisser," Bobby lies.

"No," Ivy declares.

Relief fills me.

I need to trust her.

Trust her?

Trust no one.

I'm losing it tonight.

Avery chirps, "See? I told you this party's too intense for her. Ms. Goody-two-shoes once more."

"Shut up, Avery," I order, but there's no stopping my sister.

"Why are you here if you're going to be such a downer, Dax?" Marcey accuses.

I give her a nasty look.

Cindy steps closer. "Ivy, I think you forgot something."

"What's that?"

Cindy slides her hands over my face and tries to kiss me. I jerk my head so her kiss lands on my cheek, barking, "Get off me. I told you I'm not interested in you anymore."

Ivy's eyes narrow.

Cindy locks her hands around my neck, whining, "Don't be like that."

Bobby asks Ivy, "Are you going to let Avery win all the time?"

"Yeah, she can't handle it. She's a hillbilly and always will be," Avery sings.

Ivy shouts, "I am not—"

Bobby plants a kiss on her before she can say anything else, sliding his tongue into her mouth and holding her head so she can't escape.

My gut dives. Bile rises in my throat. Cindy holds on to me tighter, and I push her off me. She falls to the floor.

"Jesus, Dax!"

My insides tremble. Paralysis hits me as I stare at Ivy in Bobby's arms, his tongue pushing in and out of her mouth.

Those are my lips and tongue, not his to touch.

Ivy pushes against Bobby's chest, but he's holding her hostage. But then I see it. A moment where her fingers relax, and she kisses him back.

My paralysis eases, and I yank her away from him, snarling, "What the fuck are you doing, Bobby?"

Ivy's breathless. She gives me a worried look and then glares at him.

Bobby grins. "Why are you being a party pooper, Dax? I just wanted to see what it is you see in her. But I think Avery is right. I think she's nothing but a hillbilly."

Ivy's face falls, and tears fill her eyes.

More anger rages inside me.

I tug her tighter into me, and I'm no longer pretending. "All of you, stop being cruel to Ivy."

"Since when are you a prude, Dax?" Cindy asks.

"I'm so over you, Cindy. If I never see you again, it won't be soon enough," I seethe.

Hurt fills Cindy's expression.

Bobby crosses his arms. "Is this really who you want to be with?"

Why can't they understand I don't want to play this game right now?

He adds, "Cindy's right. She's a prude and turning you into one."

In the past, this situation would be perfect. Right now, it's only making me ill.

And pissed off with a rage I've not felt in a long time.

I step forward and push Bobby.

He pushes back, shouting, "What the fuck's gotten into you?"

"I'm over this and you."

Avery interjects, "She can't handle being here. You shouldn't have brought her."

"Would you shut the fuck up?" I bark.

Avery crosses her arms and pins her gaze on me. "Fine, I'll shut up. Or I'll shut up, and I'll never talk about any of this again."

And here's the wild card.

I cautiously ask, "If what?"

But I shouldn't. I know better. I just stepped into Avery's trap.

She glances at Ivy, then me. "I won't make fun of Ivy ever again. I won't even claim that she doesn't belong here. I'll be nice to her."

"You're a liar," I state.

"Why am I a liar?"

I stay quiet.

"So you don't want that for Ivy?" she taunts.

I glance between Ivy and her. In a normal game, I want Avery to keep harassing Ivy. Yet everything in my head is screaming for her to stop.

"Guess Dax doesn't care about you that much," Avery says to Ivy.

I blurt out, "Of course I want you to stop."

"Good. Then Ivy only has to do one thing to earn my approval."

My gut drops to my toes. "What's that?"

Avery turns fully toward Ivy. "Ivy, show us you aren't a homophobe. Kiss me."

"She's not kissing you."

"Jesus. You've changed, Dax," Marcey accuses.

"I have not changed," I say, not wanting to have to explain this to Ivy.

"She's already kissed Bobby. What's the big deal? Besides, I'm a girl. It's not like I have a dick to compete with yours," Avery adds.

"I didn't. He kissed me," Ivy claims.

"You kissed him back," Avery states.

"I did not," she insists.

Marcey smirks. "You did. I saw your hands relax and your tongue twine with his."

It wasn't just me.

She did kiss him back.

Jealousy and fury flare at a new high throughout me.

"That's not true," Ivy insists, but now she's lying.

Maybe my little innocent slut isn't so innocent after all.

"Oh, but you did. So make your decision. Kiss me, and we can become friends, or keep me as your enemy," Avery demands.

"I didn't kiss him," Ivy repeats.

My chest tightens with the truth. She did. And now, she's going to have to pay for that mistake.

Ivy 18

JUST ONE KISS

Ivy

Avery steps forward and softens her expression. She drags her fingers over my collarbone and studies me the same lustful way Dax usually does. The scent of her floral perfume flares around us, intoxicating me. She lowers her voice and says, "One kiss. We can be friends, Ivy. Don't you want to be my friend?"

My insides quiver. I open my mouth, but nothing comes out.

She moves closer, leaning into my ear. Her fingers dip lower, grazing my top. She slinks her other hand behind my back and caresses my spine. Tingles explode under her hot breath. She murmurs, "Let's be friends. Don't you think that's best?"

I inhale sharply, unsure why my body's tingling and what to do.

I'm drunk. That's what's happening.

"Ivy, please," she breathlessly begs, pinning her gaze on my mouth.

Dax yanks me away and quickly maneuvers me out of the room.

I can barely stay on my feet. My head buzzes.

What just happened?

Why did I take those shots?

Was I actually considering kissing Avery?

Dax continues moving me through the crowded room, and I grab him tighter, crying out, "Dax, slow down."

He doesn't. Rage flares around him.

I don't know why.

I kissed Bobby.

No, he kissed me.

Dax pulls me into another bedroom and slams the door. He spins me against it. He snarls, "Is that who you want? Bobby?"

There's something other than anger in his tone. Is it vulnerability?

Maybe I'm making it up since I've been drinking.

No, it's there.

"Well?" he questions, and it sounds a tad desperate, making me feel guilty and horrible.

But I've never wanted Bobby's lips on mine, so I object. "I didn't kiss him. He kissed me. I tried to push him away, but he wouldn't stop. You saw it!"

"Didn't look that way to me," Dax claims.

"No." I shake my head and then I wince. It's painful and makes me dizzy, and I curse myself for letting Bobby pressure me into the shots and then downing his.

"You kissed him back," Dax states.

"I didn't."

"You did. Marcey saw the same thing I did. Your fingers relaxed on his chest."

"What? No," I deny, but Dax keeps his narrow gaze pinned on me in disapproval.

I cry out, "It's Avery's fault. She wouldn't stop. I just want to be good enough to fit in here. But every time I turn around, everybody's out to get me. I don't understand why."

"Didn't look like you were that mad at Avery a minute ago," he accuses.

"That's not true!"

"Isn't it? Pretty sure you would have played tongue tag with Avery had I not interfered," he claims.

"Not true," I declare, as tears fall down my cheeks. And I can't stop them.

Dax stares at me a moment, then takes several slow breaths. My waterworks continue, and the fire in his eyes doesn't cease.

I'm scared I'm going to lose him. "Please. I love you. I don't want Bobby or your sister. I want *you*."

He doesn't reply.

My silent tears turn into a sob. I'm so confused and frustrated. Dax is the only person who's been kind to me and welcomed me. Now he thinks I don't want him.

Something changes in his expression. He pulls me into him, and I keep sobbing until his shirt's soaking wet. I slowly look up, sniffling. "I only want you, Dax. I love you!"

He takes a deep breath, then turns his face away from mine, grinding his molars.

Did I just say I love him?

My insides quiver harder.

"Dax?" I question, not wanting him to be done with me. He's quickly become my everything, and all I want is him.

Why did Bobby have to do that?

Why did I let my fingers relax?

Dax turns back to me. "You say you love me?"

"I do," I claim.

"Then prove it."

Hope flares in my chest. "How?"

"Let me really have you, Ivy," he asserts.

"You do have me."

He puts his finger over my lips. "Don't say I have you if I don't. Make sure the next time you tell me I have you, I have all of you."

I swallow hard. I don't understand what he means.

He removes his finger.

I blurt out, "You have my soul, Dax. My heart. Everything. Don't you know that?"

"Great. Let's go." He grabs my hand and turns, dragging me through the house, avoiding the others.

Everything's a blurry fog. My head keeps spinning, but Dax tightens his arm around my waist, pushing the tight crowd out of the way.

Bobby calls out, "Where are you going, Dax?"

He finally stops. He glances over at him. In a dark voice, he states, "The boathouse."

Bobby's lips twist, making my gut drop. He glances at me, then back at Dax. "Checkmate, brother."

Dax gives him another look I can't decipher.

What does checkmate mean?

He moves us faster through the house, and we step outside into the darkness. He pulls me farther from the music and steers me onto a dirt trail curving through the woods.

"What did Bobby mean by 'checkmate'?"

Dax shrugs, tightens his grip around my waist, and answers, "No idea. Ignore him. He's an idiot."

"He's your friend."

"So? He's still an idiot," Dax claims.

I don't say anything else about it. I let him lead me down the trail until we approach a small structure next to the lake.

He opens the door and points. "After you, gorgeous."

I hesitate. "Where are we?

"The boathouse."

"Is it safe?" I question, peering into the darkness.

Dax chuckles. "Why would I take you somewhere that's unsafe?"

I don't answer.

His face falls. "You still don't trust me, do you?"

"Yes, of course I do," I insist.

"Then go inside."

I swallow hard. I don't know why. Something tells me not to go in, but I do. I carefully step through the doorway, but I can't escape the dread in my stomach.

Dax follows me inside and flips a switch. A soft glow lights up the space. Tongue-and-groove-stained wood walls, a concrete floor, and covered windows appear. Boats, long paddles, and life vests are stacked neatly in piles all the way to the ceiling.

"Not so scary, right?" Dax questions.

I softly laugh, relaxing. "No. I don't know why I was so worried."

"What exactly did you think would happen?" he asks.

"I don't know," I admit.

He steps in front of me and slides his hands on my cheeks. "Are you afraid of me, Ivy?"

"No. I'm not afraid of you. You would never hurt me."

Something twisted crosses his expression, and surely I'm mistaken. I've just been drinking too much alcohol, I tell myself, when his expression morphs again.

"That's good. You're right. I could never hurt you." He

pecks me on the lips and leads me into a different room. He flips another switch, revealing a bed, nightstand, and tall dresser.

More anxiety fills me. "Does somebody live here?"

"No, but why do you look scared, my little slut?" he questions, the lewd expression Avery gave me moments ago appearing on him.

My pussy throbs. I put on a brave face. "I'm not scared."

"Good, but you look it."

I take a deep breath and attempt to lift my chin to appear confident, but my head feels heavy.

"Have you had too much to drink tonight?" he questions.

I stay quiet.

He continues, "You probably can't handle your alcohol the way everyone else can."

My stomach churns. His statement makes me feel like Avery is right. Her voice torments me, saying I can't handle what everyone else can.

So I shake my head. "No, I'm fine."

"Are you?"

"Yes, I am," I insist.

He studies me for another moment.

"Stop it, Dax. I'm fine."

He nods. "Okay. You're the judge of that."

"Yes, I am," I affirm, then smile. I put my arms around him. "I'm glad we're alone."

"Are you?"

"One hundred percent," I chirp.

He chuckles. "That makes me happy, my little slut. You know I'm crazy about you, right?" he asks, grinning, and it feels like Dax is back.

My Dax—the one who can't get enough of me.

I laugh. "Yeah, but I feel the same about you, Mr. Sexy."

He arches his eyebrows. "Mr. Sexy?"

I giggle, raising my voice. "Yeah. You're the sexiest man alive!"

His grin widens, his eyes softening. "Guess that's good since you're the sexiest little whore on Earth."

"I am?" I beam, pride filling me.

"Yeah, baby girl. And I'm yours. But I want to know that you're mine, Ivy."

My face falls in frustration. "I am yours. And you know I love you."

He stares at me, and I wait, willing him to say it back, but he doesn't. He leans into my ear, and I think he will, but instead, he murmurs, "Do you really love me?"

"Of course I do. I wouldn't say it if I didn't."

"How many boys have you said that to?" he questions.

I jerk my head backward. "None! I've never met anyone like you. And why would you think I'd say that to anyone else? I told you I never slept with anyone besides you. How could I have said that if I didn't even sleep with them?"

His challenging blues meet mine. "So you love me and enjoyed having me inside you?"

"Yes," I breathe, my butterflies fluttering harder. I caress the side of his head and suggest, "We can do it again if you're up to it." I bat my lashes the way I saw Avery do it, hoping I look sexy.

His expression softens. "You want a repeat, Ivy?"

"Yes," I eagerly reply.

"Then you're still mine?"

"Of course I'm yours. I'm always going to be yours."

"You kissed Bobby."

"I told you—"

"Shh. I don't want to argue about it. I want to forget that ever happened."

"But I didn't kiss him!"

"Do you want to argue about this all night?" he questions.

I snap my mouth shut, debating about convincing him or letting it go for now.

He tugs my skirt up and palms my ass cheek. "I know what I'd rather do."

I giggle and nod. "You're right. Then let's forget about it. But I didn't want to kiss him. I didn't, and I didn't like it."

He stares at me for a minute, and I feel as tiny as an ant. But then he says, "I want to know that you only love me, Ivy."

"You are the only person I love. Who else would I love?" I question.

Satisfaction appears on his face. "Good. Then there shouldn't be any issue for you to prove it to me."

"How? I'll do anything. I'm not a prude," I quickly add.

His expression shows his approval at that. He slides my skirt down, and it falls to my feet. He reaches around my body and releases the button on my tube top. He bunches the material in his fist and tosses it across the room.

Tingles race down my spine, right to my core.

He declares, "There are only two questions I need answers to."

"What are they?"

"Are you ready to give me all of you?"

"You already have all of me."

"Do I?" he questions, his eyes turning to slits.

"Of course you do."

He claims, "I don't have all of you right now, gorgeous. So I need a yes or no to my question."

"You do," I insist.

"I've not come in you," he declares.

I gape at him.

"I need it, Ivy. You and me as one."

My pulse quickens. I stutter, "I-I-I d-don't want to get pregnant. I thought you didn't want me to either?"

He nods. "I don't."

I add, "You said the shot would take a few weeks to kick in."

He strokes my cheek. "When did you get your period last?"

I ponder his question, then answer, "Last week."

"So you're not ovulating."

I slowly shrug. "I don't know."

"You aren't."

"How can you be sure?" I ask.

He firmly asserts, "It's day fourteen of the first day of your last period. So I can come in you and you won't get pregnant. We'll have to be careful for a few days next week before the shot kicks in."

"Ummm...why don't you use a condom?" I suggest.

His face falls, revealing more hurt. "You don't want all of me?"

"I do!"

"Then I need to come inside you."

My heart thumps hard against my chest.

He slides his hand through my hair and kisses me so intensely I get dizzy. I whimper, and he retreats. "I need you, Ivy."

Dax needs me.

"Don't you need me, baby girl?"

"Yes. I need you," I whisper.

"Then let me give you all of me. Give me all of you," he murmurs.

I slowly inhale.

"Please, gorgeous," he pleads, then adds, "I'd never let you get pregnant. Not until we're ready to start our family. I promise. I'll only ever protect you."

My heart soars. I lean into his ear. "Okay, Mr. Sexy." I try to take a step back but almost fall.

"Whoa!" He steadies me, holds my face in front of his, and disapproval fills his gaze. "Maybe you're too drunk."

"I'm not drunk!"

"I don't want you to regret me."

"I won't!"

"If you're too intoxicated—"

"I'm not too intoxicated. I told you, I'm fine," I insist.

He slides his hand on my head and strokes his thumb over my cheek. I close my eyes, leaning into his warmth. I mumble, "I love how you make me feel, Dax."

He cups my pussy, and tingles explode everywhere. "You do?"

"Yes. Please, Dax. Give me all of you," I beg.

"Ivy, I need all of you. But I need all of you when you can handle it."

Avery's voice haunts me, singing, *You can't handle it.*

It makes me feel crazy. And desperate to prove I can handle anything Dax gives me—anything he needs from me.

My eyes refill with tears. I cry, "You believe the same thing Avery does, don't you?"

He tenses. "Of course I don't."

"You do. You just said it. You think I'm not good enough for you."

"That's not true, Ivy. I've never said that or thought that. I've told you that's not true several times. So stop talking. Stop making things up. You're being paranoid again."

Am I paranoid?

I can't help it and accuse, "You didn't even want to bring me to the party."

"No, I wanted to go home and spend the night with you in bed. Is that so bad?"

Guilt fills me, but part of my insecurity still questions whether Dax didn't want to bring me here. It only makes my desire to please him stronger.

He asks, "What do I have to say for you to get it through your head?"

I blurt out, "Tell me you love me back."

He clenches his jaw, staring at me.

My embarrassment hits a new high. My cheeks instantly turn to fire.

Oh jeez.

"I'm sorry. I shouldn't have said that." I turn to avoid his look.

He spins me back into him and tugs me closer. He slides his hand behind my head. He firmly holds it so his face looms over mine. His tequila-filled breath hits my skin. It's hot and sweet.

My mouth waters, craving his lips and tongue like nothing I've ever desired. I admit, "Dax, I don't know what I'm saying. All I know is I love you. I'm not drunk. I'm fine. And I want to prove to you that I belong here with you." I once again speak too much of my truth. But the amount of alcohol I drank tonight isn't allowing me to stay quiet. Any thought or insecurity that comes to my head is coming out, so all my cards are on the table.

Dax's gaze flits to my eyes and lips and then back to my eyes. He orders, "Tell me whose slut you are."

I clench my thighs together, lift my chin, and can't stop my smile from growing. "I'm your slut, Dax."

His lips curve. "That's right. Now, tell me that you always want to be my dirty whore."

In a louder voice, I confidently declare, "I always want to be your dirty whore."

He runs a finger over my breast and then pinches my nipple.

"Yes," I whisper.

He circles it with his finger, and it grows harder and harder.

Every cell in my body lights up.

His tone deepens. "You know how much I love these fucking C cups."

Giddiness mixes with dizziness, but I push through it.

He loves me.

That's not what he said. He said he loves my boobs.

No, he loves me. He does.

"Ivy, you made me feel insane watching you kiss Bobby."

My defenses return. "I didn't kiss him. He kissed me. I didn't want it!"

Anger laces his tone once more. "Your lips were on his. Your tongue was in his mouth."

"I know, but it's not my fault," I claim.

"We always have choices. Cindy tried to kiss me. I pushed her off."

"You're stronger than her. Bobby's stronger than me. That's not a fair comparison," I state.

He studies me for a moment. He finally concedes. "Okay, maybe that's true."

"It is," I insist. I lace my fingers around his neck and try to sound sexy. "I thought we weren't going to argue about this all night. I thought you wanted all of me." I tilt my head, trace his lips, and murmur, "What do you want, Dax? Me to be your little slut or to disagree all night?"

His mouth twists. My butterflies go crazy, and he nods. "Okay, my sexy whore. Prove to me you love me. Give me everything I need."

"You can come inside me. I-I want you to," I claim.

What am I saying?

It'll be okay.

Dax would never get me pregnant before we're ready. He promised.

"That's not all I need, Ivy."

"No? What else do you need, then?"

He steps back and points to the ceiling. "Do you see those green lights?"

My heart races. "Are those cameras?" I cover my breasts with one arm and move my hand to my pussy, fretting, "Are you recording me?"

He nods. "Yes. I'm recording you. I want to see you give all of yourself to me."

Shock fills me.

He continues, "I want to watch it with you, and I want to watch it when you're not with me. You're mine, and I want a reminder that you love me even when you're not in front of me."

My insides quiver. I glance around the room again, realizing my ass is on full display.

Dax drags his knuckles over my ass cheek. "Are you going to give all of yourself to me, or is this where it ends, Ivy?"

"You're going to break up with me?" I cry out, unable to comprehend that he would do that just because I disagree with being on video.

He shakes his head. "No. It'd be you breaking up with me."

Panic smacks me. "That doesn't make sense!"

"It does. I told you, Ivy, I'm not vanilla. There are things I need...things I crave. If you can't give them to me..." His voice trails off.

"Then you'll break up with me?" I ask in horror.

He shakes his head. "No. Like I said, it'll be you choosing it."

"But I'm not choosing it!"

"You're choosing to torture me, Ivy. I can't date you and be my best self if I don't have all of you. And you deserve my best self. Do you understand what I'm saying?" He strokes my cheek.

My insides quiver. I attempt to process what he said. Confusion, warning bells, and desperation to keep him swirl so fast in my mind, my head spins.

I can't lose him. No matter what, I can't.

I blurt out, "I don't understand, but I do."

Dax kisses the curve of my neck, and zings rush to my pussy. He adds, "There's one more thing."

My anxiety intensifies. I ask, "What's that?"

He states, "You're holding back, Ivy. I'm an all-in or all-out man. What are you?"

I assert, "I'm all in with you!"

He stills, then puts his face in front of mine and asks, "Are you all in, Ivy? Do you really want me? Do you really love me?"

"Yes, I do. Why do you keep asking me this?"

"Then are you ready to give all of you to me?"

"Yes, I already told you so. You can come inside me and record it. I know you won't show it to anyone," I acknowledge.

"Then I need your full trust," he declares.

"You have it. I've done everything with you," I point out.

He grunts. "Ivy, you've not done everything with me. We've just sliced the cake."

I stare at him, perplexed.

He adds, "I need you to let me guide you. I'm the one with experience. I'm the one who knows what you need even though you don't know it. And all of it will make you feel higher than you've ever felt. From now on, I'll make sure there are no boundaries between us—no limits we can't reach together."

I swallow hard, not quite understanding how anything

could feel better than how he made me feel in the dressing room.

"When you leave this boathouse, everything will have changed, Ivy. You'll no longer be pretending to be mine. You *will* be mine."

I open my mouth to argue that I'm not pretending to be his.

He gives me a stern expression.

I close my mouth.

Dax challenges, "Ivy, this is the last time I'll ask. Are you ready to give me all of you?"

Dax 19

EARN MY KISSES

DAX

Ivy swallows hard.

I wait for her to answer. I've guilted her, tapped into her insecurities, and threatened to end our relationship. I've leaned into every manipulation tactic I've perfected over the years.

This is the moment of truth. Tonight, I'm getting all of my innocent baby girl. I'll turn her into the dirty whore she doesn't know is inside her, the one I'm craving so much I'm in constant pain.

There's no more holding back. And as upset as I was at Bobby, I'm now mentally giving him a fist bump. Hell, I'm even grateful for Avery. They played their roles, and I suddenly wonder why I was annoyed.

This is who I am—what I do.

"I'm ready, Dax," Ivy finally answers.

Adrenaline pounds through me. "That's my sexy baby girl. Now, wiggle those hips and tease me with your fat ass cheeks."

Her eyes widen, and her voice cracks. "Fat?"

I grin, peck her on the lips, and answer, "Yeah, my little slut. Your fat, sexy, I-can't-keep-my-eyes-or-hands off, drive-me-crazy ass cheeks."

Her lips twitch.

I point to the bed. "Give me a good show, my dirty whore."

She sways her hips as she walks to the bed. She sits on it and looks at me.

I order, "Sit back and put your heels on the edge of the mattress. I want to see that tasty cunt."

Her cheeks heat, but she obeys.

I clap. "Bravo, baby girl. You just made me super happy."

She beams.

"Now, circle that pretty clit of yours until I get back."

Her eyes widen. "Where are you going?"

"Bathroom. But you better be coming when I walk back in the room," I state.

She licks her lips, then puts her fingers on her pussy. She slowly plays with herself and asks, "Like this?" She bats her eyelashes.

"Yeah. Now, I'm stepping out of the room. I better hear you when you start to come," I demand.

Her lips purse together.

I tear my gaze off her, go into the bathroom, and open the medicine cabinet.

I'm taking all of her in all ways. When the sun comes up, I'm still going to be fucking her.

I pull out the erectile dysfunction medication I stole from my father. I put some water in my hand and swallow two pills.

Unlike my father, I don't have any issues with my dick. But if I'm going to go nonstop and come inside and all over her in the next eight hours, I need some assistance. The first time will be quick. After that, it'll take me longer to come, but I'll still be able to get hard again. By the time morning arrives, she won't be able to walk.

I wait until I hear her moaning. It's not loud, but the speakers I installed years ago will pick up a pin hitting the floor.

My endorphins spark to life. I lean against the wall, closing my eyes, listening to her pleasure heighten.

It's another obsession I've acquired. When she comes, it's raw. There's nothing fake about Ivy, and she doesn't try to sound any certain way.

Ivy is just...Ivy.

The other girls around here always put on a show, even when they come.

It's annoying as fuck.

My delight grows as I hear her murmur, "Dax. Oh gosh, Dax!"

My baby girl's thinking of me.

Fucking little slut tease.

I'm going to show her what the difference is between her fingers and my cock tonight.

I go to the bedroom and stand in the doorway.

Ivy's skin glistens. She has her eyes shut, and her dark hair fans the covers. Her mouth's in an O, her body trembles, and she's moaning.

I quietly creep toward her and drop my clothes on the floor. I watch until her orgasm subsides, then cage my body over hers.

She opens her eyes, her breathing ragged.

I stroke her cheek, praising, "You're such a good little whore for me."

The fire bursts in her eyes.

I push her leg up and slide into her.

"Oh gosh!" she blurts out.

I put my hand over her mouth, and her eyes widen. I thrust quickly inside her, grunting. "Isn't this better, my little slut? Me inside you?"

A muffled "mmm" escapes her. Her eyes flutter.

I lick her lips, keeping several inches from her mouth so only our tongues meet when she tries to kiss me.

"You have to earn my kisses, my dirty baby girl," I growl, thrusting faster into her pussy.

Her cunt clenches my cock.

I suck on the curve of her neck, and her insides grip me tighter. I groan, accusing, "Your pussy's super greedy. It's going to make me come too soon."

"Dax...I...I...oh good Lord!" she cries out, her eyes rolling. Sweat pops out on her skin, and she grips my head.

I grab her wrists and hold them above her head, thrusting faster, trying to prevent myself from coming even though I know I'll be sinking back inside her as soon as I'm done. I grit out, "What do you want to be to me, Ivy?"

"Your...oh, Dax!" She moans, her body convulsing harder.

I lift her leg higher, hold her wrists so tight they'll bruise, and pound into her with all my effort, demanding, "What?"

"Your slut!" she cries out, her gaze refocusing on mine.

I don't break it, keeping up my violent thrusts, taunting, "My whore likes it rough, doesn't she?"

She opens her mouth, and her hot, ragged breath hits mine.

"Answer me," I order.

"Yes!" she shrieks, another tremble moving through her.

My cock swells and heat encompasses me. A bead of sweat rolls down my forehead.

"Dax!" she whimpers.

I lean down and kiss her, finally letting her frantically roll her tongue around mine.

"Tell me you love me again," I order.

Why did I just say that?

"I love you," she mumbles against my lips, then adds, "Only you."

A giddy high hits me, and I thrust another time.

Her pussy clenches me in a hard spasm, and I lose it.

I explode inside her, calling out, "Fuuuck, baby girl."

She cries out, and for the next few minutes, the room disappears. My ears fill with animallike sounds. I thrust until I can't anymore and then collapse over her, breathing hard.

I slowly release my grip on her wrists and kiss the red mark on her neck, then suck a bit more to ensure she's marked as mine.

She whimpers and shivers, and I move down to her perfect C cups and suck on her pink tits.

She grabs my hair, writhing under me.

I suck harder, and she shrieks.

I don't let up, and her nails dig into my skull. She widens her legs and pushes her hips into my frame.

I back off and circle my tongue around her nipple, and she moans. I declare, "I know what you need, gorgeous."

"Yes," she breathes.

I keep working the same tit until she's quivering. I retreat, admiring my mark, murmuring, "You're mine."

"Only yours," she replies.

I move my mouth to her other tit, then sleds three fingers into her pussy. I scoop my cum out of her and swirl it over her marked tit, continuing to suck her other one.

"D-Dax," she whispers.

I scoop more out of her and wipe it over her lips. Her tongue flicks my fingers, and I shove them into her mouth.

She sucks without me directing her.

I groan, then mumble against her tit, "Fucking dirty whore." I resume my attention on her breast until she cries out, convulsing against me.

I move my mouth to her pussy, teasing her clit with my tongue, flicking slowly at first, then like an angry snake.

"Please," she begs.

"You want to come, my little slut?" I taunt, slowing my licks.

She pushes my head against her pussy, repeating, "Please!"

I chuckle, inhaling her scent deeper, then nibbling her clit.

"Oh Lord!" she cries out.

I chuckle some more, feeling higher than a kite, pleased beyond my own belief. I suck, lick, and nibble until she's violently writhing under me, screaming my name, and lying in a pool of sweat.

I rise on my knees, fisting my erection, my eyes darting between her puffy lips, the purple bruises forming on her tits, and the slowing of them rising and falling.

She glances at my cock, tosses me a needy, exhausted glance, then refocuses on my dick, licking her lips.

"Oh, you greedy slut. Don't worry, I'm not done with you," I declare.

She swallows hard.

I lift her legs past her hips so her ass is tilted up, grip her ankles, then spread them apart. I instruct, "Don't move your legs," then slide my knuckles through her slit. I trace her forbidden zone.

She inhales sharply. Fear flashes behind her eyes.

"You said you were all in, right, Ivy?"

She furrows her eyebrows and opens her mouth, but nothing comes out.

I push a finger past the hard ridge.

She clenches her bottom.

"Relax," I command.

She releases an anxious breath and blurts out, "You won't fit inside me, Dax."

I burst out laughing so hard my eyes tear.

Her face falls.

"Is that what you think?"

She bites on her lip.

I narrow my gaze, challenging, "That's not what a sexy slut would say."

A tense moment passes. I wait her out.

She asks, "What would they say?"

"'Fuck me in the ass.'"

She gapes.

I inch deeper and challenge, "So you're not all in with me, baby girl?"

She takes a few anxious breaths.

I swirl my finger inside her and ask, "This doesn't feel good?"

She opens her mouth and hesitates.

I circle faster. "Answer me."

"I-it feels g-good."

A new high pummels me. I demand, "Then be my good little slut and tell me to fuck you in the ass."

She caves. "F-fuck me in the ass."

I pull my finger out of her. It's not good enough. She's going to beg me to do it.

I kiss the side of her thigh, then drag my knuckles over it, and slowly trace the curve of her ass. "I'm not sure you really want me to. I'm worried you really aren't all in, gorgeous."

"I am," she insists.

"I don't know. I'm not convinced you fully trust me."

"Dax, I do!"

I lean forward and stroke her forehead, placing my lips near hers.

"Dax, I'm yours," she states.

"Are you, Ivy? Or are you a tease?"

She firmly claims, "I'm not a tease!"

I study her.

"I'm not," she softly insists.

I deeply exhale. "Good. I would die if you were. Tell me again what you want me to do."

She blinks a few times, then says, "Fuck me in the ass."

"Louder, my little slut. Please. I really need to know you want all of me." I give her a chaste kiss.

She licks her lips, takes a deep breath, and states louder, "Fuck me in the ass."

I grin and kiss her again. "I'm going to make you feel so good, baby girl. I'm going to fuck your slutty asshole until you're crying with pleasure, and I'm marking you as mine with my cum."

She swallows hard.

I press my mouth to hers and explore it with my tongue, loving every second of how she eagerly shows me she wants me.

She breaks our kisses. "Dax?"

"What, baby girl?" I reply, returning to her lips.

She continues kissing me, mumbling, "I'm scared."

I retreat, pinning my gaze on hers. My heart races. I'd normally be stoked about her admission. For some reason, I'm not. I ask, "Of me?"

She shakes her head. "No. Just..." She bites on her lip, wrinkling her forehead.

"Tell me," I demand.

She blurts out, "I don't want to lose you."

My heart soars. I stroke her cheek and state, "I couldn't let you go if you wanted me to."

Her lips curve. "Really?"

"Yeah," I answer, kissing her again.

Play the game.

I reprimand myself for losing myself in her kisses. I murmur, "It's time for us to truly be all in, baby girl. Roll over."

Ivy 20

TRUST ME COMPLETELY

IVY

Jitters fill me. My mouth turns dry.

Tell him no.

I'm not losing him.

"Trust me," he repeats.

Stop being a baby.

Dax will never hurt me.

"I do," I claim, and turn onto my stomach, grimacing when my breasts slide against the duvet. I grip the top of the mattress.

Dax puts his hand over mine and moves it next to the other. "Relax, gorgeous. Your knuckles are white. And why did you wince?"

"I didn't," I lie.

He turns my head so I can't avoid him, pinning his blues to mine. "You did."

My belly flips.

"Tell me why."

I blurt out, "My nipples are sensitive."

His eyes light up. "Ah, yes. Once we get going, they'll feel better."

"They will?"

His lips twitch. "Yeah."

"How?"

He drags his fingers over my spine, and I shudder. His grin widens. He claims, "There's a relationship between pleasure and pain. You'll see."

I don't understand what he means, but I drop it, feeling naive and hating it.

I curse myself again for being a prude in high school. I don't want to admit it to anyone, and I never thought I was one, but I now see it.

If sex is so pleasurable, then why would anyone not want to have it?

Dax studies me.

I get agitated. "Did I do something wrong?"

He shakes his head, dragging his fingers over the crease of my ass. "No, baby girl. You're doing everything right."

"I am?"

He kisses me. "Yeah. Now give us what we both need."

My butterflies erupt into a fluttering mass, mixing with my anxiety. I don't know how Dax knows what we need, but he's not been wrong about anything so far.

He demands, "Beg me to fuck your slutty ass."

My pussy clenches, and I don't understand why. I was taught not to cuss. Before now, I don't think I've ever said the f-word. Now, I'm using it and calling myself a slut.

Dax loves it.

Don't be a prude.

I purse my lips how Avery does and narrow my eyes. I don't know why I'm replicating what she does, except everyone thinks she's sexy. And I want to be nothing less for Dax.

He doesn't speak.

In a breathless tone, I plead, "Please fuck my slutty ass."

"Louder. And make sure you make me believe you want it—that you're as desperate for me as I am for you."

He's desperate for me.

My adrenaline resurfaces.

I stick my ass in the air, lean my head back, then meet Dax's gaze. In my most desperate voice, I beg, "Please, Dax. Fuck me in my slutty ass. I-I need it so badly."

"Fuuuck, you dirty little whore. I'm going to make you come so hard you can't sit down for a week," he declares.

Horror and excitement swirl in my gut. I swallow hard, unsure how he's not going to hurt me.

He murmurs into my ear, "If you want to make me happy, then you'll do something for me when you come."

"What?"

"I want you to yell, 'I love it when you fuck my slutty ass.'"

Something sordid inside of me gets more excited. I bat my eyes. "Is that what you want?"

"Yes."

I find my courage. "Then why aren't you fucking my slutty ass right now?"

Dax's eyes light with approval. He grunts. "Fucking A. You're fucking perfect."

My heart soars. I wiggle my ass, shoving my nerves down, trying not to wince from my tits grazing the covers.

He smacks my ass, and it echoes in the air. I yelp, and a sting erupts, and he rubs his palm over it. His voice turns darker. "You're a teasing little whore right now, aren't you?"

Pretend you're Avery.

I hate her.

She would know what to do.

I fall into my role, surprising myself at how easy it is to carry this conversation with him. I lick my lips and answer, "Yes."

His expression turns wicked. My pussy clenches and he suggests, "Maybe I shouldn't fuck your ass. Make you crave it instead."

"No!"

"No? Why no?"

"I need you to," I declare.

"You need me to what?" he taunts, then slaps my ass again.

"Oh!" I breathe out, arching my back.

"Tell me what you need." He rubs his palm over the sting.

"I-I need you to fuck my slutty ass!"

This is going to hurt.

Dax wouldn't hurt me.

He's not going to fit.

He cages his body over my back, his hard, warm frame pressing against it. His hot breath hits my ear, and zings fly down my spine and burst through my tits. He warns, "I need you to relax. Understand?"

I take a deep breath.

He asserts, "Be all in. Trust me completely."

"I am. I do!"

"Good. Now, do you remember how your greedy cunt desperately sucked my cock earlier?"

More adrenaline bursts in my core. Nothing's ever felt so good. I answer, "Yes."

He moves his fingers over my neck, tightening them, but not so I can't breathe. He firmly holds my head so my chin rests on the pillow.

Excitement begins to override all else.

"Your ass is just as greedy. Now promise me you're going to do what I say."

Anxiety swirls with curiosity, fear, and the desire to do whatever I have to in order to always keep Dax as mine. I vow, "I promise."

He kisses my cheek and wraps his fingers over my hands, which are still above my head. "Good. Relax."

I do my best to obey him.

He lifts his body off mine. I instantly miss his heat. He slides his forearm under my hips and tugs me up. "Get on all fours."

I obey and lift my torso off the covers.

He slides his hand up and palms my breast.

I shiver, inhaling sharply. A sharp tingle goes straight to my pussy.

"I love your body, my little slut. Your C-cup titties..." He cups my pussy. "Your greedy little cunt..." He places his other hand on my ass cheek, adding, "And this fat, sexy ass."

Fat?

Am I fat?

No, he explained that.

He chuckles. "Relax, baby girl. I love these curves. I'm so tired of bony girls."

My jealousy flares, but I'm also happy he loves my body. I hate thinking about him with anyone besides me.

As if he can read my thoughts, he states, "Don't be jealous. Think of all those other girls as practice so I know how to please you."

I stay quiet.

"I please you, right, my sexy slut?" He licks my lobe.

"Yes. So much," I confess.

"Then relax. I only have eyes for you, my little whore. Now, take a deep breath."

He only has eyes for me!

My nerves dance in my belly. He lifts my hips higher, and I close my eyes. I slowly inhale, and Dax shoves his cock into my pussy.

"Wh-wh-what," I breathe out.

"Fuuuck! You're always so wet and tight, you dirty slut." He groans, slamming his cock against my walls.

"Dax," I cry out.

He thrusts so deeply I can feel it in my belly.

"Greedy cunt." He grunts.

Once again, Dax is right.

My pussy spasms, desperate to cling to his cock. Endorphins build in my cells. I'm about to orgasm, and Dax pulls out.

"Please," I beg.

He flips on his back and tugs me so I'm straddling his hips. He positions my body so the tip of his cock hits my forbidden zone.

Fear reappears. "Dax—"

"This is the moment you trust me, baby girl." He slides three fingers into my pussy and swirls his thumb on my clit.

"Oh Lord," I mumble as the sensations I'm starting to get addicted to flare once again.

He reaches for my breast and plays with my sensitive tit.

"Dax," I cry out.

"Sink on my cock and tell me you love it when I fuck your slutty ass," he orders.

I don't move, closing my eyes, pummeled with sensations from his hands.

"Don't disappoint me, Ivy," he barks.

I open my eyes.

He clenches his jaw. There's a challenge behind his eyes. He works my pussy and tit more intensely. He growls, "Now."

I inch down but pop back up when I feel the pressure.

"Keep going. Prove to me you love me as much as I love you, baby girl," he orders.

He loves me.

Dax Carrington just said he loves me.

My heart soars.

"You love me?" I question, just to make sure he said it.

He kisses me, then mumbles, "Yeah, gorgeous. I fucking love you. Now, do what I need you to do. I can't take it anymore. You've been teasing me with this fat ass since I first laid eyes on you. My cock hurts all day thinking about you giving all of yourself to me. So relax and take all of me. Please. I need it now," he begs.

I close my eyes and push past the hard ridge.

He circles my clit faster and then leans up, sucking my tit hard.

My back arches, and an orgasm explodes inside me, mixing with the initial pain of him entering me.

He grabs my hip, continues to work my pussy, and moves me up and down on his erection.

Within a few minutes, the pain subsides, changing to a new sensation that teases me with pleasure.

I whimper, and Dax brings his lips to mine.

He urgently kisses me. He pulls his fingers out of my pussy and retreats, sliding them into his mouth and groaning. Then he shoves them in my mouth.

"You taste and feel good, my greedy little slut. Now, tell me how you feel." He pulls his fingers out of me.

"I-I...oh Lord, Dax. I feel so good," I admit, no longer needing his hand to guide me. I push my knees into the mattress, sinking deeper over him.

He puts his hand on my cheek, placing his mouth close to mine. "Always trust me, baby girl. Promise me you always will."

"I promise," I barely get out.

He grips my hip with one hand, holds my head firmly with the other, and pushes his forehead against mine. He moves me faster and grunts. "You're almost there, gorgeous."

I don't understand how he knows, but adrenaline explodes in all my cells. I cry out, "Oh! Dax!"

He seethes, "Say it!"

My eyes roll as I mumble, "I love it when you fuck my slutty ass!"

"Again!" he roars, his crazed eyes burning with fire.

"I love it when you fuck my slutty ass!" I say, louder this time.

"Again," he shouts, and I lose track of how many times I yell it out.

I can't think. Violent convulsions rack my body, making me light-headed.

Dax's cock swells, and I lose the ability to hold myself up. I fall against his muscular torso.

He holds me tighter, continuing to thrust into me, never letting my orgasm die.

Sweat slides down our bodies. He sucks the sensitive spot on the curve of my neck, and a long groan vibrates against my skin.

His erection throbs over and over. Hot liquid fills me. He sucks harder while grunting, squeezing me with his forearm.

We come down together, staying in the same position for several minutes, breathing hard and quivering.

He murmurs in my ear, "Thank me for fucking your virgin asshole."

Shock hits me again, but I push it away. I don't always like what Dax makes me say, but it makes him happy. And I don't want to be a prude.

I hold his head and lock gazes with him. I confidently say, "Thank you for fucking my virgin asshole."

His lips twist.

He moves me off him and says, "Wait here."

I lie on the bed, staring at his naked ass until it disappears through the doorway.

After a few minutes, he returns and stands in front of the mattress. He points, "Your ass is leaking all over."

I glance at the wet puddle under my bottom. My cheeks burn. "Sorry."

"What are you sorry for?"

I open my mouth but am unsure how to answer.

"Ivy, you like to bathe in my cum, don't you?" he taunts.

"What?"

"Don't lie to me, you dirty little whore. You love to have my cum all over your body, don't you?"

I stare at him.

He arches his eyebrows, demanding, "Admit it."

I don't understand why he loves talking like this so much, but every time I agree with him, I earn his approval.

I reply, "I love your cum all over me, Dax."

His expression darkens.

My core lights up again.

He curls his finger at me.

I get off the bed and step in front of him, my belly filling with nerves, knees wobbling.

He slides his hands over my cheeks and presses his body against mine. His erection digs into my stomach. He states, "You look exhausted."

I nod, smiling. All I want to do is curl into him and go to sleep. "You've worn me out."

He narrows his eyes, studying me.

My butterflies flutter. I ask, "Aren't you tired too?"

He shakes his head and puts my hand over his cock. "You feel that?"

"Yes."

"Good. Your night isn't over, Ivy. When I said you wouldn't be able to walk, I meant it."

I gape at him. Exhaustion truly is setting in. How is he not tired?

"Are you thirsty?" he questions.

I realize my mouth is dry. "Yes."

He steps over to the dresser, picks up a fifth of whiskey, and opens it. He takes a large sip and then holds the bottle out to me. "Here, baby girl. Take a sip. It's all we have."

I'd prefer a bottle of water, but it's not a choice. So I take a sip. The warm liquid slides down my throat and coats my belly.

Dax takes another and orders me to take one more. I do it and he sets the bottle back down. Then he steps back in front of me. He orders, "Go out to the main room. Lean over a boat and spread your legs."

I stare at him in confusion, but when he doesn't say anything else, I obey. I step in front of the large hanger, lean over an upside-down boat, and spread my legs. I lift my head and panic.

I see a small green light. The camera sits two feet from my face.

Calm down. It's only for Dax and me, I remind myself.

He comes up behind me and presses his cock to my ass cheek. He lays his palm over my spine, slides it up my back, then grips my neck. His voice darkens, and he declares, "I'm fucking you all night, you dirty whore. This time, you're going to suck me off before I come. Now, be a good little slut, look into the camera, and get creative while you tell me how much you love the taste of me."

As tired as I am, another wave of excitement hits me and a bit of courage resurfaces. I purse my lips like Avery, stare into the camera for a brief moment, then declare, "I love your cum, Dax. I love being your slutty whore. I love it when you fuck my pussy, mouth, and ass."

He smacks my bottom.

I yelp.

He rubs out the sting and says, "I'm going to fuck you now. You're going to remind me how greedy your pussy and mouth are, then thank me for filling you. Understand?"

I push my anxiety away and stare at the camera, telling myself everything is fine.

It's just Dax and me. He'll always protect me. There's nothing to stress over.

I bat my eyes, asserting, "I'm your sexy slut. I need your big cock in my greedy pussy. Please, Dax. Fuck me until I can't walk."

Dax 21

TIME TO MAKE MAGIC HAPPEN

One Week Later

"Dax, please. We've been through this. You have to give me a few days," Ivy pleads.

Anger boils inside me. She's lived with me all week. We've been inseparable, and I've done everything possible to further my plan.

I've loved every minute of using her.

We've boated, skinny-dipped, and fucked all over this estate. I even made her do everything possible to me in her dad's room. Before I let her, I made her beg me to record it with my phone. She resisted at first, but once we got started, my little slut was into it more than I could have ever imagined.

Throughout it all, I've recorded her. Every statement, every sound, every expression on her face—it's all been captured.

I want more.

Normally, I'd be semi-bored by now. Yet, I'm the farthest thing from it. My addiction to Ivy has only grown stronger, my curiosity for how she'll respond to my next move never dimming.

I sigh. "I don't want to go to school without you. Tell your father about us, and I'll pick you up."

"Dax, you know it's not that easy. I can't. And you promised me that you'd give me a few days so I can figure out how to talk to him," she reminds me.

I stare out the window and shake my head, pissed that I agreed to let her have a few days. She needs to be here with me.

I point out, "You're an adult. Tell him, then move in with me."

Silence fills the line.

The hairs on my arms rise.

What am I even saying?

She softly asks, "You want to live with me?"

I don't even consider what I'm saying. She's only been gone an hour, and I feel off-balance. "Yes. I need you here with me. I miss you."

Her voice is softer when she admits, "I miss you too."

"Do you?"

"Yes."

"Then tell your father and pack your bags."

She sighs. "Dax, I can't right now. Give me the time you promised."

I close my eyes and lean against the wall.

She begs, "Please. I love you. I don't want to be without you either. I promise you I'll tell him this week like we discussed."

Play the game.

I tug my hair, not used to not getting my own way and

hating it. I stare at the outline of her cottage. The day's turning into night, and the moon is barely visible.

"Okay, Ivy. But, baby girl, you have to tell him."

"I will," she firmly states.

I stay quiet.

She adds, "I have to go. I'll talk to you later. I love you."

I don't give her the satisfaction of telling her I love her. I've only done it once, and every time she tells me, I avoid saying it. It's clear she wants me to say it back. She's desperate for it. I see it in her eyes and hear it in her voice. But I'm going to keep her that way, willing to do anything to appease me, just to hopefully hear those words.

Besides, I don't tell girls I love them. I'm not sure why the fuck I said it a week ago anyway.

I was drunk.

No, I wasn't.

Instead, I reply, "Get some rest." I hang up and tear my eyes off her cottage.

Time to edit.

I sit down at my desk and open my laptop. I pull up the footage from all the different places we've fucked. There's footage from the dressing room, the boathouse, her father's bedroom, my place, my car, a few greenhouses, and the boat.

"The shower. Where is that?" I mumble, searching my drive. Then I find it, and relief hits me.

I replay all the footage, turning hard instantly. I unzip my pants. I palm my cock and play with myself, allowing myself to quickly cum.

I grab a rag and wipe up, then hit play for the next video.

I instantly get hard again.

"Jesus, how does this little slut do this to me?" I grumble.

I'm unable to tear my attention off the screen. The video of us in the shower ends, and I click on the footage I took of us on the boat.

I stare at the screen until it's over. I double-check I've seen everything, then debate.

Stop being a pussy.

It can be for us only.

Pussy.

What am I thinking?

Time to make magic happen.

I carefully review each video, editing different parts and splitting up what Ivy says or positions she's in. Then I merge it into one video, rearranging the frames how I like them.

I spend four hours on my project and then watch it. I get hard again. I pick up my phone and text Ivy.

Me: What are you doing?

Ivy: Lying in bed thinking of you.

I groan.

Me: Are you playing with those slutty pink tits?

Ivy: Should I be?

Me: Yes, and you should play with that dirty pussy of yours.

Ivy: I prefer you to play with it.

Endorphins flood my system.

Me: I'm sending a video over. I want you to watch it and touch yourself. I'm going to watch it at the same time. Okay, baby girl?

Ivy: Okay.

The video's too large to send in a text, so I put it in a Google Drive and send her a link. I turn on the TV, press a button on my phone, and pull up her bedroom. When it says delivered, I double-check.

Me: Did you get it?

Ivy: Yeah, I'm about to watch it.

Me: Good. After it finishes, tell me how many times you came.

Ivy: Okay.

Me: And spread those legs, my little slut. I'm watching you.

I glance at the TV.
She looks at the camera, biting her lip.
My cock throbs and my chest aches.
Fuck, I miss her.
She texts.

Ivy: I forgot you put a camera in my room.

Me: I just turned it on. Now, be my good sexy slut, and don't hold back.

She beams at the camera, pursing her lips, and slides her hand over her thigh several times, never touching her pussy but getting close.
Fucking tease.
I didn't even have to train her to do that.

Me: Turn on the video.

She obeys.

I split the screen on my TV, adding the video to the second one. I hit record, then play on the footage. My eyes dart between Ivy in her bedroom and the footage of the last two weeks.

It's a masterpiece.

I lean closer, palming my cock, breathing hard, unable to keep my eyes on one screen longer than a few seconds.

I'm lost in her the same way as the last four hours.

Ivy screams on the video, "I love being your dirty little whore, Dax. Fuck me harder."

I groan.

Clapping pulls me out of my trance and I jump up.

"Bravo!" Bobby applauds, standing in the doorway with a grin on his face.

I turn the TV off.

"Hey, why'd you end the show?" he questions, walking toward me and lighting up a joint. He takes a deep breath, holds the smoke in his lungs, then offers it to me.

I realize I haven't smoked in a week.

Ivy's kept me on a natural high.

I grab the joint and deeply inhale, letting the smoke sit in my lungs for as long as possible before I slowly exhale.

"Turn that back on," Bobby demands.

My gut dives. "No."

He raises his eyebrows. "No? What do you mean no?"

"It's not for you," I declare before I can think about that statement coming out of my mouth.

Bobby's eyes narrow. He crosses his arms. "Since when do you hide videos of little sluts from me?"

Ivy's not a slut.

"Don't," I seethe.

He jerks his head backward. "Don't what?"

His question hangs in the air. I can't blame him for his confusion. Bobby and I never keep anything private between us. Any video we've ever done, we've always watched together.

My heart beats faster. To shut him up, I claim, "It's not finished."

"So what? Let me see what you have so far."

"No."

He peers at me closer.

I hold the joint out to him. He doesn't take it, not tearing his gaze off mine.

My pulse skyrockets. The last thing I want to do is explain my feelings for Ivy to Bobby.

Feelings for Ivy?

What the fuck am I thinking?

His expression turns disapproving. "Are you falling for that hillbilly?"

"She's not a hillbilly," I declare.

He chuckles. "Now you're going to defend her? You're going soft."

"I'm not going soft."

"You sure about that?" he questions, giving me a challenging stare.

I inhale deeply on the joint again, then hold it out, stating while the smoke's still in my lungs, "You going to smoke this or what, you pussy?"

He grabs it. "I'm not the pussy. It looks like you've become one." He inhales a deep lungful of smoke and holds it just like I do. We release it simultaneously, and the glassy feeling my eyes always get starts to take hold.

"Not true. So, what have you been up to?" I question.

He grunts. "What have *I* been up to? Isn't it more like, what have *you* been up to? You've totally disappeared on me the last week. What the fuck is that all about?"

I nod toward the TV screen. "I've been busy getting my footage."

His lips twitch. "Yeah, I can see that. But normally, you keep me in the loop."

"Not always."

"Bullshit. I'm always part of your game. But all I've been doing is wondering where the fuck you are and what's going on," he declares.

"Yeah, well, life gets boring if you don't mix it up," I claim, then walk into the kitchen. I open the fridge and pull out another beer. I hand one to him and take one for myself.

"Are you ready to go?" he questions, taking a sip.

"Go where?"

He jerks his head back. "Are you fucking kidding me right now? Where the fuck are you, Dax?"

I rack my brain, then scrub my face. "Bobby, I'm tired. Let's not play games. What the fuck are you talking about?"

He shakes his head and answers, "God, what is happening to you? It's the night before school starts."

"So?" I question.

"So? So we need to go to freshmen hall, look at the new coeds, and figure out our new project."

"I don't need a project. I have Ivy," I tell him.

He shrugs. "So what? When don't you have multiple projects going on at the same time?"

I can't deny it. I normally break several girls at once. Sometimes, I break them together, letting them pleasure me in threesomes or even with Bobby. I'm a master at confusing them about their sexual orientation and where they draw the line regarding sex.

When those situations happen, it's beautiful. Both girls will try to please me, each competing and trying to top the other in satisfying me.

The entire time, I'll encourage them to do things they usually don't want to do to each other. Yet they'll do it to appease me.

And I'll record it all to hang over their heads when the time is right.

But that all seems boring right now.

Bobby announces, "There's a coed named Lilly I saw the other night who's staying in McPherson Hall."

"Yeah?" I ask, not interested but wanting to keep the conversation moving so Bobby gets off the topic of Ivy.

His eyes light up. "Yeah. All I keep thinking is she'd look fabulous with her tits in Ivy's mouth. I could fuck Ivy from behind. You could fuck Lilly from behind. It'd be a great video."

My stomach churns. Normally, this would be right up my alley, but there's no way anyone's touching Ivy—including Bobby.

Still, I choose my words carefully to avoid getting into it with him. "What's so special about this girl?"

His grin widens. "She's got long red hair, and guess who her daddy is."

I shrug. Bobby's got a thing for redheads. I couldn't care less. "I don't know, who?"

"Guess," he repeats, taking another hit of the joint, then holding it out toward me.

I take a swig of my beer and another hit, then shake my head, holding in the smoke, stating, "Don't know, Bobby. Who's her father?"

His expression turns wicked. "Senator McBean."

My eyes widen. "No shit. I thought that girl was going to Harvard."

Bobby shakes his head. "Nope! Apparently, daddy had an issue with an agenda on their board. Conflicted with his policies. She told me about it when she got drunk the other night."

"Damn," I say, still not overly interested.

He adds, "Anyway, she's into a lot of things daddy wouldn't be so proud of based on his platform and voters."

"So?"

He narrows his eyes. "Earth to Dax."

"Don't be dramatic, you pussy."

He shakes his head. "Wake up. Think about it. A girl like that who's willing to do anything on video is priceless. Imagine what we can do to hold over her dad's head. Fuck, we can influence decisions in the Senate."

I can't fault Bobby for thinking that way. He's actually being smart. I'd usually applaud him.

A video on a senator's daughter? We've never done anything like that before.

She's not Ivy.

His plan is genius.

I ask, "What's she into?"

Bobby's excitement shows in his voice. "Everything. I mean, *everything*. Avery already sampled her. She claims she knows what she's doing too."

My gut dives. I hate fucking women after Avery's already fucked them. I shake my head, "No. It's a no-go for me."

"What? Are you crazy?" he questions.

"Yeah, I told you, I'm done fucking coeds that Avery already got her paws on."

"Who gives a shit? Get your head back on straight. If we get footage of Lilly, her dad will do anything, and I mean anything, to make sure it never comes to light. We'll call the shots for the rest of his career. This is power unlike anything we've ever had."

She's not Ivy.

What the fuck am I saying? Bobby's right.

I don't want to fuck anyone else.

Jesus, what's happening to me?

Bobby steps closer and stares at me, his eyes turning to slits. He lowers his voice and points to the TV, accusing, "This is about that hillbilly from West Virginia with way too much weight on her, isn't it?"

"You're fucking crazy. Ivy's curves are amazing. She doesn't have too much weight on her. And all these girls around here with their skin and bones and fake everything, just suck. Jesus, aren't you over it by now, Bobby?"

He shakes his head. "No fucking way. These girls around here are fucking hot. And wait until you see Lilly. She's got it going on, for real."

"She's been with Avery."

"So what? Get over it. Avery said she licked her pussy until she came like a freight train. A girl like that, with her powerful father...fuck. We'll have more fun than we've had in a while. And then we're going to have real power. Not the pretend power we have now."

"What are you talking about? We own most of the coeds in this town," I declare.

He scowls.

I add, "Except for the ones we've run out of town."

His voice grows louder. "Dax, we're talking about the United States of America Senate. We can influence laws, rules, and agendas. Why are you not jumping on this?"

I stay quiet.

Anger fills his face. "Get that fucking girl out of your head. She's not the long-term type. She's just for fun. There's nothing she can offer us. Break her and be done with her."

Normally, I'd agree, but letting Ivy go isn't something I'm willing to do.

Not yet.

"She's a nothing," Bobby seethes.

"She's not a nothing."

"What are you saying?" he explodes, fuming.

"Don't," I warn.

"She is a nothing. Her father's a nothing. The only thing you can get from her is your dick serviced. Play the game, then move on."

Rage fills me. I'm tired of this conversation. "Bobby, I'm not interested. Now get the fuck out, I'm tired," I say and shove past him.

"Bros before hoes! Or did you forget that?" he calls out after me.

I ignore him. I go into my bedroom, shut the door, and turn on the shower. I take off my clothes and put my phone on the counter. There's a missed text. My gut dives.

> Ivy: I didn't know what it would be like to watch us, but that was hot, right?

> Dax, are you there?

> Dax?

I reply.

> Me: Sorry, baby girl. Bobby stopped by.

> Ivy: Did he see it?

> Me: Of course not. I told you I'd always protect you. You know I would never show it to him or anyone else.

> Ivy: Thanks, Dax.

> Me: How many times did that greedy pussy of yours come?

> Ivy: Four.

I groan, then call her.

She whispers, "Hey."

"Only four times?" I question, my lips curling and my cock hardening.

She softly laughs, replying, "Yeah, I'm sure if I watched it with you, I'd come more."

"Your slutty little greedy pussy would be sore by the time we got through it," I confidently state, grinning.

She giggles.

I add, "I'm picking you up tomorrow."

The line turns silent. My hard-on goes limp. I question, "What's wrong?"

Ivy sighs. "You can't pick me up, Dax. My dad will see you."

Anger fills me. I snarl, "I told you to talk to your dad."

"You promised me you'd give me a few days. Why are we going over this again?"

I'm tired of this conversation, just like Bobby's. I'm not going to stay away from Ivy. So I declare, "I have to get in the shower." I hang up on her.

She calls back, but I don't answer. I step under the water and stay in there for over twenty minutes.

What the fuck's happening to me?

Bobby's right, I'm going soft.

I should take advantage of the situation with this new coed. He's right. It's power we don't have that will reap long-term benefits.

I get out of the shower, and there are several texts.

Ivy: Please don't be mad at me. I love you. I promise you I'll talk to him this week like we discussed.

Bobby: Don't go soft on me, Dax. You'll regret it for the rest of your life if you don't take advantage of what's in front of you.

I stare at both text messages. Guilt fills me, and I realize I'm letting Ivy get under my skin.

She's a pawn in a game, nothing more, I tell myself.

Bobby's right. I'll always regret it if I don't take advantage of this Lilly situation.

Me: Put it in motion.

NOT A BUG BITE

IVY

"That's not a bug bite," my father roars.

My gut drops.

Dax: I'll be there in five minutes to pick you up.

I quickly reply to Dax's message.

Me: You can't. You know I have to talk to my father first. I'll see you at school. Do not come here.

I put the phone in my pocket. My nerves are shot. Who knows what my father will do if Dax shows up right now.

"Ivy," Dad seethes.

I turn back toward my father, lying, "It is a spider bite. It was worse earlier this week, and I couldn't stop scratching it."

He scowls, pointing at my neck. "That's a hickey, not a bug bite. Stop lying!"

"It's not a hickey," I reiterate, covering it up and trying not to wince. More heat burns my cheeks.

Dax sucked on my neck all week. I loved every minute of his lips consuming me, and I never worried about my father seeing it. He was out of sight, out of mind, and all I could think about was Dax.

When my father got home last night, I was in bed. It was late when he popped his head inside my bedroom door to tell me he was back. So it was only this morning when I got out of the shower and panicked.

It doesn't help that we're getting abnormal weather for the end of summer. It'll be almost 100 degrees today, so wearing anything but a tank top is out of the question. I tried to put makeup on the bruise, but it wouldn't fully cover it.

The moment I walked out of the bedroom, it was like my father had a sixth sense. He homed right in on my neck, and a chill ran down my spine.

"I'm going to be late for my first day of classes. We need to go," I assert, grabbing my bookbag.

A loud knock tears my father's scowl off me.

I rush past him and open it. Shocked, I blurt out, "Avery, what are you doing here?"

She's wearing a designer sundress and heels, nothing I'd ever contemplate wearing to class. But then again, I've dressed differently this last week, wearing all the things Dax bought me. Even today, I'm wearing one of the new tank tops and shorts he selected.

Avery beams, chirping, "I came to pick you up, silly. Didn't you get my text?"

My pulse skyrockets. I tug out my phone and glance at the screen. There's nothing from her, but it's not surprising. I've never given her my number.

I study her, wondering what she's up to.

Dad grabs the door and opens it wider.

Avery focuses on him, her smile widening. "Are you Mr. Ford?"

"Yes," Dad answers cautiously.

"Oh. I'm Avery. My dad's told me all about you. He says you're really talented and a great addition to his team! And Ivy's talked so highly of you too. It's really nice to meet you." She holds out her hand.

My father glances at me and then back at her. He takes her hand, and she offers him her dainty handshake, which should bug him.

It doesn't faze him the way it normally would. He replies, "It's nice to meet you too, Avery. Your dad tells me all sorts of good things about you."

I hold in my disdain. How dare Dax's father speak poorly about him and good about Avery? She's the devil. Dax is nothing but wonderful. I tell myself to hold my thoughts in, wanting to explode but not wanting to get into another conversation with my dad.

My dad releases Avery's hand.

She asks, "Are you ready to go, Ivy? We don't want to be late on our first day."

I'm unsure how to escape this situation or why she's even here. But riding to school with Dad seems like a bad idea as well.

"Is something wrong?" she questions when I don't move, her face full of concern.

Just go with it. She's better to deal with than Dad right now.

"No, sorry." I turn and hug my dad. "Have a good day."

"I was going to take you to school," he states.

"It'd be kind of silly for you to go all that way when I'm going to the same place," Avery interjects.

My dad smiles. "I guess you're right."

"Don't worry. I'm a safe driver. I'll bring her back to you before dinner," Avery claims and winks.

My dad chuckles, and my gut flips.

Is he seriously falling for Avery's act as well?

"Bye, Mr. Ford. It was great meeting you," she says, giving him another beaming smile.

"You too," he agrees, and I want to toss my cookies.

She gives a final wave and goes to her car.

"Bye, Dad," I say, following her. I slide into her Mustang.

She carefully pulls away.

I turn toward her, accusing, "What are you up to, Avery?"

Her eyes widen. "What do you mean? I'm taking you to school."

"Why did you just show up on my doorstep? What's up your sleeve?" I question.

Her face falls. She turns down the estate driveway, remaining silent, and drives toward the large metal gates.

"Avery!"

She pulls through the gates, gets to the next street, and veers off to the side of the road. She puts the car in park. "Ivy, I wanted to apologize."

I stare at her, unsure if she's telling the truth.

"I've acted very badly toward you. I'm sorry. I'm very protective of my brother."

"So you decided to be a witch to me?" I ask.

She squints, offering, "I think you mean a bitch."

I gape at her.

She sighs. "Ivy, a lot of girls have come onto our estate. They've taken advantage of Dax."

Jealously flares. *Dax has been with other girls who've lived on the estate?*

Avery claims, "My claws come out sometimes. I'm sorry. I-I was wrong about you."

I just stare at her, unsure if she's really sorry.

She puts her hand on my arm. "I really am sorry. Dax told me how much he loves you. He's never loved anyone either!"

My heart soars, and the jealousy fades.

He's only loved me?

She continues, "I want to be friends. I know everything's my fault. Please, can we start over?"

My heart thumps so hard in my chest that I'm sure she can hear it. My mouth turns dry. I'd love to be friends with Avery. I'm sure it's better than being her enemy. Yet I'm not sure if I can trust her.

"Please. I want to be friends. You'll see. I'm actually a really good friend," she says and smiles.

I soften. "Okay. I'd like that too."

"Really?" she questions.

I admit, "Of course I would. I've never had an enemy before. I wasn't quite sure why you were so against me."

She shuts her eyes and rubs the heel of her hand on her forehead. "I'm sorry." She opens her eyes and turns toward the back seat. She grabs a huge box and hands it to me. "I got this for you to say I'm sorry."

A gorgeous red bow secures the lid. It reminds me of Dax's gift, except this box is bigger. I blurt out, "Avery, you didn't have to get me anything."

"I know, but I was shopping yesterday and saw it. It's like it was screaming to me, 'I belong to Ivy,'" she giggles.

My lips twitch. I stare at the box.

"Well, don't be silly. Open it," she demands.

I laugh. "Okay, if you insist."

"I do. You're going to love it," she claims.

I untie the bow, lift the lid, and gape at a Louis Vuitton book bag.

"Well, don't just stare at it. Pick it up. Check it out," she encourages.

I jerk my head toward her. "Avery, this is beautiful, but I can't accept this."

Her face falls. "Why can't you accept it?"

"This is thousands of dollars."

She rolls her eyes. "Ivy, you realize I'm the beneficiary of a very large trust fund, right?"

My chest tightens.

She groans. "Sorry. I didn't say that to throw it in your face. I'm just saying that I have a lot of money. Oh, shoot. That sounds bad too."

I stay quiet.

"Look, I'm not even going to notice the money out of my account. But I wanted to get you something nice and, like I said, I thought it belonged to you. It literally was screaming on the shelf, 'I'm Ivy's. I'm Ivy's. I'm Ivy's.'" She grabs my hand and puts it on the leather. "Feel it. It's nice, isn't it?"

I can't help but laugh again. " Avery, it's beautiful. I've never had anything like this before."

"Well, it's time you did," she asserts, pointing to my book bag and adding, "Maybe you should retire that. What do you think?"

I glanced at the bag I'd had all through high school. It's tattered and ripped in places. I even put a patch on one spot. "Are you sure?" I question, looking at the bag again, loving how the leather feels against my fingers.

"Yes. Don't be silly. Here. Change it out before we get there." She grabs the box, tosses it in the back seat and then puts the car in sports mode. She speeds off, reminding me again of how Dax drives.

I ask, "Does Dax know you picked me up?"

"Duh. Who do you think asked me to get you?"

"He did?" I question, my nerves reappearing in my belly.

Why would Dax do that?

"Yes." She puts on her blinker and veers left. "We had a really good conversation last night. I got to his house today, and he was upset that you hadn't told your dad about him."

Dax told her that?

"Sorry. I walked in, and he was all upset, and I told him before he could say anything more that I was coming to get you."

I hate I've upset Dax, but my father is a tricky situation. I state, "Well, thank you. That was nice of you."

"Well, you don't want your dad dropping you off at college. I mean, your dad's really nice, and he's quite the looker too, isn't he?" she adds.

I groan. "Avery, come on. He's double your age. Plus, he's my dad."

She laughs. "What? I can't say that he's a good-looking guy?"

"Yes, that's fine. As long as it doesn't go further than that," I declare, wondering if she would actually do something with someone my dad's age.

She wrinkles her nose. "I go for people our age. I'm not really into the whole daddy thing and wrinkled balls," she says, wiggling her eyebrows.

"Eww, gross." I mock gag, then laugh. Relief fills me, not that I think my dad would do anything, but still, everyone around me, including my dad, seems charmed by Avery.

"Plus, we're friends. Do you really think I'd want to jeopardize our friendship like that?" she questions, glancing at me.

More relief fills me. "No, that'd be a bad thing."

She accelerates down the road and questions, "So, are you going to rush my sorority?"

"Sorority? I have no plans of rushing any sorority. I never even thought about it. Besides, I don't have the money for that," I confess.

"Don't be silly. Dax will pay for you."

"I-I don't want him to pay for something like that."

"Ivy, you have to pledge! You'd have a definite in with me," she states, once again, glowing.

I nervously laugh. "I'm not sure sororities are my thing, Avery."

She sucks in a dramatic breath of air. "What are you saying? You're going to Clifton University. You live in Connecticut now. Of course sororities are your thing. Besides, you'd love it. We do all sorts of good stuff. Charity work and all. Plus, we have great parties. And once you're part of the sisterhood, you have lifelong friendships. Sisters who will always have your back!"

I admit, "Well, I don't have a sister, at least a blood one."

"Neither do I. It's nice," she quietly states.

I think about what she's saying. I can't argue with it. I've always wanted siblings. Still, is the sorority life really my thing?

"Just come to the rush meeting with me later this week. And we'll have a rush party in about a month. If it's not your thing, then so be it, but I really want you in our sorority. All my sisters are going to love you," she claims.

"Really?" I ask, unsure that I'll be accepted that easily.

"Yeah. What's not to love about you? You're beautiful." She flashes me a slightly lewd look—so much like Dax's—but it quickly disappears and turns into a friendly smile. I wonder if I imagined it.

I shift in my seat.

Avery pushes, "You don't think you're beautiful?"

"I didn't say that," I said.

"So you do think you're beautiful?"

I laugh. "I didn't say that either."

She puts her hand near my knee, declaring, "You are beautiful, Ivy. You need to claim it."

I glance at her hand, unsure if I should remove it.

Surely, she's just being friendly and not hitting on me like before.

I have to get these thoughts out of my head.

Just because Avery likes girls and tried to kiss me doesn't mean she'll always be hitting on me.

She only did that to protect Dax, I remind myself.

She moves her hand. "I'm sorry. I didn't mean to make you uncomfortable."

"You didn't," I lie.

"It looked like I did."

"You didn't," I insist.

She slows down and comes to a stoplight. She turns toward me. "I'm sorry about the other night when I tried to get you to kiss me. Like I said, I just don't want anyone else to hurt Dax."

"Has he been hurt a lot?" I question, not able to fathom how any woman could hurt him.

Her face falls. She nods. "Yeah, he has."

"What have they done?"

She opens her mouth and shuts it. She looks at the steering wheel, pauses for a minute, then shifts her gaze back to me. "You'll have to let Dax tell you that. It's not my business. You understand my secrecy, right?" She puts her hand back on my leg.

I resist the urge to look at it, and nod. "Sure. That's fair."

The light turns green. She continues driving toward campus and asks, "So, who's your first class with?"

I pull up my schedule on my phone. "Professor Dyer."

"Ooh. You're going to have fun with him."

"Why?"

She smirks. "Professor Dyer is gorgeous."

"Well, I'm with your brother," I remind her, thinking it's strange she said that when she just told me she didn't want him to get hurt.

She laughs. "Duh. Of course you are, but it's still better to look at somebody hot during class than have a dweeby professor. Professor Dyer keeps it interesting."

I relax. "So I'm not going to be bored in his class?"

"Nope! Eye candy every day," Avery exclaims.

I laugh. "You're funny, Avery."

"That's me. Funny, funny," she chirps and then pulls into the school parking lot. She chooses a spot and then points at my bag. "You haven't put your stuff in it yet."

"Oh, sorry," I say, flustered. Then I quickly take the little contents I have in my book bag and put them in the new Louis Vuitton. I add, "This is really nice, Avery. I really don't deserve this."

She scoffs. "Don't deserve this? Ivy, you need to change your thinking. We deserve the best." She beams again.

I laugh. I like this new Avery. She puts her hand on my thigh again and leans toward my face. Her light floral scent flares in my nostrils. Tingles pop up along my skin under her fingers, confusing me. I force myself not to remove her hand.

It's just Avery's positive energy.

That scent is intoxicating.

She lowers her voice. "There's something I should tell you though...about campus."

"Oh?" I question, wishing the tingles would stop.

She nods. "Yeah." Her thumbnail grazes my skin, and I stiffen. Butterflies softly flutter in my stomach.

What the heck is happening to me?

I clear my throat. "What do I need to know about school?"

"Well, Dax, Bobby, Marcey, Cindy, and I... Well, we kind of own the place."

The mention of Marcey and Cindy makes my gut churn.

Avery leans back. "Hey, what's that look for? I was trying to tell you that you're in good hands. We'll all make sure you get into the good groups and meet all the right people. And if you have any professors that are crappy or just boring, we can help you get into the right classes."

I release a breath. "That's nice of you."

"Then, why the long face?" she asks, tilting her head with concern.

I shake my head, forcing a smile. "No reason."

She stares at me and snaps her fingers. "You're worried about Cindy and Marcey?"

I hold my breath, feeling ridiculous and caught like a kid with her hand in the cookie jar. Plus, they're her friends.

Avery pats my leg. "You don't need to worry about them. I already talked to them last night. They're going to be nice. They want to be friends too."

"Then, why were they acting how they were? And Cindy was with Dax. She still wants him," I blurt out, then my face turns to fire.

Avery rolls her eyes. "Cindy is obsessed with Dax, but he only has eyes for you. He's made it clear he doesn't want her. I've told her she needs to get past it. She promised me she'll let it go and won't hold your relationship with Dax against you. And Marcey actually really likes you. They just... Well, you know how friends are. They protect each other. Like Dax protects you. You know what I'm saying?"

I hesitate, then nod. "Yeah, I understand."

"Okay, so when I get defensive over Dax, they get defensive. Makes sense, right?"

I can't claim otherwise, so I affirm, "Yeah, it makes sense."

"Good. Well, let's all be friends. I promise you everyone wants to be."

Hope fills my chest. "That's good."

"You want to be friends with us, right?" she questions, her forehead furrowing as if she's worried I don't want to be.

"Yes, of course. I don't want to be enemies with anyone. I've never had enemies," I admit again.

She pats my thigh. "Good." She gets out of the car, and I follow.

She links her arm through mine and leads me through the parking lot. She declares, "Now, one of the things you need to know about Professor Dyer is that he gives extra credit."

"What kind of extra credit?" I question.

"He'll offer special projects, the opportunity to help him grade papers in his office, things like that. His tests are really hard, so if he offers out extra credit, you definitely should take it," she advises.

I make a note. "Okay. Thanks for the heads-up."

"No problem. He'll also have a sign-up form today to get on his teacher assistant training list. You should consider it. There's a small stipend, but he'll give you extra credit for that role too."

"Hopefully, I'll do well and not need any extra credit," I say.

Avery shakes her head. "Ivy, at some point, everyone needs it. He will get you on an exam. It doesn't matter how smart you are. His tests are really hard, and his questions are tricky, so I advise you to take as much extra credit as you can."

"Okay. I will," I state.

She leads me through the lawn until we get to a classroom. She points. "There you are. Have an awesome first class."

I smile, grateful that she wants to be friends. "Thanks, Avery."

"No problem." She hugs me and then retreats. "Meet me at noon in the courtyard. We'll all have lunch together. I'll make Dax come too."

Is this really happening? Is she really letting me into her group?

My gratitude fills me. "Sounds good."

"Good. Now, go sign up for that TA spot!" She points at the front desk and then takes off down the hall.

I enter Professor Dyer's class and find the form on the desk. It shows a stipend of fifteen thousand a year and that twenty hours a week are required.

That's more than I'd make picking up any job, I think, reminding myself I had plans to find part-time employment once I got settled into my classes.

I sign my name under the other students and pray he chooses me.

Dax 23

GOOD GIRL

Dax

Ivy still hasn't told her father about us, but that's my fault. I've made sure he works eighteen to twenty hours a day.

It's brilliant, really. It keeps Ivy guilty and tension between us when I want to use it to my advantage. I get lots of time to do whatever I want with her.

Every morning, I make sure John's out the door by 4:00 or 5:00. Then he gets home almost every night after midnight. He's barely getting any sleep.

Ivy's worried about him, and I keep hinting that I can have my father hire more help if he's incapable of running things. But then she assures me that he is and it's not necessary. Then I reassure her that his job is secure.

My phone dings. I pick it up and look at the screen.

Bobby: Lilly saw you and Ivy on campus. She
was practically salivating.

Me: Over Ivy or me?

Bobby: Both of you.

Excitement and warning bells swirl around me.
I can't do it to Ivy.
Yes, I can.
What am I saying?
Stick with the plan.

Bobby: Avery has everything set up at the
sorority house tonight.

My gut flips, but I do my best to ignore it.

Me: Good to know. See you later.

I end our chat and start another with Ivy.

Me: Wear a skirt today, my little slut.

Ivy: Which one?

My cock hardens. Every time Ivy asks me what to do, my
ego skyrockets. She pleases me beyond my wildest dreams.

Me: The mesh one. Wear the gold thong
under it.

Ivy: Isn't that for a bathing suit?

Me: No. And wear the gold sweater. Your tits
against that cashmere drive me wild. No bra.

Ivy: Dax, are you sure? It's pretty revealing for school.

Me: Have you looked at what the other girls wear?

A tense moment passes.

Me: Make sure you wear those gold stilettos with them.

Ivy: It'll be hard to wear those shoes and walk around campus.

Me: You did fine in the last pair.

Ivy: But these are six inches.

Me: You have your sorority rush party tonight. We don't have time to come home and change. I want us to grab a bite to eat before it starts. That outfit's perfect.

Over the last month, I've convinced Ivy to rush the sorority. She keeps telling me she doesn't think it's for her, but I keep telling her how she'll make connections that will help her for the rest of her life. In a normal situation, that'd be true. But it won't be for Ivy.

I get ready to argue with her about the outfit when she doesn't respond right away, but she finally replies.

Ivy: Okay, I'll wear it.

Relief and adrenaline hit me. I get a rush to my head, feeling almost dizzy.

Me: That's my good little sexy slut. I'll pick you up in a few.

I whistle as I finish getting ready for school, then get in my Porsche. I go over to Ivy's and pick her up. We make small talk in the car until we get to campus.

I park and get out. I go around to her side of the car, open the door, and help her out. I slide my hands over the mesh on her ass.

"You look fucking incredible," I tell her. And she does.

Apprehension fills her expression. "I still think it's a little too much." She glances around.

"Ivy, you're wearing more than most women here. It's fine. And if you got it, you need to strut it," I tell her and wink.

She nervously laughs.

I groan. "Tell me you're not going to worry about this all day."

She sighs. "Okay, I won't."

"Good girl." I squeeze her ass, give her another kiss, and lead her to Professor Dyer's classroom, stopping outside the door.

"I'll see you around noon?" she asks.

"Absolutely," I reply, giddy with what I have up my sleeve.

I leave and wait fifteen minutes. Then I text her.

> Me: Meet me in the library, floor 4, near the women's literature.

> Ivy: What time?

> Me: Leave now.

> Ivy: I'm in class.

> Me: So? I've already paid someone to take notes for you.

A moment passes.

Ivy: You're crazy.

Me: Crazy about you, you filthy whore. Now, show me how dirty you are and meet me. I need you, my baby girl.

More minutes pass. She finally caves.

Ivy: Okay, I'll see you soon.

I cross campus, enter the library, and wait for her.

She finally finds me and meets me in the middle of the aisle.

I whistle. "You're fucking sexy as shit, you know that?"

Her flush fills her face, and she beams. In a quiet voice, she asks, "Dax, what are we doing here?"

I push her against the bookcase. I take my arm and move it across the shelf so the books fly to the floor. They hit it with a loud bang.

"What are you doing?" she whispers, eyes wide.

I spin her so she's facing the shelf and pin her so her arms are forward. I murmur in her ear, "I'm taking what's mine, my little slut."

She gapes at me over her shoulder.

I move her ankle with my foot and pull up the mesh. I move the thong over, tug her hips up, and sink my cock into her.

"Oh God," she whimpers.

It's another thing that's changed. She no longer says oh gosh, or Lord. She says God.

I glance at the library camera blinking on the ceiling. I snarl, "You like that, my dirty whore?"

"Ohhh, Dax," she says, her pussy clenching me like it always does.

"Such a fucking greedy cunt." I grunt, already feeling the rush of being inside her. It happens every time. I don't know what it is about this girl.

She turns her head and looks at me from the corner of her eye. "Dax..." Her face turns hotter.

"Tell me how much your pussy loves me," I demand.

"I love it," she says.

"That's not what I said," I bark.

"My pussy loves your big cock," she cries out.

"Yeah. How do you want it?" I question.

"Harder," she cries out, and I groan, thrusting faster inside of her, moving deeper.

I've trained her so well. She doesn't even realize it, but I have, and the crazy part is it's happened so naturally. There hasn't been a lot of planning on my part. And the biggest surprise is that I've enjoyed every minute with her—more than I've ever enjoyed anyone.

"Dax," she cries out, her voice cracking.

I hold her neck down and squeeze a little harder. "Tell me you love me," I say, pounding into her.

"I love you. I love you so much," she cries out.

"Be quiet, you filthy whore," I demand and move my finger around to her clit, adding another source of pleasure for her.

It only takes a few seconds, and her body breaks into convulsions, her pussy spasming on me with desperation.

I grunt, continuing to pound into her. "Do you like it better in your pussy or your ass?" I question.

She moans, long and low.

"Answer me," I order, slightly out of breath.

"I-I can't answer that," she admits, and it only makes me happier.

It doesn't matter how I do it with Ivy—her mouth, her pussy, her tight asshole. She loves every second. She swallows me, licks me, does anything to pleasure me, and it's more than any woman I've ever been with. They all wanted me, but there's something different about Ivy wanting me.

It's real.

She doesn't want anything but me.

The realization hits me, and I panic for a brief moment.

"Oh, oh, oh God," she cries out, tearing me out of my anxious state.

"Greedy, fucking...fuuuck," I shout, unable to handle it anymore. I come hard, drowning her pussy with my cum while she violently shakes against the bookcase. I collapse over her, breathing hard into her neck.

Her ragged breathing matches mine.

I kiss her cheek and murmur, "You are such a good little dirty whore."

Her lips twitch. "Thank you for letting me be your dirty slut."

It's another thing that makes me happy. It's crazy how that little phrase gives me so much joy, but I've trained her well. It doesn't matter what I do to her. She always thanks me with different phrases I've trained her to say.

I catch my breath and stand straight, securing my pants.

She gingerly pushes herself off the bookshelf, turns, and tugs her barely-there mesh skirt down. Her face is flushed, her hair slightly messed up, and she gives me those glassy just-got-fucked eyes that haunt me at all hours of the day and night.

I slide my hands on her face and kiss her.

She flicks her tongue in my mouth, and I start to get hard again, but then I remind myself that I have a lot to do.

I pull back. "Rush is at eight o'clock. Let's grab a burger before we go. There'll be a lot of drinking tonight. You'll need something in your stomach."

Uneasiness enters her expression.

I question, "What's the look for?"

She hesitates, then admits, "I still don't know if I really want to be in a sorority."

"We've been over this, Ivy."

"I know, but it's expensive."

"I told you I'll pay for it. You don't need to worry about that."

"It's a lot of money, Dax."

I chuckle. "Baby girl, when will you realize I have more money than God? It's not a big deal."

"I don't know if I'm sorority material."

"Stop saying that," I tell her for the hundredth time. She has to go through tonight. She'll unknowingly win a point in our game if she doesn't.

I can't have that happen.

I'll have Bobby all over my ass, and I'm tired of listening to him whine. And he's right. It's time we get what we need from the senator's daughter.

"Some of those girls are...well..." She bites her lip and looks away.

I turn her chin so she can't avoid me. "Are what?"

She cringes. "I don't want to say it."

"So we're going to have secrets between us now? That's what you want?" I scowl.

She sighs. "No. I don't want secrets between us. You know that."

"Then tell me what you were going to say."

"They're fake. I don't have a lot in common with them."

"You shouldn't. You're not fake," I state.

"Then why is it so important to you that I join?"

"Ivy, we've gone over this. Gamma Sigma Phi is the top sorority in the country. The relationships you'll make will open doors for you for the rest of your life. Your career will take off because you're in this sorority."

"But can't my career take off without me being in it?"

I laugh. "No, it can't. Baby girl, the world works this way. It's about who you know, way more than our accomplishments."

"But I'm smart," she says.

"Yeah, you are smart. But if you don't know the right people who can open the right doors for you... Well, just look at your dad's situation," I say, happy to throw her father in her face again.

Her expression hardens. "What does that mean?"

I put my hands in the air. "Nothing bad. I just meant look at how hard it was for him to find another job."

She stares at me, hands on her hips.

"Ivy, stop acting like I'm saying something bad. I'm pointing out facts. If your dad had known the right people, he could have gotten a job at any time during those few years when he was out of work."

Her anger doesn't disappear.

"Are you really going to hold this against me? I'm trying to ensure that you always have the career you deserve and doors don't close in your face because of who you don't know."

She finally caves and shakes her head. "No, I'm not going to hold it against you."

"Are you sure about that? Because I feel like you are."

"No. I just... I don't like it when you talk about my father like that."

"I just explained what I meant," I declare, although she's right. Of course I was insulting him.

She stays quiet.

I add, "You're never going to tell him about us anyway."

"Dax, please don't start this again. I told you he's been working long hours."

"And I told you I can find more help for him if he can't keep up. Maybe the position is over his head."

"It's not," she claims.

"The last guy in his spot only worked eight hours a day," I lie.

She blinks hard and glances away.

I sigh. "I can hire more—"

"No! That's not necessary!"

I groan. "Ivy, if you're not going to let me find more help for him so he can work fewer hours, then I don't know what you want me to do."

I can see her internal debate in her expression. I let her struggle for a moment and then declare, "Listen, all I was pointing out was that who you know helps you in life."

"That doesn't seem fair," she claims.

I groan. "The world isn't fair. Surely, you know this?"

A frustrated breath escapes her.

"Ivy, promise me you'll do whatever it takes to get into Gamma Sigma Phi. I promise you it'll change your life."

She throws her hands in the air. "Okay, fine, I'll go through with it."

"You promise me?"

"Yes."

"Do you vow on our relationship that you will do whatever it takes to get in?"

"Yes, if it means that much to you."

"It does," I insist.

She nods. "Okay, then."

"Whatever it takes, Ivy," I remind her and then add, "I wouldn't ask you to do it if I didn't know it would be life-changing. Remember, I'll always protect you. I'll always take care of you. And I know this world. You need this."

"Okay, Dax."

"That's my baby girl."

"So I'll see you tonight?" she questions.

Bile rises in my throat, surprising me. I swallow it down.

Stop being soft, dammit.

I tug her into me, kiss her, then vow, "I wouldn't miss it for the world, my sexy little slut."

Ivy 24

SOON-TO-BE SISTERS

"This is your big night," Dax declares, beaming with excitement when we pull up to the Gamma Sigma Phi house.

My nerves reappear, but they're not as bad as they've been. Dax took me to dinner. We had burgers, fries, and two lemon drop shots.

He parks the car, gets out, comes around, and reaches inside for me. I take his hand, and he pulls me out. He slides his palms on my cheeks and studies me.

I squeeze my legs together. It's the look he gives me I can't resist. It awakens all my cravings for him.

He quickly kisses me and states, "I'm so proud of you."

"What for?" I question.

"Tonight. You're going to be a Gamma Sigma Phi. You're going past your comfort zone and doing what it takes to ensure you have everything you need in the future."

I smile, wanting to only make him proud of me. "If you insist I need to do this, then I will."

He puts his fingers over my lips. "I do. You have to trust me. You're never going to have an opportunity like this again. This is really big, Ivy."

The alcohol flows through my veins, and I'm grateful he gave it to me. It's helping me relax, and he's right. I need to gobble up any opportunity I can.

He states, "There's no point in working hard through college if you're not going to set yourself up for the best possible outcome in the future."

"You're right."

He gives me another kiss. "I know you're real, and a lot of these girls are fake, but sometimes we have to do things we don't want to do to get ahead. And I'm so proud of you for doing whatever it takes tonight."

I beam at him. Anytime Dax is happy with me, it creates a joy within me I've never felt before.

He gives me a long kiss, slipping his tongue into my mouth.

I slide my hands through his hair, holding him close as he tugs me closer. I return all of his affection, feeling like the luckiest girl in the world.

Dax Carrington is mine. Everybody in the sorority knows it. And ever since Avery picked me up the first day of school, Marcey, Cindy, and anyone around them have been nothing but kind.

Dax pulls back. "Are you ready, gorgeous?"

I swallow my remaining nerves and lift my chin. "Yes."

"That's my good little slut," he teases with a wink.

He slides his arm around me, then leads me up the driveway and onto the front porch. He opens the door and steers me toward the main room.

"Ivy's here," Avery chirps, then comes over and hugs me.

I hug her back. It's amazing how awesome she is, and I'm so glad she's no longer out to get me. We really have become friends.

Her smile widens. "I'm so excited you're going to be my sister."

Something deep inside me that I've always craved lights up. I've always wanted a sister, and I can already see how the sorority is a sisterhood.

She leans closer to my ear, lowers her voice a tad, and declares, "But it will be legal someday when Dax marries you." She leans back, beaming.

I can't help but grin. I can't even describe how happy the thought of marrying Dax makes me feel. It would be my dream come true.

Dax confirms, "Yeah, baby girl. Someday."

My insides dance with giddy joy. My cheeks heat.

"Well, let's not stand here. Come on. We have to get you ready," Avery states.

"Let her have a drink first," Dax orders.

"There's my man," Bobby calls out.

Dax and I turn toward him.

Another freshman named Lilly is on Bobby's arm. I've also gotten to know her over the last few weeks. Her father's a senator, and everybody is vying for her attention, but she and I have become genuine friends.

They step next to us.

Avery hugs Lilly and then Lilly hugs me.

Bobby wiggles his eyebrows, declaring, "Our two girls will be Gamma Sigma Phi's after tonight."

Dax slides his hand on my ass, and tingles explode underneath it. "Yeah. I'm so proud of Ivy."

Every qualm I had about joining a sorority disappears. It's

obviously important to Dax. And every time he tells me he's proud of me, I can't help but feel amazing.

A waiter in nothing but a silver G-string and matching bow tie appears with a tray of champagne. I recognize him as one of the freshmen in Dax's frat. He offers, "Drinks?"

Avery takes two, hands them to Lilly and me, then grabs one for herself.

Dax and Bobby each take one too.

Avery holds her glass out and says, "To my new sisters," then she leans into us, asserting, "I know you're both going to make it through the night. Don't worry about anything. They'll try to scare you, but I promise there'll be no harm. It's just to ensure you're strong enough to be a sister. Because once you're one of us, it's a bond that will never be broken."

My stomach flips. *Why would they try to scare us?*

Dax chuckles. "Don't look so scared, you two. All sororities and frats try to scare you. There's nothing weak about either of you, right?"

Lilly laughs. "Nope! I'm not weak."

Dax turns toward me.

"No, I'm not either," I declare, telling myself again that I can and will do anything. Again, this is important to Dax. He claims it'll change my life. So why would I want to mess that up?

"That's right. You're not," he affirms.

"All right, you two, get out of here," Avery orders, taking her two fingers and motioning for Dax and Bobby to leave. "I have things to do with my soon-to-be sisters."

She slings her arms around Lilly's and my waist and leads us out of the room and up the stairs. She guides us down the hall and into a bedroom.

Cindy and Marcey stand in the room with flutes of champagne in their hands. They're both wearing little black dresses, just like Avery.

"You look amazing," Cindy gushes, coming up and sliding her fingers over my gold mesh skirt.

"Thanks," I reply. She's been nice, but I'm still cautious around her. She used to sleep with Dax, and I don't know how she could ever get over him, even if Avery has claimed several times she has. But she's not done anything since Avery warned her, so I should stop being hesitant around her.

Marcey steps up next to her. She reaches for my top and slides her finger over the side of my breast. "Wow, this material is amazing. Where did you get it?"

I ignore the fact that she touched my boob, telling myself it was innocent. I shrug. "I don't know. Dax got it for me."

"Of course he did," Avery says, and for a moment, I'm not sure how to take it. She adds, "He's so in love with you, all he thinks about is you. He's hiding several more boxes at my house to surprise you after tonight."

I arch my eyebrows. "He doesn't have to keep getting me gifts."

Avery puts her hand on her hip. "Yeah, he does. You're his woman."

I laugh.

"Plus, he's so proud of you." She smiles, opens her mouth, then shuts it.

"Is there something you want to say?" I question.

Her face brightens. She hesitates again, but her smile widens.

"What is it?" I ask.

She shakes her head. "I shouldn't tell you."

"Tell me what?" I fret.

She glances at the others.

"Avery!"

Marcey groans. "That's not fair, Avery. Tell her."

Avery releases a breath, then steps closer. Her floral scent flares around us. She lowers her voice and states, "You can't tell Dax I told you."

"Told me what?"

"Promise you won't tell him."

I blurt out, "We don't have secrets between us."

"You sure about that?" Cindy asks.

I snap my head toward her. I open my mouth, but Avery puts her fingers over it.

She softly laughs. "It's not bad."

I wait, my insides churning.

"Tell her," Marcey urges again.

Avery leans into my ear. Her hot breath hits my neck. She whispers, "I saw the ring."

My butterflies take off. I cautiously ask, "What ring?"

Avery moves her face in front of mine, her expression full of excitement. She reiterates, "*The* ring."

I freeze.

She adds, "Tonight's going to be perfect. Every man in our family has married a Gamma Sigma Phi since the early 1900s. Now that you're going to be one...well..."

I gape at her, my heart soaring.

She continues, "It's gorgeous. Dax helped design it."

My butterflies flutter harder.

"You have to promise not to say anything to Dax. He's saving it for Christmas."

I continue to stare at her, my jaw on the floor.

She urges, "Promise me!"

I nod, barely getting out, "I promise."

Dax wants to marry me!

Avery claps. "Not only will we be Gamma sisters, but we'll be real sisters once you two get hitched!"

I grin bigger than I ever have. "That'll be awesome."

"Yeah it will!" she affirms, hugging me, then adds, "Just make sure you get into the Gammas. My father won't let anyone into our family who isn't one!"

Anxiety flares in my gut.

Dax's voice floods my head. *Do whatever it takes.*

It all makes sense why he was so adamant I get in.

Giddiness fills me.

"Okay, time to get ready. Oh, I need you to sign this really quick." Cindy grabs a clipboard off the desk. There's a ton of paper on it with several sign-here stickers attached in different places.

"What's this?" I ask.

Cindy waves her hand. "Just the normal paperwork that you're going to agree to abide by the rules, that you know the sisterhood song, that whatever happens in our sorority is confidential, and blah, blah, blah. We can't break the circle of trust now, can we?"

"No, of course not," Lilly answers.

"Great." She holds a pen out to me. "Sign it so I can take it downstairs."

This all seems silly to me, but it is what it is. I quickly glance at the paperwork and start signing, initialing that I know the pledge. The next form declares I know the song, and I soon tire of reading stupid forms. I blurt out, "This seems a little excessive."

Avery scoffs. "Yep! Don't waste your time reading it all. It's boring shit."

"Here." Cindy opens each page to where I have to sign or initial.

I stop scanning and just initial and sign my name where needed. When I'm done, Cindy sets it down and grabs another clipboard. "Your turn, Lilly."

Lilly signs.

Cindy grabs the clipboard with my papers on it. "I'm going to take this downstairs. See you later." She leaves.

"So what's next?" Lilly questions.

"Well, you know that our brotherhood frat, Alpha Omega Tau, is here tonight, right?" Avery answers.

My stomach flips. I'm unsure why. I question, "The entire frat?"

"Yep. They're always at our rush parties, just like we're at theirs. Oh, don't worry. Their party's next week, and you're going to have the front row sitting next to me because you're going to be part of the sisterhood," Avery beams again.

A mix of excitement and uneasiness fills me. Part of me wants this. But part of me still is unsure.

I have to be a Gamma to marry into Dax's family.

He designed my ring!

His voice pops into my head again. *"Promise me you'll do anything to get in."*

I push away the uneasiness and focus on my excitement.

"Awesome, I love frat parties," Lilly states.

Marcey laughs. "Yeah, we've seen you at enough by now."

I'm unsure what she means. I've only been to the one frat party with Dax. He's not taken me to anymore, but most of the time we spend together, we're wrapped up in each other, and I'd much rather do that than go to any party.

Marcey states, "Are you going to give it to them or wait all night?"

"Hold your horses," Avery reprimands, then steps into a closet. She comes out with two big boxes. "These are for both of you."

They have bows on them, but it's the type of box where you just lift the lid. So Lilly and I remove the lids and pull out matching skimpy thongs and bras. The soft red crocheted material reminds me of the whore red polish Dax loves me to wear.

"It matches your nails perfectly," Avery points out.

I glance at the lingerie and declare, "This is beautiful."

Dax is going to love me in this.

"Okay, what are you waiting for? Put it on," Marcey orders.

I stare at the see-through material and gaze at her. "Now?"

"Yes, now."

"But—"

Avery puts her finger over my lips. "You can't argue tonight, Ivy. Whatever we say, you have to do it. Please don't ask questions. There's nothing to be scared of. Remember, I have your back," she says, but there's a pleading look in her eyes.

I stay quiet.

She adds, "Dax and I need you in the sisterhood."

Lilly announces, "I'll put it on. This is gorgeous."

I look at the risqué bra and thong. I finally voice, "I don't think Dax will like me walking around in this."

Avery claims, "Dax picked it out for you."

"He did?"

"Yes. Every pledge has to wear something similar, but he made sure he picked this out."

I stare at it again, not understanding why Dax would want me on display for all to see.

Marcey interjects, "You get more than I did. I only got a pair of thongs."

"Me too," Avery says.

"Really?" I question.

She nods. "Yep. Dax insisted you get a bra too."

I'm suddenly grateful Dax picked this skimpy outfit for me to wear.

Marcey's alarm on her phone rings. She turns it off and states, "Time is ticking. Get dressed, ladies."

Marcey and Avery take seats on the armchairs across from Lilly and me, sipping champagne.

Lilly and I remove our clothes and put on the lingerie. I'm slightly uncomfortable with Marcey and Avery watching me, but I push it away, telling myself I'm being ridiculous.

There's a knock on the door.

Another server from Dax's frat comes inside, wearing the same silver thong and matching bow tie. He carries another tray of champagne and hands me one. "Bobby said to give you this."

My nerves reappear. Ever since Bobby kissed me, I don't fully trust him. But he's Dax's best friend, so I'm trying to let the incident at the frat party go.

"Perfect timing," Marcey says, grabbing two drinks and handing them to Lilly and Avery. Then she grabs one for herself.

"Can I get you anything else?" he asks.

Avery steps up to him. She puts her hand on his bicep. "Your name's Brad, right?"

He glances at her like he wants to eat her up and nods. "Yeah."

"Your father runs the oil company in Texas?"

"Yes, ma'am," he says in a thick drawl.

"Hmm," she says, dragging her fingers across his chest and down the side of his torso.

He swallows hard.

"How do you like Connecticut so far?" she questions.

"Right now, I'm loving it," he answers, his lips twitching.

She slides her hand down, stopping on the front of his thigh near his cock.

He glances down at it, then back at her.

"Good. I hope you pass your initiation next week."

He nods. "I will. Just for you," he says and then winks.

She steps back and then motions for him to leave the room.

He turns and walks away, shutting the door behind him.

"Well, he's a sexy piece of Texas," Marcey states.

Avery spins back to us. "Sure is. All right, ladies." She holds her glass up again. "To my soon-to-be sisters."

We clink glasses, and I take a sip. Lilly downs half her glass, as does Marcey and Cindy.

Marcey nods. "Drink up, Ivy. We have to go soon."

I finish the champagne, and within seconds, my nerves disappear.

I'm going to be Mrs. Dax Carrington!

Cindy reappears, directing us to leave the room. She leads us down the stairs and through the main room, but nobody's in it.

"Where is everybody?" I question.

"We can't tell you that," Marcey answers, then leads us down the staircase into the basement.

It's dark. I've never been down here before, but it's set up as a theater with dozens of seats. Smoke, similar to that at the frat party Dax took me to, hangs thick in the air. The smell of alcohol mixes with the haze, but I can't see anybody in the chairs. Still, I know they're there.

My nerves reappear.

Avery leads us through the darkness and up four steps. My heels click on a wood floor. I barely make out a curtain in front of us.

"Lilly, did you memorize your script?" Marcey asks.

"Yes. I was up all night, but I have it down," she answers.

"What script?" I question.

Avery pulls me aside. "Every sister has to do this. You might not want to, Ivy, but it's just one night. It's just one scene. And if you get through it, you'll pass the first stage. You won't ever have to do it again. But you'll be judged on your performance and how accepting you are."

My gut dives. I question, "How accepting?"

"Yes." She sighs. "When we pulled the cards..."

More anxiety fills me. "What cards?"

She pulls me farther away from the others, replying, "Let me explain how this works. The sisters get together, and there are different cards of scenes. Every single pledge has to act out a scene. You and Lilly got paired together."

My mouth turns dry. "And what's my scene?"

"Well, when they pulled the card, it said we had to keep you in suspense."

"I'm not following, Avery."

She studies me, making me more nervous, then confesses, "Crap. Ivy, when they pulled the card, I knew you wouldn't like it."

My insides quiver. I repeat, "Avery, what's the scene?"

"Just remember that you only have to do this once and then you'll be a sister for life. Dax is right. It's worth doing anything you have to do because we'll always have your back. You'll get places in life you would never be without the connections here. Plus..."

My heart races faster. "Plus what?"

Her eyes light up. "My father will be able to give Dax his blessing to marry you even though you don't come from a prominent family."

My insides quiver. I gape at her.

She sighs. "It's not fair, Ivy. I know it's not, but this is how my family works. Even with our wealth, we still need these connections. It's why Dax is in the frat and I'm in this sorority."

I stand speechless.

"Ivy, I'm telling you, I just need you to play this scene,

okay?" She puts her hand on my arm. "I promise you every-thing will be fine. You'll have the entire world at your fingertips."

"Avery, what's the scene?" I ask again, my voice shaking.

She releases a heavy breath. "You're surprised and unsure, but then realize it's what you actually want."

"What do I want?" I question, my gut spinning faster.

"You want Lilly."

WORLD AT YOUR FINGERTIPS

Ivy

Avery's floral scent swirls around me, making me slightly dizzy. She steps closer. "It's not a big deal. Just go do it."

I open my mouth, but nothing comes out.

Avery adds, "You're not fucking her. Just so you know, it won't go that far."

"How far is it going to go?" I ask.

Am I contemplating doing this?

No. I'm not doing it.

"Just a little bit of petting. It's just acting," Avery insists.

"Why do I have to act? I'm not an actress."

Sympathy fills her expression. "Ivy, everyone has to do this. We all get scenes. My scene was..." She shakes her head.

"Your scene was what?"

"Nothing. I'll tell you about it once tonight's over, but I

can't tell you before. I would break my oath to the Gammas if I told you before you were sworn in."

My chest tightens further.

"I've already disclosed too much, but I've done it because..."

I stay quiet.

She puts her hand on my heart. The bottom of her palm touches my tit.

I inhale sharply.

She says, "Dax loves you. You know how good that feels, right?"

"Yes, of course," I admit.

"Okay. You're going to have dozens of sisters loving you too. Women who will do anything to help you and make sure you're okay at every stage of your life. Isn't that what you want?"

I ponder her question.

"It's not?" she asks with sadness in her eyes.

"No, that's what I want," I confess.

"Good. Hold on a minute." She disappears for a quick second.

I stare into the darkness around me. My heart pounds harder.

She returns and hands me a shot. "Here. One final toast to you."

She clinks my glass and shoots hers back.

I hesitate, then empty the glass. The warm, sweet liquid slides down my throat and into my stomach.

Avery puts her hand on my arm again. "I got you something too. I want to give it to you."

"What is it?"

She steps behind me and moves my hair over my right shoulder. Then she dangles a gold necklace in front of my face.

It's an I with a vine of ivy leaves wrapping around it.

Her breath hits the back of my ear, and a shiver full of tingles runs down my spine. "I had it made for you when Dax designed your ring. Do you like it?"

"I love it," I gush, touched she'd make something so personal for me.

She whispers, "You're already my sister forever." She secures the necklace and then steps back in front of me.

I'm overwhelmed. I touch the pendant. "Avery, this is too much."

She shakes her head. "No, it's not. Ivy, please tell me you'll do the scene. I really want you in Gamma Sigma Phi. We're going to have so much fun!"

I take a deep breath, double-checking, "I don't have to fuck Lilly?"

She shakes her head. "No. Of course not."

I release a breath. "Okay, but I don't understand what part I'm playing."

She glances around and says, "I can't disclose much. Your character is supposed to be confused about your sexuality. That's all I can tell you. But, like you said, you're not a real actress, right?"

I giggle. Maybe it's the alcohol or my nerves. I reply, "No, I'm not."

Avery chirps, "Then it should be easy for you to play the part."

I sigh.

"Please do it. It's just a quick scene," she pleads.

I touch the pendant again, giving in. "Okay. What's my name?"

"Ivy."

Ivy?

"I don't get a different name for my character?" I question, still trying to believe I'm even contemplating doing this.

Avery laughs. "No. We've changed names in the past, but it's harder for non-actors to remember them. The sisters decided it's easier for those rushing to play their parts if they're just called by their real names."

I release a deep, anxious breath.

"So you're going to do it? You're going to become my sister for life?" she asks with excitement in her eyes.

I can't believe I'm going to do this.

Dax's voice pops into my head. *"Promise me you'll do whatever it takes to get in."*

I answer, "Okay, Avery. I'll do it."

She claps. "Good. Once tonight's over, you'll have everything you've always wanted. I promise. Plus, you know how excited Dax is going to be. It will break his heart if you can't get into Gamma Sigma Phi."

I glance down at my outfit. "Are you sure he's not going to be upset that I'm prancing around in this?" I ask, revealing my insecurities.

She scoffs. "Yeah, he bought it for you. He's dying to see you in it. Don't you understand?"

"Understand what?"

She traces the edge of the bra, and once again, tingles explode along my skin.

It's the alcohol.

"Dax wants to show you off. And he's never wanted to show anyone off before. You've changed him."

"Changed him? I don't want to change him," I declare.

"Not in a bad way, silly. In a good way."

"How?"

"I don't know. I can't explain it. He's just... Well, he's so in love with you. And he's so proud that you're his."

I smile.

She hesitates, then says, "Ivy, can I say something without you turning weird on me?"

My butterflies slowly flutter. "Sure."

"Promise?"

I nod. "I promise."

Anxiety fills her expression.

"It's okay. Say whatever you want," I push.

She blurts out, "I find you very attractive, Ivy. That day that I wanted you to kiss me... Well, I wanted you to kiss me because I wanted to see what it was like—what Dax was so obsessed about, but I already understood it. You're gorgeous. You're different from everybody else around here, and that's... Well, you're just a treasure. And I'm not saying this so you kiss me. I'm just telling you the truth."

I gape at her. Avery is the gorgeous one. She has everyone eating out of her hand too. Since we've become friends, I've realized that if I could be more like anyone, it would be her.

She drags her finger over my cleavage and down to my belly button.

I freeze, except for the throbbing in my pussy.

She leans closer. "If you were into girls, I would take you away from Dax."

I stare at her.

She giggles. "I told you not to get weird."

My butterflies flutter harder, confusing me.

She giggles again. "Don't get weird. I know we're just friends. But I'm telling you because you need to own your power. And Dax is proud of you, so you need to go out there and strut it and not show any signs of homophobia, okay?"

"I'm not a homophobe," I state.

"I know you're not. But you have to go prove it to the sisterhood."

"They think I'm a homophobe?" I ask in horror.

She glances around us, then lowers her voice, admitting, "Only two girls think that."

"Who?" I question.

"I can't tell you. But they heard about what happened on the lake the first day you met Marcey and Cindy. It was before we were friends. I'm sorry. It's my fault. Please don't be mad at me." Her eyes turn glassy.

My insides rage. I hate remembering how they called me a homophobe. I reaffirm, "I'm not a homophobe."

"I know you're not. So go out there, play the role, and show the sorority you're not. When tonight's over, you'll be in the sisterhood. You and Dax will own the campus. And my father will welcome you into our family with open arms."

Something about owning the campus with Dax excites me. I don't know why. I've never needed to be prom queen or even popular. But knowing Dax's family will welcome me makes me determined to do whatever it takes to become a Gamma.

A bell rings.

Avery leans into my ear, and more tingles appear under her hot breath. "I'll give you a final piece of advice if you want."

"Please do."

"Pretend you're kissing Dax. That's all you have to do. Pretend that Lilly is Dax."

I swallow hard at the thought of kissing Lilly.

She puts her fingers over my lips, firmly restating, "Ivy, pretend Lilly is Dax."

A tense moment passes, and the bell rings again. She chirps, "Got to go. You're going to do great." She gives me a quick peck on the lips, surprising me, and takes off before I can say anything.

Nervousness floods me. I want to run, but my brain won't let me. My feet won't move.

I have to do this.

It's just a stupid scene.

Lights turn on, peeking through the curtains, and a girl's voice says in the microphone, "Time to start. Will the actresses please take the stage?"

I remain frozen in place.

Lilly steps next to me and grabs my hand. "Come on, Ivy, let's get this over with."

I turn toward her. "You're okay with this?"

She shrugs. "Yeah. No big deal. Let's get it done and then we'll be part of the sisterhood forever."

I bite my lip, shifting on my feet.

She adds, "My father's a senator. You know that, right?"

I nod. "Of course."

"He claims the most important thing is that I get into this sorority because it'll change my life. So if he's saying that, this is important for us in our future, okay?"

I say nothing.

She adds, "Besides, it doesn't mean anything. We're just going to go act."

I finally agree. "Okay. You're right."

"Great. All right, go out first. I'll follow soon," she instructs.

I take a deep breath, willing my legs to stay steady, listening to my heels click against the wood. I peer past the curtain, looking for Dax, but all I can see are the top of heads, no faces. The lights are too bright.

It's now or never.

Don't do it.

I force myself to walk across the stage. It's so quiet you could hear a pin drop.

Pretend she's Dax.

Do what Avery would do.

I fix my expression to one that I feel she would use, then try to appear sexy and confident, strutting across the stage until I reach a standing-height table without chairs. My pulse skyrockets when I see the bed and couch several feet away. I grip the edge of the table, and my knees wobble.

Lilly steps out from behind the curtain in the same outfit I'm in, and I can't help but wonder, *How does everyone see her compared to me?*

Her breasts are flawless, at least two sizes bigger than mine. Her body's a lot like Avery's. There's no fat on it anywhere. Her long red hair swings in perfection as she walks.

Lilly's green gaze narrows as she struts across the stage and stops as close to me as possible. She picks up a martini glass and hands it to me. "Thanks for making my favorite drink, Ivy."

My insides quiver. I take it from her, grateful for a distraction.

She picks up the other one and clinks it against mine. "To tonight."

"Tonight?" I question, my voice cracking, unsure what to say. I drink more than normal until half the martini is gone.

"Yeah. Tonight." Lilly kisses my shoulder, then takes a sip.

A shiver runs down my spine. I giggle, then nervously stutter, "Wh-what are y-you doing?"

She sets her glass down, swallows hard, and grazes her fingers over my hand. She declares, "I have to admit something to you, Ivy."

My chest tightens, and my voice shakes. "What's that?"

She drags her palm up my arm, over my neck, and onto my cheek. Nerves fill her expression. She blinks hard a few times and states, "You're one of the most beautiful women I've ever met."

My mouth turns dry. I swallow hard.

She steps closer, and her scent smells just like Avery's. It's intoxicating, like always, and my core lights up. My breath begins to turn shallow. My heart races faster.

Lilly steps closer, and her tits graze mine.

I inhale sharply. My insides tremble.

She begs with desperation in her voice, "Ivy, tell me you feel it too. I know you've never been with a woman, but tell me you feel this between us."

"I..." I can't complete my sentence, overwhelmed by Avery's scent and Lilly's intense gaze.

What is happening?

She slides her hand over my stomach, and zings fly to my core.

I squeeze my thighs together.

She steps even closer. Her mouth moves an inch from mine. She confesses, "I dream about doing a lot of things with you. Do you want to know what they are?"

I gape at her, paralyzed.

She takes her finger and traces my lips.

I stand there like a moron, doing nothing.

She takes my hand, instructing, "Come with me, Ivy." She tugs me.

I follow, almost falling.

She steadies me, teasing, "Maybe we'll lay off the drinks a little bit, huh?"

I nervously giggle. "Yeah, that would be good."

When she's assured that I'm on my feet, she leads me to the bed and says, "Here, sit. This is more comfortable."

I obey, and my butterflies reappear.

Instead of sitting beside me, Lilly straddles me, putting both knees beside my hips.

I fret, "What are you doing?"

"Shh," she purrs, sliding her hand into my hair and leaning

close to my ear, murmuring, "Pretend I'm Dax. Let's get through this. It's just a scene."

She's right.

I bite on my lip.

She moves her finger down my neck to my chest and then slowly swirls it around my nipple.

It hardens, and my pussy clenches.

I'm not into girls, I scold myself.

"Ivy, I know you want me too. Don't be scared. Just tell me you want me," she demands.

I open my mouth, but once again, I can't speak.

She whispers in my ear while sliding her hand over the curve of my waist, "Ivy, play your role. It'll be over soon." She gives me a look, urging me to agree, and breathlessly begs, "Please tell me you want me."

It'll be over soon.

I blurt out, "I do."

"You do what, Ivy?" she questions, moving her hand between us.

Pretend she's Dax.

Be Avery.

I lift my chin and purse my lips, staring at her.

"I need to hear it," she says, her hot breath merging with mine.

"I want you, Lilly," I lie.

Her lips curve as she quickly kisses me.

I stare at her, my heart beating so fast I think it might push out of my chest.

She drags her finger over my spine, beaming. "That wasn't so bad, was it?"

I shake my head and giggle.

Why was I worried?

That wasn't a big deal.

She surprises me, once again pressing her mouth to mine and flicking her tongue with urgency against mine.

I freeze.

"She's a homophobe," a girl declares from the crowd, reminding me we're on a stage.

"I'm not—" I try to turn my head.

Lilly firmly grasps my hair, holding my head so I can't move, and whispers in my ear, "It's just a part, Ivy. Don't give her the satisfaction." Then she slides her tongue back into my mouth.

"Homophobe," the girl hurls again.

My insides quiver.

Pretend it's Dax.

I force myself to kiss Lilly back.

She tightens her hold on me, and I do my best to kiss her how I would kiss Dax.

She moves her fingers between us and grazes the top of my thong, kissing me deeper until my head spins, and I whimper.

Endorphins rush through me.

She grinds her lower body. The heat from her pussy penetrates mine. She pushes me back.

I lose my balance, falling to the mattress. She never takes her mouth off mine.

I close my eyes, my body throbbing, confused as to why I'm not disgusted. I tell myself to end this, but I don't do anything to stop her from kissing me.

Lilly moves her mouth down my neck to my breasts and licks my nipple.

"Oh God," I murmur and slide my hand in her hair, pushing her against me just like I do Dax.

As more adrenaline hits me, her mouth moves lower, and she kisses my pussy through the crocheted material.

What am I doing?

I push her away, sit up in the bed, and scoot back, a cold chill running down my spine.

She jerks upward. Her face falls. "Ivy, what's wrong?"

I glance toward the stage, looking for Dax, wanting him to save me, and wondering why I'm doing this.

Dax 26

PASS THE TEST

My dick strains against my zipper. I don't think I've ever been so hard watching any two girls go at it.

Not that Ivy let it get too far, but she still got farther than I thought she would.

Her eyes turn glassy. Her lip quivers. She gazes at Lilly as Lilly stares at her in confusion.

Jesus, Lilly plays her part perfectly.

Lilly reaches for Ivy and says, "Your—"

I clap and shout, "Bravo!" as loud as possible to stop the scene.

The others in the room soon follow until I can't hear my own applause.

Bobby looks at me, accusing, "What the fuck are you doing? It's just getting good."

"Chill out. The night is young," I remind him, knowing I

need to get Ivy off that stage. It was hot, but I can't take her tormented look anymore.

At least not in this public setting.

The room gets louder, and the lights turn on.

Ivy turns and stares with a tear dripping down her cheek.

Lilly beams on stage next to her.

The entire frat and sorority stand, clapping louder and whistling, but I can tell Ivy's petrified and confused.

It doesn't give me the satisfaction I thought it would.

Ivy searches the crowd and finally pins her gaze on mine.

I smile at her in approval, continuing to clap, which helps ease her anxiety.

Avery interrupts our stare off, stepping next to the girls and declaring, "That was brilliant, both of you. Pass or fail?" she yells out to the crowd. Almost everyone yells, "Pass."

A few of the bitchiest sisters shout, "Fail."

My gut sinks.

Ivy furrows her eyebrows and puts one arm over her chest, trying to cover herself.

Avery shrugs. "Time for a vote. Pass, raise your hand, sisters."

All of the sisters raise their hands except for two.

Avery adds, "Fail, raise your hands."

The bitches raise their hands.

Avery turns back toward Ivy and Lilly, beaming. "You've passed the first test. Congratulations, ladies."

The room erupts in applause again.

Avery helps Ivy off the mattress and slides her arm around her. She moves her off the stage, and Lilly follows.

Step two.

What am I doing?

My gut tightens, mixing with endorphins, and I don't

know why I feel like this. This normally makes me beyond giddy.

"Are you going to puss out?" Bobby questions as if he can read my thoughts.

I scowl. "Of course I'm not going to puss out. Shut the fuck up," I bark and move through the crowd.

Bobby follows close on my heels, and we go up the stairs.

At the top, I glance around, but Ivy's not there. I have to give my sister credit. She knows our routine better than I do sometimes.

I nod at Bobby, and we move down the hall and into the den, not bothering to knock.

We walk in as Avory chirps, "That was perfect, Ivy. Really."

Ivy frets, "I don't know."

Bobby begins to clap. "That was perfection, you two. Good little sluts!"

Ivy looks at him in horror.

That's right. I'm the only one that gets to call you a slut, I think to myself in satisfaction. I love how she hates it when Bobby says it but loves it when I do.

"Do you need a minute?" Avery asks Ivy with concern in her expression.

Ivy arches her eyebrows. "A minute for what?"

"To move forward."

Ivy blinks hard, then glances at me. I rush over to her and tug her into my arms, stroking her back, gloating, "I'm so proud of you. You were amazing up there. So strong. Those bitches who said fail can eat shit."

She softly laughs.

I add, "I promise you, tonight's going to change your life forever."

"I-I..." she stutters, her lip quivering.

"I can't tell you how proud of you I am," I repeat, sliding my lips against hers.

She clings to me tightly.

I kiss her with everything I have, over and over again until her body melts against mine and she's whimpering. I murmur against her lips, "That's my baby girl. You looked fucking gorgeous up there."

She hesitates and asks, "You're not mad at me?"

I chuckle. "No, why would I be mad? You played that part perfectly."

"I did?"

"Yeah."

Her lips slowly curve. "I—"

I put my fingers over her mouth, stating, "Ivy, stop trying to explain anything. You played the part perfectly. You passed the test. You're one step closer to being a Gamma Sigma Phi. I'm so proud that you were mine up there."

She blinks hard, takes a deep breath, and nods. "You were?"

"Yeah, baby girl. And this outfit..." I slowly lower my eyes, checking her out. "Fuck."

Her expression lights up.

And we're back on track.

I shouldn't be doing this.

Stop being a pussy.

I slide my hand around her waist and turn, tugging her closer. I offer, "Lilly, you did a good job too. Congratulations."

She grins. "Thanks. Ivy, you're not mad at me, right?"

It takes Ivy a second to answer her question. She shakes her head. "No."

Lilly releases a breath, but I know it's fake. She loved every minute of that scene. "I'm glad. I wouldn't want you to be mad, especially because we're going to be sisters for life."

Ivy nods, and I kiss her on the forehead.

"It's time for round two," Avery sings, catching my eye quickly, then redirecting her gaze between Ivy and Lilly.

"What's round two?" Ivy nervously asks.

Avery shrugs. "I don't know. I have to go ask the sisterhood."

"Why don't you know?" Lilly questions.

"That's how tonight rolls, ladies. I'll be right back." She steps in front of Ivy again and grabs her hand. She pins her admiring expression on her and softens her voice. "You really were amazing up there."

Ivy swallows and then softly replies, "Thanks."

Avery squeezes her hand and then leaves the room.

I kiss Ivy again, trying to make her forget what just happened so she's ready for the next portion of the evening.

It'll change her life forever.

That's the game.

I shouldn't let her do this.

Marcey and Cindy come into the room. Cindy cheers, "Bravo!"

"Yeah, that was fucking hot," Marcey declares.

"Well, I'm glad I pleased you ladies," Lilly chirps.

Bobby reiterates, "Oh, you pleased us all right. Every dick in that room was hard."

Ivy shifts on her feet.

I tug her closer and murmur in her ear, "Every dick in that room was hard knowing they can't have you because I do."

She turns toward me, her face flushing deeper, and gives me her innocent smile.

I repeat, "I really am proud of you. You were fucking amazing up there."

She takes a deep breath.

One of the new freshmen rushing our frat enters the room.

He's wearing the same silver thong and bow tie as the other servers. He has a tray of drinks with smoke rising off them.

"What's this?" I ask, pretending I don't know, but I've had it often.

"Rum & Smoke. I was told that only those who survive get it," he answers.

"These are good, Ivy. You're going to love this," Lilly declares.

I pick one up and hand it to her. Everyone else takes one, and I grab one for myself. I hold my glass in the air. "To passing the first test and being one step closer to making all your dreams come true."

Everybody clinks the shots together.

I instruct Ivy, "Don't sip it. Take it all at once." She nods, and we all toss our shots back. The alcohol travels down my throat and warms my belly. I get an instant buzz. It's the strongest alcohol we have, and it's guaranteed to give Ivy more liquid courage to do what I want her to do next.

Avery returns to the room almost as if on cue, announcing, "They're eliminating all the other steps for you two."

"Really?" Ivy questions.

"Why is that?" Lilly asks.

"Well, all but one," Avery adds.

"So then we only have to do one more thing, and then we're sisters?" Lilly questions excitedly.

"Yes. You two got lucky. You just get to have fun in this next part."

"We do?" Ivy asks with relief in her voice.

"Yeah."

"So what do we have to do?" Lilly inquires.

"Bobby, Lilly, Dax, Ivy—you're to stay in this room until the sun rises," Avery states.

"And?" I question, as if I don't know what's going to happen.

She drops the bomb. "Bobby's in charge. Everyone has to follow his orders and do whatever he wants."

Ivy glances around the room at the couches and several pieces of sex furniture that I'm pretty sure she has no idea what are used for. Fear takes over her expression.

"Sounds fun." Lilly smirks.

Avery motions to Cindy and Marcey. "Come on, ladies. Let's leave them alone so they can finish their rush requirements."

Marcey and Cindy follow Avery out of the room, and the door shuts. The click of the lock fills the air.

For the first time ever, the hairs on my neck rise.

Ivy grabs my arm.

Bobby goes over to the stereo and turns on the music. He goes to the bar, fills four glasses with scotch, and sets them on a tray. He brings it back over to us.

"I'm okay," Ivy says.

Lilly giggles. "Nope! We have to do whatever Bobby wants!"

"Seriously? Why does Bobby get to make the decisions?" I complain. But once again, I'm full of shit. It's exactly the way we rehearsed this.

"I think I'm okay," Ivy says.

"Uh, uh, uh," Bobby says, wiggling his finger. "I'm in charge."

"Bobby," I warn, knowing Ivy's probably close to her limit. I really don't think she needs any more.

He sets the tray on the table and crosses his arms. "You're forgetting who's in charge."

"Bobby," I warn again, giving him a look.

One thing Bobby and I utilize is alcohol to loosen up the

coeds. But we can agree we don't want them so drunk they can't consent to what they're doing.

He concedes. "Fine, you can drink half of it, Ivy. But, Dax, you take the rest. Don't abuse our alcohol."

I clench my jaw.

Maybe this wasn't a good idea.

Of course this wasn't a good idea.

What was I thinking?

Stop being a pussy. This is exactly what was always supposed to happen.

I encourage Ivy. "Come on, baby, a few sips and then you're done for the night."

She steps in front of Bobby. Something hard forms in her expression. She leans down, picks up a drink, and downs it, then tries to hide her grimace.

His face erupts in approval. He claps. "Bravo."

She sets the glass down and struts over to the stereo. She turns up the volume. "If we're going to be in here, we might as well have some fun."

I grin. "That's my baby girl."

Lilly steps next to Ivy and grabs her hand. She starts to wiggle her hips, and the two dance.

Bobby and I sit on the couch so we're practically touching.

"Ivy," I call out, curling my finger.

Bobby does the same and directs Lilly, "Get your hot ass over here."

Lilly and Ivy giggle, strutting across the room, and it's clear Ivy is now officially drunk.

I pat my lap, and Ivy straddles me.

Lilly does the same with Bobby.

I swirl my finger over Ivy's tit. "I think this one's sad and needs attention."

She giggles. "Why?"

"Well, Lilly only paid attention to the other one, didn't she?"

A flush builds on Ivy's cheeks, and her face falls. She quickly glances at Lilly and Bobby, who stare at her. She turns back toward me.

"Suck her tit, Dax," Bobby states.

Before she can resist, I sink my mouth over her tit, sliding my tongue between the mesh and circling it, then adding just enough suction.

She shivers and whimpers. I suck her harder and tug her pussy closer to my cock.

"Fuck, that's hot," Bobby says.

I stop and look at him to remind Ivy that he's in the room, ensuring she's uncomfortable.

"That is hot," Lilly agrees.

I stroke Ivy's back. "My baby girl isn't just hot. She's sexy as fuck and my dirty slut. Isn't she?"

Ivy's cheeks turn redder.

"Yes, she is," Bobby states.

Lilly nods, adding, "Plus, she's a great kisser."

"I am?" Ivy asks.

"Of course you are," I declare, tugging her closer.

"Show me again how you two kiss," Bobby orders.

"Wh-what?" Ivy splutters.

I continue to stroke her back and assure her, "It's okay. We have to do what Bobby says, remember? Besides, you already kissed Lilly. It's not a big deal."

She furrows her brows, staring at me.

"Come on, baby girl. We need to get through this."

"But I already kissed her. I passed that test," Ivy protests.

Bobby grunts. "Yeah, and this is the second test. I want to see it again. Unless you think you're better than Lilly?"

Ivy jerks her head back. "Of course I don't."

"You don't think she's beautiful?"

"Of course she's beautiful," Ivy confirms.

He orders, "Then just lean over and kiss her. Come on."

Ivy glances at me again.

I encourage, "It's okay, baby girl. It's so fucking hot."

"Don't be a prude," Bobby tosses out.

Ivy blinks and bites her lip.

I lean into her ear. "Be my sexy slut. I really want to see you kiss her while you're on my lap." I pull back and stroke her cheek.

"You do?" she quietly asks.

I grab her hand and put it on my cock. "Yeah."

Lilly giggles. "Come on, Ivy, let's show him how it's done. What do you say?"

Fire lights in Ivy's eyes.

I kiss her on the lips, mumbling, "It'll make me so fucking hard. Will you show me again?"

Her lips slowly curve. "Okay. For you, Dax."

My dick throbs.

She glances down at it and then her lips twist. It reminds me of Avery, which turns me off for a brief moment. Ivy turns toward Lilly.

Lilly puts her hand on Ivy's leg, and Ivy sharply inhales.

I put my hand on Ivy's back and slowly push her toward Lilly.

She slides her hands on Ivy's face, and within seconds she presses her mouth to hers.

Ivy tenses at first, but I stroke her back with my thumb. "That's it, baby girl. Be my little whore."

She relaxes and kisses Lilly.

I move my hand to her lingerie top and unhook it. It falls between her and Lilly. I slide it out and toss it on the floor.

Bobby does the same with Lilly's bra, and I catch his eye, but then we both gaze back at the women.

Bobby declares, "Fuck, that's hot. Now, Ivy, touch Lilly's tit."

Ivy stops. Her panicked expression reappears.

"You have to do what I say," Bobby reminds her.

Ivy glances at me with ragged breath.

"You're fucking making me so hard, my little slut. It's okay. I'm so proud of you. Go ahead, do what he says."

Ivy's glassy expression morphs, but I'm unsure what to make of it.

"It's okay. I'll touch yours too. Then you're not the only one," Lilly coyly suggests.

"Yes, do that," Bobby states.

I groan. "Fuck, that's hot. God, I wish you understood how fucking sexy you are," I reiterate.

She turns back toward Lilly and reaches for her breasts.

Lilly puts her fingers on Ivy's.

I put my hand on Ivy's head and push her toward Lilly's, and they're soon making out again.

I slide my hand down around Ivy's waist and slide my finger underneath the mesh, stroking her clit.

She whimpers.

I hold her head firm so she can't escape Lilly's kiss.

Bobby does the same with Lilly, sliding his hand around her body and into her delicate thong as well.

We rub their clits, and both of them begin to moan, the intensity of their kisses growing.

Ivy shudders first, her body rolling into an orgasm, her thumb caressing Lilly's tit.

Then Lilly joins Ivy, trembling into a high.

Bobby's expression darkens. He glances at me quickly before refocusing on the girls.

The night's just beginning. It's everything I've been planning since I laid eyes on Ivy. My dick has never been harder.

Their cries intensify, and I murmur into Ivy's ear, "Say it."

She mumbles against Lilly's mouth, "I'm your dirty slut, Dax."

Bobby grins and then yanks on Lilly's thong until it snaps.

She yelps into Ivy's mouth, arching her breasts into her.

Bobby's wicked expression grows. He declares, "Let the games begin."

A mix of endorphins and hesitation fills me. It's never happened before.

Bobby nods.

I take a deep breath, yank Ivy's panties until they rip, and tell myself to stop being a pussy.

REMIND ME THAT YOU'RE MINE

Ivy

"Oh!" I gasp as Dax snaps my thong off my body. He holds my head firmly, and Lilly's tongue flicks back into my mouth. He circles my clit quickly, and everything spins with a new high.

Adrenaline pounds through my cells. Endorphins explode so intensely that I almost black out.

"Fuck, my little slut. No one's as sexy as you," Dax murmurs in my ear.

Lilly's tits slide against mine, but I'm no longer worried. I'm too engaged in what's happening to even think. Plus, Dax continues to encourage me, praising me every step of the way, his cock hard against my pussy.

"I am so glad you're not a prude," Bobby booms, pulling me out of my trance.

Dax's hands pause, and I retreat from Lilly.

I glare at Bobby. "Stop calling me a prude. I'm not."

"I said I'm glad you're not," he reiterates, his lips twisting in a mischievous grin.

Dax kisses my shoulder, and tingles run down my spine. "Ivy's not a prude. She's my sexy little slut, aren't you, baby girl?"

Heat flares hotter on my cheeks. I quickly glance at Lilly and Bobby, then back at Dax.

He's never called me a slut or a whore in front of anyone before. It takes me a minute to recover.

He strokes my cheek. "My sexy slut."

"Lilly's a good little slut too, aren't you, baby?" Bobby chimes in.

She giggles and then squeezes my breast. "Yeah, it's way more fun being that than a prude, right?"

I glance back at her.

She smiles bigger.

She continues, "I don't understand why people are prudes. Life is so much better having orgasms, isn't it, Ivy?"

I can't deny her statement. I nod. "Yeah."

Bobby moves Lilly off of him and rises, ordering, "Ivy, come here."

My stomach flips. I move closer to Dax, my pulse skyrocketing.

Bobby shakes his head. "You don't take directions very well. You're supposed to do what I say and not ask questions. Now, stop being scared. Come here."

"Go ahead, baby girl," Dax directs, squeezing my ass.

I stare at him.

He chuckles. "Well, go on. Don't piss Bobby off when he's in charge."

"Yeah. Don't piss me off, Ivy," he practically sings.

Lilly groans. "You're such a control freak."

"I'm proud of it," Bobby declares.

She rises and grabs my hand. "Come on, Ivy. I'll go with you. He's not a big bad wolf like he wants to be."

I laugh, her statement seeming funnier than it is, and I realize I've drunk way too much tonight.

We step in front of him, and Bobby points. "Ivy, you see that chair right there?"

I stare at the oddly curved lounger. "Yes?"

"Go lie down on it."

"Why?"

He puts his finger over my lips. "Stop asking questions."

Lilly releases my hand.

My chest tightens, but I obey and go to the chair. I sit on it, swing my legs over the bottom of the curved part, and lie on my back, realizing I'm now completely naked. I nervously ask, "What now?"

Dax demands. "Spread your legs so your heels are on the very edge."

I gape at him.

He gives me his commanding look that drives me wild. He drags his eyes over my body, then back to my face. "I said to spread those sexy legs, you little slut. Don't disappoint me now." He purses his lips.

Pretend I'm Avery.

Pretend I'm Avery.

Pretend I'm Avery.

I try to look as sophisticated and sexy as she does, slowly sliding one foot to the edge and then the other.

"You're lucky, Dax. Your pussy's beautiful," Lilly blurts out.

I glance at her. My heart thumps faster.

"Sorry, but it is," she quickly adds.

Bobby moves over to stand in front of me, gives me a lust-filled look, and a shiver runs down my spine. "Nice and pink, just like those nipples."

Dax rises and walks over to the side of the chair. He kneels down and strokes my hair, asserting, "I told you, you're the most beautiful girl on the Earth. No offense, Lilly."

She giggles. "I normally would take offense, but I agree. Ivy's gorgeous."

"I am?"

Bobby adds, "I see why you've been so crazy about her, Dax."

My head spins. Part of me is elated that they're praising me, but the other part panics.

What am I doing?

"Time for body shots," Bobby announces.

My stomach dives. I arch my eyebrows. "Body shots?"

He chuckles. "Yeah. Don't worry. You don't have to do any more shots."

Relief fills me. "I really shouldn't drink anymore."

Dax strokes my head, affirming, "You're not, baby girl. Relax."

Bobby selects a bottle of brown liquor from the bar and comes back. He kneels on my other side, then hands it to Dax. "You do the honors."

Dax gives me another heated look, then kisses me gently. I reach for him, but he retreats.

Bobby pats Lilly's ass. "Kneel next to Dax."

She obeys.

Dax leans into my ear. "You know what I love for you to scream when we're having sex? When I'm making you come?"

"Yes," I breathlessly answer.

Lilly moves her hands over the curve of my waist, and Bobby's palm slides up my inner thigh.

I shift on the lounger.

Dax orders, "I want you to scream it. Remind me that you're mine. That you'll always be mine and show them. And one day, when we're walking down the aisle, and they're standing up in our wedding, they're going to remember how turned on they were listening to you scream."

My lip quivers. I stare at him, breath ragged, unsure what'll happen. My chest rises and falls faster, but I remind myself I trust Dax and he'd never hurt me.

He demands, "Be a good baby girl."

I nod.

He adds, "Fuck, you make me happy. So fucking happy."

Elation runs through my body. The floral perfume I always smell on Avery once again flares in my nostrils. It mixes with Dax's musk, intoxicating me to the point my head spins.

"Relax, gorgeous, and enjoy yourself." Dax leans back and holds the bottle of liquor over my body. He drizzles it from the top of my neck through my cleavage, over my belly button, and onto my pussy.

I gape at him.

Before I can object, Lilly's tongue runs down my neck and through my cleavage.

Bobby's lips suck on my belly button and then move lower.

"Dax," I fret.

"Shh. Everything's okay. Fuck, you make me proud. So fucking proud you're mine," he repeats.

"But—"

He puts his lips to mine, slides his tongue in my mouth, holds my hair tight, and kisses me.

I once again fall into the world of Dax Carrington.

"Pretend it's Dax," Avery's voice whispers in my mind.

I kiss him back, and it's no longer Lilly or Bobby's tongues and hands on me. It's Dax's.

His tongue thrashing around mine, incoherent sounds

muffled between our lips. He mumbles, "You little slut tease." Then he kisses me with more intensity.

Bobby and Lilly's tongues push me higher and higher, flicking across me until sweat pops out on my skin. More adrenaline drowns my cells.

Dax kisses me until my body convulses, and I'm writhing underneath all of them. Dax leans into my ear, glances at the others, and murmurs, "Look at them working over my whore. You know what makes me happy. Say it."

Bobby sucks on my clit. Lilly places the same amount of pressure on my tit, and I come harder.

"Say it," Dax demands.

"I love being your fucking slut," I choke out.

"Louder," he demands.

"I love being your little fucking slut!"

"Switch," Dax states, sliding his palm on my other breast.

Bobby picks his head up and wipes my juice off his mouth with his forearm.

I look away.

What am I doing?

Oh God!

Dax holds my chin firmly so I'm staring at him. "Don't be a prude, Ivy."

"So far, you're passing, Ivy," Bobby calls out.

"What about me? Am I passing?" Lilly questions.

I glance at her.

Bobby smacks her ass, and she yelps. He replies, "Yeah, you are. Now, get your face in her pussy."

I object, "But—"

"Wait!" Dax orders.

My heart beats faster, and my pulse throbs in my neck. Tension fills the air along with the music, and Avery's damned floral scent continues to swirl around me.

Dax leans closer, stroking my cheek. "I'm only going to ask you once, Ivy. Do you want to quit? Do you not want to be part of the sisterhood?"

I furrow my brow and try to speak, but he places his finger against my lips, adding, "This is one night only. I want to see them pleasure you, and I want you to get into the sisterhood. I want you to have everything in life—in *our* life—the life that we're going to create. Now, either tell them no or choose to say yes to everything in front of you."

The room feels like it gets smaller. I glance at everyone.

Dax leans to my ear. "Baby girl, don't be a prude. Everything's fine. It's okay to be pleasured in lots of ways. All I want is for you to experience everything life has to offer. This is part of it. And I promise I won't be mad at you afterward."

My head swirls with alcohol and confusion.

He brings his face in front of mine so I can't see the others. "What's it going to be, baby girl? Are you going to tell us to stop? Or are you going to tell Lilly to lick your pussy?"

"Don't be a prude," Bobby mutters loud enough for me to hear.

"I'll do it right, Ivy. Better than Bobby," Lilly adds.

He grunts. "Doubt that."

"I will," she insists.

"Only if she's not a prude," Bobby hurls out.

Dax keeps his challenging stare pinned on me.

Lilly twirls her fingers on my clit, and I inhale sharply, my entire body lighting up.

Bobby sucks a bit more alcohol out of my belly button, and I arch my back off the chair.

"It's okay. We can stop," Dax states, disappointment growing in his expression.

Panic hits me. I reach for him. "No."

"No, as in stop?" he quickly asks.

I swallow hard and then shake my head. "No, I didn't mean it like that."

"Then what did you mean, Ivy? Be very clear what you mean," he orders.

I swallow hard as Lilly swirls her finger faster, and adrenaline coats my cells. "It's okay."

"Tell Lilly to lick your pussy," Dax demands.

I open my mouth, but it doesn't come out.

She takes her fingers off me.

"Ivy—"

"Lick my pussy, Lilly," I blurt out.

"Say please," Dax demands.

"Please," I call out, my voice cracking in a desperate plea.

Satisfaction lights up Dax's face, followed by something dark. Then it disappears.

She giggles, then takes her tongue and slowly licks from my hole to my clit, and I shudder, moaning.

Bobby sits back, muttering, "I'm going to watch this."

I glance over at him.

Dax moves my head back to his. "Enjoy it, and remember what I love to hear you say." He kisses my cheek and then sits on the other side of me, his hand stroking my tit.

Bobby puts his hand on my other breast, mimicking Dax. All of us stare as Lilly eats me out.

It doesn't take long. I come within seconds, adrenaline rushing through me, my head spinning to the point everything turns white. I cry out without even thinking, "I love being your little slut, Dax. I love it. Please don't ever let me stop. Please. Please." A tear runs down my cheek from the power of my high.

He slowly wipes it away with his thumb. "Shh. You're making me so hard, baby girl."

Lilly continues to eat me out, never letting up, and it's

unlike anything I've ever experienced. And I don't know why everything feels so much more intense.

"Enough," Bobby directs.

Lilly doesn't stop.

He yanks on her hair, pulling her back. "Greedy little whore. I said stop."

She looks up at him, breathing hard.

He orders, "Lie on Ivy and kiss her."

Dax slides behind me, massaging my shoulders, kissing the back of my head, and praising me. "You're so fucking hot, baby girl. Everybody wants you. Tell me you're still mine."

"I'm still yours, Dax," I declare, as Lilly slides her hot, naked body over mine and then her lips are in front of my face, my orgasm all over her breath.

She flicks her tongue at my mouth but isn't close enough.

I instantly flick mine to meet her.

She stays planted for a few moments while we barely touch each other's tongues, giggling.

I giggle too.

Dax presses Lilly's head so her tongue's in my mouth, and we're slowly kissing.

Bobby slaps her ass, and she jumps. Then Dax holds her body down on me.

Bobby slaps her ass again.

She whimpers in my mouth, and I kiss her more urgently, not understanding why any of this feels so good, but it does.

"Fuck, I'm hard." Dax groans.

"Are you hard?" Bobby bellows.

"Fuck, yeah, I am," Dax replies.

Bobby tugs my thigh up.

Dax tugs the other.

Lilly grinds her pussy against my clit.

I moan, quivering.

Dax murmurs into my ear, "Such a good little slut."

"Time for the real fun," Bobby announces, tugging Lilly off me, holding her up, and trying to steady her.

Dax pulls me to my feet and slides his arms around me, kissing me as needy as ever.

I melt against him, soaring in how amazing his body feels next to mine. I retreat and blurt out, "I love you."

He holds my face in his hands and pins his dark gaze on mine. Something passes over it once again. If I didn't know him, I'd be scared.

Moments pass as his stare intensifies.

Desperation hits me. I beg, "Tell me you love me. Please."

He stays quiet, disapproval filling his expression.

"Dax?" I cry out.

He leans closer to my ear. "Shh. I love you more than anything, my sexy slut."

Relief hits me.

He adds, "Remember that night in the boathouse when I promised you that you wouldn't walk the next day?"

"Yes?" I breathe.

He slides his fingers through my hair and tugs on it so my head faces the ceiling. He leans over me and warns, "That's going to look like nothing by the time this night's over." His lips tip up into a wicked grin, and I have to wonder again what I'm doing and why.

Dax 28

GAME POINT

Dax

My sordid self can't decide if I like this or not.

She's mine.

Why did I let anyone else touch her?

Ivy bashfully smiles at me, her breath ragged, and I kiss her, then release her. I go to the window and stare out into the blackness.

I need space to collect my thoughts.

It's going exactly as planned.

This isn't right.

Bobby hands me another glass of scotch.

I take a few sips, trying to calm my racing heart, breathing in the scent of Ivy's arousal and Lilly's perfume. It reminds me of Avery.

I wish it would disappear along with Ivy and me.

What am I thinking?

I can't do this.

She's going to regret it.

That's the whole point. Stop being a pussy and win the game.

Bobby suggests, "I think it's time we actually had some fun, don't you, Dax?"

I glance at him, alarm bells ringing in the back of my mind.

He gives me a look and clinks my glass. It's the same look he always gives me when he tells me not to wimp out, which never used to happen before Ivy entered my life.

"Yeah," I affirm against my better judgment.

He nods.

I swallow the rest of my drink and force myself to return to Ivy. I tug her into me and lead her toward Bobby and Lilly. I ask, "Do you like my cock in your pussy or your asshole more?"

Her flushed cheeks turn maroon.

She deserves better.

Play the part.

My stomach flips. I chuckle and take another sip. "It's okay, baby girl. We're among friends. You and Lilly are sisters."

She blurts out, "Just because I'm from West Virginia doesn't mean I'm into incest!"

I put my finger over her lips and chuckle. "I didn't mean it like that."

Worry fills her expression, and I kick myself.

"Of course he didn't mean that," Bobby proclaims.

Ivy's body relaxes. "Okay, sorry."

Lilly steps next to her and drags her nails down Ivy's arm.

She shivers.

Lilly adds, "You're so sexy, Ivy. I wish I could be more like you."

Ivy furrows her brows. "What do you mean?"

"You don't realize how hot you are or the power you hold over all of us," Lilly states.

Bobby was right. This girl knows her game.

She was the perfect one to break Ivy with.

Why did I ever start this? She doesn't deserve it.

Ivy's eyes widen. "Thank you. That was nice of you to say."

"It's true. Everybody on campus wants you."

Ivy's expression shows her disbelief.

I jump in. "It's true, baby girl. Everybody wants you. I see it. I am glad you're finally owning your power though."

She turns to me, her eyes glassy from alcohol, asking, "What do you mean?"

I cup her pussy and hate myself for it, repeating what I've told at least a hundred girls. "You're owning your power. You're not letting any boundaries stop you from taking what's yours or getting the pleasure you deserve. And you're earning your spot in the sisterhood. You're going to have the world at your fingertips."

She bites on her lip.

"But we're all having fun, aren't we?" I add, wanting her to convince herself that all this is fine and she should keep going.

She ponders my question for a minute and then smiles, admitting, "Yeah, I'm having fun."

I kiss her. "Good. So am I."

Am I though?

Bobby drops his pants to the ground. His belt hits with a clank.

Ivy's eyes dart toward him. She gapes.

I step back and drop my pants. My belt hits the floor just as loud.

She redirects her gaze to my cock.

I chuckle. "Whose cock do you like better? Bobby's or mine?"

Her eyes dart between both of us.

"Are you both the same size?" Lilly blurts out.

Bobby grunts. "No, I'm bigger than Dax."

"Bull-fucking-shit you are," I declare.

Ivy bursts out laughing, as does Lilly.

Lilly slides her arm around Ivy's shoulder. "Men and their cocks. It's a never-ending battle."

Ivy continues to giggle, then puts her hand over her mouth.

Lilly laughs harder, and Bobby and I begin to chuckle as well.

When the laughter subsides, I step in front of Ivy so my cock's against her stomach. I tug her hair back so her face is tilted toward the ceiling. I hover over it, studying her.

She bites on her lip. Her chest rises and falls faster.

I ask, "Who's my sexy slut?"

"I am," she quietly claims.

Bobby steps behind her.

My gut dives.

I shouldn't be doing this.

But this sets me up for game point.

Bobby slides his hand around Ivy's neck.

Her eyes widen.

He puts his lips near her ear. "I heard you tell Dax that you like it up the ass, Ivy."

She scrunches her forehead. Embarrassment fills her expression again.

Bile crawls up my throat. I swallow it and insist, "It's okay, baby girl. Be a good little slut and tell him what you like."

She hesitates.

Lilly volunteers, "I love it up my ass and my pussy."

Ivy looks at her from the corner of her eye. Bobby keeps his firm hold on her neck.

I snap, "You're going to wait your turn, Lilly. Ivy's earned first dibs. Understand?"

"Dax," Ivy whispers.

"Shhh. We're just having some fun."

"But you're mine, Dax."

My lips twist. "Yes, and you're mine."

"But—"

I kiss her, my tongue urgently flicking across hers. My cock hardens further against her stomach.

I need this.

I groan and pull back, demanding, "Ivy, do you like it better in your pussy or your ass?"

"I...I..." She shakes her head.

I chuckle. Satisfaction fills me, and I state, "You've never been able to choose. Have you, baby girl?"

Ivy bites on her smile and slowly shakes her head.

"Fuck, that's hot," Bobby says, and she blinks a few times.

"Now, you know I own you, right? You're mine, and I'm yours?" I remind her.

She nods, swallowing hard. "Yes, Dax. I'm only yours."

"Good." I lean into her ear. "I want to give you a gift, gorgeous. A gift money can't buy. And I want you to accept my gift and say thank you."

"What..." She stops and takes a deep breath. She nervously questions, "What's the gift, Dax?"

Bobby interjects, "I'm going to take you in the ass, and Dax is going to sink his cock into your pussy. We'll let Lilly play around with you how she sees fit."

He's said it too many times to count, and I always love the expression that fills women's faces. Sometimes, it takes me by surprise. Sometimes, I expect their reaction. But Ivy's is fucking priceless. It reaffirms that we're meant to do this.

I swirl my finger around her hardened nipple, reassuring her, "It's my gift to you. Be a good little slut and say thank you."

She opens her mouth, but no sound comes out.

Lilly breathes, "That's such an awesome gift. I wish I had a boyfriend who would do that for me."

Fuck this girl. How the fuck did she end up at Clifton University?

Bobby was right.

Her father won't like what she's saying or what he sees when he gets this video.

I give myself a high five in my head.

Tonight's going to have lifelong consequences.

In my favor, I remind myself.

Time to lay it on the line.

"You don't like my gift?" I accuse Ivy, giving her my hurt puppy-dog expression.

She scrunches her face and opens her mouth again, but nothing comes out.

I put my hand on her pussy and ask, "You don't trust me anymore?"

"I didn't say that, Dax."

I push more guilt on her, claiming, "I would never hurt you or put you in a position to do anything that wasn't in your best interest. Or don't you believe that anymore?"

"I-I—"

"Maybe she doesn't want to be a Gamma Sigma Phi," Bobby suggests.

A perplexed expression fills Ivy's face. She's never really wanted to be in a sorority. I know she's only doing this because I keep pressuring her.

I continue to push. "You're so close, baby girl. And I wanted to give you a gift. Something I couldn't buy since you're always telling me that you don't care about my money and I shouldn't be buying you gifts. I wanted to show you how much I love you. But I see—"

"That she's a prude," Bobby asserts.

"Shut up, I'm not a prude," she says, jerking her head toward him and glaring.

"No? Then prove it. Do what I say and join your place in the sisterhood. Let Dax give you a gift and be grateful instead of acting like a prude."

"I'm not a prude," she insists, angrier.

"Aren't you?" he questions, giving her a look of disapproval.

It's brilliant, but it makes me feel ill.

Stop this now.

Don't be a pussy. Stick with the plan.

Ivy looks back at me.

Lilly grabs her arm and softly says, "Take the gift, Ivy. Be the little slut that you are."

Ivy looks at her.

Lilly beams. "So much better being a slut than a prude." She slides her hand on Ivy's ass and lowers her voice, leaning closer to her, adding, "If you love having one cock in you, imagine how good it'll feel with two."

Ivy blinks a few more times.

I shake my head in disappointment. "It's okay. You don't have to do it. I'm sorry I misjudged what I thought you'd love—"

Bobby grumbles, "She's a prude."

"Shut up, Bobby!" I bark.

Tense silence fills the air.

Bobby narrows his eyes.

My pulse quickens.

Ivy tugs on my arm.

I turn toward her.

She whispers, "Okay."

Mixed thoughts plague me.

"I-I'll do it, Dax."

"Tell him the right way," Bobby orders.

I stand paralyzed, wanting to take her out of the room and wanting to stay and win my game.

She swallows and locks her intoxicating eyes with me. "Let me be your slut, Dax."

"You are my slut."

"Tell him what you want, "Lilly encourages.

I state, "You don't have—"

"Please fuck my pussy and let Bobby fuck my ass like the good little slut that I am," she states, lifting her chin and squaring her shoulders. But her lips tremble.

I shake my head, my conscience screaming not to do this. "No, Ivy, it's fine. No, we don't have to."

"Please, Dax, I need it," she says, giving me her challenging stare.

"That's a good little slut," Bobby states.

Ivy cringes, and I once again notice how she doesn't like it when anyone calls her a slut except me.

That's because she's my slut.

"Desk, now. And thank Dax," Bobby demands and steps back.

I stay planted.

Ivy steps forward on her tiptoes, kisses me, and says against my lips, "Thank you, Dax. I'm going to be a good little slut for you now."

Shock fills me. I didn't expect this twist of events. While I wanted her to agree, I didn't expect her to step into the role this willingly. I wanted her to be more conflicted about it.

Maybe she wants to fuck Bobby.

What am I saying? I put her in this position.

Before I can say anything, Lilly grabs her hand. "Come on, Ivy." She leads her over to the desk where Bobby's sitting.

"What the fuck am I doing?" I mutter, standing there, feeling helpless.

Bobby sits on the desk. He pats the desk behind his body. "Stand on the desk, behind me, Lilly."

"Really?"

He chuckles. "Come on." He holds his hand out, and she grabs it. He palms her ass and boosts her up so her knees are on the desk. She slowly moves to a standing position above Bobby so her pussy's right over his head.

"Good little whore."

Lilly beams. "I am a good little whore, aren't I? Ivy, I'm a good whore, right?"

Ivy laughs. "Yeah, Lilly, you're a good little whore."

"Good." She smirks and glances over at me.

"Dax, move your ass," Bobby demands.

My heart races faster.

Bobby scowls. "Is there a problem?"

I don't want to do this.

What am I saying?

"Checkmate," Bobby calls out, snapping me out of my wayward thoughts.

He's right.

Move forward.

"What does that mean?" Ivy asks.

Bobby locks eyes with her. "It means it's an awesome night, that's all."

"You say weird stuff," Lilly states.

"Do I?" He turns, reaches around her body, and slaps her ass.

She yelps.

"Dax, get over here," Bobby orders.

I force myself to play my role, stepping closer. The scent of arousal mixed with Avery's floral perfume, makes me want to hurl.

Get it together.

"Dax?" Bobby arches his eyebrows, as if he knows what's going through my mind.

I push it away.

This is our moment to solidify everything.

I'm so close to winning the game.

I suddenly wonder if this is what I really want. I reach for Ivy and stroke her cheek, hoping she can decide for me. I ask, "Is this what you really want, baby girl?"

Say no.

"Don't be soft," Bobby mouths.

I scowl at him.

Ivy takes a courageous breath and nods. "Yes, Dax. I want to be your good little slut."

Bobby demands, "Take your position."

My gut falls.

He grabs Ivy's hips, but I state, "No, you only enter Ivy when I say."

Ivy's smile grows, but nerves dance across her expression.

My erection throbs.

This is going to feel so fucking good.

I stroke her cheek and praise, "You're such a good slut for me."

She nods.

I admit, "You're the best little slut ever. I fucking love you." It comes out of me before I know what I'm saying.

Bobby grunts.

I ignore it.

A light in Ivy's eyes ignites. "I love you too, Dax."

"Let's give her what she wants," Bobby declares, pinning his challenging stare on me.

I stay silent.

Ivy takes it the wrong way. She murmurs, "Please, Dax. I didn't mean to be ungrateful."

"You're not."

"I'm not a prude," she adds, slightly slurring.

"Time to make Ivy come," Bobby demands.

"I'm next," Lilly volunteers.

Ivy's face scrunches.

"Shut up, Lilly," I order, then murmur in Ivy's ear, "It's you and me, baby girl. Okay?" I hold her face in front of mine.

She nervously smiles and nods. "Yes." She puts her hand on my cock and breathes, "I can't wait for you to pound into my greedy cunt."

Jesus.

Bobby groans and mutters, "You've trained her well."

Ivy furrows her forehead.

Do it before Bobby ruins everything between us.

I kiss Ivy and murmur, "Come and get your gift, gorgeous."

She hesitates, swallows hard, then smiles. "H-how does this work?"

I kiss her again and direct, "You're going to straddle me, and I'm going to lean back so Bobby has access to your ass."

"Then what do I do?" she nervously questions.

I kiss her again. "You enjoy yourself, baby girl. Bobby and I got you, okay?"

She inhales and exhales deeply, and the fire in her eyes grows hotter.

I motion to Bobby, and we help Ivy get into position so her knees rest on the desk, on both sides of my hips. Her wet pussy teases the head of my cock as it pulses with anticipation.

Bobby moves behind her.

I demand, "What are you waiting for, baby girl? Take me."

She sinks down on me, and her eyes close. A moan rolls out of her.

"Hold on to me," I tell her, wrapping my arms around her.

She laces her fingers around my neck, sliding her hands in my hair, and I shut my eyes for a minute, pretending it's just her and me.

Why am I doing this?

Stick with the plan.

Fuck, she always feels good.

Ivy works my cock, and I groan.

Bobby steps closer, warning, "Get ready, Ivy."

"Bobby," I mutter, but Ivy presses her mouth to mine. Before I can say anything else, he slides inside her, and an incoherent, muffled sound flies out of her mouth, vibrating against mine.

"Oh my God, this is so hot," Lilly breathes over us, stepping closer so her knees are on the sides of my head.

Bobby and I fall into our rhythm. Every time I slide out of Ivy, he slides in.

"Dax," Ivy moans, her eyes fluttering.

Lilly strokes her head, then kisses her neck.

"Oh God, oh God," Ivy whimpers.

"Fucking little slut," Bobby grunts, pounding into her harder.

It feels better than I dreamed. I should be giddy with excitement. But all I want to do is kill Bobby for touching her.

Ivy violently convulses between us.

"Fucking whore," Bobby snarls, his face red.

She's just a girl from West Virginia. A pawn in my game.

She's more than that.

I love her.

Emotions overpower me. I kiss Ivy as hard as I can. She

ends our kiss, her mouth forming an O and her body trembling in an out-of-control state.

Lilly uses the pause to step between us.

Her ass hits my face. She shoves her pussy in Ivy's.

Bobby grabs Ivy's head and demands, "Suck on Lilly."

Ivy says something I can't comprehend.

Don't let her.

My cock swells bigger. Zings sit on the edge of my cells.

"Please, Ivy. Please. I need it. Lick me," Lilly desperately calls out.

"Do it," Bobby says and holds her face to Lilly's pussy.

"Wait, Bobby," I call, but Ivy's fingers appear around Lilly's waist. She digs her fingers in her ass and, to my shock, begins to eat her out.

"You're such good fucking sluts," Bobby praises.

I shut my eyes, unable to stop the testosterone flowing through me, continuing to thrust inside her.

Sweat rolls down my face, and the smell of Avery's perfume continues to torture me, mixing with Ivy and Lilly's arousal. It grows thicker and thicker until I can barely breathe.

Lilly pushes on Ivy's head and declares, "I can't take any more. I can't."

"Get out of the way," I say, pushing her away.

She falls to her knees on the desk. "What the fuck, Dax!"

I ignore her and reach for Ivy's head. Lilly's pussy is on her breath. She doesn't give me any time to say anything. She doesn't hesitate and locks her lips back on mine, sliding her tongue all around my mouth. Then she retreats and moans against my lips, "I love being your slut, Dax. Tell me I'm your favorite slut."

"You're my favorite slut, baby girl," I reassure her.

"Harder. Fuck me harder," she cries out.

Bobby and I both pick up our speed.

"I'm not going to last much longer," he warns.

Before he can, I shove him away, flip Ivy over on the desk, and push her thighs up.

"What the fuck are you doing?" Bobby yells out.

I pound into Ivy, my palm on her chest, her eyes wild with fire until they roll back, and her body convulses violently once more against my cock.

Then I explode into her, crying out, "You fucking little whore. Fuck, I fucking love you, you fucking dirty slut."

"I'm your slut. Oh God! I'm your slut, Dax," she screams just as I've trained her to.

I continue thrusting until I have nothing left and collapse over her. Her arms wrap around me. Her ragged, hot breath pushes into my ear.

"What the fuck was that, Dax?" Bobby shouts.

"Oh my God, that was hot," Lilly breathes.

"Dax," Bobby demands, but I ignore him, kissing Ivy, wondering again why I ever allowed anyone else to touch her.

Ivy 29

TAKE ME HOME

My body quivers underneath Dax's. I hold him tighter, my heart trying to slow, but it doesn't seem to. The high from the rush of endorphins continues to keep me buzzed.

He mumbles, "I'm sorry."

The realization of what I just did hits me. "Wh-what?"

"What the fuck was that, Dax?" Bobby snarls.

Dax kisses my neck and pries himself off me. He slides one hand under my back and grabs my other hand. "Come on, baby girl." He helps me to my feet.

"Dax, what the fuck was that?" Bobby demands again.

"We're leaving," Dax announces.

Panic hits me. I shouldn't have done this. What was I thinking?

Lilly interjects, "You can't. Ivy won't be part of the sisterhood if you do."

"Fuck the sisterhood," Dax bellows, leading me past Bobby.

"Dax, what the fuck is going on?" Bobby booms again.

Dax picks up my risqué lingerie and then shakes his head, disgusted. He tosses it, then grabs a blanket from the couch and wraps it around me. He tugs me into him and kisses the side of my head. "Ivy, let's go."

"But the sisterhood," Lilly cries out.

His father won't let him marry me if I'm not a Gamma.

I freeze. "Dax, what are you doing? She's right. The sisterhood."

He barks, "I said fuck the sisterhood."

Confusion fills me.

Bobby scowls with anger. He steps between us. "What are you doing?"

Dax shoves him out of the way and steers me toward the door. He gets to it and tries to open it, but it's locked. He shouts, "Open the fucking door."

"Dax?" I ask.

"We're all here for the rest of the night," Bobby claims.

"Bullshit," Dax spouts. "Stand back, Ivy," he orders, moving me several feet away. He pounds on the door. "Open the fucking door, Avery."

Nothing happens.

Dax continues to pound.

Bobby grabs his arm. "What are you doing, man?"

Dax shrugs out of his grasp, steps back, then hurls his body at the door several times, utilizing his shoulder until it breaks open.

I stare at him in horror, unable to move.

He reaches for me. "Let's go." He keeps me close to him as he maneuvers me through the sorority house.

We reach the front door, and Avery asks, "Dax, what's going on?"

"He doesn't want Ivy to be in the sorority," Bobby declares.

"Shut up," Dax says. "And this isn't Ivy's choice. It's mine." He flings open the front door and moves me outside. The cold air hits my face and feet.

He leads me off the porch.

"Ow," I cry out, stepping on a stone.

Dax looks down. "I'm sorry, baby girl." He picks me up, carrying me toward the car.

Avery follows him. "What are you doing?"

"Leaving," Dax says.

"Why?" she questions.

He spins. "You know why, Avery."

They glare at each other.

My pulse quickens.

He breaks Avery's stare and takes me to the passenger side.

She scoffs. "You seriously have to be kidding me."

He ignores her, opens the door, and gently puts me inside. He gives me a quick kiss on the lips. "Are you all right, baby girl?"

I nod, confused about what's going on.

He slams the door, hurls something at Avery I can't hear, then stomps to the other side of the car. He opens the door, slides in, and turns the key. He revs the engine, peeling out of the driveway.

"Dax, what's happening?" I question, my head spinning and trying to focus on him.

He doesn't take his eyes off the road. "We're going home," he claims, speeding up and maneuvering through traffic.

"Why? Are you mad at me?"

He glances over. "Why would I be mad at you? Because you let Bobby take you in the ass or because you sucked on Lilly's pussy?"

I jerk my head back. "What? You told me to do it," I declare, my chest tightening.

"And you liked it, right?" he spits.

I gape at him, my heart feeling like it'll explode. Then tears fall, and I can't stop them, no matter how much I try.

He clenches his jaw. He says nothing, and we finally pull into the estate through the gates.

I demand, "Take me home."

He glances at me. "No."

"I said to take me home."

"You're in no shape to go home. Your father won't be happy," he says.

I look out the window, crying harder, knowing he's right. I can't go home like this. Why did I drink? Why did I do all that? Why did I care so much about that stupid sorority?

He'll never marry me now.

I turn back to him and beg, "Dax, please. Talk to me. I only did what you told me to do. I didn't..."

"Fuck, Ivy," he says, slamming his hand on the steering wheel. I flinch and cower toward the door, suddenly afraid.

He closes his eyes and sighs, pulling into his driveway. He turns off the engine and then takes several deep breaths. His gaze drifts toward the ceiling and stays there for several tense moments. He finally turns toward me. "You didn't do anything wrong, Ivy."

"Then why are you mad at me?"

"I'm not," he claims.

"You are," I accuse.

A defeated look fills his expression. He shakes his head. "I'm not." He gets out of the car and comes around to my side. He slides his hands under my body and pulls me out of the car, carrying me into his house. He locks his door and then takes me to the bedroom, setting me on my feet.

I steady myself, holding on to his forearms. "Dax, I don't know what's happening." The blanket falls to the floor.

He drags his eyes over my body.

I blurt out, "You're still naked."

He glances down at his body and back at me. "So are you."

We stare at each other for a minute and then I can't help it and laugh, pointing out, "You drove home naked."

He finally cracks a smile and starts chuckling.

Tears fall again until it's not funny anymore. I wipe my face, and we stare at each other in tense silence again.

More panic hits me. I put my hand on his chest and plead, "Please don't be mad at me. I only did what I thought you wanted me to do."

He blinks a few times and steps forward, grabbing my hands, curling his fingers around them and holding them over his pounding heart. He softly states, "You told me you wanted to do it, Ivy. Are you trying to say that I made you do it?"

I shake my head. "No, of course not. But you told me it was your gift to me. You said you wanted me to do it."

He opens his mouth and then snaps it shut. A perplexed expression crosses his features.

"Dax, please. You have to believe me. I only want you." I start to sob again.

He tugs me into him, kisses my head, and holds me tighter. "As long as that's the case, and you really do only want me."

I cry out, "I do. You're the only person I've ever wanted. And I don't know what happened tonight. I just... I'm so confused," I admit, sobbing again.

"Shh. Everything's fine," he claims.

"Is it?"

"Yeah. Everything'll be fine," he repeats.

But my gut tells me everything won't be fine.

$\mathcal{D}ax$ 30

GAME OVER

DAX

The sunlight fades, trying to set into darkness. It's four in the afternoon, and I haven't slept one wink.

Ivy's passed out in my arms. She hasn't woken up since we got home late last night.

My soul's tortured. I used to think it was a dramatic expression stated for attention, but now I truly understand it.

All I see is Lilly kissing Ivy on that stage, Bobby taking Ivy's ass, or him pushing her face into Lilly's pussy. It's everything we planned and nothing we haven't done before.

I hate myself for all of it.

I don't know what's wrong with me. I've never hated it before. I've always gotten a high better than any drug could give me when I get to this point.

I'm winning.

Ivy's demise is near.

This is what I've worked so hard to accomplish.

Yet I've never been unhappier.

It's a hard realization slapping me in the face. I glance at my baby girl. Everything is different with her. I'm in love with her and can't deny it anymore. So I make a final decision.

I'm not doing it.

Game over.

Bobby and Avery can take the win.

I stroke my thumb over her hip and kiss her forehead.

She stirs.

"Shh," I tell her, not sure why she's so exhausted but wanting her to get rest.

Her eyes flutter. She barely gets out, "Dax."

"Yeah, gorgeous. Everything's fine," I assure her, even though everything inside me says it's not.

She blinks harder as if she's trying to wake up.

I shouldn't let her drink so much.

She slowly focuses on me. "What did we do last night?"

My heart races in panic. "You don't remember anything?"

She swallows hard and then nods, squeezing her eyes shut. Her voice shakes. "I did things..."

I pull her closer to me, kissing her forehead again. "Everything's fine, baby girl."

"Are you mad at me?" she frets.

"Shh. No. Why would I be mad at you?"

Her eyes widen. "Because I did things with other people. Lilly... Bobby..." A tear rolls out of her eye and down her cheek.

I swipe at the wetness, insisting, "It's fine. Everything's fine."

"But you made us leave. I didn't get into Gamma Sigma Phi." More tears fall.

I don't give a shit about that sorority. I'm glad she didn't get in. As much as I pressured her to do it, it was only to continue the game. Now, I'm stopping this sordid situation. I repeat, "It's okay, baby girl."

"But our future..."

I put my finger over her lips. "Our future is fine. You didn't do anything wrong."

"Are you sure?" she questions, sniffling.

I kiss her on the lips. "Yeah. Go back to sleep."

She hesitates.

"Everything's fine," I reassure again.

She swallows hard. "Are you sure? The things I did. I..." She scrunches her face and looks away.

"You didn't do anything wrong," I tell her again in my firmest voice.

She releases an anxious breath.

I order, "Now go to sleep. You need rest."

She closes her eyes and snuggles back into me, and my anger and hatred grow.

I hate that I let Bobby convince me to go forward with the game. I detest that I put Ivy in a situation I know she would never have been in without me pressuring her. And I loathe myself on a deeper level than ever before.

Ivy falls back asleep.

My phone dings. I grab it, and bile creeps up my throat. I swallow it down, rereading the text.

Avery: The sisters decided they're accepting Ivy into Gamma Sigma Phi.

Another text pops up.

Bobby: Has she come to life yet?

I have to breathe through the rage since Ivy's sleeping on my chest.

I fire off replies, first to Avery.

> Me: She's not joining.

> Avery: What are you talking about? Of course she's joining. The sisters have decided, even though you left. What the fuck were you thinking?

> Me: I said she's not joining.

> Avery: We'll see about that.

> Me: The game's over.

> Avery: Is that what you think? That you have the power to just stop it at any time?

> Me: I mean it.

> Avery: So do I. Checkmate.

My gut sinks.

Checkmate.

She's got me. She knows she's got me, and I don't know what my next move is to gain control again.

Another text pops up.

> Bobby: Don't tell me you're sleeping. I didn't drug you too.

The hairs on my neck rise.

> Me: Tell me you're fucking joking.

> Bobby: Nope! It was way more fun.

I fist my hands, wanting to kill him.

Me: I told you I don't fuck women who you slip that shit to.

Bobby: She needed to loosen up.

Me: You fucking bastard.

Bobby: Stop being a pussy.

Me: You're the fucking pussy, needing to stoop to that level!

Bobby: Don't act like the moral police now.

Me: You know I don't approve of drugging our pawns!

Bobby: So what? I do. You enjoyed it. End of story.

Me: You asshole!

I turn my phone off and toss it across the room. It slides across the wood floor.

Ivy stirs. "Dax?"

"Shh. I'm sorry. Go back to sleep." I snuggle under the covers with her and hold her as close as possible.

"Your heart's racing," she murmurs into my chest.

I kiss her head. "It always does when I'm near you."

She looks up and gives me a soft smile.

"Go to sleep," I tell her again.

She closes her eyes, and I close mine as well, trying to breathe through my rage.

Bobby's father owns a pharmaceutical company. They created a drug that the meat industry buys. It's liquid, meant to be added to water. They use it to drug animals so they have sex more frequently and produce more offspring. It's cheaper than artificial insemination.

The first time Bobby showed it to me and told me what it was, I made it clear he was not to use it. I told him I wanted no part of it. He's bragged a few times about using it with his girl-friends, but I told him to stop that shit.

He claims they agree to take it, but I don't fully believe him. And anytime he brags about his drugged-up conquests, I reiterate I'm totally against it.

And I've done my research on it. The drug makes people do things they would never normally do. It gives them a high more intense than normal when they orgasm. If used too much, an addiction forms, and they just want more, turning them into a nymphomaniac. Alcohol only speeds up the process.

Everything about the drug makes me cringe. It's not my style. I want my sluts to make their own decisions. Alcohol is fine to a point, but even that I have a limit on.

Bobby knows I disapprove of it and would never have agreed. I even warned him not to use it on Ivy, which I do every time we play with a new coed.

He assured me he didn't have it on him. And I don't have many boundaries, but this is one of them, and he knows it.

How dare he use it on Ivy.

I'm going to fucking kill him.

No wonder she did that with Lilly and him.

No wonder why she's so worried.

She's going to hate herself.

Bile crawls up my throat. I do my best to swallow it, but I can't.

I pry Ivy off me, run to the bathroom, and throw up.

"Dax," she frets, entering the bathroom after several minutes.

"Get out of here. I'm sick. You don't need to see this," I insist.

"No, let me help you," she says, grabbing a towel and running it under the water.

I hurl again.

How could he have done this?

Why did I trust him?

Ivy puts a cold cloth over my neck. She crouches down by me and strokes my head.

I squeeze my eyes shut, feeling like I might need to hurl again.

"Are you okay?" she questions.

I sit back and slide against the wall. She follows. I put my arm around her, my skin covered in sweat, breathing hard. "I'll be fine."

"Did you drink too much?" she asks.

This has nothing to do with alcohol, but I nod. "Yeah, I must have."

She sighs and puts her head in the curve of my neck.

I slide my hand over her ass, wondering what the fuck I've done and how I'm going to reverse this. But there's no going back. I know it deep down.

I sit there for several minutes and then make Ivy get up. We go back to the bedroom.

Her phone lights up and vibrates on the table. She grabs it, then exclaims, "Oh my gosh, Dax!"

My stomach dives again. "What is it?"

"I got in."

It's a stupid question, but I ask it anyway. "What do you mean you got in?"

"To the sisterhood! Avery just texted me. She said they accepted my bid. They're excited to welcome me into Gamma Sigma Phi!"

I feel like I can't breathe. My chest tightens, and the air in my lungs turns stale.

Ivy peers at me closer. "Why do you look like you aren't happy?"

I stay quiet, trying to figure out my thoughts. Emotions I don't ever have plague me, and I wonder why I no longer want this.

It will be the beginning of her demise.

No, I'm going to stop her from joining.

"I don't want you accepting it," I tell her.

She jerks her head backward, scrunching her forehead. "What do you mean? I only rushed because you told me to. Everything I did last night was because you told me to do whatever I needed to in order to get in."

Her words are a slap in the face.

"Why aren't you happy for me? We left before Bobby said we could leave the room, and they still want me."

I stay quiet, unsure what to say or how to explain myself.

Ivy's voice shakes, but there's a firmness in her tone. "Don't tell me I did all that for nothing."

I'll figure out later how to get her blackballed.

I release a breath and force a smile. "No, baby girl, I was just teasing. Congratulations."

Her smile returns.

I pull her into me, stroking her back, wondering how the hell I'm ever going to keep her as mine.

The end is near.

I should be elated.

I'm not even close to being happy. This situation isn't like anything I've created before.

I no longer want the ending I planned. Yet I'm unsure how to stop the others from scoring the winning points.

Ivy 31

I DID ALL THOSE THINGS FOR YOU!

Ivy

One Week Later

An estate employee hands me a bouquet of roses.

Dax is spoiling me again.

I deeply inhale the floral scent and set the vase on the table. I pick up the envelope and pull the card out.

Ivy,

We're sooooo excited to welcome you into Gamma Sigma Phi! Put on your best outfit. Avery will pick you up for the brunch induction ceremony in thirty minutes.

XOXO,

Your Sisters for Life

Excitement fills me. I pick up my phone and text Dax.

> Me: The Gammas sent me roses! They told me to wear my best outfit for the brunch induction ceremony. What should I put on?

Several minutes pass, and the hairs on my neck rise. Things have felt off all week with Dax. He's as attentive as ever, if not more, but every time I mention Gamma Sigma Phi, he seems to not like it.

Guilt continues to eat at me about what I did that night. My conscience says I shouldn't have done what I did. I worry it's created a wedge between Dax and me, even if he's not admitting it. Yet every time I say something to him, he assures me it hasn't.

> Me: Are you there?

> Dax: Wear your pink dress. Everyone will be in Gamma colors.

> Me: Duh! I should have known.

> Dax: I miss you.

I smile. I left his bed only an hour ago.

> Me: I miss you too.

> Dax: I'll pick you up soon.

> Me: The note said Avery is taking me.

> Dax: I'll tell her I am.

Me: I don't want to disobey the Gammas before I even get in.

More minutes pass.

Me: Please don't be mad.

Dax: Fine. I'll see you over at the house.

Relief hits me.

Me: Okay. Love you!

Dax: Love you too, gorgeous.

Joy fills me. Dax no longer holds back his I love yous. He's constantly telling me, even when I don't say it first.

I send him three kiss emojis and go into my bedroom. I slip on the pink dress and matching heels, put on the pendant necklace that Avery gave me, and trace the ivy leaves. Every time I wear it, I smile. It was such a thoughtful gift.

I glance at my reflection in the mirror and have flashbacks of my night with Lilly, Bobby, and Dax. I close my eyes, trying to push them away.

I hate thinking about it.

I still can't believe I did it.

Dax might always assure me I didn't do anything wrong, but I wish I could erase the memory.

I got into the Gammas.

I did what it took.

My stomach flips. It's weird when I see Bobby. He looks at me differently now, and it's almost like he's too nice. Plus, he always hugs me, which makes me cringe.

Oddly enough, Lilly and I went back to our normal relationship. Nothing seems to have changed. I thought it would feel different, but she's her normal self.

I go into the bathroom and apply my makeup. I'm finishing putting on my whore-red lipstick when there's a knock on the door.

I open it, and Avery's there, wearing a pink shift dress. She beams at me, chirping, "There's my newest sister. You look gorgeous."

I glance down at my pink dress. "Thanks."

She hugs me, and her scent fills the air. I inhale it, loving it as much as I always have, and starting to feel the little bit of the intoxication it always brings.

She questions, "Are you ready to go?"

"Yes."

We leave the house and I get into her car. It doesn't take long to arrive at the sorority house. Only six girls I rushed with are in the dining room.

"Where's everyone else?" I ask Avery.

Her lips twitch. "They didn't get in."

"Oh."

She leans into my ear, "Only special women become Gammas, Ivy. And you proved you belong here."

I smile, forcing away the sympathy I have for the others.

Avery's breath hits my ear as she adds, "Prudes aren't allowed in our sorority."

They didn't do what I did.

My gut churns at the thought.

Stop it! You're a Gamma!

They picked me over the others. This is a happy time.

Dax's father will accept me.

Lilly spots me. She waves as she approaches me, and we hug. She exclaims, "I'm so excited!"

"Me too."

She grabs my hand and tugs me over to an empty chair. "Here, sit by me."

A few girls stare at us, and I get self-conscious. But their gazes quickly move on, and I don't know if I'm imagining things.

Why am I feeling guilty?

If Dax is okay with it, I should be too.

It was only one time.

It's better than being a prude.

The servers enter the room. It's the pledges from Dax's frat. Today, they're wearing pink thongs and bow ties, and I realize all the other girls are wearing pink dresses like me. Satisfaction fills me. Dax always knows what to do. I'm glad I asked him what to wear.

The servers set mimosas in front of us. I reach for mine, but another guy scoops it up.

I glance at him. "What are you doing?"

He hands me another. "That glass is chipped."

"It is?"

"Yeah. I don't want you cracking your teeth or splitting your lip open."

"Oh, thank you," I say.

Avery clinks her spoon on her flute and rises. Her smile is full of excitement. She glances at all of us new girls and then pins her eyes on me. "I can't say I've ever been so excited to induct anyone into Gamma Sigma Phi. You are the most gorgeous, sexy, interesting women we've ever had in this house, and we welcome you into the sisterhood for life."

My butterflies flutter hard.

She keeps her eyes pinned on me as she sips her mimosa.

I smile at her and take a sip.

Avery and I have gotten closer in the last week. I even confided to her that Dax has been acting a little strange, and she told me not to worry about it, that he goes through moods. I asked her if she thought it was because of what happened the night of the party, and she rolled her eyes. "No, you're not a prude. Do you really think Dax Carrington wants a prude?"

I decide she's right and push my guilt away again.

I take several sips of my mimosa. Within a few minutes, my cells start to buzz.

Platters of food are set on the table. Eggs, bacon, salmon, and sausage fill the girls' plates, but no one touches any carbs.

I grab a piece of toast and pass the platter to Lilly.

She states, "You're so lucky you can eat that."

"You have no fat on your body. A few carbs won't hurt you," I point out.

She glances at herself in disappointment and shakes her head. "No, I can't."

A server refills my mimosa even though half is left.

Avery tells Sarah, the girl beside me, "Go sit in my spot."

She obeys.

Avery slides onto the seat next to me. She holds out her mimosa, beaming. "We're finally sisters."

Pride fills me. I did it. I got into the best of the best. I made Dax proud, and now I have a sisterhood for life. Sisters who are going to help me achieve things I never could have achieved without their help.

Dax is going to propose to me at Christmas!

Avery clinks my glass again, and I drink half of it, suddenly really thirsty. When I set the flute down, I start to laugh.

Avery slides her hand on my thigh, rubbing her thumb underneath the hem of my dress. "What's so funny?"

Tingles burst underneath her touch.

Lilly leans closer, and their intoxicating perfume flares around me.

I giggle harder, and tears start to run down my eyes.

Lilly giggles, too, and puts her hand on my other thigh.

I glance down and then at Lilly. She laughs harder.

I don't know what's funny or why I can't stop laughing, but zings fly to my core. I squeeze my thighs and shift in my seat, trying to get ahold of myself. Then I turn to Avery and start to crack up again.

She moves her hand higher on my thigh and giggles.

"What are you guys laughing about?" Dax booms, walking into the room.

I turn my head.

He steps behind me and snarls, "Get your hands off her!"

My giggles stop. My face falls. I arch my eyebrows. "What's wrong?"

"Nothing." He bends down and kisses me.

Lilly moves her hand.

Avery moves hers even higher on my inner thigh. "Why are you being such a downer, Dax?"

"I said to get your hands off of her," he seethes.

I scoot my chair out, rise, and stumble.

"Wow, baby girl. How much have you had?" he questions.

I slide my hands around his neck, giggling, "I'm so glad to see you."

Concern darkens his expression. He palms my ass and tugs me closer to him.

I kiss him as hard as I can. Then I slur, "Maybe we should have some more fun." I look around the room and then catch Avery's eye.

Bobby walks in and slides his hand on my back. "Hey, Ivy."

"Hey, Bobby," I reply, then my giggles hit me again.

Dax's eyes narrow. "You're drunk."

"No, I'm not," I claim, laughing harder. I've not had that much to drink. My tolerance has grown way higher than this, so I can't be drunk. I add, "I'm just excited about this occasion."

"She's fine. It's just a little mimosa, right, Bobby?" Avery states.

Dax freezes, and the color drains from his face. His voice turns so cold, a shiver runs down my spine. He demands, "Bobby, tell me you didn't."

Bobby crosses his arms and stays silent.

Avery interjects, "Stop being a downer, Dax."

"We're leaving, now!" Dax asserts, pulling me toward the door.

I stumble, and he pulls me closer.

"Dax, what are you doing? She can't leave. We're inducting her into Gamma Sigma Phi," Avery shouts.

"Bullshit," he says, tugging me closer to the front of the house.

"Dax, no!" I object.

He continues to maneuver me, leading me to the front door and yanking it open.

"Dax, stop! I have to get inducted!" I slur.

He doesn't listen.

"Dax!" I pull on his arm, and he spins to face me.

He picks me up and throws me over his shoulder.

I shriek, "Dax! What are you doing?" I knee him in the chest.

He takes his hand and smacks my ass. "Don't do that."

"Dax!" I shout again.

Avery and Bobby say something, but I can't make out what it is. Everything starts to spin.

Dax gets to his car, opens the passenger door, and puts me inside. He buckles my seat belt.

I try to push at him. "What are you doing? You're ruining my day."

"You'll thank me later," he claims, then shuts the door.

I don't have the energy to try to get out. I suddenly feel extremely intoxicated.

Dax gets into the car and peels away from the sorority house.

I stay quiet, my head spinning.

When we pull up to the cottage, he turns to me. "Ivy, you can't return to the sorority house. You're not going to be part of Gamma Sigma Phi."

"What are you talking about? Of course I am," I declare, unbuckling my seat belt and finding a new surge of energy.

He grabs my arm. "I mean it. You're not joining."

I shrug out of his grasp and get out of the car. "I don't know why you're talking like this. I am joining Gamma Sigma Phi. You wanted me to. I did all those things for *you*!"

He grinds his molars.

My pulse picks up. "Why did you ruin my induction? I worked hard to get in there."

His nostrils flare as he exhales hard.

My mouth turns dry.

I need another drink.

He opens his mouth, but nothing comes out.

"You have nothing to say?"

He stays silent.

"Fine. I'm leaving." I take off, stumbling across the yard.

He follows me and grabs my arm. "Ivy, you can't go home."

"Yes, I can."

"No, you can't!"

"Leave her alone!" Dad barks.

I freeze, and my heart pounds so hard I think I might have an attack.

He steps out from behind a tree. "I said to leave her alone!"

Dax steps closer to me. "This is between Ivy and me. Stay out of it."

My father's eyes turn to slits. He steps forward. "Ivy, we're going. Now!"

Dax doesn't release his grip on me. He orders, "Go back to work, John."

My father glares darts at him. "Let go of my daughter, right now."

"Yeah, let go of me, Dax," I say, upset about how he's acting. I did all those things for him and then he didn't even let me enjoy the moment of everyone's acceptance.

He looks at me pleadingly. "Ivy."

"No. I don't want to talk to you right now," I say.

"What did you do to my daughter?" my dad snarls.

"Nothing. Stay out of it!"

"Dax, go home. I don't want to see you."

Dax's eyes widen.

Tense silence fills the air.

My father seethes, "You heard her."

Dax finally shakes his head. "Fine. We'll talk later, Ivy."

"No, you won't. You'll leave her alone," Dad insists.

Dax chuckles. "You're clueless, old man."

"Dad, let's go," I say, not wanting things to get worse.

He takes another moment, keeping his scowl on Dax, and then leads me to his golf cart.

I get in, and he takes me home.

When I step inside, I move toward my bedroom.

Dad barks, "How much did you drink, Ivy?"

I freeze, my insides quivering.

"Look at me," he orders.

I close my eyes and hold on to the doorway.

"Ivy."

I slowly turn toward him. I start, "I don't know what—"

"Don't you dare lie to me!" he spouts.

I sigh and attempt to lift my chin, but it feels heavy. "Dad, I'm going to sleep. We'll talk later." I go into my bedroom, then shut and lock the door.

I slide into bed, wanting to forget everything about this day. I close my eyes, but my dreams haunt me. My nightmare spins on a constant replay of me sandwiched between Dax and Bobby, breathing in Avery's scent and Lilly's arousal, and my voice repeating, "I earned my spot and I did it for you, Dax."

Ivy 32

YOU DON'T KNOW YOUR POWER

Ivy

When I wake up, it's dark out. My phone rings. I glance at the screen, expecting it to be Dax, but it's not.

I answer, "Hi, Avery."

She laughs. "It's about time you woke up."

"What do you mean?" I ask, sitting up.

"You've been asleep for over a day."

Panic hits me. "What are you talking about?"

"You must've just been tired, but it's Monday night."

"Monday! I missed school?"

"Don't worry. I talked to your professors. Everything's fine," she declares.

"Really?"

"Yeah. I came over and checked on you. Girl, your dad's upset."

I close my eyes, trying to remember the interaction between Dax and him and me.

Dad knew I was drunk.

I didn't drink that much.

Avery adds, "Don't worry. I told him it's the first time you've had any alcohol, and it was just a mimosa to celebrate. I said that it probably went to your head. And I apologized and took the blame."

"You did?"

She chirps, "Yep! I also told him you were awake early this morning, and I picked you up for school. He doesn't know you missed it."

Relief fills me. "Thanks, Avery. You're such a good friend."

"No problem. I'm outside, though, so take a quick shower, put some clothes on, and get out here," she orders.

I glance out my window and see her headlights. "Where are we going?"

"We're going to celebrate your induction."

"But I didn't get inducted."

"That was Dax's fault. The sisters agreed to let you take your vows next time you're at the house."

"They did?"

"Yes. But get your booty out of bed. I have a surprise for you. Dax isn't going to ruin your achievement."

My heart hurts thinking about Dax. I question, "Is he okay?"

Avery groans. "Of course he's okay. He's moping over you, but you two will work it out. Don't worry. Now, put on something nice. I'm taking you somewhere special."

"Okay." I slide out of bed.

She adds, "It's a really awesome dessert place. You're going to love it."

Excitement fills me. "Sounds fun."

"Oh, it's going to be. Now, get your sexy self out here," she demands and hangs up.

I put my hair in a claw clip, jump in the shower, and quickly freshen up. I get out, dry myself, and put on a little bit of makeup. I stare at my closet and then select a black dress and heels. I get dressed, go outside, and get into Avery's car.

She leans over and gives me a kiss on the cheek. "You look great." Her eyes dart over me, reminding me of how Dax looks at me.

My insides light up. Her scent swirls around us. My cheeks heat, and I suddenly feel a bit shy. I reply, "Thanks, so do you."

"Of course. I always do." She smirks, then laughs.

I laugh too, wishing I could be more like her. Avery comes across so confident. I make a silent vow that I will be just as sure of myself one day.

She whizzes through town and pulls into a fire lane, just like Dax, and I laugh.

She arches her eyebrows. "What's so funny?"

"You and your brother. There are so many things you do that remind me of him."

"Well, he's learned them from me," she claims.

I laugh again. "I'm sure he'd claim the same."

"Yep, he sure would," she says and gets out. The valet opens the door for me and I step out onto the pavement.

Avery comes around, links her arm around mine, and we walk into a dimly lit restaurant.

"Ms. Carrington, so good to see you," a young man coos.

Avery replies, "You too, Peter."

"Perfect timing. I have your table ready. Follow me," he chirps. He picks up two menus, leads us to the back of the restaurant, then stops.

Avery motions to me. "After you."

There's only one bench for the booth. The other side is a wall, ensuring privacy. Candles flicker on the table.

I slide into it, and Avery sits next to me.

The host sets the menus down.

"We don't need those," Avery states.

"No?" he questions.

"No. We'll have two glasses of chocolate pinot noir and the carrot cake. Right, Ivy?"

I grin. "Carrot cake's my favorite."

"Good. It's to die for here," she claims.

The host laughs. "Well, then, I'll tell your server."

"Great, thanks." Avery scoots closer and turns toward me.

Peter walks away.

I stare at the wall and then gaze past Avery. There are no other booths around.

My butterflies take off again, and I inhale her scent deeply. "This is a nice place. Very, um, quaint," I say, searching for the word.

"It's rather romantic. Don't you think?"

An uncomfortable feeling fills me. "Yes."

Disapproval fills her expression. "I can't believe Dax hasn't brought you here."

"Well, he's taken me to many places," I say, defending him.

"I know, but he should have brought you here by now. Don't worry, I'll tell him to," she adds.

A server comes over and sets two huge wineglasses down. Chocolate oozes over the rim and runs down the sides. Pinot noir fills half the glass.

He leaves.

Avery holds her glass up. "To us."

"To us," I repeat, clink her glass, and take a sip, moaning. The pinot noir hits the chocolate perfectly and explodes on my tongue. I swallow and add, "Wow, this is so good."

"You have to keep drinking. It gets better," she claims and takes another large sip.

I do as well, and a buzz fills me again. It's the same feeling I felt at the sorority house.

"There's nothing like a little hair of the dog," Avery chirps.

I set my glass down. "Maybe I shouldn't be drinking after how drunk I got."

"You weren't that drunk," she claims.

"How was I not that drunk? I slept for several days."

She shrugs. "There's a nasty twenty-four-hour virus going around. You probably caught it, and that's why the mimosa hit you so hard. But you obviously were exhausted and needed to rest. And I'm sorry again for my brother. Dax had no right to take you out of there like that."

My heart sinks again. I confess, "I don't understand why he got so angry. He wanted me in Gamma Sigma Phi so badly. He convinced me to do it."

She puts her hand on my leg, and her thumb slides under my hem like the other day. She caresses the inside of my thigh, and tingles explode everywhere, going right to my core. I shift, but there's nowhere to go. I'm surrounded by walls and Avery's intoxicating scent. My nerves mix with endorphins, confusing me.

Concern fills her expression. She coos, "I'm sorry. I don't know what's gotten into him."

I calm inside, reminding myself that Avery's my friend. She's just concerned.

I take another sip of wine and admit, "I don't know either. I feel like since..." I release an anxious breath and take another mouthful.

"You feel like what?" Avery asks, her thumb inching higher.

More adrenaline hits me, and I smile, feeling giddy. "This is really good."

Avery nods. "Yes, it is." She clinks my glass again. "To good wine."

"And chocolate." I laugh, then finish the glass, as does Avery.

A server appears with another round. "Assuming you want more?" he says.

"Wow, are we on video?" I tease.

Something passes in his expression but quickly disappears. He claims, "I'm just that good of a server." He hands a glass to me.

Avery takes hers, and he once again disappears. She leans closer, positioning her face an inch from my ear. Her hot breath sends fresh tingles down my spine, and my insides throb. "To the sisterhood. I'm so proud of you, Ivy. You did everything you needed to do, tapping into all the desires you've always had but you never knew you craved." She lightly grazes her nails over my skin, closer to my slit.

Adrenaline pools in my cells, mixing with more anxiety. I question, "What do you mean?"

She licks her lips, studying mine, and deeply inhales. She tilts her head, then raises her other hand and traces my mouth. "Do you think I'm sexy, Ivy?"

I squeeze my thighs together, trapping her hand between them, and blurt out, "Of course I do. You're the sexiest person I know, Avery."

Fire lights in her eyes. She shakes her head. "No, I'm not."

I nod, insisting, "Yes, you are."

She squeezes my thigh, and I inhale sharply, my insides quivering. She states, "I've never met anyone as sexy as you. You turn everyone on."

"I-I do?" I question, unable to fathom her statement.

She kisses my cheek, licks my lobe, and assures me, "Yes, Ivy. Everyone wants you. That's what made everything you did at the sorority house so much better." She pushes her hand against my thigh, spreads my legs, and drags her hand down the inside of my thigh, past my knee, and then my calf.

I swallow hard, whispering, "Avery..."

She slowly moves it back up.

Zings explode throughout me and I whimper.

"Do you really think I'm sexy?" she questions, her scent intensifying.

My voice cracks. "Yes. You're super sexy."

Her lips twitch. "You know what I think?" Her finger grazes my pussy so lightly I wonder if I'm imagining it.

"What?" I barely get out.

Her tongue hits my lobe as she murmurs, "I think you're the most gorgeous woman I've ever met. You don't know your power. I want to show you how to claim it."

I open my mouth, but no words come out. I'm paralyzed.

She flicks her tongue on my lobe and states, "I want to pleasure you, Ivy. In ways that no one else can. Then you'll be even sexier."

I swallow hard.

She strokes my cheek, quickly circles my nipple through my dress, and seductively asks, "Isn't that what you want? To be the sexiest version of yourself?"

"Yes," I whisper, stuck in a trance, my body throbbing with want and need.

Confusion fills me.

I'm not into girls.

I need an orgasm.

"Avery—"

"Keep your legs spread," she demands.

"Wh—"

Her lips crush mine. Her fingers slide over the thin material of my panties. Her thumb pushes against my clit, and three fingers slide inside me.

I fight her only for a moment and then find myself kissing her back, grinding my lower body on her palm.

She fists my hair the same way Dax does, circles my clit faster, and slowly pumps her fingers in and out of me until I'm shaking against the back of the booth, moaning loudly.

"Tell me you're my sexy slut," she orders.

"I'm your sexy slut," I barely get out.

"Louder," she commands, working my pussy harder.

"I'm your sexy slut," I cry out.

She murmurs against my lips, "Good little whore. I'm going to make you feel better than Dax does."

Dax.

Oh my God. What am I doing?

I grab her hand and find the energy to push her off of me.

She slides off the seat, barely catching her balance in order to not fall on her ass. Shocked, she angrily accuses, "What are you doing, Ivy?"

Flustered, I reply, "I-I... No, Avery, no. The only person I love and want to be with is Dax."

"Not true," she claims, smoothing the skirt of her dress.

"It is," I insist, rising to my feet but tripping. I grab the wall so I don't fall.

"Ivy—"

I turn to her, declaring, "I love Dax, Avery. Only Dax. He's the only person I want to touch me."

She puts her hands in the air. "Fine. No reason to get all upset." Her lips twist, and my gut drops.

My ragged breath doesn't cease. "Why are you looking at me like that?"

Her expression changes. "Sorry. I-I think I misread our situation."

"Yeah, you did," I claim, storming through the restaurant.

She follows and grabs my arm when I step outside. "Ivy, wait."

I spin, fighting my buzz. "What?"

"I-I'm sorry. I-I really value our friendship. I'm sorry I misread things."

I stare at her.

"I am," she softly states.

I release a breath and nod. "Okay."

She cautiously smiles. "So we can still be friends?"

I stay quiet.

She grabs my hand. "Please. I promise I won't ever mistake our friendship for anything else again. It means too much to me."

I relax and firmly reply, "Of course we can be friends. But that's it, Avery. No more, understand?"

"Yes," she agrees, but I can't shake the feeling something is off.

Dax 33

SHE'S BROKEN ME

Dax

"Ivy, where are you?" I shout, storming into Ivy's house. I'm tired of her ignoring me. It's been over twenty-four hours, and she's not returning or answering my calls or texts.

I glance around the empty space.

Where is she?

I pace their tiny living room, then stop in front of the window, staring into the blackness. No matter what I've done to contact her, she won't respond to me, and it's driving me nuts.

I text her again.

> Me: Where are you, baby girl? We need to talk.

She doesn't reply, and my anger surges.

Where is she? I have to work things out with her. Even if I

have to come clean about things I've done, I will. I can't lose her.

And this game is over. Ivy's unknowingly won.

Bobby and Avery can go fuck themselves.

Ivy's stolen every piece of me. Anything that mattered in the past no longer does.

I pace faster, tugging at my hair, listening to the clock tick. I finally sit on the sofa, tapping my hands on the armrest, continuing to wonder where Ivy's gone. I glance around and freeze.

A worn, tattered, leather-bound notebook sits on the table.

I mutter, "What is this?" I pick it up and open it.

A man's handwriting fills it. The front page reads, Property of John Ford.

Every page has a date. It goes back twenty years. At first, it seems like nothing but a bunch of formulas, but then I realize it's more than nothing.

Hybrids for new flowers fill the book. One's dated during the time John was between jobs. Scribble marks state "$10,000 - patent attorney."

My adrenaline picks up. I take a snapshot of all the pages with my phone, deciding this is the insurance I need. The next time Ivy's dad tries to come between her and me, I'll create an offer for him he can't refuse.

I shut the book, return it where I found it, then rise again. I pace some more until my phone dings.

I glance at the screen, hoping it's Ivy, and bile rises up my throat.

Avery: Checkmate.

A slew of pictures comes in, and I get sicker and sicker. She and Ivy are at the dessert restaurant.

Avery: Since you didn't bring her here, I decided I would. Checkmate again.

Pictures of them kissing and one of Avery's hands between Ivy's thighs pops up on the screen.

"Bitch," I seethe, my pulse skyrocketing.

Maybe it's not Ivy's leg.

I peer closer, and my gut sinks. The faint outline of the birthmark near Ivy's pussy proves I'm wrong. And Avery's wearing the ring my grandmother gave her.

My chest tightens, and I feel like I can't breathe, to the point I think I'm having a heart attack. I put my hand on the windowsill, trying to steady myself, and staring at the photos.

A video link appears. Before I hit play, sweat pops out on my skin. I force myself to watch.

Avery and Ivy kiss. Avery orders, "Tell me you're my sexy slut."

"I'm your sexy slut," Ivy whispers, her eyes fluttering, lips trembling.

Avery's hand on Ivy's pussy flashes on the screen.

Bile creeps up my throat.

"Louder," Avery commands.

The video zooms in on Ivy's face. She cries out, "I'm your sexy slut."

Avery murmurs against her lips, "Good little whore. I'm going to make you feel better than Dax does."

I punch the glass. It breaks, and blood streams down my hand.

"No, no, no," I yell, fighting tears.

The cold air bursts into the room, but I barely feel it. Unable to help myself, I watch the video again, my world crashing around me.

I'm losing this game, but in a different way than I thought I would.

Avery has her. It's the point in the game when I usually let my pawn go.

I can't this time.

All I want is Ivy.

I stare at the video again, wondering how I got here. The goal was to break her.

But she's broken me.

Ivy 34

ALL EYES ON ME

Dax won't return my texts or calls. After Avery dropped me off, I stumbled across the estate to his place.

He wasn't there. I stayed all night and eventually fell asleep. As far as I know, he never came home.

My panic hits an all-time high. I step out of his house and pull my phone out of my pocket.

> Me: Dax, please call me.

Avery pulls into his driveway. "Why aren't you dressed for school?"

"Have you seen your brother?"

She shakes her head. "No."

"He's not returning my calls or texts."

She shrugs. "He's pouting still. Get ready. You can't miss another day of class."

I close my eyes, then go into Dax's house. I grab a clean outfit from his closet and join Avery in the car.

Her intoxicating scent fills the air. It makes me uncomfortable remembering what happened the previous evening. And I still want to be her friend. I admire her, but I don't want anything else past friendship.

I only want her brother.

I barely comprehend what Avery's chirping about on the way to campus. We arrive, and I force myself to sit in Professor Dyer's class.

He rises and puts his hand through his salt-and-pepper hair. He puts his black glasses on and announces, "I decided who the teacher's assistant will be."

My ears perk. I had forgotten I applied, but I still want the job. The $15,000 stipend will pay my sorority fee. Dax insisted he would, but I need to figure out what's happening between us.

Professor Dyer pins his eyes on me. "Ivy Ford, you got it."

Excitement fills me.

I can't wait to tell Dax.

If he ever talks to me again.

The excitement quickly fades. My heart hurts thinking about the possibility of my relationship with Dax not lasting forever. And I don't even understand what I did to upset him so much.

No, whatever I need to do to keep him, I will. Once we talk, things will be fine, I tell myself.

The room erupts in applause, and Professor Dyer says, "Okay, time to get to work. Ivy, see me in my office after class."

I nod.

He clicks a button on his remote, and his presentation pops up. "Today, we're going to talk about hybrid seeds."

I lean closer. This is what my dad does. It's always interested me. Maybe it's because we've had so many conversations about it, but I want to specialize in it.

"One of the things you're going to learn—" Professor Dyer clicks the screen, and it goes black for a brief moment. He clicks another button. "What the..."

A video pops up.

My voice rings out from the speakers. *"I'm your dirty slut."*

My gut drops. The class bursts out in laughs and whoops.

A nightmare reel begins.

Professor Dyer clicks his button and declares, "I can't turn it off."

Every fear I've ever had is coming to life. My gagged mouth and naked body bent over for the entire world to see, lights up the big screen.

Dax's voice booms, *"You're going to take all of me, Ivy. This will only hurt your virgin pussy for a minute. Then your greedy cunt's going to feel like it's Christmas, and Santa left his entire sleigh of presents under the tree."*

The whoops turn so loud my ears ring.

Scorching fire singes my cheeks. I put my hand on my stomach, feeling like I'm going to get sick, and more panic fills me.

Flustered, Professor Dyer declares, "Someone turn this off. I can't get it off."

Dax booms, *"Fuck, your pussy's wet, you little slutty tease."*

The class never quiets. All eyes on me.

I'm dying inside but can't take my gaze off the screen.

My nightmare continues. All the things Dax ever said to me or wanted me to say to him about being a slut and a whore, blares into the room. All the personal, intimate moments we had are now out there for the world to see.

I'm learning how to strip in his room. We're skinny-dipping in the lake. I'm making out with him in his Porsche, sucking his cock with the whore-red lipstick, and taking it up the ass.

I swallow the bile trying to escape my throat.

"Nice ass," the guy sitting next to me says.

My insides quiver harder.

Then it gets worse.

I'm on stage with Lilly. I'm kissing her and then I'm licking her pussy while Bobby's fucking me in the ass. Dax's taking me in my pussy.

"I love it when you fuck my slutty ass," I cry out.

The students holler louder.

The screen splits. Dax's cock thrusts into my ass. My face appears on the other screen, where I wince.

He thrusts faster, then I'm coming hard, shouting, *"I love it when you fuck my slutty ass."*

Whistles, applause, and laughter taunt me.

The screen splits into dozens of images of me. My voice never stops, and all the things I've ever said hurl at me.

One screen turns to Avery and me kissing. The other of her hand up my pussy. Then I'm declaring, *"I'm your sexy slut."*

The guy behind me leans into my ear. "Who said you're sexy? Rather full of yourself, aren't you?"

Tears fly down my hot cheeks.

Dax's voice barks, *"Admit you love tasting yourself after I've been inside you."*

My breathless voice admits, *"I do."*

Dax asks, *"Have you ever thought of being with a girl?"*

I reply, *"No, but I'm not a homophobe."*

The class starts chanting, "Homophobe, homophobe, homophobe," and my tears turn to sobs, blurring the screen.

"Thank you for letting me be your dirty slut," I cry out the night during the foursome.

"Want to meet me in the bathroom after class?" the guy on the other side of me asks.

I crumble further, muttering, "Stop it. Please."

The footage of me with Lilly and Avery pops up again. Then it zooms back to the sorority house. Bobby's pushing my head into Lilly's pussy. A slow motion of my tongue flicking her seems to never end.

I can't handle it anymore. I grab the Louis Vuitton bookbag Avery gave me and rush out of the room.

Professor Dyer calls after me.

I don't stop running, but he catches up and grabs my arm. "Ivy."

I can barely make out his face through my tears.

He tugs me into his arms, stroking my head. "Shh."

My knees give out. I clutch him, weeping harder than I ever have, including when my mom left.

Then Dax grabs me, spins me into him, and seethes, "Are you fucking him too?"

Dax 35

CHECKMATE

Dax

Dyer's arms around Ivy is another blow, horrifying me further.

How did he get to her?

Avery. It had to be Avery.

My game once again played me, but I'm too hurt and full of rage to dwell on it. I snarl, "You are, aren't you?"

Shock fills Ivy's expression. She sobs, "No!"

Dyer holds out a hand. "Nothing's going on, Dax."

"Sure it's not," I bark, knowing exactly how Dyer works.

"It's not. There was a video," he innocently claims.

"You bastard," I hurl.

"Dax—"

"You couldn't help yourself, could you? You had to take what was mine," I claim.

Ivy interjects, "Dax—"

"Don't deny it! I caught you," I assert.

"There was a video," Dyer states again.

"So you say," I fume.

"You were in a lot of it," he adds, continuing the charade we've played too many times in the past.

Only this time, it's not a charade.

Ivy catches her breath and then realization crosses her face. She narrows her eyes at me. "You did this, didn't you?"

"Of course I didn't!"

"Y-you did. You were mad at me, so you decided to destroy my life," she accuses, more tears falling.

"You don't know what you're talking about," I state.

"You... I trusted you!" she cries out, then sobs.

Professor Dyer tugs her back into his arms.

Rage fills me. I push him away. "Get your hands off of her." I slide my hand around her waist.

"Don't touch me!" Ivy orders.

Anger builds within me. "Ivy, I didn't do this."

"Everything we've done! Everything!" she yells.

Dyer maintains his innocence as he explains, "It came up on the screen. I couldn't get it off."

I curse myself. I should have taken all the footage we had and destroyed it or put it in my safe. I mutter, "I'm going to kill you."

Ivy sniffles. "How could you do this to me? You said you would always protect me."

I step toward her, and she backs up. She pushes my chest. "Don't you dare touch me." She rushes down the hall.

I follow her.

She exits the building and rushes down the steps toward the parking lot.

I catch up to her and grab her arm.

"Don't touch me!" she shrieks.

I pull her into me. As always, she feels like she's meant to be in my arms.

We'll work this out.

Even if she fucked Dyer, we'll work it out.

She fucked Avery.

I'll keep my sister away from her from now on.

Ivy sobs for a minute and then pushes me away again, seething, "How could you? Just because you're mad at me?"

"I'm not mad at you."

"Stop lying to me. I know you're mad at me, but you made me do all that stuff," she declares.

A new rage fills me. I accuse, "I made you fuck Avery?"

She gapes.

"Yeah, don't worry. I knew about it before today."

Through her sobs, she stutters, "I-I—"

All my jealousy and hurt skyrockets. "You had to have her, didn't you? You got a little taste of Lilly, then you had to have my sister too," I hurl, unable to contain my thoughts.

"I didn't," she cries out.

"Liar," I accuse.

"I didn't. You're a monster," she shouts.

"I'm a monster," I repeat, but I know I am.

"Yes, you did this. You set me up," she claims.

I freeze. This would normally be my glory moment, but there's nothing joyous about it.

Her eyes widen. She shakes her head in disappointment, and I've never felt so low. "Dax..."

I stay paralyzed. For the first time in my life, this hurts.

More tears fall. She brushes past me.

Avery's car pulls up. She demands, "Ivy, get in."

"Stay away from her," I order.

Avery smirks and Ivy jumps in her car. Before I can do anything, Avery peels away.

I run to my Porsche and race out of the parking lot, soon catching up with Avery.

She pulls through the main gates of the estate and heads toward Ivy's house.

I follow, my insides shaking. The moment I park behind Avery, I jump out. I rush toward them.

"Stay away from me," Ivy cries out.

"Yeah, Dax, stay away," Avery gloats.

"You stay out of this," I seethe.

Ivy opens the door.

John's tall frame looms in the doorway. He questions, "What's going on?"

"I can't tell you," Ivy sobs, and he pulls her into him.

"What did you do?" he accuses, pinning the blame on me.

"Nothing," I lie. Not that I did anything with the video, but I know what my role's been.

"You're such a liar, Dax," Avery states.

"Shut up," I bark at her.

Disgust fills John's face. He turns toward my sister. "What happened, Avery?"

"Like she's going to tell the truth," I hurl.

"Don't tell him," Ivy begs.

"Tell me now, Avery," John demands.

My sister puts on her fake little act, and I want to smack her. She reveals, "A video was released throughout campus today—"

"Throughout the entire college?" Ivy sobs in horror.

John holds her tighter. His cold, firm voice, asks, "A video of what?"

Avery shakes her head. "Mr. Ford, with all due respect, I don't think you want to know."

"I do."

"No, Mr. Ford, you really don't," Avery insists with sympathy in her voice.

"Dad, please just drop it," Ivy declares.

His phone dings. He doesn't pull it out of his pocket. It dings again.

"Maybe you should get that," Avery states.

My gut sinks further. I blurt out, "No, don't."

It's the wrong thing to say.

He gives me another look of death. He takes out his phone, and his thumb moves across the screen. The color in his face drains as Ivy sobs harder in his arms.

Her voice fills the air. *"I'm your dirty little whore. Fuck me harder."*

He watches for several seconds longer, then turns it off. He slides his phone into his pocket and pushes Ivy behind him. He steps toward me.

"Dad, don't," Ivy cries out.

"It's okay, he deserves it," Avery urges.

"Dad!" Ivy screams.

I don't move, unsure how to flip the situation around.

John takes his fist and pounds it into my face.

Blood bursts everywhere. I fall to the ground, my face hitting the dirt.

"Dad!" Ivy screams again.

"You fucking piece of shit," he snarls.

Ivy rushes over to me and crouches down. She puts her hands over my cheeks, sobbing, "Dax!"

"You're super sexy, Avery." The muffled sound of the video continues.

My insides crumble.

More panic fills Ivy's expression.

She fucked my sister.

"Get off of me," I seethe.

"Dax, no!"

John yanks her away from me, ordering, "Don't you ever talk to my daughter again, you disgusting piece of shit."

All my anger and jealousy come to a boiling point. It fuels me. I slowly rise, rub the blood across my forearm, and bark, "You're fired. Get off my property."

"What? Dax, no! You promised me you'd never fire him!" she cries out.

I turn toward her. "Then you should have thought about that before you fucked my sister."

"I didn't fuck Avery."

Horror fills John's face.

Avery declares in her fake good-girl voice, "She didn't. What are you talking about, Dax?"

I bellow, "Shut the fuck up, Avery. Stop lying."

"I'm not lying. Why would I do that? Ivy and I are friends," she claims.

"You did! You know you did! You even sent the video to me!" I boom.

Ivy shakes her head. "Dax, we're only friends."

"She taped you! She set you up! But you had to fuck her, didn't you?" I scream, out of control.

Confusion fills Ivy's face. She glances at Avery, then me, and pleads, "Please, Dax! You—"

"I don't want to hear it, Ivy! Leave now or I'll have you arrested. Your shit will be mailed to you," I state.

"Dax, no!" Ivy begs through tears.

I get in my Porsche and slam the door.

She rushes over and bangs on the window, but I don't open it.

I reverse out of the driveway and take off, done with all of it.

There's no coming back from this. What's done is done. I know the game, and I got played.

Once you're in the position I'm in, there's no winning.

I've lost, only this time, I've lost it all—the game; my top position on the scoreboard with Bobby and Avery—but I don't even care.

Everything now's burning with flames.

None of it matters except one thing.

I lost Ivy.

And I know the game better than anyone. There are no do-overs.

My insides shake harder. I park my Porsche, go into my house, and grab a beer. To torture myself, I pull out my phone to look at photos of Ivy.

I don't get far. The first picture that pops up isn't of anyone.

John Ford's writing stares at me, and a crazed chuckle flows out of me.

I've been operating under a false assumption.

It's time to change the game.

I was wrong about do-overs.

I scroll through my contacts.

This isn't the way to handle this.

Go get Ivy back.

Bullshit. She's never coming back to me.

I stare at the name on the screen, then hit the call button.

It's time to stop being a pussy and finish the game.

Avery thought she won.

She didn't.

This has always been my game. I hold the cards.

It's time to stop being a pussy and conquer the game.

**Are you ready for the mind-blowing conclusion of the
Wilted Kingdom duet?
Dying to see Ivy get her revenge?
Grab Thorns of Malice at your favorite retailer or grab it
along with discounted paperback bundles on
maggiecolebookstore.com**

Thorns of Malice

From International bestselling author Maggie Cole comes the mind-blowing conclusion of the Wilted Kingdom dark romance duet.

For ten years she's been under my skin and out of my grasp.
The last time I saw her, I decimated her and everything she valued.
Not a day passes that I don't crave one more dose of her.
And Ivy Ford's everything I remember.
Beautiful. Graceful. Seemingly innocent.
I wish that were the case.
There's only one reason she's reinserted herself into my life.

Revenge.
It's nothing new in my world except for one thing.
Ivy learned from the best.
Me.
It's clear there's no longer anything naive about her.
She's an uncontrollable stalk of poison spreading all over me.

**Are you ready for the mind-blowing conclusion of the
Wilted Kingdom duet?
Dying to see Ivy get her revenge?
Grab Thorns of Malice at your favorite retailer or grab it
along with discounted paperback bundles on
maggiecolebookstore.com**

Thorns of Malice
Chapter One

Thorns of Malice has not been edited yet, so please excuse any grammatical errors.

CHAPTER ONE

Ivy Ford
10 Years Later

Jaxon Savoia presses me closer against the dirty, white, peeling painted wall, his hot breath against my ear, ordering, "Cum now, Ivy." He thrusts harder, over and over, until adrenaline finally releases throughout me.

It's a teaser, giving me only a moment of relief. The high I'm desperate to experience, the one which should have faded into a mere memory by now but is stronger than ever, stays buried deep.

"That's my girl," he grits, pumping everything he has into me until he's spent.

His ragged breath is fiercer than mine. He stays planted, his chest filling with air against my spine until it's almost normal. "We have to stop doing this," he reminds me, spins me to face him, then steps back, pulling up his pants.

"Spoken to the choir," I mumble, grabbing wet wipes from my purse and cleaning myself up. I tug the hem of my dress over my hips.

He secures his belt and reaches into his sports coat. He takes a swig of Scotch and hands it to me.

I take a sip, barely grimacing as the hot liquid warms my throat.

"You wore that dress on purpose today, didn't you?" he accuses, his eyes narrowing in a bizarre ironic state of disapproval and approval.

My insides quiver, my pussy throbbing once again in need. Jaxon's expression briefly reminds me of the only man I ever loved.

I'd do anything to forget Dax Carrington, yet nothing will let me. And every time I see that look in Jaxon's eyes, no matter how quickly it comes and goes, Dax's face lights up all the memories I crave to relive and hate to remember, torturing me further.

Jaxon steps closer, pushing my face toward the ceiling, demanding, "Admit it. You planned on derailing me again."

"Did you expect any different?" I question.

His lips twist, and it's probably another reason I allowed myself to get into this situation with him. There's something sadistic about his mouth, reminding me once more of Dax.

I have to stop thinking about him.

He destroyed me.

Jaxon's phone buzzes, and he releases me. He pulls it out of his pocket, taps the screen, and motions for me to go first.

I whine, "You're such a party killer."

He grunts, "Last week, you were the one who insisted we attend the meeting."

I begrudgingly open the door, carefully step out into the alley, and get slapped with a gust of wind. I hustle around the building and up the steps of the church, brushing past the smokers and hating myself further.

"Ivy," Ben greets me, giving me his welcoming smile.

"Hi, Ben," I say, then sit on the cold metal chair.

Several of the smokers come inside, and Jaxon follows. He plops across from me, avoiding me and making small talk with the woman beside him.

"Welcome to Sex Addicts Anonymous. It's good to see you all. It looks like we don't have anyone new today, so let's get started," Ben states, sips his coffee, and sits inside the small circle. As if he knows what I've been up to, he directs, "Ivy, why don't you start today."

My guilt fills me like every meeting. Most of the time, I wonder why I allow Jaxon to force me to attend these meetings. I've never abstained for more than four days, and I confess my last encounter in every meeting. No matter how I attempt to do better, I can't. And over time, my addiction has only gotten worse.

Jaxon nods in encouragement, and I want to slap him. We met in this room years ago, the first day I attempted to rid myself of my impulsive behavior. We sat side by side. I quickly learned he was the CEO of Blooming Gardens, a national wholesale floral corporation, and it led to a long conversation about botany. By the end of the month, we had not only formed a friendship, but he offered me a job and a scholarship to finish my schooling.

It felt too good to be true, like when my father told me the Carringtons would put me through Clifton University. So I resisted at first, but Jaxon finally won. My father was barely making ends meet, and we needed extra income. It was my fault he lost his job. What Jaxon offered for my monthly wage was more than Dad made in six months.

It's another thing that torments me. My father's never gotten a decent job again since Dax fired him. So the only thing I could do was accept Jaxon's job and be grateful.

Over the years, he's been a great mentor, boss, and friend. But our weaknesses run deep.

Maybe it's because we know the other's demons, but it didn't take long until we were feeding the other's addictions. No matter how much we try to stop, we can't.

At first, I thought he needed it more than I did. He constantly tempted me until I caved, which didn't take a lot of persuasion.

Lately, I can't stop pulling him down the rabbit hole. Every move I make centers around getting my next fix. And the fact I keep coming back to this church tosses my hypocrisy in my face once a week.

I wouldn't have come today if it weren't for Jaxon's one rule. I have to show up to every meeting, or I lose my job. It's his non-negotiable.

The one time I didn't take his threat seriously and skipped, he suspended me for a week with a final warning. Then he sat me down, and we had a long discussion about the importance of beating our addictions.

After I signed a form promising to attend future meetings, I batted my eyes how Avery Carrington used to, seduced Jaxon, and he pinned me down on his desk and fucked me hard. When we finished, we once again said it was the last time and went off to our meeting.

"Ivy," Ben repeats.

Anxiety appears as it always does, mixing with my shame. I'm a 28-year-old woman who can't let go of the past. I pay for it daily, as does my father, who never forgets. He may not speak about what happened, but anytime he looks at me, it's always with pity. He tries to hide it, but I see it.

Jaxon nods at me again.

I swallow hard, then admit, "I'm Ivy, and I'm a sex addict. It's been..." I glance at my watch and then loathe myself further, continuing, "...six, maybe seven minutes since I've indulged in my addiction."

"Hi, Ivy," the room offers in unison, with no judgment.

Ben asks, "How did it make you feel?"

I bite my lip, fidgeting with my fingers, trying to think of something more creative than my typical answer, especially with Jaxon, who's been so good to me sitting across from me.

I can't. I take a deep breath, lock eyes with him, and admit, "Empty. Disappointed."

Jaxon gives me the same look he always does. It's full of compassion and understanding, which somehow makes me feel worse today.

"What else?" Ben asks.

Without thinking, I keep my gaze on Jaxon and blurt out, "Unable to attain the high I crave but ready to try again."

His eyes turn to fire. He licks his lips, his chest slowly rising higher, and his fingers dig into his knees.

"Ivy, look at me," Ben directs.

I wait a calculated moment, knowing what it does to Jaxon, pretending I'm Avery and hating myself further. She's another person I want to forget but can't. The fact that I replicate so much of what she does makes zero sense. Yet I can't help myself.

Jaxon shifts in his seat, and I finally turn toward Ben. He questions, "Do you believe you'll find what you desperately want if you indulge in your addiction?"

I shake my head, knowing I won't. It doesn't matter who I

fuck, where, or how. There's no recreating what I felt with Dax. Or that night...

I squeeze my eyes shut as a flashback torments me. Bobby's pushing my head into Lilly's pussy, while Dax and Bobby's cocks thrust in and out of me in tandem, my body violently convulsing with pleasure. Then Dax is pushing everyone off me, caging his warm, hard body over me and creating another hit of adrenaline so intense I blackout for a brief moment.

"Ivy, come back to us," Ben firmly orders, tearing me out of my flashback.

I blink hard and swipe at my cheek, realizing I'm crying. I sniffle, "Sorry."

"It's okay. Everything you're feeling is okay," he reassures.

But it's not. It'll never be, and I know it.

I stay silent for several moments, and Ben finally says, "Carrie, why don't you go next."

I barely hear her or any of the others. When the meeting ends, I rush out of the building with Jaxon on my heels.

"Ivy," he calls out, grabbing my arm at the bottom of the steps.

"Not now," I warn, not looking at him.

"Ivy—"

"I said not now," I shriek, spinning into him, full of another emotion I never escape—raging anger.

He slowly lifts his hands in the air. "I'm here if you need me."

I say nothing, hightail it down the street, and jump on the bus before it pulls away. I find a seat toward the back and get lost in my self-loathing.

It's dark by the time the bus driver stops in my neighborhood. I keep alert, rushing past anyone I encounter, relieved when I enter my front door. I lock it and call over the TV, "Dad, I'm home."

He doesn't reply, which is unusual.

The hairs on my neck rise, and I repeat, "Dad?" turning the corner into the family room.

A choking sound fills the air. Dad's in his armchair, holding his chest.

I rush over to him, fretting, "Dad!"

Sweat covers his purple cheeks. His widened blue eyes glisten.

"Dad!" I cry out, grabbing his cold hand.

His eyes roll, and foam spills past his lips.

My insides quiver. "Dad!" I shriek, pull my phone out of my purse, and try to turn it on, but my gut dives further when I realize the battery's dead.

"No, no, no!" I sob, glancing at the table and patting Dad's empty pockets.

The purple deepens, more foam falls, and I tug him into me, weeping, "Dad!"

He freezes, his eyes wide open.

"Dad," I shriek, my hands on his cheeks. "Dad! Breathe!"

He doesn't take in any more oxygen. The warmth leaves his body, and his face turns harder.

I tug him into me, sobbing until I have no more tears. Numb, loud music fills the air.

I slowly turn, and then paralysis hits me.

Avery Carrington sits with her legs crossed and perfectly manicured hands in her lap, beaming at talk show host Winter Sophia.

"Welcome back. If you're just joining us, we've been discussing the newest scent developed by Avery Carrington. Tell us more about how you created Seducing Ivy," Winters asks, holding up a bottle of perfume. A red, diamond-encrusted I, with a vine of ivy leaves, wraps around the gold.

Whore red.

My stomach churns. It's the same design as the necklace she gave me the night of my demise. The color of the I matches the nail polish and lipstick Dax used to insist I wear.

Avery chirps, "Well—"

"I think it's best if I explain, don't you, dear sister?" a voice calls out, and my insides shake harder.

The camera turns, and an older, sexier, more filled-out Dax Carrington appears. He leans down, kisses a surprised Winter on the cheek, then does the same to his sister and plops on the sofa beside her.

Avery quickly gets over her surprise, and her smile reappears. "Dax."

"Well, isn't this a surprise! If you don't already know, this is Dax Carrington, CEO of Carrington Enterprises and Avery's oldest brother," Winter gushes.

Dax grins, and my world continues to fall apart. It's haunted me for ten years, never fading. He states, "I wanted to support my sister's latest venture. I hope it's okay to join you?"

"Of course!" Winter exclaims.

Avery's expression never changes and I can feel her seething underneath, but it's something the rest of the world wouldn't ever pick up on.

Dax nods. "Great. I think you asked how we created Seducing Ivy?"

"She meant how Avery Carrington Scents created it," Avery corrects.

Dax nods at her and grins wider, agreeing, "Touche." He repositions his gaze on Winters, stating, "As a subsidiary of Carrington Enterprises, we allowed Avery Carrington Scents to incorporate in their latest perfume our newest, and soon to be highly sought-after hybrid seed."

Winter arches her eyebrows, "Love you're confidence for your new flower."

Dax confidently grins. "Yes, well I don't ever make statements I can't back up."

"Fair enough. So tell me, what's so important about this new flower?" Winter questions.

Dax continues, "A lot, Winter."

"Like?"

Avery answers, "The—"

"For starters, the new hybrid creates a vibrant red blooming flower. The scent is incredible and the blooms stay alive 80% longer once they're unattached to the root. I anticipate it'll cut the demand for roses in half before the end of the year," Dax interjects.

Winter gapes.

Avery adds, "What my brother means—"

"I mean every floral shop in the world will want the new hybrid," he declares.

"So you have a new million dollar product," Winter gushes.

Dax chuckles. "Try over a billion dollars."

Winter's shocked expression appears again, but she recovers faster this time, stating, "Sounds like we should show our viewers what this newest craze-to-be looks like!"

The TV fills with applause.

A pop-up screen shows ivy crawling up a wall with gorgeous red flowers dancing around it.

"How did you create this new hybrid?" Winters asks.

Dax starts, "I—"

"He's always had a knack for knowing how to take the winners to the patent table, haven't you, Dax?" Avery interjects.

Something passes on Dax's expression, but it fades. He nods, claiming, "It's why my grandfather chose me to run Carrington Enterprises. He knew I'd continue to grow it."

Hatred fills Avery's expression, but she quickly recovers,

and her sugar-laced voice adds, "And my grandfather saw how my enterprising ideas would take the assets Carrington Enterprises have and expand them into billions of dollars worth of profits."

Winter beams, "Such brains between you two."

Avery leans closer to the camera and lowers her voice as if she's letting me in on a secret, keeping my trance fixated on her, claiming, "Seducing Ivy is the most important project we've ever worked on, isn't it, Dax?" She slowly glances at him.

A brief flash of disgust fills his expression, and then it turns to agreement. He pulls me in just as Avery did, answering, "If I'm telling the truth, Ivy's the only thing that's ever mattered to me."

My insides crumble. A new wave of heartache, rage, and grief hits. I grab the rose paperweight on the table and hurl it at the TV.

Glass shards land several feet in front of me. I wrap my arms around my father's hardening corpse, wailing.

I don't know how much time passes before I calm. I take my phone to my bedroom, put it on my charger, and look around the house for my father's cell, so I can call 911, unsure what I'm supposed to do with his body.

I can't find it anywhere. I grab my charger and phone, return to the living room, and plug it into the outlet. I set my cell on the table and sit beside Dad, still in shock.

Several moments pass. I turn to see if I can make a call and freeze.

Dad's worn, tattered, leather-bound notebook sits next to my phone. He's used it for as long as I can remember to write down all his ideas. I pick it up, stroking the leather, tearing up again.

I wipe my face, open it, and cry harder seeing his handwriting. After a few moments pass, and I calm. I review each page, remembering how excited he'd get when he thought he was onto something new.

Halfway through the notebook, I turn the page and discover a white, folded piece of paper. I open it, muttering, "What is this, Dad?"

It's a printed page from the United States Patent and Trademark Office. As I read it, four words cause bile to creep up my throat.

Seducing Ivy.

Patent granted to Daxton Everett Carrington V.

My pulse skyrockets.

Why is this in my father's notebook?

In a new state of shock, I read the paper again, then stare at Dad's notes, focusing on several words.

Red blooming Ivy.

$10,000 patent attorney.

My eyes dart between the printout and my father's handwriting of a date from 15 years ago until the truth becomes clear.

How did Dax get Dad's notebook?

This is my fault.

Dad knew what he did.

I stare at the broken TV, an onslaught of new guilt soaking my entire being until I'm drowning in grief and self-hatred.

There are no tears this time. A snowball of something new rolls at lightning speed, growing bigger until I can't see straight.

It's the need for revenge.

I put my head on Dad's hardened chest, squeezing his freezing hands, muttering over and over, "I'm sorry. I'll make him pay. I'll make all of them pay."

How?

There's no room to be weak or feel sorry for yourself, Ivy.

I straighten up, squeeze Dad's hand, and pick up my phone. I take several deep breaths and dial 911.

A woman answers, "911. What's your emergency?"

My voice cracks. New tears fall. I state, "My father's dead."

Are you ready for the mind-blowing conclusion of the Wilted Kingdom duet?
Dying to see Ivy get her revenge?
Grab Thorns of Malice at your favorite retailer or grab it along with discounted paperback bundles on maggiecolebookstore.com

Can I ask you a huge favor?

More by Maggie Cole

Wilted Kingdom Duet (A Dark Bully College Billionaire Romance)

Seeds of Malice (Book One)

Thorns of Malice (Book Two) - February 15, 2024

Mafia Wars Ireland

Illicit King (Brody)

Illicit Captor (Aidan)

Illicit Heir (Devin)

Illicit Monster (Tynan)

Club Indulgence Duet (A Dark Billionaire Romance)

The Auction (Book One)

The Vow (Book Two)

Standalone Holiday Novel

Holiday Hoax - A Fake Marriage Billionaire Romance (Standalone)

Mafia Wars New York - A Dark Mafia Series (Series Six)

Toxic (Dante's Story) - Book One

Immoral (Gianni's Story) - Book Two

Crazed (Massimo's Story) - Book Three

Carnal (Tristano's Story) - Book Four

Flawed (Luca's Story) - Book Five

Mafia Wars - A Dark Mafia Series (Series Five)

Ruthless Stranger (Maksim's Story) - Book One

Broken Fighter (Boris's Story) - Book Two

Cruel Enforcer (Sergey's Story) - Book Three

Vicious Protector (Adrian's Story) - Book Four

Savage Tracker (Obrecht's Story) - Book Five

Unchosen Ruler (Liam's Story) - Book Six

Perfect Sinner (Nolan's Story) - Book Seven

Brutal Defender (Killian's Story) - Book Eight

Deviant Hacker (Declan's Story) - Book Nine

Relentless Hunter (Finn's Story) - Book Ten

Behind Closed Doors (Series Four - Former Military Now International Rescue Alpha Studs)

Depths of Destruction - Book One

Marks of Rebellion - Book Two

Haze of Obedience - Book Three

Cavern of Silence - Book Four

Stains of Desire - Book Five

Risks of Temptation - Book Six

Together We Stand Series (Series Three - Family Saga)

Kiss of Redemption- Book One

Sins of Justice - Book Two

Acts of Manipulation - Book Three

Web of Betrayal - Book Four

Masks of Devotion - Book Five

Roots of Vengeance - Book Six

It's Complicated Series (Series Two - Chicago Billionaires)

My Boss the Billionaire- Book One

Forgotten by the Billionaire - Book Two

My Friend the Billionaire - Book Three

Forbidden Billionaire - Book Four

The Groomsman Billionaire - Book Five

Secret Mafia Billionaire - Book Six

All In Series (Series One - New York Billionaires)

The Rule - Book One

The Secret - Book Two

The Crime - Book Three

The Lie - Book Four

The Trap - Book Five

The Gamble - Book Six

STAND ALONE NOVELLA

JUDGE ME NOT - A Billionaire Single Mom Christmas Novella

About the Author

International Bestselling Author

Maggie Cole is committed to bringing her readers alphalicious book boyfriends and fiercely strong heroines.

She's been called the literary master of steamy romance. Her books are full of raw emotion, suspense, and will always keep you wanting more. She is a masterful storyteller of contemporary romance and loves writing about broken people who rise above the ashes.

Maggie lives in Florida with her son. She loves tennis, yoga, paddleboarding, boating, other water activities, and everything naughty.

Her current series were written in the order below:

- All In (Stand Alone Billionaire Novels with Entwined Characters)
- It's Complicated (Stand Alone Billionaire Novels with Entwined Characters)

- Brooks Family Saga- A Dark Family Saga – Read In Order (Each book has different couples)
- Behind Closed Doors-A Dark Military Protector Romance – Read in Order (Each book has different couples))
- Mafia Wars (Stand Alone Novels with Interconnecting Plot and Entwined Characters)
- Mafia Wars New York (Stand Alone Novels with Interconnecting Plot and Entwined Characters)
- Club Indulgence Duet-A Dark Billionaire Duet – Read in Order (Same Couple)
- Mafia Wars Ireland (Stand Alone Novels with Interconnecting Plot and Entwined Characters)
- Wilted Kingdom Duet-A Dark Bully College Billionaire Duet-read in order (Same Couple)

Maggie Cole's Website
authormaggiecole.com

***Get your copies of Maggie Cole
signed paperbacks!***
maggiecolebookstore.com

Instagram
@maggiecoleauthor

TikTok
https://www.tiktok.com/@maggiecole.author

Feedback or suggestions?
Email: authormaggiecole@gmail.com

www.ingramcontent.com/pod-product-compliance
Lightning Source LLC
Chambersburg PA
CBHW061106310726
48974CB00002B/409